The
Psychopomps

The Psychopomps

Sean Byrne

Apprentice
House Press
Loyola University Maryland

First Edition

Casebound ISBN: 978-1-62720-401-9
Paperback ISBN: 978-1-62720-402-6
Ebook ISBN: 978-1-62720-403-3

Printed in the United States of America

Design by Maria D'Agostino
Edited by Hannah Schaub
Promotion plan by Claire Marino

Published by Apprentice House Press

Apprentice
House Press
Loyola University Maryland

Apprentice House Press
Loyola University Maryland
4501 N. Charles Street
Baltimore, MD 21210
410.617.5265
www.ApprenticeHouse.com
info@ApprenticeHouse.com

A teacher once told me I didn't have to struggle to write.
Well, she sure as hell was wrong. So I dedicate this book to
my family, who has seen both the ugly and less ugly side
of me and stood by me through it all.

Thank you so much.

1

Thirty miles an hour down the Jones Falls Expressway had never felt so amazing. Janzen raced southbound into the city faster than anyone, and with each increasing number on his speedometer, he reached something closer to freedom. Big metal bodies around him flashed by in blurs. The surrounding rush hour traffic pushed foot-by-foot into Baltimore with thrusts of red-lit propulsion. With his chest nearly parallel to the road, the only resistance he faced came from a late summer breeze off the Chesapeake, and he squeezed in his elbows and dropped low on his bars to combat such a force.

The issue – one of the many, really – was that Janzen's disposition simply didn't allow him the benefit of a vehicle. For someone deemed directionless for much of his life, to be labored with the necessity of direction often left a driver like him, well, enraged. Ever seen a wolverine caught by the leg? Now light it on fire.

Even the air conditioning during Decembers did little to temper his encased spirit. How many others out there were like him? Flying in between and around the cars, he recalled his days in the driver's seat. He was curious who else had contested the amount of pressure it took to dislocate a steering wheel from its column. Were there those who sat at red lights counting the number of dents in the roof's sheet metal? Why was it that one of the four humors stained so much? For him, these weren't just ruminations but were the results of his confinement.

It was too much. During particularly onerous bouts of traffic, he had always unconsciously fingered the Darwin's point of his ear, possibly triggering the rage he had inherited from ancient descendants. Maybe the roots of his family tree crossed paths with a young Phaethon, who dared drive his father's chariot. Janzen had driven his father's Subaru. Both vehicles ended up in flames, the Subaru from an abused catalytic converter. The car tested Janzen. It was an oven; so instead, he rode a bicycle. And this evening, he rode it right onto the expressway.

The only recognizable indicator of the job he had left twenty minutes earlier was the frayed necktie knotted tightly around his forehead, a pale blue number that whipped violently behind him, flagellating his back with the dips and turns of his head. His buttoned-down shirt and scuffed loafers had been placed one on top of the other in the lost and found box behind the unmanned security desk of his now former employer, Tappert Publishing. The corduroy pants he wore to work were cut at mid-thigh, and he was shirtless despite the likely road rash.

He had given his two weeks notice a month earlier, so this final day was filled with the requisite hugs and handshakes from a few well-wishers wishing they remembered his name. "It's Janzen," he told one of the higher-ups, "one of your content editors, but it's on to the greener."

"Freelance, right?"

"We all are, sir."

"Excellent. Well, good luck, son," said the suit, extending his soft palm.

Janzen had bypassed the polite farewell and went in for a full-on hug. Thanks to years spent in the wrestling room, he was well versed in the Greco-Roman pummel, and after a few precise movements, he managed to secure a firm double underhook. He laced his arms under the armpits and around the man's tensed upper back and rested one temple softly on a taut shoulder. A flexed gluteus staunchly drove Janzen's hips towards the opposing pleats. Of course, had this been a huggable situation between two men, a more acceptable embrace called for the standard one-arm-over, one-arm-under technique, but impending death sure had a way of shaking things up.

But fear not. Janzen harbored no death wish during his final ride from work. In fact, his plan was to take his usual route back home, zigzagging his way through county suburbs until he hit the city. The highway's entrance, unfortunately, proved too tempting. It swallowed him right up until he was bombing his way down the ramp and into the evening slog of traffic. He wanted that stretch of roadway, and he took it. Or it took him. True, he was off his meds, but they didn't govern his ability to turn left and right. He was sick of his slow, fuzzy life. He wanted to fly.

He loved his new toe clips, a final gift to himself for the last few rides. The connection between shoe and pedal was a perfect convenience for a man who took at least some pleasure in being uncomfortable. While one foot drove down, the other pulled up, and he hit forty with the declivity. The errant horns and growling traffic whispered softly behind the music playing through his ear buds. John Adams' "Loops and Verses" compelled his quads and lungs through the burn, and the relentless repetition was a perfect soundtrack for his impulsive journey. Tears streamed from the corners of his eyes, their provenance presumably due to that pesky wind.

Riding a bike had filled part of the masochistic void when sobriety finally became the last option. At 29, he was just over two years without the drink. He had never been in better shape and never thought more clearly, the latter of which scared him shitless.

He passed 43 on his 25 mm tires. There was no give when rubber touched road. That morning, he had filled both inner tubes beyond capacity. It was a rough ride but fast. At this speed, a pothole was as lethal as a pickup.

In the past year, two IEDs had blasted apart gaping sections of Baltimore's highway system. The second assault resulted in the 695/70 interchange collapsing after the coordinated attack. Several surviving witnesses reported backpacks thrown from moving vehicles seconds before the explosion. Compared to other major metropolitan areas, Baltimore ranked somewhere in the middle for number of lives lost; consequently, the roads were cracked or cracking, relegated to gravel in sections. Funds dedicated to improving an already decaying infrastructure were now stowed away for the next catastrophes, ones everyone had grown to accept as part of civilian life. More and more of these attacks were decimating the U.S. highways, so regular upkeep soon became something of the not too recent past.

Janzen knew the work that went into laying road, and the fractures he dodged and hopped that evening required from him a little something extra. It stung to see such disrepair, these roads held hostage that needed fixing. There were still so many Baltimoreans who needed these jobs, but they sat around, waiting for the next disaster.

A relatively smooth patch opened before him, and he pinched the top tube between his knees to check for what dripped off his elbow. The color on his fingertips confirmed a collision with a side view mirror, an unnoticed injury and further evidence of the bicycle's wonder.

With his speed dropping, Janzen's mind wandered the course of a fleeing hare. He grabbed the corner of his consciousness and held fast to the roadway beneath him. The condition of the JFX ushered in an immediate heaviness his bike would not detect. Before spending the previous two years at Tappert Publishing, he had worked for a string of smaller, locally run construction outfits. Years in the business had callused his hands and provided him a sense of accomplishment at seeing something through to the end.

His father reacted to his son's vocational path with a lift of his one eyebrow and a snide comment about the difference between a métier and a trade. For Janzen, that was fine, coming from a man who often yelled at men and women alike. He preferred his father's more subtle expressions of scorn when compared to his loud fits. He considered that lifted eyebrow a graduation gift from the old man when he finished up his MFA from the University of Maryland. Through that educational journey, Janzen read the good book but preferred satanic verses; he slogged through Chaucer to Fowles; he bulls-eyed meter, and his participles dangled not. He had laid his literary foundation, so he figured he should learn to pour concrete. The first thing he wrote after finishing grad school at 23 was a cover letter to C and J Construction looking for work. If Howard Roark had his granite quarry, then it was time for Janzen to toil.

And toil, he did.

Adams' crescendo was an assault, and the grade now climbed past seven percent. He was up off the seat, and his drop bars flew from side to side under his bared chest and sidewinder arms. This acclivity demanded the white-hot. His speed slowed and he pumped and pumped. The drenched necktie around his head retained all it could until he no longer saw clearly with the new sting in his eyes. He saw stars along with the cars. He bit into his lip knowing the metallic taste would clear his vision and drive the legs.

He reached the top of the incline, and a flick of his ankle released the toe clip. His foot touched ground, he sucked in air, but his leg held steadily. His muscles reacted well, and a series of smacks to the quads warned the lactic acid to retreat. Two stalled lanes of traffic lurched on either side of him. Those heading north on the other side of the divider enjoyed three car gaps and speeds over sixty – off to the county or across state lines where the number crunchers from Pennsylvania justified their daily commute.

The siren in the distance carried well that early evening, but Janzen's head bobbed to an old Double Dagger cut, perfect for an impromptu excursion among the working folk. Janzen reveled in Strals's raw delivery, and while he caught his breath, the colors around him tightened and swirled. The view was swathed in his favorites. Sheeler crafted the vehicles perfectly, right down to the lug nuts, each side a different shade. Estes handled the surrounding cityscape, applying textures of coarseness to the old bricks that played prettily against the sheen of the vivid windows and their popping reflections. Redon took over at the horizon and filled Janzen's canvas with warm hues that could aptly be described as evocative.

"Is you crazy, muthafucka?"

Janzen removed an ear bud and tracked the voice as the one coming from the young black male steering the Land Rover. "Evocative isn't it?"

"There ain't no pedals on the light rail, bruva," said the other fella in the passenger seat. Coasting alongside the vehicle, Janzen clipped back in and grabbed the corner of the SUV's open window.

"Ask me about miles per gallon on this thing," said Janzen, enjoying the arterial conversation.

"Yeah, well, my honey ain't jumpin' on no pegs come the weekend, bruh." The driver smiled and checked the rearview before turning down the stereo. "You gonna wait around to see if them sirens are singin' for you?"

Janzen pushed away from the SUV and scrolled

through his watch. "I have something better."

"Man, is you crazy?"

Janzen grabbed the door panel again and answered as if being deposed. "I'm not psychotic…I don't think." He readjusted the tightness of the knot at the back of his head. "In a clinical sense, you know…all that axis one bullshit. I can tell you that my psychosis probably does *not* require immediate hospitalization. Manic, though, yes. I'm manic as fuck."

"Well Mercy's right down on St. Paul, but you wanna go to Sheppard Pratt, bruh. They check yer head when it ain't bleedin'."

"I didn't like the vibe there," said Janzen. "You see, I require the freedom to roam!" He swooped an arm out in front of him. "Ah! My egress comes a-calling gentlemen." He nodded his goodbye and pushed away from the SUV. He caught a straight line and powered the bike through the traffic, ass off the seat until his thighs sizzled the appropriate sizzle. He built up to his favorite speed: lights out fucking nuts. He wanted to scream a magnificent scream, but he'd save that.

Is you crazy?

To the casual observer, a bicyclist pushing pedals down a major metropolitan freeway during rush hour may elicit similar conventional responses. It was a little over two years ago when Janzen finally questioned his sanity shortly after quitting the drink. Not a sip of alcohol had passed his lips since then, but it was on his mind tonight while he tested the limits of his body and bike. He flickered his fingers off the drop bar, and the trails of the scars on his busted up knuckles took him back to the times years earlier when he first opened those wounds against the likes of brick walls, refrigerator doors and swerving foreheads. He drifted off and pedaled without effort, fueled by that big diesel engine in his chest.

In his clouded artistic process, Janzen had drunk the wine with Fante and the whiskey with Bukowski. He drank and read; he drank and wrote; he drank and fucked; he drank and fought. It became sloppy, and the lowest common denominator went from quotidian to daily, poetic to obligatory – a necessity for the shakes in place of a pathway to the sublime. The romance had soured.

Years of the elixir gave way to three slow-motion days of the cold turkey. The fevers, chills, vomit and fetid sweat were a reprieve from his restless legs stabbed over and over with invisible metal spoons. He found no sleep and lived within the fist of nausea. At one point he rolled over but realized he was on the floor. He tasted blood and his tongue swelled in his mouth. He thought he had some plague or best-case scenario: Covid-19. It turned out to be a seizure. On the fourth day of his newly sober world, he stomached half a sub sandwich and then lost touch with the reality he had been struggling to set right.

Voices not his own spoke the thoughts he was about to think. The hallucinations turned tactile. What was tactile grew razor-edged teeth and armored bodies. Who knew maggots bit so hard and drew so much blood? On that fourth day, everything started to shriek. The broken bones and kidney stones of yore whimpered off his podium of pain. A new king of torment was crowned. The problem was physical and supernatural; the problem was audio and visual; it turned spiritual and psychological.

He had worked enough jobs in the Baltimore area to know Sheppard Pratt was the psychiatric establishment he needed. He didn't drive, so he took a sufferer's route along sidewalks through a night rain infested with sharp and slimy things. Some were insects he didn't recognize. They sprouted from the downpour and moved like locusts. They invaded every open orifice. He rolled in the grass and on driveways and ran his exposed skin against tree bark, but nothing stopped them. It was in this condition that Janzen walked to the hospital grounds, acknowledging every home he passed as another haunted house.

Mile four of four turned into one of those rain-drenched, soul-searching, thousands of wasps dive-bombing into the eyeballs type of walk. Luckily, a discarded pair of eyeglasses he found near a curb at least forced the battalion of wasps to negotiate a barrier before they burrowed one after another into his eye sockets. That was a new kind of venom. The cracked glasses blurred his path, but they were his only defense. Some of them bounced off his drenched body, but they flew back under his shirt where they found other access points down below. Others crawled into his mouth and tore at his tongue, so he chewed and chewed and tasted their blood, which flowed down his chin and shirt. He swung his arms, and the pounding of his heartbeat shook some of them off – a driving bassline scored from the fluttering wings of a coked-up hummingbird.

His hold on reality was fleeting but grounded in a single word: asylum. He needed someone to make sense of the sinister voices yelling at him and the insects' infestation of his body and their piercing stings. Were they speaking to him? Was he the new host for their larvae? Why was it so important that the pain they inflict be so severe? These questions had only confused him when his only focus was sanctuary. The University of Maryland had been the oldest institution he held onto as his own, the respected cornerstone of his literary pursuits; however, that night saw Janzen straining to grasp at anything worth remembering. In its place, the words and sentences and structures he had honed with so much precision scattered in shrapnel and led him elsewhere towards institutionalization. The neural pathways he blazed in College Park had finally dead-ended or short-circuited. What was once fertile ground had pickled. He needed asylum that night. He needed help.

Overwhelmed by the expansive sprawl of Sheppard Pratt's Towson campus, he tried opening door after door until a wary security officer took him into one of the resident buildings. Janzen confessed to a nurse that he was being possessed. Years of focused atheism dissolved in the rain that night. The nurse had tried to calm him, and if his full awareness hadn't failed him, he would've seen a woman frightened for her safety. He repeated and repeated his concern about the availability of a priest who would both sanction and perform his exorcism. He kept asking whether Sheppard Pratt was considered a secular mental health facility. Was it true that only the Vatican could approve an exorcism? He asked if she could see the bugs all over him. The nurse yelled promises of a priest if he would just wait quietly in his seat so that she could arrange for a doctor to see him first. Janzen tore off the soaked shirt that clung to his torso. He tied it around the glasses as another blockade for the wasps and whatever else wanted in. A shard of the shattered spectacles freed the blood that soon flowed down his face, dying the shirt and eventually the tiled floor.

Cheap labor on the job site had led to Janzen's fluency in Spanish. Three days in an ICU taught Janzen his only Latin lesson: *Delirium Tremens*, the diagnosis made at Sheppard Pratt.

"Fuck you and your Stone Age language!" yelled Janzen upon hearing the diagnosis. "My blood's drawn with a syringe, not a leach, you fuck!" His confusion and anger stemmed not so much from the words coming out of that doctor's mouth. More precisely, it was the invisible children's choir singing songs of ancient curses that proved to be so disconcerting. He ran back through the hallways of the building and out into the rain. He sprinted across the hospital's grounds and crossed Osler Drive until he found another hospital with a revolving door. That St. Joseph's waiting room employed another frightened nurse and more agitated security guards, and the one with the clipboard arranged for Janzen to see a second doctor who repeated the same diagnosis.

"Sir, when did you last drink?" asked Dr. Number Two. It was four days ago, and it was his final Tullamore D.E.W. "Are you currently taking any medication?" To this question, the reply came quickly. "Lamictal and Trazadone. Abilify and fluoxetine. Dentyne and Thunderdome." At first, the words tramped from his mouth with a militant march, but the more he repeated them, the more loosely they came out until they next found a rhythmic cadence and the march turned to melody. "LaMICtal and

TRAAAzadone SeroTOOOOnin hydroCHLOOOORide." It was a perverted verse bent over the lap of withdrawal. His hummingbird heart slowed to a quavering warble. It was as if Janzen's nervous system had anticipated the influx of benzos about to flow into his bloodstream.

Another seizure was a possibility, so the nurses were all vitals and drips and anticonvulsants. In his volatile state, he tried yanking the IV line from his arm because its insertion was just one more stinging insect. He waved his arms and fought them off the best he could, but his swats eventually connected with nursing staff, who were shadowed and blurred and resembled the half-formed spooks flying off the walls to haunt him whenever he blinked in certain intervals.

Those on call were mostly sympathetic to Janzen's condition, but one of his backhands drew blood so leather cuffs chained to the underside of the gurney kept his wrists and ankles in place. They were padded against his skin, but he strained against their grip with grunts and howls. The veins in his neck and forearms rose like inverted furrows of a living and mutating land forgotten on some abandoned tract. He struggled with everything he had knowing he was now rendered a defenseless organism for the evolving waves of pestilence.

There was no stopping them. Once he gave in, the shadows, parasites and night stalkers struck in their horrifying syncopation. It was over. He was theirs now. It went on for hours until hours turned into days.

The youngest and largest of the nursing staff had maintained a cherubic affability and christened this patient 'Doozy' because of the doozy of a job the poor young man had done to his liver. Blood was drawn, and tests revealed enzymes and protein counts endemic to a much older and tenured drinker. "You gotta shoot for them stars, Nurse Ratchet. You just gotta shoot for them stars." Janzen saw her name tag that read Vanessa Williams, but she didn't mind the Ratchet references. For the next two days, she was both anchor and engine amid the rocky sea and rogue waves of his horrors. When she could have returned to her station between rounds, Vanessa sat in the darkened room at his bedside. She would always return to stroke his clammy forearm while he twisted and flinched, held tightly to the bed with the restraints. Her touch was tender and possibly inappropriate by some clinician's handbook, but she was there with her softness when everything else was jagged with backbones or segmented bodies and nasty intentions.

Lying there, largely immobile, Janzen found himself in waking nightmares, and Vanessa's voice became a beacon to a kinder place. He sometimes spoke in rolling incoherent incantations and rambled on about his future plans with a swollen, chewed up tongue. She was mostly left to her own digressions, and the lilts and timbre of her words were more important than their meaning. His flinches and choked whimpers were coaxed and nuzzled with her humming. In her touch and her voice, Janzen recognized something familiar. There was a depth both tight and taught, stretched across every waking second of her day until it was resigned to that shallow and transparent courage she showed the world. For Janzen, her sounds, that touch and her courage filled her history that she either revealed or he invented.

Vanessa Williams was not yet thirty. She also might have been imaginary. The burgeoning crease in between her eyebrows was of a noticeable depth and was assuredly contoured over years of contemplation or was perhaps the result of that smirk she could not yet define. She moved with a lightness of foot, motion that belied the extra weight she carried while hinting at years of rigorous training in mirrored studios. She wore no rings and applied her makeup to be seen from afar. When she hummed, she hit every note, and her voice rose and fell and skipped across Janzen's dark seas. Her melodies were sometimes improvised; some belonged to others – to the soprano Dawn Upshaw and to other symphonies of sorrow. Her fellow nurses called her by different names, and her scrubs were fresh and new. She tried hard to appear eager. Sitting next to Janzen, she hummed softly and switched her feet between first, second and third position.

After 72 exhausting hours in the ICU, Janzen approached a clarity he was on the trail of days earlier. On day four, he and Nurse Williams embraced outside the empty hospital chapel. Janzen loved her for what she did for him, and with his sensor on the fritz, he had no problem telling her just that. She cried enough to shake her round frame. She also made Janzen promise to look for love in less life-threatening ways. He asked for her information, all of it. He finally had an emergency contact.

That specific hospitalization took place a little over two years ago, and now that Janzen was sober and healthy, the memories played like a sentimental clip show on TV after a long, celebrated run. But what was that terrible noise interrupting such a broadcast? It was a howl the folks of Baltimore knew well. The siren had, in fact, been singing his song. The congestion on the JFX was an uninspired peloton with Janzen on the breakaway and the cop car now yo-yoing behind. Either expressway shoulder provided passage for the black and white, whose pursuit provoked heads out of many a car windows. Janzen muted his music to better gauge the distance that remained between the cop and him. Encouraging motorists shouted for him to "Ride, mutha-fucka! Ride!" and the speed brought back his tears. The flick of his finger found a bigger gear, and his legs and lungs pumped. He tucked down tight on his drop bars when the car appeared alongside in the outer lane. The policeman manhandled the wheel at ten and two, his forearms cords of ferocity twitching under his skin. The officer yelled something unintelligible, and his angry gestures were met with a smile, a flick of the eyebrows skyward, and then a hard left in front of the cop car and through a gap in the freeway divider. Weaving through the oncoming traffic was all Frogger and fortune as he flew up the ramp past the merging vehicles. Homeward to Hampden!

Janzen overshot his row home and cruised down the switchback to Falls Road from Wyman Park. He wasn't done riding yet, and he always enjoyed the presence of the Jones Falls stream alongside him. He removed the tie from around his head and squeezed out the wetness before putting it back into place and yelled playfully toward whatever brown trout might be swimming along with him. He had ridden this stretch of Falls hundreds of times in the past few years, and he slowed his speed and dropped into a more appropriate gear, one that would allow for a moment of nostalgia. He would miss these roadways. He'd even miss parts of Hampden, though it was more of the neighborhood's history that endeared it to him rather than the availability of sous vide dog food and flavored compost material.

In the years before the Civil War, gristmills and a busy harbor initially drew many of the poor white farmers north to the Hampden-Woodberry area where they settled around the Jones Falls watershed in the row homes lining the meandering, dirt-packed roads. Given Baltimore city's majority black population nowadays, the Hampden neighborhood had retained its own little white enclave due in part to that Southern lineage, a population that boomed in the latter 1800s and had somehow maintained its bloodlines throughout the decades until those mill workers, farmhands and cotton swappers of old begot and begot until the fathers of babies eventually gave birth to baby daddies. If the ghosts of those descendants walked about Hampden today, they'd see their families still white as white talking black as black. These young men now walked around with their sagging pants and were sons of other young fathers who had hung onto the words and movements of whatever *Yo! MTV Raps* broadcasted. And now what fathers remained watched on at the parade of endlessly pregnant teenagers with skinny legs and loud mouths, whose main role revolved around manicuring the boys' tight fades and pushing around their hand-me-down strollers.

The middle-aged meth-heads were a throwback to

decades earlier when the neighborhood's kitsch was still a ways off, but the restaurants soon came one-by-one. Coupled with rent control and the wide expanse of Jon Waters' cinematic shadow, Hampden eventually played host to a hipster infiltration, a population that clashed with the old-timers and their grandsons and grand-daughters in a most silent and segregated way. Janzen had straddled the line between blue-collar grunt and one of the harbingers of gentrification. Ultimately, the books he read and the music he listened to and the beer and coffee he drank all formed a cultural undertow that drew him further and further away from the tool belts and Firm Grips of years past, but it was a gap he bridged with his daily struggle. In truth, he wasn't out in the mix like he used to be; his sobriety assured him of that. He preferred his isolation and took in the neighborhood's changes mostly from behind his second story window.

Janzen made his way up Roland Ave. and took a right onto 36th Street, The Ave. as the locals knew it. Hampden's main drag offered its patrons Michelin star restaurants, head shops, mom-and-pop bookstores and barbers, consignment shops, a terrible Mexican joint, and everything else one might expect from a townie's town thrust in trendy directions that most locals would've pre-ferred have happen to nearby Charles Village.

The Avenue shimmered on this early August evening. The sidewalks were busy with people making their way to eat while the lookie-loos held tightly to their purses and window-shopped through the less fashionable window fronts. Some of the locals sat on the bus stop benches and fanned themselves. Baltimore's heat was only oppressive to the uninitiated; that's not to say it wasn't hot as hell, but one was bound to run into some weather south of the Mason-Dixon. Janzen loved the heat and believed himself baptized after every ride. Tonight, the neighborhood sparkled in such a way because he'd no longer call it home. He always enjoyed Hampden at about twelve miles an hour; any slower and Smalltimore reared its ugly head. He hooked a right on Chestnut and dodged a family full of fatties spread out across the intersection like drugged slugs on the wrong 'shrooms, too involved with their artisan ice cream to take notice of incoming traffic. In their defense, The Charmery made a delicious cone.

Janzen cruised to a stop and led his bike over the curb and into the hallway of his row home. It was the time of year when the humidity swelled the laminate flooring beneath his feet, and he bounced his way down the hall and up to the second floor, his home for the past few years. To describe his apartment as spartan would be generous. There was a single beach chair opened for business in a room typically used for watching television. A card table rested in front of the chair, shimmed for steadiness with Salinger's *Nine Stories*. On the table rested a computer. Past the laptop on the wall hung the one remaining decoration: a framed headshot of John Kennedy Toole. Every other piece of furniture had been sold or given away weeks ago. He spent the last few nights chasing dreams in the sleeping bag he used as a child.

Janzen had scrubbed the place floor to ceiling because his soon-to-be-former-landlord was a peach of a woman, who frequently left salted brownies outside his apartment door in an effort "to fatten up them cheeks, hon." Janzen had helped her find a replacement tenant, showing her how to navigate the new online sites with sortable credit scores and background checks.

He flipped the computer alive knowing there awaited a final unread email, one he had received a week earlier. The subject line in his inbox gave no indication of its contents, but if it read like the others, he'd no longer have any further need of the computer, which he intended on passing along to his landlord. He clicked on it.

Mr. Hakkinen,

Your novel details a rich tapestry of emotions woven into a dynamic narrative, but what it lacks is a singular focus we here at Top to Bottom Press feel is imperative to thrive in this current market. Tawdry Fields is a work bathed in the boiling water of solipsism, whereas what we publish here is more akin to a water slide at an amusement park. The opening is rife with action and consequence, but the concern is that the readership will not follow the protagonist and his self-referenced bi-polar perspective.

While your voice is unique and thought-provoking, there were more questions raised than answered, and I wonder if it would behoove you to reconsider Teezer's final decision to turn himself in when there are obviously no charges brought against him. I found it courageous that Teezer attends the "Preserve the White" rally of Senator Howley to confront that or whom he loathes the most in the face of his recurring dream of torturing and killing the politician. (I offer this as an aside: are two protracted chapters necessary to evoke the brutality of these sadistic acts of torture? I do applaud your attention to detail, but the exercise becomes a horrific lesson in mutilated anatomy and the tensile strength of the senator's fingernails, eyelids and select organs.)

These two chapters do raise interesting comparisons to the effectiveness and morality of state-sponsored techniques, which your protagonist repeatedly mentions, as he believes his deeds to be for the greater good of society, but where are you really going with this manuscript? Please consider submitting any future work to my attention.

Good luck, Janzen.

Cordish Mayweather

That Cordish could write, and his response was far from the form rejections that had been trickling in over the past few months. He asked the right questions, too. Janzen knew they were coming, and he knew where he was going with this manuscript: Formstone Avenue.

2

At about the same time Janzen had quit drinking, William Hallorann hanged himself from the limb of a tulip poplar on his family's plot of land in rural Harford County. He was 47. Though the two decisions were made by men who did not know the other, that didn't mean the ripples of either act didn't in some way finally connect them down the line in a most unbelievable way.

William had lived on the twenty-acre property with his brother Wirt, one of his two living relatives. Along lacquered bar tops in the county, the two were known as The Drunk and The Devil. There was a third brother, but he lived in a sparsely populated hunting and trapping village in northern Alaska having once claimed that "until the Bering freezes over, Teller allows for the farthest distance between me and my two dumbfuck brothers."

The Devil, William, was a masters division-winning taxidermist known for his savage representations of mammals and gameheads. The Drunk, Wirt, drank Natty Boh all day and shot squirrels for stew with his .22. He also cared for the landscaping, maintained a garden and

the house's upkeep, and often conveyed fraternal correspondence with his brother through their unofficial communication liaison, the Harford County Sheriff's Office.
See, the two fought like bacon grease, not anything
that'll kill you, but it'll leave a mark. Three constants
remained true to the end of the duo's relationship: they
always fought, one of them always called the cops, and
no one ever pressed charges. The deputies were used by
the brothers on more of a consultation basis than anything else. William and Wirt were more interested in the
clarity of the law rather than the enforcement of it. For
example, would the convergence of the sniffing end of
a stuffed beaver and the flared end of a flintlock blun-
derbuss be considered a hostage situation? The answer,
they found out, was no; however, charges of vandalism
and willful destruction of property could have been filed
after Wirt's eventual squeeze of the trigger that ensured
the obliteration of said beaver. But, of course, no charges
were pressed, and the deputies had witnessed nothing.

Before his foray into the blue yonder, William
excelled not just in the field of taxidermy. He was also
quick with a pen and offered a prodigious stream of correspondence to Maryland's elected representatives. The
trademark ferocity that characterized his mounts was no
less apparent in the strike of his ink on paper. Most folks
along those aforementioned lacquered bar tops surely
assumed William's political leanings would angle in a certain direction due to his inexorable and vocal contempt
for those elected in the historically blue state. Others
might also point to William's penchant for donning the
Confederate colors and his pride of having been named

after a gray-clad brigadier general, but it was that rebel blood flowing through him that necessitated not the obedience of a singular political allegiance inasmuch as an adult-long commitment to righting anything that did not sit so well with him. Being the vexed type, there was little that escaped the choler of a man who found stimulation in being red-faced and pissed off. He was progressive in the fact that party lines meant as much to him as a spit in the well.

William wasn't a numbers man in that he struggled with math coming up in school. History was complicated on account of the dates. Sometimes he remembered to charge for his taxidermy services; other times, not so much. He kept a cardboard box filled with receipts and purchase orders that he delivered to an accountant around tax time every year. He did not know his own telephone number, and he recognized his birthday around the end of August. Even with these numerical aversions, William had memorized the addresses to the offices of Maryland's congressmen, numerous editors of *The Baltimore Sun*, and the home addresses of the six Harford County city council members. These numbers were learned by rote through the simple act of repetition and eventually came as naturally to him as the cleaning of his Colt revolver. Diatribes, inquisitions, remonstrances, reflections and prognostications filled the pages of these correspondences.

The final piece of mail sent by William Hallorann was addressed to Mrs. Caroline Borden, editorial director of the news content for *The Sun*. Years ago, Caroline had begun saving William's letters and smiled at their closings regardless of the invective-laced language and the continuous charges of journalistic impropriety in *The Sun's* local political coverage. She had told colleagues at lunch or over a cocktail that mixed in with the letters' combative strain were glints of sensitivity and equanimity. She appreciated his effort and the self-referential way he recalled earlier points he had made in his other letters. Yes, he was a mean, crusty man, but he cared deeply about Maryland and its political direction. He made such a particular and peculiar impact on her that she would always remember the day of his passing despondently.

A deputy report estimated that his noose was affixed at a height of around 130 feet. William had scaled the mighty tulip tree using the zest of a cantankerous ideologue and the antique climbing spurs left to him by his father. It was speculated by those at the scene that his last action before his hanging was to wrap electrical tape, later found at the base of the tree, around either hand in such a way as to ensure the projection of his two longest fingers.

His brother Wirt had called the sheriff's office non-emergency line not until 11 that morning because he figured, "Where the fuck was he gonna go anyways?" Wirt had stood by quietly throughout the entirety of the retrieval. He watched while the authorities brought in a city-works cherry picker, which spun its tires as soon as it reached the wet grass fifty feet from the tree. The fire department then tried to angle the ladder on their truck only to have the hydraulic turntable fail with the ladder pointed far enough away from the tree to be deemed useless. Wirt had shook his head as television crews appeared, and a swelling crowd waited for a climber with a specialized set of skills. Hour seven of the body retrieval saw such a man fasten a harness to a swinging William. The belay end of the rope was thrown over the same branch from which William swung with the idea of slowly lowering him down.

The noose was cut, and William immediately flipped head to feet. The harness had a tenuous grip on the body that wouldn't hold for long. With William's head leading the descent, it absorbed countless thwacks and bumps on branches and limbs, which left Wirt rubbing the creases of his forehead. He claimed that the only reason he stuck around for the full rescue was "to get my goddamned climbing spikes back." The equipment was ultimately taken to the morgue along with the body. Wirt had walked alongside the gurney and patted his brother's chest before he was lifted into the silent ambulance.

In that final letter to Caroline Borden, the opening paragraph was similar to many that came before it – a chastisement on an inconsistency in a quote or a misused semicolon. But what followed was a list of 22 assorted antiques, gewgaws, curiosities, and a few select mounts that he asked to be passed on to various organizations, companies and museums around Baltimore. There was no direct reference made to his suicide, though those with a bent for the cryptic would probably beg to differ.

Word of the actual suicide eventually came back to Caroline in her office, and it was then that the pressed tulip accompanying that final letter made more sense. She had heard talk about a man hanged from an enormous blooming tree a day earlier but never made the connection. She revisited the letter and reread the closing salutation, which read "Thank you," instead of the customary "Get your shit together," and she found it unexpectedly necessary to close her office door to collect herself. She reread the postscript and vowed to follow through with his final appeal: "My one brother's a sonuvabitch and the other's a drunk. I would appreciate if you found the homes for the above mentioned pieces and be sure my brother Wirt gets the climbing spikes and my taxidermy equipment."

Upon receiving word of his brother's death through Wirt, Jeremiah Hallorann took a plane out of Nome and made it back to Baltimore in time to see his younger brother interred. There was no ceremony, just Wirt digging a hole in the ground next to his mother and father's plots. William did not want his remains displayed but had made the instruction on multiple occasions that his ashes be "buried next to ma and pa in some Tupperware so I'll stay good for a lil longer."

Once back in town, Jeremiah laid claim to William's skinning and tanning equipment and mentioned to his brother that he'd make good use of it when back on Alaskan soil. By this time, Caroline had been in contact with Wirt and made him aware of his deceased brother's final letter. She wrote that she intended to find the proper destinations for everything on William's list in spite of Jeremiah's intentions. A fistfight between the two remaining brothers and an ensuing appointment with a probate judge followed.

A decision was made in favor of Caroline and a newly sober Wirt. Jeremiah would not move on from his brother's death empty-handed, though. As per William's instruction on that final letter, number 19 stipulated that his older brother would be the new proprietor of a plastic bag full of "a once steaming pile of horse shit best used as sustenance to smolder and fuel those cold, soulless Alaskan nights." Wirt had even included a fresh addition to the bag's contents before he sealed and sent it.

The case was covered locally and caught the public's attention and discussions about the legality and necessity of final wills and testaments soon followed, a product of a city and state facing a silent and steadily growing epidemic. With the unexpected spike in suicides, the non-profit group out of Harford County, Solemnly Departed, grabbed the baton and ran with it until "Bill's Will Bill" was law, making notes written of the suicidal variety legally binding if a number of statutes were met. One: the letter must be notarized. Two: the letter must be signed at the time of the notarizing. Three: proof of identification must be provided. Four: a second witness is required at the time of the signing. And five: any sign of intoxication or duress leading up to the final signature would preclude the notary public from certifying such documents.

Years and years ago, a person of a well enough maintained mind and disposition might find this law morose, superfluous, and overly encumbered in terms of both its purpose and execution, but what began as a Baltimore whisper had expanded into a swelling beat that pounded across city streets and rolling Maryland hills alike. What was once ho-hum to the unaffected could no longer be ignored. Bodies had to be removed, communities were unnerved, and some spoke of an infection while others recognized something deeper, a city's residents being swallowed up whole from so many flaws and so many failures. There was, though, one man at one particular location along Formstone Avenue whose ears were tuned in to the movement. His involvement was spurred by the loss of a loved one and led to the first and only one-stop-shop for those wishing to pass on to whatever came next.

3

The building at 1923 Formstone Avenue climbed eleven stories and could have been inspired by some maenadic madness. The man who commissioned its construction, Mr. Wayland Selby, had surely indulged his lavish yet limited architectural knowledge. It was a building with eight sides but not like a stop sign with eight equal sections; rather, it was a building with four sides of ample length to accommodate rows of windows facing four quarter clicks of a compass. The other four smaller sides cut into what would have been the building's corners. The raised and rusticated ground floor boasted an entranceway capped by a broken pediment, bridged and surmounted by the splayed limestone legs of Persephone. It was reported that the Greek's head was replaced by another version because her gaze was not originally upward as mandated by Mr. Selby. Sculpted pomegranate and other clustered fruit decorated the upper cornice while diamondback terrapin shells and black-eyed Susans adorned the keystones.

For every decorative wonder was its foil – a *what the fuck* to go with a *what a sight*. Those with aesthetic eyes and acerbic tongues mostly assailed the building's ninth floor. It bucked whatever convention remained at that height where huge glass panes on each of the four major sides interrupted the sedimentary flow above and below. From a great distance, it was a blindfold on a boulder. *The Sun*'s article covering its 1995 opening was titled "A Shock to the Senses." The architectural choices were certainly suspect, but there were genuine bits of elegance to behold. At the ribbon cutting ceremony, the breeze was soft and brushed gently past the gorgeous flowers that climbed from the second story on up. It was reported that Mr. Selby's young wife was responsible for the blossoms festooning each of the four smaller sides of the building. She had hired a local sculptor to twist and mold wrought iron into tortuous paths up each of the four sides, curving and winding its way around the singular windows installed on each floor of each side until each section reached the rooftop. She insisted that the artist allow for the connection and weight of beds of soil from which the flowers and vines would grow. During the winter months, the iron was designed to resemble the vines they supported during the spring and summer, and they appeared to grow out from the concrete to which they were attached. But the May opening saw the anemone clematis in full bloom on two of the sides. On the others were the greens and reds of the crimson glory vine. The beflowered ten-floor irons brought life and movement to the building. The writer covering the opening devoted an entire section of his article to Mrs. Selby's contribution but was unable to obtain a single quote from the shy woman who spoke only to her clinging young son.

It was a building out of time and out of place, and the conglomeration of materials used in its construction assured its lack of grace. Mr. Selby's allegiance to Maryland and his promise to use only materials "within her beautiful bosom" surely won him points with the locals. The first floor exterior was made of Baltimore gneiss. The marble used in its interior was excavated from the same quarry that supplied the materials for the Washington Monument. The concrete that flowed from the second floor up was in part made of the crushed rock drilled from the very land on which the building sat. Mr. Selby had bought out the quarry that operated at this location for the previous fifteen years. The grounds were cleared of any reminder of that operation and in its place sat Selby's grand headquarters. For almost three decades, it served as the central hub of Selby Industries, the name stamped on shower drains, lighting fixtures, heating panels, door hinges, doorknobs and vents that supplied, returned and exhausted. The name was imprinted in the residential and commercial – a name and company whose origins took hold in Baltimore years before.

After the opening of the building, *The Sun* published a follow-up feature on the designer and owner, Wayland Smith Selby. In the piece, he was heralded as the local boy who rooted himself in the community and who thrived in the city that helped raise him.

The Sun's article reached back to the days of Selby's youth as the son of a brilliant contractor who had worked the greater Baltimore area for decades. The elder Selby was a man known affectionately as "Hammer" due to his prowess with the tool. It was reported that the mother had died from complications with Wayland's birth, and Hammer's inimitable work ethic and unyielding devotion to his wife guaranteed young Wayland's status as an only child.

The gist of the article went along these lines: Wayland recalled one of his earliest impactful memories, wandering through the forest with his father, who carried an axe at his side. Wayland was around seven years old at the time and was told that the man whose property they were on was a client of his father. As Selby lore had it, the client had fallen on tough financial times and could not pay his father for his previous work. The man alternatively offered him an afternoon on his property and any tree he could fell with an axe as payment for the work. The memory of those eight hours or so of his father's harvesting tree after tree with mighty, precise strikes stayed with the boy. "The swing of that man set a standard for me that no Oriole could ever eclipse. He was the first idea of a hero for me, and that image of him chopping endures to this day." The lumber that came from the black walnuts were processed by his father's homemade bandsaw mill and became the structure for the home Wayland loved from his youth through his adolescence.

His father had the strength of a brute, but the elegant flairs of their stained banister and sculpted fireplace mantle told the story of an artist. Wayland grew up surrounded by his father's passion. He remembered the first time he saw mass-produced picture frames sold in a store and had wondered at how many his father had given the business to sell. After all, didn't the world's supply of picture frames come from his father's workbench? It was the childhood home filled with his father's skill that eventually took hold of Wayland and told him what he was to do with his life.

He went on to earn an MBA from Towson University and began paying off his school loans with the money he made every summer working alongside his father. The month after his graduation, Selby Industries began out of the Selby station wagon, a 1980 Buick Estate. In the article, Wayland remarked "that the Buick had, in fact, been my entire estate. I sunk everything I had into those first few years." He had driven from one work site to the next – from one home furnishing business to another – carrying a leather-bound portfolio of his father's work under his arm, a tie around his neck and the boast of hand-made products and competitive prices. It was the closest he came to an evangelical life, Selby claimed. The first order he took was for a bundle of shingles for a neighbor's doghouse, a commission no less important than anything that had come before it in the construction trade.

Wayland had enlisted the full-time help of his father, who admitted his excitement at the idea of a partnership with his go-getting son. Hammer transitioned from contractor-for-hire to designer-fabricator. What his father could not manufacture in his garage, he only needed to pick up a phone and call one of scores of people willing to offer access to heavier, stronger equipment.

The first year of Selby Industries was a financial loss, but it provided the time to stockpile merchandise for the coming summer. Wayland learned to pinpoint his sales efforts, and first orders from clients typically led to others.

Over dinners, he often directed his father's storytelling towards the names of contractors and foremen he had worked with in the past for possible leads. While he often worked alone, Hammer cemented a reputation as an eccentric but effective hire. He built quickly and to code. He taught his trade secrets to anyone who worked hard enough. He problem-solved and massaged crews when communication broke down. He was known to name his tools after their perceived personalities and handled a pickaxe with the dexterity of Marin Alsop's baton, a movement he was indeed familiar with given the number of times he took his son to see the Baltimore Symphony Orchestra perform. He drove nails in single strokes to the ticks of some inner metronome. And he was trusted to see a job through its foundation, construction, wiring, and plumbing up to its inspection, which he never once failed.

Wayland told *The Sun*, "My father's greatest gift was the ability to see when something wasn't on the level." Hammer told his son that there was a tug inside of him that was his secret to success as a man, and it was also the reason he could see one of Wayland's ears was slightly higher than the other. At lunches on the job, the grunts would lay two-by-fours between a-frames and challenge Hammer to spot the incongruity. They'd insert miniscule shims to offset the bubble of a level in an attempt to throw off Hammer in the hopes of sullying his gift. The man, though, always knew the exact position of that bubble.

Wayland also attributed any gift of salesmanship to advice passed down by his father. Hammer had told his son that the key to an effective conversation was to approach it the way a blacksmith would his material. "He always spoke of listening to the steel, detecting temperament through its color and movement," the younger Selby said, having grown up sharing time with his father in their backyard forge. He learned that the material could speak in tinny tones or with depth. The final product was ultimately the goal, so it was imperative that the blacksmith listened to what was offered.

It was during that interview when Wayland admitted to a secular upbringing, but the forge had become something spiritual to both of them, father and son working together on Sunday afternoons. No choir was necessary as long as one of them swung a hammer, a sound rooted in archaic harmonics. As a boy, he knew some Old Testament stories and found the parts about the world's creation entertaining and the wrath and violence glorious, but when he finally reached the seventh grade, he grew partial to another god. Strong yet crippled, Hephaestus would become Wayland's choice for their company's name had his father not hinted at his aversion to such grandiosity.

A college degree, a genuine smile and a humble belief in his products warmed Wayland's sales pitch. Hammer's craftwork and history added a layer of oxide. Guaranteed delivery and affordable pricing stoked the flames. And soon, the Selby name produced more and more special products, and in turn, the company slogan changed three times over the next twenty years. First stenciled and spray painted along the Buick Estate was: *Baltimore Through Selby*. Years later, the first storefront in Towson read: *Maryland Through Selby*. And still later, the tag on the TV spot featuring then Baltimore Oriole second baseman Brian Roberts read: *The Mid-Atlantic Through Selby*. Finally, the freight of tractor-trailers heading west was emblazoned with *The U.S.A. Through Selby*.

The tone of the newspaper article had painted Wayland Selby as a man deserving of success the way a true Baltimorean should have earned it, through gritty persistence. Selby said, "I consider my success like a fisherman holds his catch. There's some pride, and it's okay to see it for a moment or two, but if you spend too much time admiring what you got, things get to stinking real quick."

4

Janzen was diagnosed with bipolar II during his junior year in high school. Upon hearing the news, he thought about how much he loved *Empire Strikes Back*, *T2*, and *Aliens* over their respective predecessors. He lacked focus at times. He had just seen *Wrath of Khan*, and while the psychiatrist spoke of medication and psychoses, Janzen asked him about that gnawing feeling. "Hey Bones, about this gnawing feeling…"

That question was Janzen's only external investigation into that burrowing agitation that crept and clawed throughout his system. Over the years, it gnawed at him, and he screamed. It gnawed at him until he drank it away. The bounce of a breast on a television commercial incited it, and it gnawed differently until he came. It would eventually come back and he would have to cum again. It gnawed for hours and hours until days and nights were wasted and relegated to profligate compulsions. Before the prescriptions, the gnawing encompassed every passing minute. It was a rollercoaster ride; it was a jail cell; it was the only thing at the time, a burning immediacy begging to be released. Early on there was cutting, and the spreading of skin gushed forth stopgap relief. The cutting gave way to drugs, drinking, fucking, and fighting. The fallout of each typically yielded an inactivity that cloaked him heavily. During those times, he thought of himself as catching dust – the only activity found in the verb itself. He caught dust until his bladder intervened or his alarm went off for work.

The gnawing began as a teen. It was there through his twenties. And it was there at 29 when he arrived at 1923 Formstone Avenue.

Janzen followed the news and was hooked years earlier by a story on one of the passed legislations of Maryland's General Assembly. Senate Bill 728 established the legality of the final will and testament of a "suicide participant" given proper documentation and witness substantiation. Bill's Will Bill also cleared culpability of present executors as long as the drafting was notarized and completed in the absence of coercion, duress or deception. Later added to the law was an option to designate from a growing list of charitable organizations a destination for the "suicide participant's" property and possessions – both monetary and material – in lieu of said participant's spouse and/or kin.

Janzen had been listening to WYPR when he first heard of the law's passing. For him it provided an incentive to finish the writing he was working on. It gave him a hope and drive to write those final two words so many others had written. He wanted to write those words in good conscience so that he could finally rest, and he had done just that. He put in the effort.

The chain-link fence Janzen now gripped had been installed the week after Selby's headquarters closed its front doors for the final time – right after her suicide. That was two years ago.

An intercom system projecting from its cylindrical concrete anchor faced Formstone, a two-laned leg of an original bypass route for truckers traveling east and west hoping to avoid traffic on the beltway. The roadway was now filled with potholes so deep that locals with any savvy avoided it. Deprived of the hundreds of employees buzzing about the building and grounds, this stretch along Formstone lay in ruin with its eleven-story anomaly serving as its worn and faded toe tag.

The building was set back about seventy feet from the road. What appeared to be a guard shack sat as an afterthought at the heel of the monolith. The patch of grass in front of the building had been cut recently, but weeds grew through the beds of years-old mulch.

Janzen gripped the fence and peered through to the sculpture of Persephone, once a symbol for a thriving business and now a repository for bird shit. He empathized with her captivity and abandonment and took the warm summer breeze as an exhale of her understanding. He waited for her to blink. He waited, too, for something wet to roll down his cheek, but he wasn't sad. He wasn't anything.

He breathed in the air and shivered. The scent of asphalt and dust kicked a little something loose. Maybe it reminded him of days out at recess on the blacktop, and suddenly the dry breeze wasn't simply a gust of wind; it was a confluence of Chesapeake zephyrs landing sulfuric kisses along his salty nape. Janzen swelled. The building and the scene played well with the Arvo Pärt now in his head. There was now a little wetness, and the big structure in front of him sparkled with an infinity of mirrors.

His bike rested stolidly against the same section of fence he held onto and interrupted his abstraction. From his pocket, he produced a pen and a Moleskine. He wrote, "For whomever needs it" on a blank page. He worked the words over again and crossed out the *m*. He tore out the note and pinned it in between the brake line and the frame's top tube and rubbed the saddle as an uncle would tousle a young nephew's hair. "Bye, bud."

Janzen approached the intercom and pressed the only button on it. He lowered his head and mumbled a hello into the recessed speaker.

Nothing.

"Anyone there?" he yelled toward the guard station. Still nothing. He traced a path up the façade on the western facing side of the building and had to tilt his head skyward to accommodate the view. The once blossoming lengths of iron were now discolored and weathered. Scraps of dead creepers hung in spots, but it struck Janzen that if he could scale his way to the second floor any of the ornamental irons would offer a winding path to the top of the building. That must've been how the others did it. Conveniently, a ladder of sufficient length rested in the grass next to the building.

Janzen found a new use for the intercom system and hoisted himself up on it with thoughts of scaling the fence. "Whoa there, my boy! Belay off! Belay off!" crackled the brushed metal system.

Janzen dismounted the device and spoke once again into the corrugated section. "I need to speak to someone, sir."

"You're doing just that, son."

"Goddammit. This is clumsier than I imagined."

Dead air.

The poetry of this day stuttered. The Chesapeake zephyrs gave way to puffs of dust that coated his mouth. "Sir, I'm interested in your depth of knowledge on Proposition 728 that was voted into law a couple years back." Janzen waited as if for a truant bus. He kicked rocks at his feet. He took in the hardness of his surroundings and was impressed at the ambitious spots of green popping up from the burlap expanse. "You know you're plopped right smack dab in a goddamn quarry?"

"Let us build ourselves a city and a tower that reaches the heavens and we'll make a name for ourselves." The allusion only irritated Janzen, but his mind was currently occupied with Roark's time with his granite, and he permitted the sedimentary to play the role of Providence, ensuring the decision he had made. This was the place.

"I'm here to kill myself, sir. I know you. I mean, I know this place. I know what you do for people, and I need your help. I'm coming over." Janzen had already reached the top rail of the fence when the magnetized latch clicked, revealing an opening entranceway. A door to the guard shack pushed open and once there, Janzen entered.

"Name?"

"Janzen Hakkinen."

"Finnish much?"

"Finish what?"

"Hmm…" The security guard opened a once water-logged notebook and began his notation: "…not responding to improvised attempt at humor." The guard stowed the notebook back into its drawer and studied Janzen like he was Luce's *Morning, Interior* propped up on an easel, staring as if all those dots were less a composite but a quandary.

The desk he sat behind was in the shape of an L and ran alongside the shack wall and out between his visitor and him. The roll of his office chair towards the telephone broke the stillness. He poked an extension and waited for a response. With the receiver to his ear, he surveyed Janzen with the subtlety of a child who recently learned to express circumspection. The guard was all eyebrows and beard, the latter of which was prodigious in volume and length. The busyness of his fluttering fingers seemed the current that controlled such an imperially ashen growth. In these whiskers, Charles Darwin and Karl Marx were contemporaries finally brought together in the form of this odd Baltimorean. The man's uniform was fit for a man living decades earlier given the length and point of the collar appearing under the beard. It had the look of new old stock, with an untailored style of something built rather than designed with enough room across the back to accommodate the latissimus flex of Atlas.

"Yes. Yes…here right now, sir. Yes sir." The guard hung up the phone and with a shove of his foot propelled himself back to the desk with the aplomb of one who had just rolled his twelfth consecutive strike; unfortunately, it was the accuracy of this move that sent him not only towards his desired destination but then some. He hit the midsection of his target with such power that one foot hit the desk's metal modesty with a wallop that abruptly straightened both spines in the room. The guard made no small move and held Janzen's gaze as the boom settled around the two men.

Holding.

"We could've named that thing," said Janzen in an attempt to incite a blink from the strange, now blink-bereft man.

"That sound?"

"The desk sound."

Holding.

"Name?"

"I don't know...'brack' or something onomatopoeic but more guttural...like the old Batman graphics but less obvious."

"*Your* name."

"*Again*, Janzen Hakkinen."

"Mr. Hakkinen, I don't know what your intentions are."

"You know exactly what my intentions are. I know from the paper that at least four people have jumped off the top of this building and each had previously met with a person on these grounds capable of notarizing their final will and testament. And I know that the man who owns this building made donations to different charities in the names of those people. I know someone is not going to leave my body here to rot and fester like it naturally should because a person innocent of my decision should not be burdened with the image of the decaying corpse that I intend to be with or without your help."

"Are you on any drugs? You sober?"

"Stone cold."

"Blow into this, please." The guard produced a breathalyzer from another drawer and read the double zero after Janzen's forceful blow. "Fill this out please." The two-sided document looked like an application for a new apartment. "Please read the fine print, Janzen." The blocks of periphrastic prolixity brought Janzen back to the months he had served as a technical writer when the construction work had dried up one winter. His tenure with that pharmaceutical company was spent holed up with factions of the company's legal team inventing circuitous language born to poke holes in the barrage of lawsuits they'd slap away one after another.

That job never sat so right with him. Some of his coworkers congratulated Janzen's adeptness at configuring and arranging the duplicitous verbiage. Janzen had never read the fine print until he actually composed it. Most of the content was promotional in nature and marketed toward the potential sales of medications, but he was part of the problem, which became another reason sleeping through the night grew exhausting. The experience was but a tiny rivulet making its way toward his rage's cataracts.

Janzen was hopeful that quitting the drink would dull his fury, but the opposite happened. What burned and seared his insides grew more focused when before it had been blunt and lazy.

It was just the other day when he called to cancel his

gas and electric, and there was no human to be reached on the other line during what was supposed to be normal business hours. The automated voice controlling the cancellation of services had taunted him with its equanimity and ignorance. There was no option for an operator or customer service technician and the main menu only led down those thorny pathways to the same dead end. Janzen had noted a hint of condescension in the computerized voice and swore he heard an exhale that he interpreted as a snicker. He was forced to place the phone down because it no longer served as a device used for speaking; it was a fucking provocation. It wasn't the lack of communication or efficiency or the fact that his FUCKING ACCOUNT NUMBER was not accepted even though he was pressing the EXACT FUCKING ACCOUNT NUMBERS that caused Janzen so much concern. It was that desperate rage. It left wakes in his life; it left gaps.

"Huh?"

"I asked if you were prepared to put this on video," asked the guard.

Gaps and gaps and gaps.

"Sure." Janzen's forearm gleamed after a swipe across his forehead.

"You get cracking on that paperwork, and I'll make a phone call for another witness over here – a law man. You logged out on me a little there," said the bearded guard. He set up a tripod and locked a camera into place. He once again picked up the phone and dialed an outside number. "Yup...first one here gets it...yup...starting now." He smiled to himself and replaced the phone's receiver. He then peered through the dusty slats of the budget blinds.

Janzen let his surroundings sink back in. The interior of the guard station conformed to what he understood to be an interior of a guard station. A poster hung on one unpainted wall detailing the correct CPR procedures. A mini fridge hummed in a corner on which a microwave rested. A charging dock boosted the life of one walkie-talkie. There were filing cabinets, a stapler, carpeting, an installed fuse box, dust, economy, deadened acoustics all wrapped up in a 12x12 aluminum sided package that when examined alone passed the part of any other prefabricated guard station in the city had it not been for one detail: what or who was it guarding? The building that had served as Selby Incorporated's headquarters had closed years earlier. So now this little afterthought of a shack-cum-notary public office stood as the lone onsite appendage of a once-thriving company. Upon entering, Janzen had noticed the minimal wear of the exterior aluminum. This office hadn't been squatting in its compatriot's eleven-story shadow for long. It was surely a late addition and was likely dropped in place not too long ago.

Janzen busied himself with his application, skipping one question and saving it for when his host was less engaged. The guard swiped a magnetized card hanging from a tether on his belt through the reader next to the desk. Janzen could hear the roll of the security gate opening for their second witness. From the bottom drawer, the guard retrieved a 750-milliliter bottle of bourbon and placed it in front of Janzen and lifted his gray eyebrows twice in quick succession to relay the information that something was definitely happening. He then moved to the camera to confirm that there was a memory card in its slot. He ambled back to the blinds to have a peek, humming a song under his breath. If a graybeard was ever considered giddy, this one was all popsicles and pussycats.

"Who's my executor?"

The guard gave no indication he heard Janzen. He separated the blind's slats like Doctor Bliss in search of President Garfield's hidden lead. "I love how this fella moves," said the guard. Janzen looked at the man as if he just dropped trou and shit where he stood. The old man gleaned the implied irritation from his visitor and explained. "Mr. Koontz was on retainer with Selby years and years ago and let's just say that his years in the field have been unkind to him. The country is overflowing with lawyers and this overflow leadeth his cup to runneth over. Each time we get a new candidate, I tell him he is one of three lawyers we have contacted and the first one to show gets the commission, a one hundred dollar check and a bottle of bourbon. He hasn't lost yet. His office is far enough down the street and he's without a car on account of his consumption. The pudgy fella will sprint the entire distance. It's really something to see."

"Who are the other two?"

"Who?"

"What if one of the other two beats him?"

"It's just him. I wouldn't have anyone else to call straight away."

"So why tell him about the other two?"

"I'm simply offering some incentive."

"Who's my executor?"

"Mr. Wayland Selby."

"With an *ie* or *y*?"

"You spell *mercy* with an *ie*, pal?" the old codger snapped like a Hotchkiss gun but regained his enthusiastic anticipation at the blinds *tout de suite*.

Living life as a jagoff for years and years, Janzen was well acquainted with the sharp reactions of affronted parties. He enjoyed taking them in stride with the affect of a dieter peeling stringed cheese. That look could infuriate. What simple pleasures he used to indulge. Janzen filled in the final blank line and finished the *y* with a flourish.

"Oh, this is special! This is really special!" The guard bounced in place. "He's on a bicycle! This is new." He unclipped the retracting security card from his belt and threw it in Janzen's direction. "When I say the word, swipe the card, Janzen. Readyyyyy..." Janzen peeled stringed cheese. "Now, son!" Janzen appreciated his excitement and was now curious as to the combination of an unfit man on a bicycle and a closing security gate. Even through the years of sobriety, three things were certain to wring a smile from Janzen's temperance: pratfalls, flatulence and primate monkeyshines. He played his part and slid the card through the reader before spreading the slats to view the spectacle.

The lawyer was an untrained grizzly in a vest and fez, perched atop a runaway trike, but a bear has neither the facial dexterity nor the unique human understanding of horror to properly convey what Janzen observed tearing down Formstone Ave. The man approached speeds even Janzen deemed unsafe, and it was apparent given this man's frightened expression and vibrating arms that control was something foreign to him at this moment. This blur of a man could have slid through the remaining space of the closing security gate, but that concern was no longer relevant. His safety and his body's ability to contain the screaming blood throughout his system given the impending collision had taken precedence. He located the rear brake and clasped the lever with the power of a cast-iron Kodiak trap because the rear wheel instantly fishtailed in a herky-jerky motion that heralds only one outcome. The impact with the adjoining fence was miraculously made without the benefit of the bicycle. He somehow dismounted the bike, which flew out from under him – ejected through the air, end over end in a rainbow's arc – and he continued his unpredictable trajectory on disintegrating soles. He maintained a posture of both upright and flailing until the flex of the linked chain put an end to what had been a remarkable act of cyclicide, a portmanteau born into the world by this one fantastic act.

Was Tutankhamen really felled by a speeding chariot? James Dean's Porsche lost a duel with a Ford Tudor. Would there be another addition to the list of those lost in transportation? The mass at the foot of the fence regained its mortal shape and the confused man looked around for answers to those eternal *What the fucks?* this world throws at folks now and again. Janzen and the guard moved not an inch lest a single twitch of a muscle would somehow cause the injured man to combust into the ether. The man wriggled appendages to ensure their proper locations within familiar sockets and gingerly raised himself back to his feet. He simply shook it off. It was an immaculate transgression against every law of physics, endurance and probability. What was it that propelled this man forth? The bottle of bourbon might provide an answer.

Guard and patron rushed away from the blinds, and Janzen found his seat facing the desk. The guard approached the camera and feigned inspecting settings and buttons. Both acted as if having left an adult theater in broad daylight, and their practiced aplomb was the only thing assuring their reintegration into conventional society. The man's wreck was his own, and it was private. The velocity and magnitude of it was such that it now became a part of his very fiber, and it surely refuted or confirmed the existence of a being either malevolent or charitable depending on his disposition. The guard nodded once to Janzen, sealing their complicity in witnessing the event. The door opened.

Mr. Koontz, Esq. moved with the composure of someone shopping for a throw rug. He took in the inventory and nodded jerkily to the guard and the stranger. But shock is a wonderful thing, and the lawyer's adrenal glands were redlining. Mr. Koontz decided that slow, perpetual movement would stem his inner turmoil. He moved deliberately from one curiosity to the next. He handled the stapler, opened and closed the fuse box, opened a file of drawers in search of a response to his present circumstance, but this was akin to throwing an Alka-Seltzer in the crater of a spewing volcano. He found the bourbon on the desk and pointed at it with a bizarre tilt of his head. What then came out of his mouth conformed to no known language. It was a loud short burst. A dropped laptop will sometimes emit a foreign succession of bleeps. The human body is no different. Inner sensors and regulators are thrown out of whack when thumped appropriately, so when Mr. Koontz opened his mouth for the first time, the part of the brain controlling the amplitude and volume of his voice simply needed a system check and a restart. Without the benefit of control+alt+delete, Mr. Koontz gulped down his solution. This swig was the antidote to his monstrously vibrating tremors.

"I am here," he managed once his reboot was complete.

"You are here, my friend. And your presence is both appreciated and admired," said the guard.

"I trust I am of the first variety?"

"If I am compelled to decipher your inquiry, then I must say that yes, you are the first to arrive. I would beg you to please sit down. Please just sit down, my dear friend."

"If you insist," said Mr. Koontz with a polite bow, the perspiration cascading off his face down to his collar.

"Janzen, if you'll please move your chair and person to the wall there, we can get along shortly." The guard clipped a microphone to the front of Janzen's shirt and ran its wire to a transmitter hooked to Janzen's belt loop. The guard donned a pair of earphones now plugged into the receiver. "Before we commence Janzen, a reminder that any dishonesty from you prevents Mr. Koontz from making this a lawful transaction and would immediately put an end to our relationship as it now stands. Do you understand that?"

"Yes, sir."

"Mr. Koontz, are you ready?"

"I am." He wasn't.

The guard turned on the power to the camera and adjusted the focus. He found Janzen peering past the lens. The guard stepped in front of the camera and quickly showed proof of his identification from his back pocket, holding up the card next to his face. He clapped once to sync the audio before maneuvering back behind the camera. "Mr. Koontz can you please identify yourself for the record?" The lawyer stood, wiped his face dry and adopted a solemn manner of comportment, clicking his heels together and reciting his name for the recording. He then found his seat once again at the desk facing Janzen. Mr. Koontz's heavy breathing accompanied the hum of the refrigerator.

"State your full name please."

"Janzen Hakkinen."

"Full name, son."

"Janzen Marko Hakkinen."

"Please state your reason for being here today."

"I am here because I hope to fill out my final will and testament."

"Why?"

"So it's legal."

"Not that. Why are you really here? What are your intentions?"

"You know why I'm here." Impending death sure had a way of shaking things up. Each question asked was met with pure openness. Where Marcus Brutus had dear Strato, Janzen had a guard and a fat man. When the Roman general was beaten to the pit, Janzen found a guard shack promising deliverance. He responded to the guard's questions with ease. He could've been in a doctor's room for a physical. This was an examination for which he had thoroughly prepared. Janzen replied to the guard's metaphysical abstractions with simple, declarative sentences. The complex sentences were left to describe his failed ambitions and regrets.

Knowing what was to come allowed his answers to flow freely, alleviating any need to self-censor. His confessions were laced with none of the shame that he had carried around for years. When his consideration of the ceiling no longer cleared his view, he would simply squeeze the wetness away with a steady thumb and index finger. He was unsure of the motivation behind the line of questioning, but what left was there to hide? Every man should have the opportunity to speak to a graybeard about life. You didn't attain those streaked whiskers without bobbing and weaving life's vicissitudes. Any young punk could withstand a few jabs. A graybeard has taken haymakers and endured.

It was over in less than twenty minutes, and after his interview Janzen sat in that plastic chair for about the same amount of time. The guard and Mr. Koontz were no longer there. The lawyer's handshake had been sure and steady, and the guard hugged Janzen even though he remained seated. Outside, the light from a fading day streaked the coral sky. A gap in the rear door lit the circulating dust. The doorway lured him through, and he rose and stepped out back. The ladder he saw earlier was now propped up against the building, allowing passage to the inset second floor from which he could reach the iron vines climbing to the top. Janzen walked to the back of the building and peered up. A huge yellow banner waved directly out to no one and covered the ninth floor window view and sent its message out to the old quarry grounds dotted with the vagrant life of acid loving pines and Japanese pierises.

In big black lettering, the banner read: *How Awesome is This Place!*

To whom did this banner speak? Tree lovers espoused the idea of their beloveds' consciousness, but this field of trunks and limbs was at best a terracotta army in a tomb. There had to be a reason for a standard of this ilk. Janzen took in the brightness of the yellow and the crispness of the corners. There were no visible frays at this distance. The black of the lettering popped in the reflecting sun. It was not an aged banner. It appeared newer than the guard shack from where he just came.

Was this the ensign of a narcissist? Did jonquils and daffodils grow under its direction? Was that the dome of someone's head peering back at him over the eleventh floor cornice? From Janzen's perspective, the ripple of the banner overhead hid the truth. It was a tiny breaker of a bump that disappeared after a blink. Was it a mirage? Quite possibly it was a beckoning.

Janzen tested the give of the slab under his feet and scanned the rooftop for any other aberrations. The foundation he stood on was solidly laid concrete and led into a loading bay, which was locked shut from the inside. Wedged at the bottom corners of the roll-up door were scraps of tawny litter, wind tamped leaves and pine needles.

Everything was in its right place. It was time. If the guard or lawyer ushered him out earlier onto Formstone, his only plan was to hop on his bike and ride until he found another suitable place. He carried enough money in his pocket to make the final few days comfortable. Nothing wrong with a bicycle, stretches of back roads and nowhere to be. Prettyboy Reservoir would've been a logical destination – plenty of props to do the job right – but he was here now.

Nothing left to do but climb. And fall.

He turned the corner from the back of the building and climbed the sixteen-footer to the second level. He had his choice of iron to climb and the two routes he was presently in between weaved different paths but would likely offer a similar scaling challenge. He edged his way toward the one closer to the front and jerked at it to test its strength. It was set firmly in place, and he swung his body out from the building to catch sight of Persephone. While her head was lifted toward the sky, she gazed directly at him. The artist had decided on a brow of someone in longing or anguish. The birds' desecration did little to impugn her grandeur. If Janzen needed any strength, he found it in her.

He was ready to begin his climb. After covering two stories in no time, his movements turned mechanical, and he found a rhythm and a pattern to the sculptor's path. The only impediments slowing his progress were the dead and slippery leftovers from the last planting. The dried up scraps of vine crushed easily under his weight and turned the iron to ice. His legs and arms shook at intervals but not from his effort; no, it was from his excitement. Exhilaration filled Janzen from his feet on up until his head was left to process its source. It was wonderful to have a taste of something strenuous before the final leap down. He would die properly: with dirtied hands and a light film of sweat.

The evening breeze cooled his skin, a final goodbye from what had been a scorching summer. He passed the mid-point of his climb when he was interrupted for the first time. He hadn't noticed the neon red of the tiny dot until he was only feet from it. The lens of the camera was mounted off to the side of the iron, and as he moved by it, he heard its electronic thrum. Its aim pointed directly down the path he had just taken. He waited for the mount to move mechanically in his direction to follow the rest of his way up, but it maintained its obstinate focus. Above him, he thought he saw a similar dot, and his suspicions were confirmed once he reached the eighth floor. He looked below and found himself now between two red dots. Had the first one swiveled? He didn't think to check the back of the unit when he passed it. The dots hurried his pace until he reached the summit, but the intimacy of his ascension was gone. Privacy had long since become an endangered species.

The top end of the iron was attached so fixedly to the building and near such a bulky plate that Janzen was able to reach over the top and lift himself up. As he crested Mount Selby, he expected to find a practical tar and gravel roof, but the smell alone told him otherwise. What wafted was pure redolence. What he saw froze him in place. It was a swath of green speckled with every color.

To call it a flower garden was an insult. While Janzen was the only human on the rooftop, there was much more alive here. It was the moss that first struck him, a carpet that crawled over the entirety of the space. A shift in the wind gave it movement like snowfall. This moss was feral but in the most refined sense. Janzen's heart pounded not from his expedition but from this sight. The wind once again transformed to zephyrs, and the minimalistic *Phrygian Gates* playing in his head reminded him of beauty's many shapes and shades. The invasive red dots were gone.

Flagstone paths of deep blues, greens and grays swerved here and there. The purple of the Siberian irises mixed with the wild Russian sages. The arching elegance of the Nanho blues clustered in small congregations. In one corner was a running granite fountain with a smiling bronze Naiad washed in its verdigris. One of the slab paths led to a single garden table with a single garden chair placed exquisitely in a flat section. Everything was back in its right place. The scene before him was both primordial and pristine. Could there be an incarnation of the hidden ancient wonder outside of Mesopotamia?

Janzen dropped into the green, and the recessed roof enveloped him. The moss climbed the surrounding height of the walls. It closed in on Janzen, a quilt made for the depths of winter. If there was a HVAC unit, it was bathed in the verdure; there was no racket of anything from the modern world, just the bubbling of the nymph in her fountain. No hatch or doorway was visible. It was just Janzen and everything else thriving around him.

This was one final gift.

He followed the flagstones and ran his extended fingers through the moss as he walked. It was soft and plush and even tickled his palm as he ran it against its nap. The greenery undulated in mounds and reminded him of a picture he once saw of the Chocolate Hills of Bohol, only these rose about waist high. He took a seat on the one chair and admired the latticework along the perimeter crawling with green until it reached the overhang swathed in blossoms.

The enclosures around his old row home in Hampden crept into mind. It enveloped similarly to the green here, but it was with malignancy, especially to someone who prized solitude. Janzen always knew when his downstairs neighbor cooked Mexican and knew how much her bowels struggled with the meal in the subsequent hours. He knew whenever his old racist neighbor next door would babysit his young racist grandson. The black clad adolescent yelled constantly at the television or into a headset about the "fucking niggers" who had wronged his video game character. The kid threw his bottles of piss outside his window, ricocheting off the brick walls, and Janzen would step on and kick them while struggling to finger the correct key with a handful of groceries. He rarely saw the neighbor on the other side, but the baying of her colossal mastiff produced tones Janzen had only heard in horror movies and experimental jazz. Cracking drywall, suspect insulation and cheap laminate flooring were acoustic choices rather than noise deterrents.

Those were old sounds now. Janzen washed them away and enjoyed the buzz of a hummingbird over the gentle roll of the water. The bird's pursuits sent it zipping from flower to flower, testing the nectars of the Turks caps, bee balms and columbines. But the crown of the head that he thought he saw earlier countered his corolla reverie. He surveyed the panorama and approximated the area where it had peeped. As the roof he now sat on was recessed to such a degree, there was only one such place someone might venture a look-see, and it just so happened that that particular place was smack dab at Janzen's approximation.

Across the rooftop out from where he sat was a pathway leading to an open gap. If the entire perimeter was an enclosing parapet, this one opening was a lowered gap over which a person of any height could peer. Before looking over the edge, he knew that he would find the hideous yellow banner waving twenty or thirty feet below him. Still farther below that was the concrete pavement entering the loading dock. Around the corner from there perched the ladder he had used to reach the second floor, its two bottom braces stuck in a strip of lawn. He remembered from his initial view from Formstone Ave. that there was another strip of green of equal width on the other side of the building.

He walked the pathway across the rooftop. When he peered over, the yellow banner was indeed below him; farther still was the concrete landing dock. From this height, he heard the snap of the yellow fabric against the window when the wind picked up. It was much bigger from this perspective and that much more confusing.

He turned and faced the loveliness of the garden and smiled at the emerald balustrade around him. Someone had invested a tremendous effort to design and maintain this strange rooftop enclave. Janzen accepted it as a gift and was thankful. He took a careful step back until his heels no longer touched the roof. He bounced on the balls of his feet, readying himself for this high dive. The wind moved the moss back and forth: a final wave goodbye. He closed his eyes and leaned back away from the building until he was weightless.

5

Years ago, Janzen found himself in a little trouble with the law. He was 25 at the time and on that particular day, he started drinking at nine that morning. The Mount Royal Tavern was one of the best early morning bars in the city because you'd never drink alone. Janzen awoke that morning knowing he could either suffer the duration of the day with both a fracturing headache and the type of nausea a young Darwin fought on the HMS *Beagle*, or he could drag himself to the MRT and throw back a few rounds of eye-openers.

His extremities had steadied by ten. Around noon he had switched to the brown stuff and was politely asked to leave soon thereafter, meaning the baseball bat wielded by the bartender was used only to suggest his exit in the same way a comma suggests a pause.

The police officers had trailed his wake of carnage for close to five city blocks before they hit the switch of their lights. They had certainly witnessed his indiscriminate thrashing of that city sidewalk and all its trappings. When Janzen turned to face the patrol car, he was armed with a broken nine iron and a metal cover of a garbage bin under which he had discovered the old club. If someone had the opportunity to capture this particular warrior stance in a frozen and miniature form, it could have easily been placed atop the loftiest trophy column and given to the golfer who had ingested the most hallucinogens.

The one officer calmly asked him to put the weapon down to which Janzen replied, "It's a nine iron, dumbfuck." Luckily, his current state of inebriation slurred the retort to such a degree that the insult had swung and missed. In so many words, the one officer asked him why he was swinging the niblick in such a haphazard way.

After dropping his saber and shield, Janzen ran the gauntlet of exercises an officer gave to a subject suspected of being under the influence. He actually scored a 100%, impressively failing every single sobriety test given, though there was one duty he was tasked to accomplish that would stick to his frontal lobes until the day he pushed himself backwards off an eleven-story building. He was asked to close his eyes and count to thirty, but he could not count out loud. He was supposed to let the officer know when the span of thirty seconds had elapsed. Janzen followed the directions and made the requested count. Once finished, he smiled and gave the officer two thumbs up and said, "That's it."

The officer asked, "Was that thirty?"

Janzen speculated, "It might have been closer to 32 or 33, but who's countin'." The officer deadpanned and showed Janzen the digital display of his phone's stopwatch. It read just over two minutes. "Motherfucker." The handcuffs clicked.

A brain preserved in alcohol is a sight to behold. Suspended by strings in a clear glass jar, the golden liquid pops well against the pale pink of the organ. A brain swimming in alcohol, though, is another sight altogether. In men, shots of it can lead to a disjointed strut possibly to compensate for engorged sets of biceps and balls. This same brain can also understand complex relativistic concepts in that it somehow simultaneously knows both everything and nothing at all.

Janzen had since wanted to forget about his trip to jail. He wanted to ignore how close he came to rushing the officer nearest him, wanting to forget that violent instinct. It was shameful and shined a light on those darker parts of him. Upon his release the following morning, Janzen drank enough to bury the memories of the cell full of bologna sandwiches, angry black men, utilitarian beds and the single seatless and doorless toilet. He was left wondering: was it really the alcohol that prevented him from correctly determining a certain block of time? How did he epically fail that officer's thirty-second test? He never again closed his eyes and wondered about the passage of seconds and minutes.

Until now.

He fell away from the building with his arms spread wide. He fell backwards because he preferred the back of his cranium make direct contact with the concrete below. How long had he fallen? Was it five seconds? Was it less? There was no shock – no pain. Was this the numbed sensation of death? He opened his eyes and was held in a fetal embrace bathed in a silky cadmium hug. "The fuck?" A deadened whir accompanied a new motion. "What the fuck!" Was he being raised? He convulsed and jerked his body to reposition his feet below him, but he couldn't grab at anything to right himself. He would've had more success picking up spilt milk between his fingertips. So there he was – the bulbous sphere of a bright yellow pendant. He was caught in the clutches of the sinister banner.

During the moments of clarity that existed when Janzen found himself cuffed to a gurney during his bout with the DTs, the memory of that indignity kept him awake for months afterwards. He also remembered slivers of embarrassment when handcuffed in the back seat of the patrol car; those slivers grew in time. Here he was again, incapacitated and shamed at failing his final act.

He kicked to vent the shock from his system. He flipped his body, and his back was now bowed and contorted. The material rearranged his face. He finally stopped struggling and gave himself over to his captor.

He was definitely gaining elevation, and the steady move upwards added pressure along his side. Then something else began to move, something close. He recognized the sound and smell of hydraulics in motion. Something else outside the banner was being lifted or lowered. It was heavy.

His ascension stopped with a jerk, and everything went silent except for the liquid-driven machinery at work. It was that slow high-pressure movement he had heard on so many backhoes and bulldozers. It was the sound of power.

How far had he been raised? Janzen was confused by yet another indeterminate number. The hydraulics finally stopped. Something was in place, either next to or below him. The whistle of the wind blew through the fabric. The yellow surrounded him, and what he understood to be the cinch of this human sack revealed nothing but more yellow. He waited. His body dropped a few inches, and he gasped in surprise. He was jerked to a stop before this frightening descent was made smoother with a steadier pace. He had no way to tell how far he was lowered until the slide of a diagonal hardness pressed against his back. He was being angled in the direction of the slant. The hydraulics kicked on once again, and the angle of the hardness below him grew steeper and steeper towards verticality. Trapped in the slickness of the fabric, he was still helpless.

The air around him was changing. The bumps of his body against the surface soon echoed. The light visible through the yellow faded to black. Was he being swallowed? His expedition up Mount Selby turned into an unknown descent. The tautness of the banner relaxed when he touched ground and found stability on all fours. He saw vague lines of light slowly disappear, and the hydraulic hum was the new soundtrack to his entombment. He pushed his arm away from the light, which gave him a glimpse of the ninth floor window shutting him inside the building. It closed with a definitive seal, locking in complete darkness.

There was enough space to spill out of the banner. He ran a finger along the tiled flooring, the surface cool, hard and smooth. "Hello?" Though Janzen never before practiced echolocation, he was confident the walls on either side of him were close. He tried flexing away the quivering of his arms and legs and willed himself to get up. He found his feet and moved away from the banner and found a wall to lead the way. He could only feel the wall, not see it. He crossed the blackness and found another wall that ran parallel with the other. He extended his arms out in either direction and could almost bridge the distance with his reach. "Fuck you!"

His final act had been robbed from under him in a most obnoxious way, now corralled and made hostage when he should've been free. Whether the glass door opened for compassion or contempt was of no importance. Does a moral argument or philosophical contention demand intervention? The move reeked of nefariousness.

A light, cool sensation moved across his face, and he understood its purpose instantly. He was transported back to the unfinished basement of his childhood home. That room had cold concrete flooring, a low exposed ceiling, and boxes of clutter he would burn years later. His basement had bare 60-watt bulbs affixed between the ceiling joists. The bulbs reacted to no flip of a switch; instead, they illuminated with the pull of their beaded strings.

"Hello, Janzen."

His skin constricted with goosebumps at the sound of an unexpected voice saying his name. In the blackness, Janzen lost his breath and reached for the ground. He was startled into dizziness and held hard to the floor beneath him for support. Spasms of voltage pulsed through his extremities. He needed to control his breathing. He wanted to respond but had to stop shaking first. His fright exhaled violently from his nose. He waited for the other to make a move, but nothing came for him.

Whoever was in there with him stood his ground.

"Who the fuck are you?"

"I see, but cannot reach the height. That lies forever in the light." The voice was deep and clear.

Janzen pushed himself back to his feet. He swung his arms to locate the beads and no longer knew from what direction the voice came. He stumbled with an ambitious step and crashed into the wall. He kept his feet but with someone else so near in this chamber, his quick breaths were only amplified. He stopped moving. He wanted composure. He slowed his chest and walked a few steps while grasping for beads. There they were again. There was a part of him that now preferred the absence of light. He pulled it anyway. It clicked.

"Jesus Christ!"

The form had its back to Janzen. The phantom was there before him, but it was incomplete. The light illuminated a large, dark bald-headed man in clothes tailored tightly to his body. His arms were held out horizontally towards each wall and reached the distance with ease, though he wasn't posed in that position for effect. He stood that way for stability's sake because what projected from his waist was one, not two complete legs. The bespoke cut of the shortened leg required a hem above the missing knee.

"I will need your help, Janzen." The man hadn't turned to face his new companion. He kept his back to Janzen, facing down the remainder of the hallway. And what a hallway it was. The walls were paneled in a modern textured material, showcasing slate-colored diamonds. The floor was of patterned marble. Janzen knew each piece would have been cut individually. There was a line of beaded metal that hung from polished antique fixtures. As Janzen approached the large figure, he peered past its body to a set of elevator doors at the hallway's end. They were industrial silver framed impressively by streaked ebony marble. Oddly enough, there was no hallway intersecting the one in which they stood. It was only the one stretch of corridor leading from window to elevator. "Please, Janzen."

Janzen sidled up to the man until they stood hip-to-hip. "If you'll please." The man wrapped an arm around Janzen who instinctively held tight around the man's waist for better leverage. "To the elevator, please." He regarded Janzen the way one would consider expired milk. He was a half a foot taller than his Finnish crutch, a black bishop and his white pawn. The duo stained the refinement of their surroundings with their plodding advance. The last time Janzen had shared space this close with another man for this duration, he had beaten him unconscious.

The labor involved in transporting a one-legged man of this size inhibited any questions Janzen wanted to ask. He'd wait for those answers; besides, he had always found acts of this variety to be palliative in nature, a fleeting serotonin boost for his own psyche.

They reached the elevator doors and the man pressed the button to take them down. "Thank you, Janzen. I know this must be difficult for you, but I promise that if you'll be patient, things will be made clear. But for now, I need to take you somewhere first, just for a few minutes. And after that, you'll get some answers, okay?"

"And if I tell you that I'm going to take this elevator down to the first floor and get the fuck out of here?"

The big man smiled. "Then I would tell you with the utmost sincerity that those plans would not work."

"And why is that?"

"Because there is only one way to exit this building, and you've already taken that route." The elevator arrived with an electronic bing. "But you're destined for something greater than what you had planned, Janzen."

"What is this place?"

"In good time, Janzen." The man toyed with his little Romanov with a Rasputin wink.

The doors parted to reveal a giddy elevator operator bursting at the seams both literally and figuratively. He resembled a pear-shaped bratwurst defrosting from its rimy hibernation. His intestine casing was a blue buttoned-down with the buttons' stitching screaming for relief. His unrestrained beaming must have involved the entire complement of facial muscles; an eyeball becomes a projectile at such an effort. A quick squeal emitted from the round man that he salvaged into a greeting, a salutation that worked as well as a pressure relief valve on a distended water heater because he soon found his voice projecting words at a normal thrust. "Hello, Janzen. I'm Samuel." The man welcomed Janzen with the spirited grip of an arm wrestler. The one-legged man seemed to enjoy Samuel's ebullience or Janzen's bewilderment or a combination thereof.

"You know where to take us, Samuel."

"That I do, Mr. Atis." The doors closed and they descended down to the third floor. Samuel plopped himself down on a stool that had previously been hidden by his haunches.

"Can you pass me my carriage, Samuel?"

"Ah!" Samuel labored off his perch and wielded a mighty backside to his riders while reaching for something in his corner, forcing his visitors once again into intimate quarters. Mr. Atis was no longer humored by the man's exuberance. "Got it!"

Samuel handed over a contraption that first resembled the size and relative shape of a unicycle; however, in place of one wheel were four smaller ones. From these wheels sprouted brackets that housed what appeared to be a gyroscope. Above this device was a gunmetal housing unit, the interior of which could have held the brains or brawn of the machine. And to top it off was a two-toned leather seat the colors of an orca. The way either of the men handled it, the weight probably didn't exceed fifteen pounds.

Mr. Atis held the apparatus upright and placed his large frame on its seat. His weight instantaneously triggered the machine to life as the wheels repositioned themselves directly under the man. The movement came with a soft purr of technology. Mr. Atis lifted his solitary leg to a modest foothold branching off a supporting strut. He adjusted the pleat of his pants, and the machine compensated for Mr. Atis's languid activity with minute adjustments.

Janzen scanned the gadget with an artless observation for a maker's mark but found none. Even with its impressive functionality, it wasn't without its Frankenstein glow. The bing of the third floor sounded, and with a slight lean forward, Mr. Atis floated between the doors before they slid completely open. Janzen hesitated, and Samuel smiled dumbly.

"This thing go all the way down?"

"No, I can show you when you get back. You won't be long. I promise." Whether or not he was telling the truth, there was such earnestness in Samuel's delivery that Janzen's single-mindedness was temporarily diverted.

A stern call from Mr. Atis pressured Janzen from the elevator; he followed. The pristine and tailored hallway was lined with ornamentally framed mirrors, pastoral paintings, and individually decorated doors with bronze knobs. Mr. Atis waited for Janzen at the only open door at the end of the corridor. The contraption he rode balanced Mr. Atis and responded to the smallest movement of his big hands.

"I'm going to leave you here with Ms. Helena Wanda March. She won't take up much of your time, and afterwards your inquisitive mind will be appeased. Is that fair?"

"It's something."

"Alright Janzen, in there and have a seat. I'm very pleased to meet you." With that, he wheeled away back to the elevator. "Very pleased, Janzen. Your kingdom awaits!"

The intensity of the light escaping the room that Mr. Atis had indicated cast a blaze on the hallway wall. Upon crossing the threshold, Janzen was transported to a professionally equipped photography studio. A snow-white cyclorama wall curved the angles and shadows of the setup. The lighting package sprouted from an army of tripods and hung from the ceiling rafters. There were tables full of camera bodies and lenses. There were apple boxes, sandbags, flash meters, ladders, reflectors and diffusers. In the middle of the focus was a single wooden stool with three stationed cameras pointed towards the lone pedestal. Behind the equipment was a separately enclosed room. An illuminated red light shone next to its closed doorway. Collapsed and stowed in another corner was a mass of materials one found in a painting studio.

Alone, Janzen walked the perimeter of the room and stopped at each camera. Like most dilettantes in the civilized world, he had dabbled in photography and experienced brief aspirations of a Helmut Newton career but was soon saddled with a Jeff Lebowski ambition; besides, he believed the written word offered so much more in terms of psychiatric trauma that it therefore became the obvious choice for his artistic endeavors. He continued his tour and found an ass-sized dolly pushed underneath a table; each of the four wheels was formed in such a way as to lie on a track that he could not locate. The little rectangle reminded him of the sugar maple boards he rode so long ago. During adolescence, Janzen's skateboard sessions proved to be a more effective panacea for his unease than any Fluoxetine capsule. He found sanctuary on a deck. He could always move away from somewhere or something. Skateboarding scattered his anxiety and recklessness in the healthiest way he knew how. The propulsive balancing act was a temporary haven for years.

Janzen picked up his board and approached the spotlight. The built-in curve of the wall was a serviceable quarterpipe, but the move would require some speed. He figured the old simile about riding a bike also applied to board sports, so the only hesitation he had concerned the transition to a manual. Once he moved the stool standing in the center of the setup, an obvious avenue presented itself.

The dolly moved at a surprisingly quick pace, and it followed the straightest of lines. The wheels were inset enough from the edge of the seat that it provided a faux-kicktail on which to pivot. He cruised up the ramp and hit a solid 180. The return trip followed the same path, but when Janzen shifted his weight for the manual, a series of blinding lights wrecked his concentration. The whirs of the cameras' shutter cycles were silent before he had fully transferred to a prone position on the floor.

"What in the fuck is this?" If degrees of contempt were bought and sold on the stock market, this particular exhibition was a blue chipper. With his vision clearing from the unexpected explosion of lights, Janzen laid eyes on a woman doused in seething fury. "What the fuck did you do to the wall! I'm going to have to paint it again." Janzen retraced the dolly's journey, and sure enough, the wheels had left an incriminating trail that popped against the white wall. The woman gripped shutter release hand-helds in each of her fists, and she restrained herself from throwing one at her new visitor.

As a tenured dipshit, Janzen was well equipped to respond with any number of dipshit retorts, but her anger-infused exasperation was a thing of beauty. It was unrestrained, held on a leash made from the braided leather of a bullwhip. She set down the two devices and wet a cloth from her supplies on a nearby table. With her nose now inches from the floor, she worked at Janzen's signature scrawled across the whiteness. He found another cloth and did the same until there was no trace of the offending trail. Helena then scrolled through the LCD screens of each of the three cameras trained at the center stool. Janzen guessed that she was younger than he was by a few years, and she hid whatever slight figure was her own in clothes much too big for her. Her militant black boots laced to the calves punctuated a declarative fashion choice.

Janzen continued wiping the floor because doing otherwise put him at the mercy of her silence. For fear of stripping the paint, he then stood up and studied her long enough to make her equally uncomfortable. "Why am I here?" asked Janzen.

"For your picture."

"No. Not that. I don't want to do that."

"It's done. Let's go. We have somewhere to be."

"I'm Janzen."

"I know."

"I think I'm going to stay down here for a while. And then I'm going to leave."

"Did they tell you there was only one way out? Up top?"

"Yes, Helena Wanda."

"Don't call me that. Do you want to see the bottom floor?"

"Yes," he responded. Helena turned off the lights to the studio and led him to a stairwell encased in rough gray cement. She descended the steps at an impressive angle and speed. Her thin arms pumped with the fluid motion of a sprinter. When they reached the door to the second floor, Janzen peered down the final flight of stairs continuing down one additional level. "So the lobby is down there?"

"You would think, but there's no door."

Janzen smirked. He continued down by himself, but when he made the final turn of the switchback, he was met with a concrete wall devoid of any entrance or exit. Even in the dimness of this bottom floor, he noticed blocks of concrete a slightly different mix from those around them. The mortar work was sloppier in the area of the discolored blocks, an obvious clue to the previous doorway.

Helena scuffed her boots from the stairway above loudly enough for Janzen to notice. He put a solid kick in the center of the newer concrete. It was dense and immovable, so Janzen climbed back up to Helena, who held the door open for their exit out the stairwell.

The view to the second floor layout was blocked. The drapery that hung from the raised ceiling followed the perimeter of the space, leaving only a few feet to follow its path. "What's under here?" Janzen began lifting the material but there was so much of it that he couldn't find the bottom. It was heavy and thick.

"There's a way in on the other side. C'mon." Helena forged ahead. They made two rights but still there was no evidence of any exit save the stairway door from which they entered. They moved through near darkness as the ubiquitous drapery absorbed any light. "Be careful here." Janzen heeded her advice as they walked up a short ramp. He noticed the different play of sound from his footfalls on this new, elevated level. There was now much more give to the surface below. The space might have opened up around them. The cascading material still surrounded, but Janzen could decipher different contours of blackness in the shadows. "Jesus. Where is it?" Helena searched for something; Janzen could only hope to locate her through the noises she made. "Wait here, Janzen. I need to find the box to flip on the lights."

"Shit!" Janzen had walked into a folding chair. He sat and rubbed his shin, kneeling low to the ground. The layout of the room had him stumped. They had walked nearly two-thirds of the perimeter, and they should have passed rows of windows and seen past the statue of Persephone. They were directly above what would have been the first floor lobby, which should have offered a view to the outside from any point along their walk.

Behind him, he could hear a line or wire drawn through what could be a pulley. The slight squeak of the stiff wheel brought to him the image of a self-propelled hospital gurney down a decaying hallway. "Helena?" The atmosphere around him changed. He tried rubbing smooth the flesh of his forearm. Something else was with them. It wasn't just the shuffle of one pair of feet.

Then came the sound of something familiar, the sound he used to hear when he plugged his guitar into his amp. It was that electric buzz made before he lay pick to strings. He heard a similar frequency now, but it was bigger in this space.

And then, the drone of the noise was silenced by his words, reverberating over unseen speakers "You must know why I'm here."

The final word echoed not because of the surrounding space but because of some effect manipulating it. "You must know why I'm here." As he sat on the folding chair in the darkness, Janzen heard his words through the speaker system. They bombarded him, but he could locate no one source. "You must know why I'm here." He had said those same words only an hour or so before in the guard shack outside. He assumed his responses were being recorded for liability's sake. What kind of warped broadcast was this?

Then his shadow finally showed. The first glimmer of light elongated his form on the chair in front of him. When he twisted in his seat to track the trajectory of the light, there was an obstruction between Janzen and the source. He sat looking at his diaphanous image on a large screen. "You must know why I'm here." He watched himself speak and then freeze. At that instant during the interview, Janzen had stared directly at the camera's lens. He now stood face to face with his projected image. "I could talk of failure or regret. And those would apply." Janzen walked toward his image. "I could talk of failure or regret. And those would apply."

The volume of his voice was increasing.

"I could talk about the energy inside me that itches all over." He walked across the floor, which gave slightly with each step. "Or I could talk about the madness." The video slowly disappeared with every step in its direction until it was only a line of illumination at this angle. "Or I could talk about the madness."

He passed the suspended screen, and the light from the projector forced Janzen to squint out its intensity. He used the crook of his arm to shield the light and turned to face the other side of it. The image of him seated against the wall of the guard shack was crisp and vibrant. "I could talk about the madness."

"What is this?" Janzen swung around and stood in front of his projected image. The singular source of light blurred anything around it. He turned and pushed the screen without thinking. "What the fuck is this?" Somehow his voice was projected through the speakers. His sight adjusted, and he saw activity out in front of him. He advanced slowly and almost stepped off the brim of the apron. His arms flailed to steady himself back off the edge of the stage. Seated at tables in front of him was a crowd of motionless spectators wordlessly practicing some primitive exercise in stillness.

He went back for the folding chair and added a Highland touch to their Druid ceremony, hurling the chair with a revolving launch. Where it landed, people scattered out of danger and Janzen jumped offstage before there was any chance for retaliation. He headed in the direction of the only exit he knew. He ripped under the drapery and found himself feet from the door he had entered.

His instincts took him back up a single flight and towards Helena's studio. He saw no light coming from the end of the hall and threw open her door but found no one inside. The screeching in his head was a violent Penderecki threnody, and he twisted the closest door-knob and found an anemic man naked from the waist up staring at him from an unevenly lit room. Janzen backed away from the gaunt figure that rose from its sitting position. It moved slowly toward its visitor.

"Janzen! In here!" Half of Samuel beckoned from inside the elevator. Janzen backed into it to be sure the emaciated man didn't follow him

"What is this, Samuel?" Janzen paced around whatever area wasn't taken up by the big man. Samuel pressed the highest number and somewhere in between the seventh and eighth floors, Janzen flipped the red *run/stop* switch halting their climb. Janzen grabbed Samuel's collar and slammed the big man into the corner of the elevator. "What's going on here Samuel? I'm not going to ask you again."

Samuel's big body shook in panic while he fumbled over his half-formed words. Janzen had seen this before from those not accustomed to such a jostling. He let go of his shirt and backed away from Samuel. "They're just like you, Janzen. Everyone here."

"Why don't you go ahead and be crystal clear."

"Right. One way in, one way out. Everyone in this building came in the same way you did and for the same reason. Well, the reasons are different, I'm sure, but you know what I mean."

"How many?"

"I'm not sure."

"How many!"

"I really don't know, Janzen. Sometimes I just stop seeing people. It's hard to keep track."

"Why?"

"I don't know. Maybe you can tell me that," said Samuel, who punctuated his sincerity with pleading hands.

"Why do you say that?"

"Because he might tell you if you ask him. You're going to see him now."

"Who?"

"Mr. Selby, of course. Wayland Selby."

"*The* Wayland Selby of Selby Industries?" asked Janzen, suddenly adjusting his body from one held in impatience to one now in suspicion.

"Yes. This is his building."

Janzen rapped the bridge of his nose with his knuckles hoping the sensation led to a more complete understanding. He sensed the skin above to give so he transitioned to shaking his head back and forth, as he believed the elevator man in front of him to either be his prophet or his Svengali.

Samuel flipped the switch that brought them up to the eleventh floor. "Mr. Atis is waiting for you." The elevator doors parted, and Mr. Atis wheeled by without looking at either man. Samuel nudged Janzen onward with an encouraging nod of his head. A biological fear still shuddered the big man's frame, a sight that quelled Janzen's anger. The poor man was a big old mutt caught out in a lightning storm.

Janzen stepped away from the elevator and was overtaken by the eleventh floor's décor. The ire he had suppressed now came scratching its way back with this offensive scheme. There were columned archways, cascading velvets, gilded tables, Aveline chairs, stylized apothecary jars and demijohns, Rococo chests and Victorian sofas with ornamental legs thicker than the round of a Holstein, and so much lacquer. The office he walked through dripped opulence. Even the Esterházy clan would have found this design to be garish. The entire floor displayed every gaudy decorative instinct from the seventeenth century on.

Janzen followed Mr. Atis towards a pair of closed pedimented doors outfitted in hyper-white stucco. "We were sorry to see you leave so abruptly, Janzen. We had much more planned for you."

"I'm not in a polite mood, Mr. Atis."

Mr. Atis knocked on the door and checked his nails, palms out. "He's been waiting for you, Janzen."

A garbled summons made it through the heavy doors. Mr. Atis politely motioned for Janzen to enter. The stickiness of the outside ornamentation had bled into this office, though a touch of the Gothic added a hint of Eastern Germanic with the crossing of two medieval weapons hung to make an X behind a massive desk. At the window, an older gentleman in a classic gray suit looked out from one window. When he turned, he revealed the beard that Janzen had seen earlier that day. It was the security guard: Mr. Wayland Selby.

"Janzen! Welcome to the family! An embrace, please." Mr. Selby walked forward with his palms out from his elbows but stopped a few feet short due to the tensed jaw muscles he saw flexing in front of him. "Easy, Montecore. Let's take 'er easy now. Please, have a seat." Mr. Selby leveled his voice and stowed his smile. "He's a live one, isn't he Mr. Atis?"

"Yes. He made quite an impression downstairs. Luckily, no one was injured."

"So what do you think? Isn't this place exquisite?"

With his arms outstretched, he presented his office.

"You've made Liberace proud," responded Janzen.

Mr. Atis flinched at the indignity. "Janzen!" yelled Mr. Selby. "Call me any name in the book, but the effort and artistic vision of what you see here is the handiwork of our very own Mr. Atis, and it is most certainly above sarcastic reproach." Mr. Atis had heard enough, and he wheeled out of the office at an accelerated speed.

Mr. Selby sat and planted his elbows on the desk and his exasperation exaggerated the hunch of his spine. "You don't know the shitstorm you just started, Janzen." He spoke through his fingers. "The tenth circle is a gay man's anger."

"That's clever."

"It's a play on the –"

"I know. Why, Selby? Why?" As he was questioned, Mr. Selby straightened his jacket and sat up in his chair. "Why the banner? Why your guard getup? Why these people? Why me, at your desk, right now?"

"All relevant questions. And you'll get the answers in good time."

"Not good enough." Janzen stood up, and his head started to shake and his voice trembled. "How do I get the fuck out of here?"

"One way in, one way out."

"And you stole that from me. What's stopping me from putting this chair through the window?"

"That's an easy one. You," Mr. Selby said calmly.

"Wrong answer." Janzen manhandled a substantial burned wood armchair as if it was made from tinder-dry twigs. He crossed the office with it raised over his one shoulder.

"I wouldn't do that," said Mr. Selby.

Janzen threw the chair with such exertion that he fell forward upon its release. At the point of impact, the armchair ceased functioning as a piece of furniture and had become nothing more than kindling. The glass absorbed the strike without even a shimmy of its constitution.

Mr. Selby pushed back from his desk and nonchalantly lifted one of the medieval battle-axes from where it hung on the wall behind him. He placed it gently on the desk and directed Janzen's attention to it with a waggle of his pointer finger.

Janzen seized the axe and adjusted the weapon to wield the heavier bludgeoning side. Mr. Selby returned to his chair and crossed one leg over the other. "Oh no. Please let my poor window be." Mr. Selby's monotone revealed not a tinge of sincerity.

Janzen struck at the window again and again, but it was like trying to fell a redwood with a flyswatter. After his third thwack, his arms could no longer take the jarring impact of the rebuffed steel.

Mr. Selby jumped up with a wicked grin. He grabbed the two handles of a large glazed pottery jar. The flowers that adorned the object touched every stop along the color spectrum. He walked toward Janzen, who was recovering from his exertion near the window.

"Janzen! Not the vase! Or jar! It's from Positano!" Mr. Selby launched the pottery with such malice, Janzen thought his aim was to throw it back to the Amalfi Coast. The shattering produced an unexpected *pop*! "Janzen, no!" Mr. Selby directed his voice towards the doors to his office. He grabbed Janzen by the wrist and whispered, "He would be heartbroken if he knew I hated it. Thank you." He lightly petted the clear glass Janzen had just attacked. "It's our new polycarbonate – super affordable. We think it'll sell well in Tornado Alley and in cities where the masses are apt to riot. Impressive, eh? Now let's talk." He grabbed another chair from the corner of his office and offered it to his frustrated guest. "I should have been straight with you, Janzen. I will not waste your time. I believe that you can help me. And if you'll give me just one week of your life to decide if that's something you want to do, then I'll respect whatever decision you make afterwards."

"Meaning I can leave?"

"Meaning you can leave, jump, stay, help – whatever you want. You have my word. I only ask that you stay here with me – with us – for one week. Aren't you curious about what's going on? I believe you're part of something special – we all are. And I'm asking for just one week."

"Who were those people?" asked Janzen.

"You'll meet them. They came in the same way as you. Everyone is free to leave whenever they want, but they're here, my man!"

"What do you want from me?"

"I want this story told, and I need someone with a particular voice and perspective. I know from our brief interactions that you think deeply. That was apparent in our discussion outside. I wanted everyone to see that side of you. That's why the video downstairs. Everyone else went through it, but I think you will understand what I'm trying to do here."

"What are you trying to do?"

"That's a big question, Janzen. I'm not trying to be evasive, but you should see it for yourself without anything coming from me. I'm assuming you don't have much faith in what I say at this point anyways. What's a week, son?"

"And if I say no?"

"I'll show you up to the rooftop right now. It's right through this door." Mr. Selby indicated the closed door in the corner of his office. "Everyone had this same choice." The man leaned in closer to Janzen. "Listen, we feed you, we clothe you, we already have your own room ready for you on the seventh. We require nothing further from you tonight. Tomorrow, you'll see the grounds, and we'll go from there. There's food in your fridge, but if you're up for something more social tonight, you can join everyone below. We'll be having..." he flipped through a pile of papers on his desk until he found the menu "...Cajun blackened salmon, cumin-butter carrots and blanched and sautéed haricots verts." His butchered Baltimorean pronunciation betrayed the sophistication of his suit and tie. "Christ, what happened to a steak and starch? There's some summer sausage and bread in your room. That would be my suggestion. Samuel will help you with anything you need. Just press the elevator button. He knows where everything is. Now shake my hand, and tell me you'll stay for a spell. Stay for a week. Just stay for a full day."

The man's pleadings were impulsive, and it was seeing this that ultimately sealed Janzen's decision. He thought of Goethe and said, "I accept."

The bearded man hopped up out of his seat. Delight can be feigned, but this was unadulterated and pure. He at once began speaking of names and locations found on "the grounds," accentuating his message with bobbles of his head and frenzied strokes of his beard. Mr. Selby moved around the desk with a fluidity of a much younger man. Grizzly Adams went full-on Gene Kelly. With a light touch on the small of the back, Mr. Selby shepherded his latest addition back through the doors and towards the elevator where Mr. Atis sat dolefully at his desk and sucked none of the joy from Mr. Selby.

The soft lumbar touch and the excited intonations of Mr. Selby's voice dipped Janzen in and out of focus. He was now forced to take on the previous solicitudes that had occupied his mind leading up to his jump off the rooftop: the continued drone attacks in Yemen, the paramilitary groups organizing across state lines, the IEDs ruining the highways, and the increasing number of murders, making a trip to the theater a legitimate threat based on the film's content. Prisons were still bloated, the war on drugs was a failure, everyone had a gun, and everyone wants a platform. He now had to reconsider the bump on his ass that could be a hemorrhoid. There was research to undertake on the provenance and appearance of hemorrhoids. He had calories to ingest and weight to maintain and water to drink. When should he resume the unregimented and/or regimented habit of masturbation? When was the last time anyways? There were the rising costs of education and his school debt. What's the point of a head start if the finish line is nothing but debt? Is $195,000.00 for congressmen too much for those who do nothing but compose sound bites, reject subpoenas while ignoring the actual needs of their constituencies? Where were the term limits? They received cost of living raises, so why don't teachers? Were there cultural reasons behind black folks littering? There had to be something behind it besides indifference. Was it a learned behavior like a gangsta's slang or a scholar's balderdash? He'd need a scale. How did a minority of Karens mobilize a nationalist movement? Mr. Atis deserved an apology for the Liberace remark. He'd still have to read *Walden*. What about riding? Would they have toenail clippers here? What do Christians believe about toenail growth in purgatory? He'd have to revisit his father and their distance and his wayward mother. Did she think she could have saved him from his father's faults? Would his mom have stuck around a little longer if he had been kinder? Would he really ever write again? He would need music. The toilet paper ply count must meet or exceed three plies or there'd be hell to pay. Would he meet those people he just threw a chair at? Why couldn't he ever remember the definition of *labile*? Was the prettiness of the word *effluvium* a compensation for its meaning? What about humping? Humping gravel made him appreciate his body and the exertion involved. He once gave a goodbye toast to his calluses when he scored the editing gig. What was this old man talking about? It was a hell of a beard. Where was he? Where did he go from here? He'd need a bathroom.

"Is there a bathroom?" asked Janzen, who found himself on the seventh floor about midway from the elevator and the end of a hallway. Mr. Selby held open a door that led to a restroom. A placard on the door read *Men*; an open stall and toilet winked back at them. "Where do I stay?"

Mr. Selby pointed at the open door across the hall. He was certain he had seen this room before. "You were just standing inside."

"That explains it."

"Right," said Mr. Selby. "Breakfast is bright and early. Find the elevator and Samuel will lead you in the right direction."

"How will I know when?"

"It'll be hard to miss. Now rest up, young man. We're happy to have you."

"One week."

"One week." Mr. Selby tapped Janzen on the forehead twice, and with that odd gesture was off and Janzen was left to inspect his room.

Unlike the eleventh floor, his new accommodations had not been a focal point of any recent renovation or redecoration. Once he shut the door behind him, a mustiness settled in. A former high school wrestler, Janzen was confident his olfactory system would adjust in no time. If the scent of dank and unbridled adolescence festering in a heated gymnasium became tolerable and then unnoticeable, a little mildew would waft just fine.

The following effects were found in the room: a twin-sized bed made to a military tightness, a metal waste bin, a thigh-high refrigerator, a yellowed poster hung on the wall with the image of a mountainscape and a caption that read: *Motivation*, a rolling chair, and a corner desk which hadn't seen a wrench in decades. The switch near the doorway controlled the rectangular fluorescent lighting suspended along with the drop ceiling.

Janzen checked the two top drawers of the desk, neither of which contained anything. He sat in the chair and adjusted its height. He opened the fridge and found it stocked with provisions. He chose the summer sausage and a brick of cheddar cheese; a plastic knife was taped to the former. He would have to give sleep another go tonight. Were there withdrawal symptoms from Tramadol?

6

There were withdrawal symptoms from Tramadol. It began as an ersatz version of the real thing, the Crystal Light of the detoxification world. His clammy skin prickled, and his legs fought the dumb electricity flowing threw them. He kicked at the sheets and flexed his legs to rid himself of that awful sensation of being chewed on by a toothless assailant. He gnashed his back molars until he split the inside of his cheek. His forearms and fingers cramped from their constant flexing, and he kept wiping his shins dry from his seeping pores. There would be no sleep that night. He kicked and fought that maw of pharmaceutical withdrawal until the percussion finally interrupted the gummy mastication.

The synthetic staccato erupted from somewhere close. He noticed that two of the ceiling panels shook with remarkable consistency and realized they were suspended speakers. The drums of the music shook his bed. The Djembe rhythm was wild and rapid. The African beats merged into something Henryk Górecki on speed would've composed. The volume violated his room, but at least it was something different. He didn't want another hour focused on kicking his pain meds. He needed out of this room. With no windows and no sunlight, his Tramadol kick turned out to be a little slice of awfulness.

He sat up and rolled his neck, and his skin stuck at its creases. He wanted a pair of pedals and a string of hills to trash his legs and condemn what ailed them. Some food down the gullet was another distraction – a little digestion for his legs' ingestion. He jumped in place, shook his head violently and snarled at the wall before throwing a straight cross against the concrete. That was better. He opened his door and the song played at a more agreeable level outside his room. He'd need to have the volume in his room adjusted. He saw unfamiliar bodies down the hall step into the elevator. He needed to keep his legs moving. Samuel saw him and held the elevator doors open.

One of the new bodies had a head that smiled at Janzen. The other body was crammed into the corner of the elevator with a chin buried in a chest. Samuel smiled and mouthed a 'good morning' over the volume of the music. On the way up to the tenth floor, Janzen tightened and relaxed his quads to the beat, which continued playing once they spilled out of the elevator.

Within a glass-enclosed room, there appeared to be some type of commissary. Most seats were occupied. Those that were untaken still might've been claimed by some of the men and women dancing in their own worlds in their proximity. A young black male yelled intermittent lyrics between his smooth and precise movements. His feet stood spread on two chairs, and the veins on his neck bulged from the strain.

Janzen followed the elevator herd through the wall of music. Some stopped near the entrance and began improvised movements now possessed by the beat. A septuagenarian rose from his chair and jerked around with them. Most of the eyes trained on Janzen the previous night were now either rolled pleasantly back in their bouncing heads or ricocheted from one enraptured form to the next. Janzen found Helena's sideways head resting in the crook of her elbow while two of her fingers tapped to the beat. The music was raw, but the sound was a contemporary rage. It fueled the geriatric hustle, an improvised Māori haka, the clenched fists, the glistening smiles, and the messaging neurotransmitters. The ending of the song was met with a release of yelps and applause, though one man shook his angry head at what he had just endured while another rapped his forehead against a tabletop.

A man waved to Janzen from a nearby table. He wore the expression of a boy waiting for the return trip of a boomerang and pointed to an open seat next to him. His head was pale and shaved to the nub, a bold roundness that accentuated the paunch in the midsection. He was perpetually in motion as if his respiration depended on it. Janzen rescanned the room before heading in his direction and sat down next to him.

"Hi Janzen. Name's Scoop. Welcome to the nuddouse. Very interesting entrance yesterday. You cost me some hooch, but iss cool. I was sure we'd get troo da video. I didn't peg ya for a crier, but I wadn't countin' on unprovoked violence. Felix nailed it. Said he recanized that glare of yours or somethin'. I had a line on a setta knives if you just ran out widout the UAV."

"UAV?"

"Unprovoked Act of Violence. Iss cool. Don worry bout it. I'll win it back. If I really need dem knives, I could prolly get 'em anyways." He jumped up from his seat to work out the details of a wager with a nearby man. A Charles Ives piece began playing quietly over the speakers. A man and a woman in complete chef's regalia emerged from a set of swinging doors at the back of the commissary. They both wore aprons spotted with flour over their checkered pants, double-breasted coats and starched white toques. Each pushed a server's trolley stacked with lidded food pans and cellophaned bowls. Along the back wall, they dropped the stainless steel pans into the line of bains-marie. They lifted the lids and removed the cellophane. The man poured two cups of coffee while the woman garnished the eggs. He passed the woman her coffee. She drew deeply from the cup. All conversation in the room hushed. She turned and nodded shyly to the group. The eager beavers formed a line at once and worked their way down the table, heaping steaming food and fresh fruit onto their plates.

Janzen was the last one through the line and when he turned from the buffet, everyone was sitting politely waiting for his return. When he found his seat, Scoop either bared his teeth in a threat or smiled towards Janzen.

"Christian and Amber, thank you for the food in front of us," said Mr. Atis, who sat at the head of one of the tables. Scoop shoved a link of sausage into his mouth before Mr. Atis stared him into stillness. "And please go out of your way to welcome Janzen. He'll be with us for a week, and we should make his stay as comfortable as possible. And please remember: beware of flying chairs." Mr. Atis tilted his head playfully but the corners of his mouth maintained their downward trajectory. Nervous glances ping-ponged between Janzen and the big one-legged man. "So we lift our glasses. Menny moppy tickle parson!" Everyone in the commissary repeated the last four words in unison. The forks then flew to work.

"Atis is a pain in da ass," said Scoop in between gobs of food. "Selby likes 'im – thinks he's got da bess in mine fer everyone, and it ain't on 'count of him bein' a cripple neither. It was his own damn fault he loss da leg anyways, and it wadn't on 'count of no runway train neither."

"That's a hell of an accent, Scoop."

"Man, I used to run from Parkville to Dundalk and everywhere in between. Spent some time ore in Jessup but that wadn't by choice – State arranged that up. I got family in the county, Balmer and Harferd. Man, dey call it Smalltimore but I been here my whole life and ain't seen but tree er four slices of da pie." While he spoke, Scoop lifted a perpetual forkload of food into his mouth. His other hand snapped an Eisenhower dollar into a spin. He'd catch the silver dollar at a dead stop and snap it right back into motion until the friction threatened the tightness of the rotation. Scoop accomplished all this while scanning the perimeter of the room, an action made more understandable considering his imprisonment in Jessup. Janzen only knew jail. This man knew prison. "You comin' to da mornin' sesh?"

"He is." Janzen and Scoop turned around to find Mr. Selby standing over them. He massaged the nape of each of their necks before he moved on to greet the other diners.

"He's a slippery one, that Selby. Like shakin' hands wid smoke."

"What's a morning session?"

"I know, right. We know we're fucked up. It don't take no magnifyin' glass to see a mountin."

"What's a morning session?"

"It's the one before da afternoon sesh."

"Thanks Scoop." The pale little man had cleared his place and left before hearing the final pop of Janzen's sarcastic *p*. He finished his meal in silence and waited anxiously for what was supposed to happen next. He kept his head down but was aware of the attention directed at him.

"Conference Room A everyone! Half an hour! Felix, you're on dishes. Daryl, you're on linens." Mr. Atis's baritone voice commanded the room's attention. For Janzen, that voice was a sparking angle grinder, one that pricked more acutely on account of the oily Tramadol slime festering over his body. Mr. Atis watched Janzen squirm for a little longer than was necessary, perched upon his rolling contraption like a proud stylite, so sure of his elevated path.

The big, dark man wheeled out of the room. Janzen sat with his empty plate long enough for most of the room to clear out. He asked one of the few remaining people about the morning session and was given a floor number and directions off the elevator, which were easy enough to follow.

Conference Room A was spacious enough to seat twenty or so people. Three of the four walls were hard-wired for different inputs. The fourth wall's hue was slightly different from the rest, and Janzen craned his neck to catch sight of an elusive pixelation. In front of the suspect wall, two men staged furniture at the direction of Mr. Atis. He kept referring to the "third hotel set" as props were carried in from another room. In came a modern couch, a matching loveseat, a mini-fridge, a swath of carpeting, a standing lamp – they kept coming in.

Mr. Atis saw the shifting of the couch by millimeters as paramount to the functionality of the room. Was this glacial shift some sadistic form of feng shui? Janzen wondered at Mr. Atis's attention to detail and chalked it up to the simple pleasure the man experienced in manipulating others. The final piece carried into the room was a tiny coffee table. When this was painstakingly placed, Mr. Atis took from his breast pocket a placard that read "Welcome" in a refined font, which he placed on the table next to the single-cup coffee maker.

No one paid much attention to Mr. Atis and his movers. Some sat slouched on a less scrutinized couch. Others had settled into swiveling office chairs while the rest were content closer to the ground, sitting propped up against a wall or stomach to the floor clutching one of the many pillows. The absence of a single, central unifying Conference Room A table struck Janzen as odd.

The woman named Amber, whom Janzen recognized as one of the chefs from breakfast, was involved in an intense conversation in the corner of the room. A man held both of her elbows while he spoke in such undulating and earnest tones; these waves of amity and warmth appeared to provide the only thoracic strength keeping her from collapse. If distraught wore a pattern, it was the houndstooth number tightly hugging her body. She confined whatever words hid behind her pursed lips. She steeled herself for something.

As if a curtain had just risen, Mr. Selby flew into the room and bounced from wall to wall and person to people, finalizing the stage design put in place by Mr. Atis. He directed the readjustment of the couch, and Mr. Atis winced at each maneuver but was assuaged by Mr. Selby's patting of his forearm. "What you have here is perfect, Mr. Atis. It's only the shadow of the couch on the screen that needs a slight adjustment." Mr. Atis made immediate calls to adjust the trajectory of lights affixed to the ceiling. Mr. Selby smiled at the man's gumption. "Places please! Mr. Atis, remind us again who's up!"

"It's Ms. Amber, sir. She promised a follow up call last week," said Mr. Atis.

"Amber, my dear! Front and center!"

The slightly creased skin at the corners of her mouth had marked Amber's face as someone in her thirties. The shy but proud body that had summoned the crew to breakfast nearly an hour earlier had shriveled and sunk as it plopped itself on the fastidiously placed couch.

"Who took the minutes for Amber's last session?" asked Mr. Selby.

Mr. Atis referenced a spiraled flipbook. "It was… Kenneth Polk."

"The Prez!" was the joyously unified response from a

few of the residents.

A short, thickset man jogged a few steps and retrieved a leather-bound album from Mr. Atis. "The minutes please, Kenneth."

"The Prez!"

Mr. Polk's beard could not hide the lifted cheeks of the smiling man. He paged forward and found the last entry with a pointed finger. "Last Tuesday, Ms. Amber promised a follow-up call to her mother."

"The Prez!"

"Quiet!" snapped Mr. Atis.

"The details, Kenneth. Give us the minutes."

"Ms. Amber, uh, Ms. Amber talked to her mom. She talked to her mom about it...about *it*," said Kenneth.

"Is there anyone here with the maturity to read the minutes?" asked Mr. Atis. "Thank you, Kenneth."

"Impeached!"

"He did not have sexual relations with that woman!" said a man sitting next to Scoop.

Kenneth passed the ledger back to Mr. Atis and jogged back to his pillow on the floor. Janzen found the man's persistent smile to represent something other than his good humor.

"Janzen, please read the minutes for us – up here now," Mr. Selby ordered rather than asked.

Janzen reluctantly obliged, took the ledger and stood in front of the staged couch. The room grew quiet and Mr. Atis indicated where he should begin from the hand-written notes. "Tuesday, August 18. Amber Vinetti called her mom for the first time after her disappearance. She asked if her mom got her emails about her being okay and staying with a friend. Her mom got her emails and got the note she left. Her mom wondered if she was still —"

Janzen stopped and looked over at Mr. Selby, who mouthed the word "read."

"Her mom wondered if she was still sticking things up her pussy for money and putting it on the internet." Janzen paused and looked for any reaction. The room was still.

"Be strong, Amber," said Christian, her cooking partner, before Janzen continued.

"Amber was sorry her parents had to see that. Her mom kept saying that it was under our own roof, that it was under our own roof that she was sticking things up her pussy for money on the internet." Behind Janzen, Amber white-knuckled the hem of her dress. "Amber will call back next week." Janzen threw the ledger at Mr. Atis while maintaining his glare at Mr. Selby.

"Thank you Janzen," said Mr. Selby, nodding to a man holding open a laptop and by the time Janzen had returned to his seat, the sound of a few keystrokes brought to life the entire wall behind Amber. In place of the beige partition with the faint shimmer was the lifelike image of a hotel wall. The newly materialized air conditioning unit from behind Amber's couch appeared to emit air that gently ruffled the high definition curtains. From the gap left between the two riffled curtains was a glimpse to a parking lot with passing vehicles.

Mr. Atis called for the projector and the man with the laptop brought it to life with the click of a remote. The computer placed in front of Amber projected its screen on what Janzen had originally thought to be a dry erase board on the wall opposite the hotel set. The room followed her keystrokes as she navigated her way to her mother. After she clicked the contact link, the program emitted a dual-gong ringer from the old rotaries that some in the room found a novelty while others were likely transported to distant childhoods. The smell of bacon grease and pancake batter crawled to the back of Janzen's throat at the sound. The ringing recalled his Sunday mornings with his mother cooking in the kitchen. His little legs had swung from his chair while she poured the batter from a plastic measuring cup. She would beckon him over to the stove, and they would laugh and jump at the spitting bacon. She would hold her palm inches from the popping grease and flinch in delight. He would ask her to stop before she playfully counted out the bubbles of the heating batter to him, who ate it up as if she herself was framed in panels of the weekend funnies. Up until a few weeks ago, Janzen had still eaten the PEZ candies from his pocket, not for their sweetness but for the saccharine flood that took him back to Ballucks, a mom-and-pop general store where sweaty men peered through rows of porno mags and where he would be treated to packs of PEZ if he helped carry his mom's sundries. The memory of teats and sweets had always warmed his core and fluttered his digits.

Amber's mom, Mrs. Vanetti, accepted the incoming call. Projected on the back screen for everyone in Conference Room A to see was the midsection of Amber's mother. She had not yet fully lifted her laptop's monitor. Mrs. Vanetti's palm held over the microphone muffled her sharp whispers to someone offscreen. She finally lifted the computer and faced the lens.

"Mom?"

The woman on the other end clearly heard Amber, but her vacant words matched her vacating eyes. The anger that might have been present a week ago was in retreat, sheathed in the disdain and disappointment only a mother or a father could brandish. She had bathed Amber and had been the caretaker of her tiny body, and her tiny genitals were a secret held closely between mother and daughter.

"I know you're not the only one to ever show yourself online, Amber." She used her name. There might be hope. Her words were measured. "It's everywhere. It's in every corner of the internet. I know that now."

"I need you to know why, Mom."

"Let me speak!" She startled some in the conference room and her volume crackled the inner-office speaker. "Why am I echoing? Where are you?"

"A hotel."

"Are you using our points?

"What?"

"Amber, are you using our points to pay for that hotel room? It's a simple question."

"No."

"Jesus Christ. What will Father Caponi say, Amber? Have you thought of that?

"Why would Father Caponi know?"

"For when you confess, damn it!"

"Where was I going to get the money, Mom?"

"Who was that man watching you?

"Mom, please."

"Your father needs to know. He sounded foreign."

"He was from France."

"What was his name?"

"He didn't have a name. None of them had any names. They were all French on a French site where no one knew me and no one knew you, dad or Father Caponi!"

Her mother looked away, relaying the information to Amber's father offscreen.

"How many were there?"

"Mom."

"How many, goddamn it!"

"Why are you talking to me like this?"

"How many?"

"There were more."

"How many more?"

There was no right answer for Amber. "More than I know."

Her mother's head fell forward. "Did he pay you?"

"Yes. Everyone paid me."

"With money?"

"Basically. It's online money."

"Hold on." Her mother leaned off camera for something before paging through a book unseen in her lap. "For certain people have crept in unnoticed who long ago were designated for this condemnation, ungodly people, who pervert the grace of our God into sensuality and deny our only Master and Lord, Jesus Christ. Jude 1:4."

"I want to know what *you* think."

"You don't want to know what *I* think."

"Mom, I'm not proud of this. I didn't think anyone

would know. You know how much I owe."

"So it's our fault that it's come to this? It's our fault your father and I couldn't afford to send you where you wanted to go?"

"No, Mom. I wanted to pay for it. It was my mistake. I'm sorry, Mom. No one is going to know."

"I know, Amber. God knows. Your father knows. Hundreds of men know. It's where the world is. I even read an article on the Virgin Mary's hymen yesterday. There's nothing sacred anymore. There's sex and lewdness everywhere, and every face and every shame and every genital out there is now yours for everyone to see. That's how I see it. I thought we raised you better, but I was wrong. We failed. And now I don't know where to go from here. A goddamn degree in French. You're Italian for god's sake! Che schifo!"

"Can I please talk to Dad?" Amber's voice slipped away down her misery's ditch. Her mother was no longer visible in front of the computer, and the conversation off camera sounded strained and distant. The inhabitants of Conference Room A waited silently and were transfixed at the drama onscreen.

Amber reminded Janzen of the ficus he had killed over the course of three months. He had mitigated its exposure to light. He had researched its water requirements and ideal soil conditions. He adjusted it only when necessary, but the plant deteriorated day-by-day until the sound of its crisp leaves hitting the floor eventually sent Janzen into a weeklong depression. His suicide note at the time read: *death by ficus*. At least he was writing.

Amber sat with her feet pigeon-toed and her elbows

buried in her lap. Her father placed himself down on the other end and revealed the origin of her daughter's softness. The computer caught his mournful eyes and the way he nervously scratched at his thick forearms. He wore a shirt that hugged him so tightly that any of his more pronounced gestures were accompanied by the fabric's scrape.

"Daddy."

"Cucciola."

"I'm so sorry."

"We thought you were dead."

"I know."

"You left that note."

"I know."

"What are you doing?"

"I don't know."

"As a parent, you don't plan for this, Amber. Your mother is hurt. If you needed money, you should've asked for it. It's hard to know what to say to you."

"Why are you wearing that shirt, poppa?"

"Your mother thinks that if she buys me smaller shirts that I'll lose weight. But everyone at the club calls me 'Salsiccia' now because I remind them of a sausage, and it makes me hungry. I've gained five pounds since you've left." Mr. Vanetti paused and then responded to a murmur off camera. "I've gained nine pounds since you've left."

"Daddy."

"When are you coming-" The connection to Amber's father was severed by a kill switch on a remote. Mr. Selby had cut power to their wireless connection. He held the device out in front of him for everyone to see. He then placed it in his front breast pocket and occupied the silence in the room with a single pointer finger in the air. Amber was still, but there was an agitation among the others that required Mr. Selby's attention.

"That's enough for now. Christian, will you please see to Amber. Let's congregate, please." This call to action triggered a synchronized rustling noise in Conference Room A that Janzen had all but forgotten – a distant memory including those slippery wooden benches, constructed in such a primitive and uncomfortable manner conceivably to invoke the suffering of their savior's crucifixion. Janzen twisted his torso and the pang in the small of his back disappeared.

Mr. Selby ran his finger along the lines of the ledger. "We learned last week that Mrs. Vanetti had undergone a complete hysterectomy years before, and that this had to play at least a tiny part of her adverse reaction to finding her daughter performing sex acts online for money. We agreed that because these particular acts took place in the bedroom in which Amber had slept as a child undoubtedly also added to the disturbance. For Janzen to better understand the situation, Amber accepted donations into an online account to stick varying implements of length and girth up her vagina in an effort to pay back the school loans on which she had previously defaulted." Mr. Selby looked toward Janzen and paused, perhaps in an imprecise taunt. "Janzen, don't rush into thinking that this was Amber's preferred employment. She was, in fact, working another job at the time - an internship that in no way offered her any financial flexibility or even so much as a living wage.

"You know, this is one of those things I've never understood and it's what's driven Amber to such desperate ends," Mr. Selby continued, closing the ledger and pinching the bridge of his nose. "At Selby Industries, we understood the worth of our employees. For anyone familiar with the inner workings of this building during the time it served as our headquarters, you'd know that the first floor was devoted to the *real* working men and women of the company and they were paid accordingly. They were paid so that they could live independent lives. When you walked through the front doors of this establishment, ladies and gentlemen, what did you see?"

The room was silent save Amber's sniffles.

"If you were a stockholder or the mailman or the janitorial staff or Wayland friggin' Selby, you'd walk right into the heart of the operation. You had Donnie on the CAEC Embosser. You had Brooks on the #35 roller. Marissa worked as hard as those goddamned machines as shift supervisor. A string of our best sellers were manufactured right below where we sit. And I know what you're thinking – yes, it would have made more sense to operate the manufacturing side of things elsewhere, but I wouldn't hear it. The heart of Selby was built on the foundation of the worker, the true-blues! They told me 'Put the Manek out there' – the old foot-operated shear my father had in his shop. They told me to put it out there on a stand with a dedication on a plaque. They said there should have been carpeting and paneled walls and smooth jazz over the speakers – make it pretty. But it was pretty. It was perfect to me. I wish I could've hired Amber to be with me back then. I know that she would've done anything for us."

Digressions are often the Rorschach of the rambler. What had begun as a sermon had turned hostage to a man's past. A few in Conference Room A might've seen the man as nothing but a moth bumping against a screen door, but certainly there had to be those whose psychoses had advanced far enough and whose sympathies extended beyond their own degradation allowing them to see a man segmenting before them into something different.

Day one in Mt. Selby had thus far offered Janzen a variety of colors from which to paint, but the near constant additions only led to the inevitability of one color: gray. But Janzen could work in grays.

"Let me get to my point," continued Mr. Selby. "Is Mrs. Vanetti's anger justified in this situation?" The air was hot with opinion with not one shared loudly enough to distinguish itself from the din. Mr. Atis called for silence but the discussions continued enthusiastically. "That's it! It's a face off!"

At Mr. Selby's proclamation, the room was abuzz with activity. Two chairs were pushed to the center of the room facing each other. Mr. Selby was on his feet pouring through previous pages of the ledger. "Who went last time, Mr. Atis?"

"We had chosen both but never started. The bell had just rung at the gate."

"We need someone to play Amber and someone to play her mother, and we need a third chair for the real Amber." A third chair was brought in on the fly, and the

occupants of Conference Room A were positioning themselves in a circle around the three chairs. Scoop, who had
buried himself in the corner of the room throughout the
previous call, had come alive with a newly found eager-
ness. He stood near the electronic whiteboard on the side
wall that had displayed Amber's parents. He asked for
power and found a stylus that allowed him to divide the
screen into sections.

Through the commotion, Christian had his arm
around Amber and quietly recommended to Mr. Selby
that this might not be the best time. The momentum and
vibrancy sparked in the room climbed. The motion set
forth by Mr. Selby caused in Janzen a seasickness that
would end only upon reaching their destination, which
in this case involved some type of face off.

"Not the best time? This is exactly what Amber needs,
some disassociation. She's too tied up in the emotions!
She needs to work with the facts!" Mr. Selby scanned the
room of its occupants. "Helena!" he declared joyously. A
cheer from the group arose.

A fever of euphoria had struck Kenneth Polk in such a
way that he was currently moving his rotund and redden-
ing figure around the perimeter of the room in a display
of exuberance no hamstring should be asked to withstand. Conversely, Helena's reticence had not betrayed
her. She was hesitant to move from her spot against the
wall; nonetheless, an admonishing finger wag from Mr.
Selby lifted her up from the wall and into one of the center chairs.

"Let's see…" Mr. Selby once again scanned the room
to the delight of many. "I need a Mrs. Vanetti." The man

was P.T. Barnum starring in a P.T. Anderson film, whose title might have been *Hocus Bogus*. "Ms. Patterson!" The reaction from the room was one of surprise and delight.

Janzen recalled seeing Ms. Patterson during breakfast. He noticed her barely moving to the blaring music. She might be an older sister to the black kid who had sung lyrics intermittently atop the two chairs. They shared the same high cheekbones and the same tiny ears that resembled the clenched fists of a newborn. Ms. Patterson moved through the crowd in the same way one walked politely by folks seated on a crowded church pew.

While Mr. Selby spoke with Amber, Scoop commandeered the role of ringmaster. He stood in the center of the room and hushed the people around him. "We got a face off between Helena as Amber and Ms. Patterson as Mrs. Vanetti. Da name of da game wull be…" Scoop shook his head and rattled things about upstairs. "Da game wull be When da Doves Cry, yo." The announcement was met with a reaction you'd expect at the blue ribbon ceremony of a Harford County rib cook-off. The men and women in the room yelled out different numbers. Scoop called for quiet while he scrutinized Amber's conduct. "Less set da parameders. Lass time der was problems when we shud'a called it. Just 'cuz ders tears don mean iss called. I been thinkin' bout dis. If an onion cud'a caused it, it ain't cryin'. Iss gotta be CTB: complete and total breakdown." Janzen was impressed with Scoop's administrative skills. "Da house has da over/under at…" Scoop once again looked at Amber, still in congress with a doting Mr. Selby. "Iss set at seven questions."

A surge of conversation once again burst forth in the

room, and Scoop was back at the board with an electronic stylus. He erased what he originally graphed and divided the board in half with a single vertical swipe. Along the top he penned the numbers one through eight; then, he simultaneously wrote initials and sums with one hand while pointing and collecting bets with the other. The left half was filled with initials of those who thought Amber would begin sobbing in six questions or less. J.H. were the only initials scribbled on the right. "Now remember yo, we're talkin' fishul answers wid eeder a yes or a no. An' if I see any innerference, yer name's off da board."

Meanwhile, in the middle of the room, Helena and Ms. Patterson sat across from each other having been cast as principals to play the roles of Amber and Mrs. Vanetti. Mr. Selby guided the real Amber to the third seat creating a triangle under the spotlight. He adjusted the sleeves of his jacket to his wrists and gave the room his ground rules. "Helena and Ms. Patterson, in a Q&A format, you must get to the root of Amber's issues as understood by each of you. Your goal in these seats is not to protect her but to help her uncover what remains unearthed. Is that clear?" The women nodded. "We go until we stop, and we always start with 'Is it possible.'" Mr. Selby backed into his chair while Amber played the part of a withered, leaning maypole. "Now let's begin. You first, Helena. You're in character now – as our very own Amber."

"Is it possible that –"

"To your mother!" scolded Mr. Selby.

Helena refocused from Amber to Ms. Patterson. "Is it possible that you're mad at me for what you saw that night?"

"Hogwash, Helena! Dig!"

Helena nodded. "Is it possible that what you saw that night will be the only image you ever have of me from here on out?"

"To the root! Well done!" said Mr. Selby, pointing at the real Amber. "Real or not?"

"Real." Amber maintained and Scoop crossed through the number one along the top of the board. Mr. Selby nodded for Ms. Patterson to continue as Mrs. Vanetti.

"Is it possible that you have always been closer to your father and this will only drive us further apart? I mean, I don't know all the facts, Mr. Selby."

Mr. Selby waved away Ms. Patterson's last sentence and faced Amber and said, "Real or not?" Amber nodded again. Two was crossed off the board. "Now back to Helena."

"Is it possible there's something else I've done that would upset you so much?"

The room's spectators shifted their attention back to Amber, who searched random parts of the room for answers. "No. Nothing I can think of." Scoop crossed off the number three.

"Serve, volley! Serve, volley!" yelled Mr. Selby. "Back to Ms. Patterson!"

"Did your mother go to college, Amber?" asked Ms. Patterson. Amber shook her head no. "Is it possible that because I never went away to school that I feel less than others, especially knowing I have a daughter I'm not close to who does these things on the internet? And it hurts you to realize this?"

Amber cleared her eyes. Scoop paced back and forth

in front of the board at the prospect of losing his money, but Amber rose back up and shook her head in agreement. Scoop took a deep breath and crossed off the number four amid the cheers in the room, now in full-throated support of Amber.

"Bingo!" yelled Mr. Selby. "Back to the inimitable Helena Wanda March!"

"Is it possible there was a part of me that was excited while doing this at first? And it was even fun, and I enjoyed being a sexual thing in front of a stranger? But everything came crashing down the night my parents found out and the idea of being sexual again has been... has been fucked?"

Amber nodded her head and reached out to Helena. They drew each other in and hugged. Ms. Patterson waited until Amber was back in her seat to continue.

"Is it possible that the problem here is me, and I that ain't made good choices when I was younger and when you was growing up, and I'm the one who needs to get over this – cuz being a mother ain't that easy," said Ms. Patterson, now looking at the young black teenager behind her. "And I may not make you proud, but I'm the only one you got and we gon' have to work through this together and maybe start from scratch knowing both of us made mistakes?" The young man turned aside.

"Amber?

She warmed at Ms. Patterson's inclusion of her own son and nodded. Scoop scratched through the number six.

"Now back to Helena," said Mr. Selby.

Helena squirmed in her seat, not sure how to proceed

but finally said, "Is it possible that this is just one long miserable ride and that we're going to be kicked and dragged through it till we're done?"

"Yes!" said Amber, finally breaking through and smiling brilliantly at this sentiment as the room hollered yelps of praise at her present transformation. The house had won and Scoop set about collecting dollar bills and receipts from the host of losers. He approached Janzen and paid out half the winnings -- $12.00 – counting out the sum for the winner's endorsement. Janzen pushed Scoop away.

"You won da money, Jay. It pushes to you. Take it. I'll win it back," said Scoop. Janzen again declined. Scoop pocketed the money, and Janzen couldn't decide if he had offended the integrity of the wager or if this was Scoop's tell that there were things to be bought inside Mount Selby. Either way, Janzen had alleviated a terrible weight when he no longer needed to fill his back pocket. The journey to reach the bottom end of the middle class had exhausted him. Where wealth might very well propel many within its reach, that drive was so foreign to Janzen that it was a novelty to be around such an affluent man as Wayland Selby.

"Ladies and gentleman, I have a presentation to make before we dismiss. The easel please," said Mr. Selby, who cleared an area in front of the group for the easel brought in from somewhere outside the room. "Everyone grab a seat so you can see this." Resting on the horizontal support was a rectangular shape draped in fabric. Janzen sensed the attention shifting to him. "Ms. Helena Wanda, as both the author of the work and our artist in residence, would you like to say a few words?"

"No."

"Very well. I should have phrased that differently. Ladies and gentlemen, I present to you the latest addition to our family, Mr. Janzen Marko Hakkinen." Mr. Selby removed the cover from the rectangle with the flourish of a matador, revealing a framed pen and ink illustration of Janzen. The unveiling triggered inhales of acclaim from the room. "Ms. Helena Wanda worked through the night, and it is my understanding that after her initial attempt of an oil-on-canvas rendition, she decided a much more understated take was necessary. Do I have that right?"

"It fit the mold of a man who took such pleasure in the destruction of someone else's things," said Helena. Her response provided a bleak counterpoint to a piece that elicited a continuous flow of compliments from those present. She had worked from a still image of Janzen on his dolly ride. The illustration captured the curvature of his shoulders extended to the side for balance. Janzen was uneasy not because of the comparing ganders shifting back and forth to the canvas and him, but the idea that someone had dedicated that amount of time and effort to capture his image held in such, well, joy – as momentary as it was.

Janzen wagered a glance toward Helena, who was focused on her shoelaces. He was at once horrified of the intimacy he unknowingly shared with the woman but also somewhat amazed that the captured image revealed something that he figured to be dead for some time.

"Of course, Janzen will join the rest of the gang on our sacred wall below. Ms. Helena Wanda, we thank you for your skill and commitment to duty. And Janzen, let this work serve as a reminder that you are now part of something that very few can claim to be a part of. You are welcome here, and we hope you give this place and us a chance. A hand, ladies and gentlemen." The group clapped warmly at Mr. Selby's behest. "Art therapy will not be mandatory this afternoon after your wonderful work this morning, but of course, the studio will be open, and we'll meet again at lunch. Enjoy the rest of the morning!"

Mr. Selby was joyful and shook hands with those around him. For some, they shook a hock of ham for all its queerness, though such an outward display of inclusion had a way of softening those with an impulse towards cynicism.

The crowd in Conference Room A exited, led by Helena. They carried with them lively conversations that matched the pace of their footfalls. Janzen was the only one left – he and his likeness. He was grateful of the image or the effort it took. He had never believed that he photographed well. The only picture he was fond of was snapped at the MVA and caught such an unbelievable depiction of rage that he kept the license even after its renewal date passed. But this one wasn't bad either.

The strangeness of the morning invigorated him and the mystique of the building got the better of his curiosity. Art therapy sounded interesting, but there was a vast frontier left unexplored begging for a reconnoiter.

On the elevator, Janzen asked Samuel for a bona fide tour of the grounds to which the fat man said simply to work his way up. Janzen had seen the blockaded first level and could only guess if there was a parking garage below that. He tossed a folding chair into a crowd on the second floor draped in its velvet mystery. The third floor was nothing but Helena's studio, a ghost-like man and hallways full of closed doors.

Samuel recommended the fourth floor as a starting point and told Janzen that it offered as much insight into the heart of this building than any other floor. Samuel squeezed his head, and his face reddened with the swimming secrets he worked to contain. Janzen did not press him before he saw things for himself, but what sprawled before him upon exiting the elevator on the fourth was pedestrian at best.

He walked through an open floor plan full of cubicles and outer offices enclosed in panes of glass. By way of a central pathway, Janzen found that while most of the cubicles and desks were free of bric-a-brac and clutter, there were still some with family photos, framed certifications, bobbleheads, stressballs and other office knickknacks.

The absence of outside light was the main curiosity. Every exterior window around the perimeter of the floor had been covered by solid pieces of composite material. The sheets were dark blue and allowed in as much light as the depths of the ocean and were affixed to the walls by heavy-duty screws that appeared to have had their countersunk heads disfigured by extreme heat to assure their permanent place. He pressed his face against the material to check its opacity and realized the only glimpse of the outside world he recalled since coming into the building was on the eleventh floor, where Mr.

Selby and Mr. Atis had their respective offices.

Janzen flicked a light switch on the wall near him, and the room was awash in neon indigo. The drone of the lights above him brought to life an eeriness that was before absent. He ran his finger along a string of desktops but where he expected a thimble-wide trail through the idle dust, he found none. He rubbed his forefinger and thumb together, and they stuck with the sticky cleanser left behind.

On the cubicle desk closest to him was a round toy penguin resting on the rim of a coffee cup. He picked it up and threw it across the room. It caromed off the far wall and crashed into something in another cubicle. He half-expected it to fly back at him, hurled by some unseen spirit. He walked the toy's path and saw it knocked over a framed photograph of a father and mother with a young child. The man wore a bored smile, and the woman appeared on the tale-end of a meth binge. The child was frightened perhaps at the surprising flash of the bulb, or would some psychologist recognize this particular expression as the boy's acknowledgement of genetic shortcomings? Janzen began filling in mysterious backstories until the hairs on his forearms spiked with the idea of something behind him. He wheeled around and found nothing. He placed the framed photo next to the computer monitor. Some truth hid away in this room.

He retrieved the penguin from underneath the desk and placed it in the leather seat of the swiveling chair before he pushed it back against the desk, concealing its location. Whatever revelations existed in this room lay hidden under a veil of normality. He passed through the fire door at the corner stairwell and climbed another flight to the fifth floor.

Even before exiting the stairwell, Janzen was met with a flurry of sounds. The door opened to blaring lights, pounding music and the electronic blinks of exercise equipment. The carpet he stood on divided a sea of tiled rubber flooring. The entire room was lined with mirrors. To the left were rows of machines aimed at honing the cardiovascular: stationary bikes, treadmills, elliptical trainers, stair climbers and rowing machines. On the opposite side were free weights and Nautilus products. If Janzen ever thought to join a gym, this one would have been out of his price range. It wasn't that he was opposed to such places, only the inhabitants that came with them, the shining breed of hulks whose dedication required immeasurable time with one's own reflection for purposes only Narcissus would find acceptable. Addicts of every shade certainly colored this world, but Janzen preferred his with body hair.

The gym's scent permeated the room – neutralizing chemicals mixed with the tainted bouquet of every unwashed area wide enough to serve as a seat. Adding to the aroma were two of Club Selby's members. One was a white gentleman in his mid-to-late forties – a gentleman no doubt because he took the time to perform an obvious full-on tuck. The elastic waistband of his elevated shorts hovered bellybutton high, and it swooshed back and forth on the elliptical. Janzen's focus oscillated between the man's rounded midriff and the equidistant headband that somehow shimmied in horizontal unison, an unbelievable feat of coordination that rivaled any motion down a West SoHo runway.

On the right was the young black kid Janzen recognized as Ms. Patterson's son. He wore a baggy shirt and skin-tight shorts, and his clay-brown skin had the hue of a wet, polished penny. His frame was still in flux in its youth, but how he shook out his lean muscles in between yoga poses spoke of a self-assured maturity. Janzen appreciated the half-moon pose he held, a maneuver left to those familiar with suffering.

The kid caught Janzen watching him and swung his suspended leg back to the ground. He approached Janzen with the nonchalance of an old cat. "Have you met Daryl?" His voice was soft and silky and came from a mile away but in a whisper.

Janzen was unprepared for a third-person conversation, but he gave it a go. "No. Janzen has not yet met Daryl." This response brought a smile to the Patterson kid's face. With an indication of his chin, he pointed at something beyond Janzen, but before he could turn completely around, Janzen was engulfed in the embrace of the man previously on the elliptical. A full-on tuck and a full-on hug joined as one.

"Meet Daryl, Janzen," said the Patterson boy. "He's a hugger." Daryl smelled of lilac.

Daryl was a man for whom speaking with a stranger pelvis to pelvis was no problem. "Janzen, I think I love everything about you. You really spoke to me during your entrance interview down in Guard Plaza. I could've just died."

"You saw?"

"We saw everything. Mr. S streams everything right

upstairs while it happens. Ain't it somethin'?" Janzen did his best version of a genteel pectoral press and created some distance between himself and Daryl, who still held on to his arms. "I've been waiting to talk to you. Is Janzen Nordic? It has to be. You look like Dolph Lundgren made love to a rosenmunnar. Will you sit down and talk to me? I have lots to ask you." Daryl brought over a padded workout bench for them.

"I can't right now, Daryl. I was trying to find my way over to some art therapy, but how about dinner together?"

"That sounds wonderful, my friend." Daryl once again grabbed Janzen by the arms. "Janzen, it's really nice having you here with us. You know that, right? I really mean it." The man's sincerity was completely absent of pretense.

"Thank you Daryl. You're kind to say that."

"It's the truth, young man. Now get along before I get rolling again!"

"One more thing, Daryl."

"Down there and to the left." The man pointed to the far side of the gym. Daryl stood there with his two feet pointing directly at Janzen, waving at his departure with not a bend in his elbow. He reminded Janzen of the blissfully confused octogenarian he once saw years ago in the Inner Harbor waving goodbye to a young child aboard the *U.S.S. Constellation*. He had overheard her repeatedly wishing the boy safe travels on the sloop-of-war that had been moored in place for some twenty-plus years at that point. She was likely waiting for her family to see the ship while she stood by on solid ground, and she kept talking to herself with quivering lips. It was probably her son onboard who kept yelling at her that they'd be right back down and to stay where she was and that they weren't going anywhere. She couldn't help herself from waving goodbye. Watching her, Janzen feared not a broken bone or a bum hip; it was the mental deterioration that frightened him most. The DTs he experienced would later spotlight the frailty of his own brain, but that was still to come. He'd still need to descend further. The old woman shook Janzen that day until he drank enough that same night to elevate his button fly to a Rubik's Cube, leading to him pissing himself as dawn broke. What a life he had led. But he got straight. He wrote his book, and he climbed this building.

Janzen followed Daryl's direction along the corridor, its walls covered with padded square panels the colors of a Maine winter. Several doors along the hallway opened to blank and empty rooms. He heard conversations at the end. One door was slightly open, and Janzen peered through the crack without attracting attention.

Inside, a few of the residents worked at their easels. Amber sat at one of the tables leading a group in origami. She laughed kindly at one's finished product and moved around the table to help adjust some of the others' work. There was a lightness about the room that Janzen found welcoming, but he wasn't ready for that. His isolation was simply another habit that needed weaning. He wanted to find someone else anyway. He moved quickly down the stairwell and found her sitting at a table organizing her supplies. He knew that she knew that he was there. He waited outside her door until she exhaled loudly enough to communicate her annoyance.

"*I know* I know you from somewhere," said Janzen.

"You don't. I never forget an asshole," said Helena.

He wasn't sure if her response was said in jest. "Are you also the resident proctologist?" She smirked, not smiled at this question, but Janzen was happy enough to adjust her interminable aloofness if only for a second. She continued working at the table. "I'm serious. This isn't a come-on or something. I know you from somewhere."

"I don't think so. We definitely didn't run in the same circles."

"Yeah? So what's my circle?"

She put down the charcoal pencil she was sharpening and focused on Janzen.

"Tell me if I'm close. Overeducated self-loathing hipster writer. You love you some social injustice, fixed gear bikes and a side of quinoa. A lone wolf type with daddy or mommy issues – not sure which one. And you love NPR, Pitchfork and most everything Wes Anderson does." She lifted her eyebrows and re-crossed her legs.

"So close, Helena Wanda."

"Don't call me that."

"But you're wrong. I love *everything* Wes Anderson does. Ha!"

"Figures." She went back to work, and Janzen appropriated her response as an invitation. "Don't come in!" Her smirk disappeared. The anger she displayed was restrained as opposed to wielded. Her leveled gaze eliminated any hint of ambivalence, and so Janzen retreated.

Years of hard drinking and drugs left Janzen with a perpetual suspicion of having already met someone. On the precipice of his full-on addiction, he sometimes wondered at the polarizing differences between two oft-muttered pleasantries: *Nice to meet you* versus *Good to see you*. During the polite and friendly phases of his drunkenness, he often mistook one phrase for the other without contemplating the potential fallout. To be forgotten was an awful pinch of life and while he forgot meeting heaps of folks, the twisted images of those forgotten continued to pin prick his consciousness. He long believed himself a dipshit through and through, but could it be he *was* an asshole?

With Vince Guaraldi's sad sack *Peanuts* music in his head, Janzen walked dejectedly back to his room. Once inside, he stewed in rejection's sting. His leap off the garden sanctuary above provided his spirit a restart, but it was this interaction with Helena that reminded him of the stale guts within this newly bathed veneer. Welcome back to life! Yes, Helena was attractive. No, attractive wasn't the right word; she had a plaintive prettiness, like an open prairie at daybreak, but razor wire surrounded those pretty pastures. She was more a mystery than anything else, and she swam in those clothes of hers. What was she hiding under there anyways and who was looking? Why were there no labels on any of the clothes here? How does one even quantify racing thoughts? The earthquake has the Richter; the body has the BMI, the jalapeño even has the Scoville. So how does an egghead tabulate darting thoughts? The breakfast that morning was actually delicious. He would make it a point to tell Amber as much when he next saw her – that Christian fella, too. Latkes was such a deceiving word, ranked right up there with effluvium. He'd show the world some effluvium. He turned to his side and offered an organic vibration. The pillow was cool, and his breathing eventually deepened. Without much effort, he slept as soundly as he'd slept in years.

7

News of the assault spread quickly and was all anyone talked about during dinner. Janzen tried piecing the information together from the scattered bits of detail he caught amid the many discussions.

"He was masked."

"He freaked out – got sick everywhere."

"Doc is up there with Selby and him now."

"He was holding something?"

"No, he's a dentist."

"He was the last one up there."

"He's shook, man."

"He just held him down. He couldn't say a word."

Janzen was still unfamiliar with most of the names mentioned outside of Mr. Selby's. In lieu of interjecting into the crock-pot of conjecture, Janzen grabbed a stool and headed for the place where he knew the information would be less diluted, and once propped up inside the elevator with Samuel, the hefty man was more than willing to divulge everything he'd learned about the incident.

The prospect of any conversation inflated the man

with such alacrity. Someone simply needed to release the dammed up information with a wag of one's own chin. Samuel had been in the elevator when he heard the screams asking for help from the fifth floor. He considered it his vocational duty to attend to what he termed a "real-life death knell." Twice during his giddy recount, he reminded Janzen that he was one of only three people in possession of the key to run the elevator. Mr. Atis occasionally filled in for Samuel when nature called or if he was under the weather. Mr. Selby held the third copy. So Samuel heard the yells, and he rushed around the corner to find Ms. Patterson dragging a hysterical Mr. McCullough from the Art Therapy room. She grasped the elderly gentleman under the arms and was heaving him towards the elevator while a gasping Mr. McCullough tossed his legs about in a panic.

Samuel conjectured that a serious panic attack was preventing Mr. McCullough from speaking. Ms. Patterson and he pulled him into the elevator and took him up a floor to the clinic. Doc Nash, who lived in the room next to the clinic, was roused from his nap by Samuel and apprised of the situation. By the time Samuel explained what he knew, Mr. McCullough had regained a slight ability to communicate, albeit in incomprehensible phrases bordering a certain Pentecostal parlance. Samuel said that Mr. McCullough was older and slower than most on account of the Alzheimer's so it always took him longer to finish eating, get around, anything really, meaning it wasn't strange that he was the last one in Art Therapy.

Mr. Selby was brought down, and Samuel remained until the old man was able to speak effectively so that he could describe the full story. Mr. McCullough had been in the room alone and was shocked to find a man in a mask with him. He said the man only watched him. He said that he was nervous so he stood to leave when the man threw something at him but missed. He kept repeating that he heard something hiss. Mr. McCullough tried to leave but the silent man cut him off with each attempt. It was then that he tried to scream for help.

"What kind of mask was it?" asked Janzen.

"Well, Mr. McCullough said it went around his entire head, even the back of it. He said that he could see the man's eyes, but then he couldn't. He had a real hard time trying to explain it on account of being so upset, but he said he tried to ask who was behind the mask but said he couldn't make the noise come out."

"He must've been scared shitless."

"That's right, Janzen! That's what I said. Mr. Selby kept asking him if he recognized the person, the clothes, anything, but Mr. McCullough said he didn't."

"So what happened?"

"Well, the man walked in real quick and grabbed Mr. McCullough, just grabbed him real tight and brought him to the ground. He kneeled real hard on his stomach and Mr. McCullough said the man in the mask just watched him try and scream and scream for help, but nothing was coming out."

"And?"

"And that was it. Apparently he just got off and left, and about ten minutes later, Ms. Patterson found him lying on the floor out of his mind. That's when *she* started yelling for help. He was still shaking when he finally told

Doc and Mr. Selby what happened."

"I don't get it."

"Yes sir. It's been months since last time, and every-one who was around for that was just starting to feel better about things."

"Months since what?"

"It was a resident. It was a former resident who's not here anymore. She woke up with someone in her room, or he woke her up and told her to keep quiet."

"Did she recognize him?"

"He was wearing a mask, too, and he didn't actu-ally say anything. Just held a finger up to where his lips would be so she knew to be quiet, you know? That's about everything we know."

"Who is this guy?"

"Not sure."

"Who do you think it is?"

"It could be anyone. No one has a real good idea what he looks like, but obviously the two are related. It could be any of us."

"So what's his game? Why terrorize an old man and just leave?"

"I don't know, Janzen."

The two men sat atop their stools contemplating the possible motives behind such encounters. Janzen and Samuel were around the same age and without realizing it, they then hit a milestone in their nascent relationship. In between bouts of speculation shared between the two were prolonged chunks of silence that passed without either recognizing it. Janzen even rode the elevator while Samuel resumed his job as "Darth Elevator," a nickname he had given himself to describe his modest and solemn persona when certain people rode with him.

Janzen was intrigued with the idea of a masked misfit; moreover, he found it the perfect opportunity to glean other information about the building and its inhabitants. Mr. Selby had collected a truly wacko troupe of actors, and Samuel was all too willing to provide a working exposition to Janzen's varied theories.

"Thanks for the intel, Samuel." Janzen stood and left his stool sitting in the corner of the elevator. "One more thing." He took Samuel's sweaty palm and held it tightly. "I feel the good in you, Samuel, the conflict."

Samuel bounced up and down. He placed his hand theatrically over his heart and said, "You underestimate the power of the dark side, Janzen!" Janzen smiled and exited the box they shared. From the hallway, a jubilant voice trailed him. "If you will not fight, then you will meet your destinyyyyyyyyyy!"

Back in his room, Janzen discovered the bulky additions at once. With no personal possessions and the austere arrangement, it was hard to miss the piles of boxes on the desk and along the far wall. Also, at his feet was a stack of white t-shirts with a note pinned to the top that read: *Come over to 618 tomorrow after breakfast for your fitting.* He couldn't decipher the signature at the bottom.

He walked to his desk and lifted a still-packaged electronic typewriter. It must've weighed 25 pounds, and the corporate model on the side wore clothes decades old. Along with the word processor was a ream of paper and replacement ink cartridges, but what took up the bulk of the space were boxes of awards, articles, merchandise, press releases, quarterly reports, copies of patent certificates – boxes and boxes of Selby Incorporated materials. Had his room been relegated to a secondary storage unit?

"Janzen Hakkinen to the top, please. Janzen Hakkinen to the top." Mr. Atis's voice came through his room's speaker system. Janzen began digging through the first box for anything interesting. "Immediately please, Janzen."

The stairs offered Janzen's thighs a quick burn, a sensation he learned to love after so much riding. He found Mr. Atis sitting in the lobby area adjacent to Mr. Selby's office. The agitated man sat behind his desk as he had evidently been waiting a minute too long for Janzen's arrival.

"I will let Mr. Selby know-"

When Janzen refused to break stride and continued straight towards the closed doors of Selby's office, Mr. Atis relented. Once in the office, Janzen found Mr. Selby at work on something behind his huge oak desk.

"Janzen! Welcome! Please have a seat."

The chair that Janzen destroyed on his first day had been replaced by an equally substantial piece. He scratched at the upholstered seat. "You guys have these coming off a line or something?"

"Chippendale."

"Excuse me?"

It's a Chippendale," Mr. Selby said. "We have everything you need here, young man, only the best. Now you must be wondering about the new merchandise in your room."

"I was curious."

"Good. You see, everyone here has a certain role to play that allows us to function at our most productive level. This isn't Sandals, you know. This is a facility. And while you are only in your probationary period – let's call it – you will nevertheless be expected to carry your own weight. Does that make sense?"

"No."

"Ah. Right. When we last met here, I told you that I needed you for a specific purpose. Do you remember what that was?"

"You told me you wanted your story told."

"Right! Well done. Now, Mr. Atis and I have assembled much of Selby Incorporated's biographical information for your perusal. I will not tell you how to do your job as I am hardly a scribe, but I assumed that you'd want to know as much about this place and what we have accomplished to fill in some of the blanks."

"But what story do you want told?

"I want the story of us. The story of what's happening now."

"Then why all the stuff about your company?"

"It's who I am, you see."

"Why?"

"Well, that's a deeply complicated question, Janzen."

"I mean, why have me write about this and learn about who you were-"

"Are," Mr. Selby curtly corrected. "For my legacy, I suppose. Who's to say I'll be breathing tomorrow morning?"

"And what if I don't understand what's going on?"

"The more reason for you to involve yourself completely in the project."

"What kind of access will I have?"

"Unlimited."

"To you?"

"To everyone."

"To you?"

"To *everyone*, Janzen." The two men shifted their weights in their chairs in the same direction at the same time. "Starting the day after tomorrow, in the morning, you will submit to me your five hundred words which will be filed away uncensored and unread to respect your artistic process. I won't read a word until you tell me it's time. The process will continue that way, every day. Do you agree to those terms?"

"What do you want written, specifically?"

"Our story. What you see. I need a reporter's eye. Stick to the facts. Conduct interviews. Front page material here. The story will take hold, but I believe that what's happening here should be documented. You have my faith and backing as long as you agree to these terms of five hundred words a day. Will you accept this challenge?

"Yes sir."

"Excellent!" Mr. Selby stood up behind his desk. "If you'll excuse me, I have some unfortunate business to attend to. Without sounding dramatic, Janzen, I think it's courageous of you to take on this challenge, and I truly believe you'll be a great fit here. So thank you, son."

"What happened to Mr. McCullough?" asked Janzen, and a gloom overtook the older gentleman, and he sat back down in his seat.

"The word is out then?" Janzen nodded his head. "It's unfortunate. We can't make much of what Mr.

McCullough told us. You see, he suffers from Alzheimer's, and the reliability of his constitution is often...in question. But according to him, there was a situation."

"I suppose a masked man terrorizing your building is a situation."

"We're not sure what to make of it. If I can confide in you Janzen, this wasn't the first time."

"No?"

"No one's been hurt physically, but there is a concern."

"Can I help?"

"Janzen, thank you, but no. This is not your problem. There shouldn't be *any* problem. Trust me when I tell you that the guilty party will be dealt with – severely. If you would, please try not to alarm anyone else about this until we know what we're dealing with."

"Do you know who it is?"

"No."

He believed everything Mr. Selby had said up until his final reply, but for Janzen, what's the big deal about truth if it wasn't for lying? Even the ripest cherry harbors a dash of poison. Janzen followed his new employer out of his office and took the stairs back down to his room on the seventh. He organized the boxed materials in piles along some space on the wall. He unpacked the word processor and loaded a fresh ink cartridge. He powered on the machine and began typing. He pushed himself for hours, and he worked until his bladder told him it was time for a break, so he stood and walked across the hallway to the restroom. It was then that the man who lay hidden underneath his bed silently let himself out of Janzen's room.

8

The next morning, Janzen met with young Monroe Patterson, who was waiting for him in 618 for his appointment. Having met a day earlier in the gym, both were comfortable around each other despite Janzen not knowing why he was there.

Monroe hunted for a specific measuring tape and displaced and placed the different sewing machines, rolls of fabric, dress forms, scissors, pressers, hams, and thread in doing so. The windows were covered over with the same dark blue material as on the fourth floor offices.

"Let's go. Arms out." Janzen lifted his arms out to his side while Monroe measured his chest. "I'm guessing no one's told you where the showers are."

"Good guess."

"Not really. You stink. I'll show you after we're done. We got a few. Spread your legs," said Monroe and Janzen followed the instructions.

"Seeing as how you're remarkably close to my balls, have I earned some leeway to ask you some questions?"

"Shoot."

"Why are you remarkably close to my balls?"

"You're funny."

"I mean, what are you doing here in this room in this building?" Janzen gave Monroe time to mull over the question while he continued with his measurements.

"I needed to change some things, and I left my moms a note and now she's right here with me."

"I don't understand."

"You will. Just give it some time. All our stories come out eventually," Monroe said, continuing to measure Janzen's widths and lengths, marking down these numbers on a notepad. "That's the mantra around here. Just stick around, you'll find out. Stick around, find out. I just think Mr. Selby is lonely."

"So just stick around?"

"What's your favorite book, Janzen?"

"Where am I when I'm reading it? What mood am I in? Am I in a hospital or on some kind of binge? Where's my head at?" Janzen had begun pacing around Monroe's studio in an effort to answer his question.

"Okay, boy. Come back here," said Monroe. "Whatever that book is, would you recommend someone read the SparkNotes instead of the real thing?"

"No. Of course not."

"So be patient. Now sit. Gimmie that neck of yours." Monroe took his final measurement.

"You're a clever one. How old are you?"

"Eighteen." He could've passed for fifteen.

"Your mom is young."

"Yes she is. Too young," said Monroe, who sat down and offered Janzen his full attention.

"How long you been here?"

"About three months."

"You're not gonna tell me anything else?"

"Not now, Janzen. Mr. Selby prefers it that way. Just be around and you'll learn – about everyone."

"So does Selby have you making everyone's clothes?"

"We all need 'em. And I know how to make 'em," said Monroe, playing with the hidden placket of his shirt, which reached almost down to his knees. "Besides, it's not like he makes me do it. I enjoy it."

"Where'd you learn?"

"Here. And from my mom a little. I taught myself some before I came here."

"Well, I prefer if everything fits extra tight so you can see my bulges."

The young clothier chuckled. "Nah. You're a preppy ass white dude who wears preppy ass white clothes."

"Are you being serious?" Janzen considered the corduroy shorts he "designed" from second-hand corduroy pants. The t-shirt he wore was paint stained and thin enough to see through. His one canvas shoe had a hole in it – one of the many open wounds he sustained a few years ago after flipping over his handlebars upon hitting a concrete divider at about thirty miles per hour.

"You definitely have a look." Monroe stood and with a kind hand, he helped Janzen to his feet. "C'mon. You're a whisker away from ripe. Let me show you those showers."

Janzen was struck by Monroe's breezy nature – how he spoke and moved; neither was practiced or contrived. He expected nutcases in the building but found only this young man's composure. He led Janzen around the corner, now serving as a tour guide. He showed Janzen the doctor's office where Mr. McCullough was taken the day before. In the room were a stretcher and an examination table and countertop full of drawers on which rested jarred instruments and gauze. Fastened to the wall, a defibrillator was hung next to a few stethoscopes. Everything about the room, including the ivory paint scheme could have been taken from a stock photo of an emergency room.

Walking farther down the hall, Monroe knocked on one of the many closed doors. He opened it and stuck his head in to say 'hi' to Kenneth Polk whom some only referred to as "The Prez." Kenneth waved an exuberant hello and goodbye to both before they moved on.

"That man can be hard to read, but he's all heart," said Monroe.

"And he came in the same way we did?"

"Yerp." They walked past a glass-enclosed office replete with white countertops, scales, vials, beakers, propane burners, an industrial sink and an eyesore of a ventilation system that had been in no way professionally installed. Its exit through the ceiling was conspicuous on account of the heavy use of duct tape keeping it sealed. "This is one of the few locked doors in the place," said Monroe.

"What do they use it for?"

"Manufacturing meds."

"For here?" asked Janzen. The young Monroe nodded. "What kind?"

"Different kinds, man. You'll see soon enough. It's about time for another hoedown real soon. You'll get a kick out of it. Now let's get you clean." He held a door open for Janzen. Inside was a converted shower room colored by the exposed unnatural reds and blues of the PEX piping. Clearly there was still work to be done if this room was going to make the brochure. Vinyl dividers hanging from the ceiling separated four showerheads from each other. Janzen had only worked on three or four plumbing jobs in the past, but he guessed that the showers were poached from a line of toilets. Monroe tugged another suspended piece of vinyl that assured the privacy of someone in the shower. Handwritten on it was the word *Dolt*. Another read *Dame*. "You, my friend, would be a dolt, so mind the company if you're sharing space. It's actually rare when you run into someone, though, so you'll be cool. Sound good?" Janzen nodded. "Listen, I'll get you some gear real soon, so just hold tight with those tees I dropped off. Anything else, just ask, man."

"Towels?"

"Right. Let me show you where you drop off and pick up your laundry."

Similes and metaphors whirled about in Janzen's head. While Monroe showed him the laundry facilities, the newest addition to Mr. Selby's collection struggled to come up with a proper word or phrase to best describe this place. The heavy velvet curtain had yet to be fully lifted on this mystery.

One image popped into his head – an old word from his childhood.

For Janzen, this place was a walrus as he now understood the word in his own special way, the meaning of which took particular hold at an early age and was an idea spawned from facts and fantasy told to him by his father. Before he even constructed a likeness of that mammal in his head, his father had read his young son the journals and notes of the naturalist Edward W. Nelson. He read about the Eskimo and Athabaskan peoples and the many ways they used the walrus. Once hunted and killed, the animal was food for man and beast alike. The fat was rendered into oil, providing light and comfort. Its skin was ripped from its flesh and stretched across boat frames. The tusks were processed and used for trading, weaponry and scrimshaw.

His father provided this information in his scholarly and detached manner, but Janzen couldn't wholly apprehend a depiction of such an animal that would provide these disparate utilities. Was it an animal so helpless that a young Inuit child his age could go and bop a walrus smack dab on the head and it would keel over on the spot?

From Nelson's writing, Janzen remembered finding himself appalled at the idea that hundreds of people from this particular group had died because a previous season's hunt was unsuccessful. Where was the fairness in that for both the walrus and the human?

There was also another element to this animal, and his storyteller's delivery transformed from David Attenborough to Vincent Price. His father took absolute delight in describing the unyielding aggression of the male adult walrus and how he often killed the younger pups in the pod because they were threats to his authority. He remembered his father telling him that it wasn't just in the Arctic where these animals were found. They were also found in little boys' dreams when they slept peacefully in their beds at night. Janzen had been horrified and confused at the thought of such an animal visiting him. His father added that the biggest among them was more than likely the meanest and most dominant, and his call was one you could hear miles away – even farther once you were asleep.

Young Janzen struggled to sleep after everything he had learned. The alien sounds of his half-dreams woke him in waves of panic, and after the third sinister night so many summers ago, he rode off on his BMX at dawn to wait for the local library to open. He would've jumped on the computer, but the internet had been out for months after the latest cyber attack. He waited hours until an elderly librarian opened the front doors. He asked for the section on walruses, and she pointed him to an aisle stocked with books on nature and the animal kingdom. It was only a few minutes until he turned the page to a photograph of that huge marine mammal propped up on his front flippers. His tusks were feet long, and his head was lifted toward the brilliant blue firmament, and it was then that Janzen refined his image of a true beast.

Ever since he was told the story of the walrus, anything – be it a situation, person or thing – now had a face split down the middle with one side tusked and the other side his father's inimical smile.

Before returning to his room, Monroe gave him some more clothes to use in case he wanted to exercise. Luckily, no one else was in the gym, so Janzen trashed his legs with some cardio and finally showered for the first time since being admitted into the building. Later in

Conference Room A, Janzen sat through another video call, but this time it was with a resident and his wife on the outside. He didn't recognize the name she kept using, the name she kept imploring to come home. He wasn't following any of it. His head was still in the Arctic with the walruses and the wilderness. Someone across from him cried or laughed at what was being said. Janzen wasn't so concerned with what he missed. It was no one's loss really – no one's loss but his.

The call ended and people moved around him and the lights were turned on. He wasn't so much snapped back to his place in the room because of this; instead, it was the unrepentant focus of Helena Wanda that finally brought him out of the wild and back to himself. Her feet, hips, shoulders and head were deliberately trained in his direction. She stared at him until he finally mouthed something to her, but her blink and turn of the head interrupted him and she was out the door before he could gather himself.

She had sucker-punched him up in Conference Room A with her attention, and she followed that up with a shot to his gut when she sat down across from him in the commissary later that night. "Would you describe yourself as homosexual or heterosexual?" she asked flatly. He spat out some of his food in surprise.

"I wouldn't really describe myself either way," said Janzen, retrieving a projected piece of filet mignon from her forearm.

"Forget it." Helena stood up from their table and scanned the room for another open seat.

"Okay. Sit down. Heterosexual." He slowly lifted

another piece of steak to his mouth and chewed carefully and deliberately. She closed her eyes and perhaps willed herself to stand in front of Janzen.

"Outside of what's going on in that head of yours, are you a relatively healthy human being?"

"Yes," he said, and she sat back down at the table.

"Do you deal with anything that a doctor would describe as contagious or congenital?"

"Benign essential tremor. And bipolar II, but I'm not sure that's congenital."

"What's the tremor?" she asked.

"My hands shake. And sometimes my head, ever since I was little."

"That's fine."

"Thank you?"

"Janzen, mah boy!" said Scoop, sitting down in the chair next to Helena.

"Scoop, can you give us a minute?" asked Helena. Scoop walked away the only kid not picked for the team. "Do you suffer from any deformities that would preclude you from living a normally functional life?"

"Preclude means prevent, right?"

"Yes."

"No."

"Okay."

"Okay?"

"I might have some more questions for you, but that's all I have right now," she said.

"I understand the meaning of those words."

"Are you being an asshole?"

"I'm being honest. I just don't know *why* you're asking

them," said Janzen.

She appeared to be deciding on which verbal assault to use from her mind's lazy Susan. "I have to go." She gathered her dinner and utensils and placed them on the conveyor belt before leaving the commissary. Janzen was left with the space once occupied by that strange creature. Even his most optimistic meanderings wouldn't sniff at anything resembling the truth of her inquiries; in fact, he wasn't even near the sands of her hidden beach that would allow him a guess at the depths of her deep blue lagoon.

He finished his meal without further interruption but was swept up by the frenetic spirit of Scoop, who had an issue that required Janzen's attention. He beckoned Janzen down a few flights of stairs to the eighth floor, and when they reached a set of heavy-duty double doors, Scoop held one open for his guest. The flooring was cement, and the walls were made of exposed cinder blocks. A single toilet and a sink were in one corner. An unmade bed was staged a few feet from those facilities. Everywhere else were piles and piles of supplies and equipment. Some of them appeared to be collected from a scrap yard: elbow joints, tubing, doorknobs, plastic buckets, tins of quick dry cement. In other piles were replacement light bulbs, hand sanitizer packs, toilet paper, aprons, and mattress box springs. Scoop stood proudly before the expanse of his reserves. The room was huge, made small only by this grand cache.

"What is this place, Scoop?"

"It's home, Big Jay."

"It's something."

"Thanks. Now here's wud I need from ya. I saw in yer video that you spent some time workin' construction. Were you bullshittin' or was you real?" Janzen assured him of the truth, and the man tugged him under a section of the exposed ceiling. "I need ta know if that thing up dere is an exhaust fan, and if it is I need ta know how to fix it. I'm pretty good with my hands but wirin' ain't my thing."

Janzen knew it was what Scoop suspected, and he repositioned a nearby ladder to check the connections. The fan itself hung crookedly from the ceiling because the one corner of the housing unit had lost the screw that kept it connected to a joist. The vibration from the device had more than likely dislodged the corner from the once humid and now-warped piece of lumber. Janzen pushed the fan back into its housing and replaced the dislodged wiring.

"Tell me you got a bunch of light switches some-where, Scoop."

"I'm a hit 'em all. 'Old on."

"One by one, Scoop."

"That's right now." The man's energy was relentless, and even when standing next to the bank of light switches he kicked his feet to temper its flow. The third switch he hit turned on the now functional exhaust fan. "Jay-man, you somavabitch. You did it!"

"Well it works, but keep it off until I come back and fix this corner, okay?"

"Sure man. C'mon down now and catch you summa dis fer yer troubles." Scoop passed Janzen a bottle of Listerine filled with a burgundy colored liquid. Without hesitating, Janzen accepted with a grateful swig.

"Damn, Scoop. That's got some heat, man."

"Go on, have yous another. You done me a solid, bro," offered Scoop.

Janzen shook the contents of the plastic container, the contents of which reminded him of his first girlfriend, Bethany, in that both were absolutely terrible for him. She had cheated on him with a guy from Timonium named Dallas, who had huge basketball hands and a full beard as a fifteen year old. With a slug from Scoop's liquor, Janzen answered any question as to whether he would ever reunite with Bethany. Really, though, the question wasn't would he or wouldn't he, but rather how quickly he'd run back to her if given the chance. "No thanks, Scoop." He handed the bottle back to him.

"So when can yous get back in here and get dis thing workin' full-time? I got some real whiskey to run and I wanna be sure ol' man Selby don' sniff what I'm up to, ya see?"

"How about later today."

"That's it, man."

"Where you getting this stuff, Scoop?" asked Janzen, who started looking through different piles of supplies.

"You are speaking to the Director of Supplies and Food and Shit."

"Sounds impressive."

"Gall damn right, now. You don' get your fancy omelets wich'er fancy mushrooms if you don' go through me. Hell, you don' wipe yer ass widout my damn terlet paper!"

"You don't go out and get this stuff, do you?"

"Nah. I get requests from da kitchen erry week or so and what dey need. I keep an eye out fer supplies we run out of troughout the buildin'. Most folks'll let me know when dey need somethin'. I get a list togedder and get it over ta Selby and he puts it through. How ya think I get errythin' I need ta run some 'shine? Yous can distill alcohol from a whole lotta stuff ya find in a store, mank. I learned about dat up in Jessup. But I got some heat here now wit some small burners an if I run some tubing up to dat fan I should be in da clear. Hell, I'm da one keepin' enough propane in this place."

"Where does it come from?"

"Selby. Then it just shows up erry Thursdee mornin' down below, and I lift it up with da winch, no problem."

"You talking tomorrow?"

"Yessir."

"You gonna let me come up there with you?"

"Jay-man, ya know I can't let you do dat. Mr. Selby finds out and then I'm off the detail, see? He don' want no one out dere wit dat glass door open."

"Scoop."

"Jay-man."

"How about I do you a solid?"

"Wha'cha thinkin'?"

"I see you got that duct work over there in a pile. You just let me see what you have going on up there and afterwards I'll run the ductwork for your still right into the ventilation and then you're really cookin'."

"Wass in it for yous, Jay-man?"

"Selby wants me writing about this place so he has a record for his legacy or something. I just want to see how this place works. Actually, I could go clear this with Selby right now and – "

"You in Jay-man. We just keep Selby outta dis as much as possible. You gonna meet me in da stairwell 'bout nine stories up at 6:30 sharp. I need to set the winch up on the roof but yous cain't come up there for dat. You gotta go up through Selby's office for dat, and he's da one that less me up. He cain't know you're up ta no good wit' me."

Scoop made the best of a given situation, a quality one hones while incarcerated. He might deliberate upon a decision – check all the angles – but there wasn't a lick of backtracking in him. "Scoop, you hear about Mr. McCullough?"

"Yeah!" Scoop disappeared behind one of his piles. He had already moved on. A frightened old man and another in a mask were of little consequence to Scoop.

Later that night, Janzen wrote about Scoop's responsibilities as the building's caretaker. He debated whether or not to include his plans about taking part in tomorrow morning's delivery. He didn't want to implicate Scoop in anything, and he didn't fully trust Mr. Selby to refrain from reading his pages despite the old man's promise not to. Janzen decided to document everything but would keep those incriminating pages for himself.

The next morning, Janzen's alarm clock was set, but he didn't need it. Years of suffering through what passed for sleep led to his ability to wake up at whatever time. An early lesson in responsibility, his paper route, was one of his birthday gifts from his father when he turned ten. "You'll be a better man for it," said his father, who had presented Janzen with a satchel in which to carry the newspapers. He was so fraught with the anxiety of missing his duties as a son and paperboy that he began to wake minutes and then hours before his alarm sounded at this early age. The lone thought of a particular time was the only alarm he needed. And at 6:30, he found Scoop right where they arranged to meet.

"Errythingo set up top. Delivery should be here in 'bout fifteen so we gotta move."

Janzen followed Scoop out of the stairwell and into the ninth floor, but he could no longer see him in the blackness. He heard Scoop knock into something and cuss under his breath. Was this really the same floor where he first entered the building? He thought back to the day of the rooftop garden and his backward plunge and the yellow banner.

Standing there in the dark, Janzen was surprised how easily he had adjusted to life without the sun's presence. He only needed a tiny red orb next to the AM on his clock to know the sun was about to come up this morning. If it weren't for his plans involving an eleven-story climb, he'd be getting up out of bed now to make it on time for his weekly editorial meeting. In the past year, much of the meeting would have served as an orientation to the new freelancers recently hired to take the place of the old ones, gone off to other jobs with benefits and retirement packages. Janzen had no such concerns. He was there to serve his time and know his grammar. He was a worker. He was an editor. He was an addict. He was a graduate. He was a problem. He was sober. He was suicidal. He was everything that meant nothing to him. So instead of being, he did. He tried. He rode. He wrote, but he wasn't a rider or a writer. He failed. He was a failure. He was a predicate nominative. He was a subject. He was both. He was so done with grammar.

The sound on the ninth floor was different from the reverberations he remembered during those first few minutes, before he had found the one-legged black figure waiting for him. Scoop turned on a flashlight, and he discovered sections of the layout through Scoop's wandering illumination. Janzen would have undoubtedly recognized the hallway that led straight to the elevator, but this was not it. From what he could tell, this floor was just another one of Scoop's hotspots to pile his junk – piles and piles stacked on pallets, some plastic wrapped, others strewn about.

"I foun' dat dolly, Jay-man. Help me clear a path." Scoop set the flashlight on a laminate cabinet, and he worked to clear crates of wiring and electrical cording against the wall.

"You're confusing the help, Scoop. Clear a path to where?"

Scoop bounced around at a frantic pace. He moved away every crate from the wall and cleared an area in front of it. He inserted a lever into the wall and pushed down on it, and the wall lifted open from the hinged upper connectors. He lifted the section and swung it out toward the cleared section. From the light of the flashlight, Janzen recognized the elevator door through the gap. While Scoop rummaged around for something on the other side, Janzen walked down the hallway away from the elevator and knew he would eventually run into one of the hanging beaded strings that would turn on a light.

He found it, and there it was: the hallway. It looked just as he remembered it with the diamond patterned walls, marble flooring, and the antique fixtures. But Janzen saw it for what it truly was, a set. It was merely dressing, an illusion of something he was trying to reveal.

Janzen heard Scoop wrestling with something on the other side and went to help. Together, they carried a heavy roll of flooring to cover the marble. The vulcanized rubber stretched the exact length of the hallway. Scoop pulled the remaining strings of beads on his way towards the entrance. From his pocket, he produced what appeared to be a C-clamp without the screw and held it against one of the wall panels. Scoop guided it until he found the right spot. The piece Scoop held was magnetized because when he drew the handle away from the panel, it opened to reveal a hidden compartment. Inside, a small rectangular device the size of a pocket dictionary hung from a coiled cable inserted into an outlet. He turned on the power to the unit and pressed the top button with his thumb. The mouth of the building opened in its slow and mechanized way, and the early light from a new day sneaked through the widening gap.

The sun was still rising, but what was there caught the underside of the passing clouds in blots of pink and orange. Janzen did not know how many days he had been in the building, and the sight struck him as foreign. Had it been only a week?

The deep blue sheets of material covering the windows in the building submerged the structure hundreds of fathoms underground, so he was unprepared for this much glory in the sky before him. He swallowed the lump in his throat and pumped his fists to contain its wonderful ache. Scoop held down the button and scratched at a stain on his pants. Dawn had always provided Janzen glints of tranquility no matter what he did hours before. Whether he was in the grips of an amphetamine bender or he simply couldn't sleep, the light of a new day always brought with it a small reprieve from the world's heaviness; of course, that was until the eight o'clock sun came and shone itself like a poisoned lollipop, but that was always for later.

A car horn honked below. For Janzen, it was a record scratch during a Georgia Mass Choir recording. A deliveryman stood beside an old box truck. The cube on the back was dirty white and devoid of any placard or advertisement. He waved up at Janzen and asked for the line. Scoop yelled at him to be patient and continued cussing under his breath. The yellow banner had been lifted and hung above Janzen on slackened lines; from afar, the drooping yellow must have looked like angry, blonde eyebrows on a huge block face.

With the building's glass partition fully opened, Scoop used the magnetized handle to open another diamond shaped compartment just above the other. In it was another control panel that operated the winch. A line of steel cable dropped from somewhere up top to the man and his truck below. He had already unloaded a plastic-wrapped pallet and was securing two tethers through the bottom of it. Janzen followed the path of the cable upwards and saw a crane arm extending out from the top of the building.

Scoop parked the pallet jack in place and leaned out the opening to ensure the fastening of the supplies went smoothly. He nodded for Janzen to take the controls, which consisted of flicking the winch toggle upwards. While the load was lifted, Scoop went to the other side of the hallway and came back with two large pieces of squared steel tubing, each welded in the shape of an L. He told Janzen to lift the pallet load to about waist high so he could slide the pieces into two slots through the floor of the entrance. Locked in place, the steel shot out perpendicularly from the face of the building and would provide a secure landing for the pallet. Scoop called for Janzen to let out the line slowly until the load was perched outside the opening to the building. Scoop could now manipulate the forks of the pallet jack into place, lift and lean the delivery towards him and tote it inside.

Scoop wheeled it back toward the elevator. The man below closed up his truck and drove away around the back of the building. Out of sight now, Scoop called for Janzen to retract the cable up toward the rooftop crane arm. The building's steel tail shortened and shortened until it was but a vestigial nub up on the eleventh floor.

Janzen wiggled his toes over the concrete slab below. He moved along the edge and kept himself from falling forward by holding the top bracing above him. Under the gentle fluttering of the yellow above him, he slid over to the center of the opening.

"Janzen, wutter yous doin'? Get offa dere!" Janzen's feet remained in place. Of course, the idea to jump was there. The idea was always there. "Janzen, you jump and then iss it for me. If yous go, I'm next man. You said yous wasn't gonna be no trouble."

Janzen stepped back from the opening and smiled

back at Scoop. "It's cool, man. Let's close this bitch up." Why involve Scoop? A bed sheet was as effective as a big leap anyways.

"Christ man. Yous got my heart pumpin' now, kid. Remind me never ta fuck wit'choo. Yous got that look about'cha sometimes, Jay-man."

"What's that look, Scoop-man?"

"Like yous 'bouta bring sum real shit."

With a wink, Janzen said, "Let's go set up that duct work."

"Fuck yeah, bro."

9

Days passed, and Janzen adjusted to a routine of working throughout the day on his five hundred words in between the scheduled sessions during the morning and afternoon. Either Mr. Atis or Mr. Selby announced whatever type of meeting would take place and their locations while the group ate breakfast. This information was also printed and displayed outside the commissary.

Mr. Selby gave no indication that he was reading the pages Janzen turned in every morning. The daily act of submitting the printed pages to the filing cabinet in Mr. Selby's top-floor office grew into an unexpected exercise in silent construction between the writer and the collector. Most mornings, Mr. Selby would be at his desk reading or working on something; occasionally, he'd be resting on the purple fainting couch with an open book rising and falling on his chest. He'd watch Janzen walk over to the cabinet, deposit his pages and leave after a quick nod. Upon each visit, Janzen took note of the model-sized foundation being constructed on top of a previously unused table.

As an only child, Janzen was presented with gifts at Christmas and birthdays that would be best celebrated by a single person: books upon books, a pogo stick, bicycles, titles of the Criterion Collection, a putter. Never had he received a baseball mitt, board games or a ping-pong table, so on that third day of submitting his work, he was not confused at the sight of the two Lincoln Logs resting next to each other on the tabletop. He had spent hours alone in his room with his set as a boy. It was that fourth day and the addition of the third Lincoln Log laid atop the first at ninety degrees to the second that made Janzen pause. Mr. Selby looked over the rim of his glasses for a beat before returning to his work.

And thus the small wooden structure grew and became – log by Lincoln Log – something resembling a home.

With no more news of anyone having been accosted by a masked man along with the full recovery of Mr. McCullough, who later doubted the veracity of his own account due to his condition, life on Formstone Avenue charged on. Janzen took to exercising on one of the two brand new state-of-the-art stationary bikes replete with drop bars, gears and video displays that took him on any mapped road across the globe. The machines had simply appeared in the corner of the workout room one morning. He had seen this piece of equipment advertised each summer during the Tour de France and knew the exorbitant cost of owning one. He asked Scoop about it but received only a wink in response. He baptized one of the machines within minutes of finding it. The display took him over the cobbled streets of the Paris-Roubaix.

He took a tour of his old neighborhood in Bolton Hill. He rode by an abandoned JCPenney in Ohio. He wanted the torture of the climb up the Alpe-d'Huez, but a route of that intensity required months of training. Still, to be back in the saddle and riding in the red was a blessing. A little was never enough. There was always time for one more hill or one more mile until he destroyed his lungs, heart and thighs.

The decision to stay past a single week came and went without an acknowledgement from anyone. The confirmation was tacitly implied as each day's missive was filed and another log was added to the structure. Janzen now looked the part of his new community. A pile of new clothes folded neatly at his door with a note instructing Janzen to "Enjoy!" fit him perfectly. Had he gone his entire life wearing incorrectly sized clothes? That Monroe was a talent. There were no labels, no advertisements, and no pit stains. When he next saw the young designer, he cornered Monroe and thanked him for his effort. Janzen's gratitude was returned with a heartfelt, "Yeah man."

The daily work on the word processor along with the exercise, regular meals and morning and afternoon sessions provided Janzen with a familiar routine. His acclimatization to the group's sessions was managed prudently. He was not again called upon to participate in any of the exercises. During the first week, he was encouraged by Mr. Selby to engage the others but only if comfortable. It was his presence alone that sufficed.

Janzen was amenable to every technique used by Mr. Selby even though many bordered the realm of quackery.

On one day, Janzen walked into a room full of disarticulated office chairs held together in reclined positions by lengths of flexible steel and all suspended from the ceiling by tethers. In here, the group lay floating in recumbent positions, each fitted with a specialized headpiece. The wiring from the nape of the skullcap connected to a central hub in the center of the room, which sent electric pulses to the different parts of the brain. During this session, the yelps resulting from a minor head fire disrupted what was supposed to be a calming atmosphere; luckily, the hair loss was modest and the balm yielded immediate comfort. The administrator of the exercise, Felix, had once dabbled in the electrician's trade and was able to diagnose the issue later that evening.

On another morning, Janzen checked the schedule outside the commissary to find a "hoedown" scheduled for later that evening in place of the typical afternoon session. He had not yet been to the room number printed on the page and remembered Monroe's mention of such a session weeks earlier. For him, the titular event ushered in thoughts of Copland's brash American style; of course, beef came to mind, too. Surely, the late composer had meat on his mind when commissioned to score *Rodeo*. There was no doubt about that. Janzen had half expected more of classical's classics for use in advertising. Perhaps, he had thought, an Alfred Schnittke dirge for a Cialis commercial? A sad song for sad dicks? Maybe Eric Satie selling affordable settees? What a fugue. Who was in charge of Copland's estate anyways? His music should be performed in symphony halls and used to score movies about Western expansion and Manifest Destiny, but no, he had become "the beef guy" to millions of TV viewers. Where was the honor in that? It infuriated Janzen. He still dealt with interspersing bouts of rage that often left him in unfamiliar locations depending on the extent of the spell. Thanks to reading the word "hoedown" he now found himself back on the fourth floor, the time capsule of an office, but he could not remember whether he took the elevator or the stairs.

He calmed himself by knocking out some pushups, but by the time he reached forty, he held himself in a plank position and dared not move. It wasn't that he heard something in there with him. He felt it – that frisson electrifying his arms and legs. He was vulnerable there on the floor.

He positioned his feet under him and slowly rose up until he could see over the cubicles around him. He heard nothing, yet the room gushed with the same foreboding atmosphere of his childhood basement. He yelled out a "Hello." He wasn't sure he wanted a response. He was frozen in the room's blue hue. He knew something circled near him, not too far from sight. "I see you, too." He wasn't sure to whom he was speaking.

Nothing responded. He waited another minute, and the place was cleared of the presence. He ran around the floor daring anything to jump out at him and did so loudly enough to discharge his nervous energy. He turned a corner and approached a familiar location. He was at the cubicle with the stashed toy penguin. He approached the desk with the same portrait and moved the chair out from under it. Nothing there. He did the same to other nearby chairs and found no penguin. He walked the perimeter of the room, and there it was – back in its original place on the rim of the same coffee cup. How it came back to its home was enough of a riddle to try the experiment again, but this time, he would make finding it much more difficult.

Janzen hadn't yet fully fleshed out the ramifications of such an experiment, though. The great thing about being irresponsible for such a long time was that it curbed the sharp edge of consequence. He was forced to adjust to so many poor decisions throughout his adult life that steeling himself against possible repercussions was damned near muscle memory. He grabbed the toy and stood up on one of the other nearby desks and was just able to reach a water-stained panel of the ceiling. He placed the penguin on the panel next to the opening before he slid the other tile back into place.

He jumped off the desk and headed to the elevator to shake loose the tendrils of this room and to pry loose any details about this evening's events; however, Samuel was unusually withdrawn while sitting there on his stool.

"The truth is, I don't really know too much about what goes on during a hoedown. I mean I can hear it going on, but I've never been to one," said Samuel.

"Is it that you don't want to?"

"It's not that. I just don't belong in there." For the first time, Samuel was less the lord of the elevator and more its captive. "Besides, I have a job to do, you know?"

"All right, big man."

Janzen thought he understood Samuel's hesitation. The kindness he typically bestowed on every resident was implacable, but tonight provided Janzen a quick glimpse into his baleful world – something that skulked under the big man's skin without him knowing. It reminded him of the disease that lurked within one of the other resident's bodies.

Leonard was the man to whom Janzen was frighteningly introduced that first night – the skeleton he had uncovered in the darkness of his room. He learned of the man's story from another resident who saw his entrance video broadcasted from the guard shack. Before joining the crew on Formstone, he was, by all accounts, a healthy man living in Mount Vernon who upon visiting his doctor following a prolonged battle with a stomach bug had received some sobering news. After some blood work and a colonoscopy, he was diagnosed with colorectal cancer, which had advanced to a stage precipitating a recommendation for a transverse colostomy that would require the use of a permanent stoma. After sitting with the news for a week, Leonard made a decision that led him to the top of Selby Tower. In the guard shack, he detailed his mother's struggles with chemotherapy and her eventual passing. Janzen had wondered why Mr. Selby would then capture him in that banner. What was his intention in prolonging this man's misery?

Back in his room now, Janzen couldn't help but worry about Samuel. He had taken to spending stretches of time in his elevator and the experience often left Janzen sinking into the floors. He was always there. He was always in the elevator with his big body and wide smile. He sometimes read a book but there were days without any reading material, which left the anticipated conversations as the only stimulation the man subsisted on.

Because the elevator did not run overnight, it was rumored among some of the residents that he simply dissipated after his shift was over. During one lunch when Samuel's ephemeral state became the topic again, Helena scolded the table for the gossip and mentioned that she saw him stroll into a room on one of the top floors. She was lovely in her own vicious way.

Hours later, on the way up to room 820 that evening, Janzen parlayed the anxiety of a new experience of a hoedown into something more optimistic. Samuel was in better spirits and much more receptive to Janzen's pressing the buttons to floors they had just passed. He'd shoo Janzen's hand away with a smack, Janzen quietly apologized, and then he pressed the next button knowing Samuel would stop at each floor on the way down.

"Sorry about that last one, Samuel."

"You're a piece of work, Janzen. Now go have fun."

"Fun? You serious?"

"I am. Now shoo."

The elevator doors shut and Janzen followed the climbing door numbers until he reached room 820. From the hallway he heard conversations of a different stock. Was that laughter?

Once he stepped across the threshold, the room was a thousand miles away. The green from the rooftop was there, but this time the hills rolled and rolled on which blades of grass whipped in the wind. Those same offshore breezes carried the scent of flowers and the ocean. The gentle tumble of the surf was audible, and it reached its hypnotic end upon a hidden shoreline. Were those the Cliffs of Moher to his right? It was magical, and it was all around him. The entire group – the entire room – and all the senses were wrapped up in the technology of these pastures of green spilling over the cliffs into a calming sea. Missing was the sun above in the clear blue sky, a proper omission considering some outlet produced its power. The floor below him was the only other betrayal to the authenticity that surrounded him. Beneath his feet was the same green of the grass, but upon each touch of his shoe or resting backside, there was a rainbow ripple of the display that popped and spread in colorful, concentric circles. The effect was dazzling. Shouts of 'hellos' flew across the room, but Janzen couldn't trace their trajectories amid the blazing digital landscape.

The haze of the technology left the residents awash in its brilliance, and every movement was followed by its ephemeral contrail. When Janzen kept his head still, he made out that most everyone had found a spot to sit along the walls. Each person held a cup of something, but not one of them drank. In the far corner of the room, Mr. Atis beckoned Janzen over with his surreal gesture. Apparently, he was the keeper of the elixir. He sat behind a tall pedestal table that provided just enough room to support a stack of plastic cups, a container filled with a red liquid and a computer tablet, which showed multiple live screens of everything Janzen saw around him.

Mr. Atis said nothing as he poured Janzen a half cup from the container. When Janzen turned away, Mr. Atis called him back and asked for his cup. He dropped something small in the container and passed it back. "Don't drink until we say so." Janzen found some free space along the wall and discovered the fan in the corner of the room. It pivoted on its base and every minute or so a soft effusion of scent issued from its tower.

Janzen had an idea of what they were waiting for, and he finally walked in wearing a handsome gray jacket and vest. Mr. Atis paused the moving images and Mr. Selby quickly tipped the brim of his Panama hat before consulting an index card from his breast pocket to address the room.

"Good evening, ladies and gentlemen." His voice echoed around the room. "It's about that time again when we allow the Fates to intervene and carry us along these windswept hills towards our destination." He nodded to Mr. Atis. "While our starting point may be familiar to some," a chorus of cheers and raised glasses around the room interrupted the man. "Yes. While our starting point may be familiar to some, the ending most certainly will not. You are free to leave whenever. There are restrooms down the hall to the left, and the rest of the microphones will turn on in a matter of minutes. If you have any suggestions concerning the scenery or the soundtrack, you have the authority, encouragement and the power to simply open your mouth. Any event is *the* event. Any tears are the group's tears. And to withhold is to deprive yourselves of the experience. There is no script, just a leap of faith. We are here for one another. Repeat that, folks! We are here for one another! Ladies and gentlemen, please lift your glass. And together -- menny meany teckle prism!" The group saluted the final four words in unison, each person offering it in his or her own way, like a born again congregation during the Nicene Creed. Down went the drinks. "Once you're done with your drink, we have some plastic straws up here for anyone who wants them," continued Mr. Selby. "And don't worry, they're clear this time! No stained mouths. And Mr. Atis has bottled water here for anyone parched. Enjoy, folks!"

Mr. Selby bowed politely to the group before leaving, and Mr. Atis took control. "I have pens for those who want them. If you have any requests, please come up and add to the playlist. Otherwise, we will resume what we used last time. The mics will be activated at once, so please keep the profanities to a minimum."

"Fuck!"

Across the room, he found her looking right at him. He blinked and heard the clacks of his lashes. His blinks had never before made such noise. Everything else was silent except for the wind's beguiling swoosh off the coast and through the whispering grass.

She brought her pointer finger up to her lips. Was she going to eat that finger? No, surely she wouldn't snack unseasoned. Sssssssssssseasoned. She was looking right at him, and she just brought that finger up to her lips and asked for silence? Whose silence? Janzen's thoughts bombarded him at an accelerated pace, though instead of their normal rattling around in his head, they pulsated with sounds best suited for science fiction. He wondered if the microphones would pick this up, or was he the only one hearing this? He scratched his arm and then his head, the latter of which produced a faint version of a piano's short, taut strings being played. Or was there music already playing? What was happening? Who was that breathing? Was the room breathing?

"What the fuck!" Janzen's words reverberated

throughout the room. Everyone rejoiced in his eruption, and the celebration and laughter of the group immediately replaced the room's breathing. Janzen heard every one of their voices even if he couldn't see them. "What is this?" His voice bounced around him.

He heard a familiar voice among the medley of flying words. "It's okay. Just be okay." Helena was with him once again, but she was missing among the shooting colors. All the words were Fruit Loops bobbing about in a bowl, there for anyone to claim and enjoy. "We need to talk," she said. Janzen leaned back and tracked the clouds passing above him. The breeze cooled his moist forehead and sent a chill down through his toes before he was enveloped in the comforting embrace of euphoria. He could find her words anywhere. She was the lone thrush amid the woozy warblers.

"Now?" The patches of white above him were tufts of cirrus. They swirled when he bobbed his head from side to side.

"No." The convergence of the other words kept their conversation hidden in the open space. The gaiety of the other sentences weaved in and around their words, and Janzen chased the tail of her serpentine responses.

"Fuck." It had been so long since he allowed any chemicals to let him simply feel. Where was this supposed to go?

"Yes."

A voice asked for the music, and the request bounced around with the other conversations. DJ Atis played a building electronic number with a Steve Reich repetition and Radiohead longing. Janzen dripped to the ground, and his back spilled over the colors below him. He flipped to his knees and kept his forehead to the plasma green of the floor. He pushed his head forward and experienced the ache of his childhood in the pull of his hair against the grass. As a boy he drove himself along the carpet this way, smashing into whatever came along.

"Is there anyone else who did this?" He wasn't sure anyone heard him. He wasn't sure he said anything. He had forgotten this sensation, one that was a touch away from pain until he felt a knock that sent a shock to his heels. He had driven his head into a corner. He turned back to the wall and his tongue grew until he willed it back to normal size. His mouth was dry, he was dizzy and any face he found was blurred before him. "Why is this?"

"Why are you?" Everyone laughed.

He sat back and found steadiness in the placid, green floor, and the scattered words finally led to sentences that fell both to the right and left of him. He was able to find the meaning in those sentences, and they provided the stability he needed. He lifted his head, and there she was, kneeling right before him, but she was there with something new. She smiled.

They sat wordlessly next to each other, Helena's exigent lure stronger than any verb or noun. Janzen was able to counteract her attraction by planting both hands at his side. When she crossed her legs at the ankle, Janzen crossed his legs at the ankle. When she held her legs to her chest, he did the same. She kicked him hard in the thigh and her burst of laughter surprised only her. Janzen did not wipe the mark of her shoe off his pants.

Helena slid Janzen her drink, and he finished it in

a gulp. More was so nice. The music played until some of the dancing stopped, and a request for a river floated by. With a swipe of Mr. Atis's finger, the green of the hillside was replaced by a river's gentle tumble. The sun was once again hidden, behind the trees this time, but its rays shone through the leaves and were dropped and lifted on the water's undulations.

Janzen was content listening to the conversations around him. Daryl, the hugger he had first met in the gym, marveled at how closely the new landscape resembled the area where he grew up. He was stunned by the similarity. He walked to a wall and tried turning over a rock but couldn't reach into the depths of the riverbed. He claimed that it was an experience on a river like this, which ultimately led him to the top of this building.

The room quieted and his story meandered. The energy changed, and Janzen sensed the room settling in to listen. "It was the strongest love I ever knew," said Daryl. As a child, he recalled finding a spot along the rill of a nearby river and said he could still feel the mud squelch in between his toes to this day. He had hiked along the stretch of water with a fellow neighbor boy and his sister. Their plan was to walk until they hit the headwaters of the river's source. The three of them were struck at the clearness and perfect depth of a particular bend where Daryl spotted some rainbow trout. The three young friends stripped to their underwear for the hunt until it became a game of catching the river's dappled sunlight. "I was ten and completely in love with them both." Their underwear eventually grew heavy with the water, and they continued the hike beneath the parted canopy without it. Daryl said the shame he normally felt while naked had disappeared that afternoon. "The water glistened off her backside but it didn't *glisten* off her backside. I knew she was beautiful and being there among the trees and the water, it was the opposite of lust – no, the absence of lust. It wasn't until much later when that lust grew into something I couldn't control. At first, I told myself that the idea of such beauty had stuck with me throughout the years because it was as pure as could be. If I thought the sight of them naked was a wonderfully freeing thing at that age, when are you not allowed to have such feelings? Adolescence only led to shame, but my feelings about that day never changed. It was that youth that became the symbol to me and it was all I could think about. And now one of the greatest days of my life has become the rope that I will soon swing from because the symbol and its meaning has changed and taken over and when I was once a child so much attracted to another child, I am now just a man attracted to the same."

Together, the group offered no contempt for the man and his secrets. If there were gusts of derision, it was hidden behind the trees and deep in the mind. In its place, sympathy flowed. Castigation was replaced by investigation – a free discussion on the differences between growing up and aging, on the biology of lust, the weight of shame, and the size of rainbow trout.

Daryl believed himself an empty vessel, and in the safety of this room, he admitted wanting to be set free when he stepped off the rooftop months earlier. He likened himself to the empty bottle thrown out to sea as waste and the hope that he'd wash ashore as something different – something that could be filled once again to nourish and help. He thought the chances small that he'd find such a place, but he was here now and sharing his story. Even so, he still considered himself the better part of trash.

Janzen appreciated the man's courage and openness. He understood the relentless desperation the man must face. How would Janzen shade the tone of this once behind the keyboard? He'd have to sit with that.

While the mood lightened, the sky darkened and the river gave way to a setting sun behind the dunes of a desert. The faces around Janzen eventually disappeared when the Saharan grains surrendered to the Greek heavens.

Janzen then experienced a tickle in his gut that caused no discomfort but rose up from deep down until it crawled up his spine, vertebra by vertebra. He brought his shoulder blades together to flex the back, and the effort centralized the tingle caught in between the triangles of the trapezii. Janzen lifted his head and then dropped his chin, and after the coolness of the inhale mixed with whatever climbed up, he spoke. "I once spent an afternoon at the Great Sand Dunes of Colorado." An hour or two later, he would mentally log this first true contribution inside Mount Selby among his previously held firsts: his first cum, his first fuck, his first ride on a bike, a journey that took him along the Baltimore sidewalks until the unsure veer of his shifting weight took him joyously through backyards, up and over curbs, across streets and traffic and ultimately into a guardrail; he'd log it up there with his first ollie, his first French kiss, his first line of coke, his last line of coke, the evening he finished *Nine Stories*, Sigur Rós at the Hollywood Bowl, that line in *Rushmore*, those two girls from Tallahassee. It was neither content nor delivery, just the facts, and it flowed from him – the sand bar to cross before the dunes, the heat of the sand, the dunes that were his own, the wind rippling his shirt, the older woman he had helped up and her story – the way she shook at his arm and how she labored, not wanting to turn back to her daughter, who waited impatiently below and who didn't want to get any sand in her shoes. Her daughter just wanted to get back home to her old room because "her ex was such an asshole" and the job was a dead end anyways. Janzen helped the woman to the top of her dune, and he climbed on to another. She wasn't just doing well for her old age; she was magnificent in her dotage. She had deserved a bit of the pretty prose.

He spoke about those dunes, and then he let the silence sink in under those stars before he adjusted to a supine state. He laid the back of his head in his clasped hands and each stretch of his body plucked the requisite fibers, vibrating the deep exhilaration of his high. The instinct to guard or censor or edit was washed away in its splendor. The compulsion to share – to elucidate and explore – took place atop his temporal hierarchy. The Great Sand Dunes of Colorado led to the Appalachian trails of South Mountain, which led to more silence and a community breathing together. His pointed toes once again plucked what was inside, and Janzen spoke of Appalachia and the people and their music and their banjo, which was really the instrument of Africa, adopted by the spiritual poor. He channeled a Rushdie tongue in a McCarthy landscape, while his hair grew wet around the ears until there were streams of it channeling paths from his forehead into his palms.

He spoke of the only Holden who ever really meant much to him, the great hairless judge, the executor of the mystic and profane. He spoke of Saturday mornings and the exploits of Wile E. Coyote, and how his rudimentary philosophical understanding began not with any categorical imperative but rather with reflections upon a being and his maniacal pursuit of an unattainable goal and how the only individual hurt in the process was the pursuer. He spoke about what it was that led to him choosing the difficult and solitary life of a would-be scribe. Was his failure to publish a fait accompli in light of his winding and convoluted prose? And why position a poster of John Kennedy Toole over the top of the laptop?

He threw these questions out to the room as the sun peeked its head over the dunes. Soon, the sky blazed with reds and pinks from a Chagall dreamscape. The breathing Janzen once heard was no longer in communion. He only detected a single other cadence amid the dawning landscape. Janzen sat up and searched the room for his audience but no one stirred. "Helena?" The reply was not hers.

"Those who stayed late thought you'd nodded off."

Janzen found Mr. Atis with his chin resting on his stacked knuckles. They were the only two people in the room. "What time is it?"

"About six in the morning."

"You've been here the whole time?" Mr. Atis nodded

his head the best he could. Janzen had never seen the man in such a fatigued state. "Why didn't you say something?"

"What would I say?"

"How about 'shut the fuck up. It's time to sleep.'"

"I don't mind the company, Janzen. I don't sleep well."

Janzen lifted himself to his feet and shin-kicked an invisible adversary to clear the cobwebs. "What are the chances you let slide one more of them drinks, Mr. Atis?"

"Here's something else." He reached for a folded envelope from his breast pocket and gave Janzen a pill. "This will help you sleep. And you'll be hungry when you wake. I'll save you a plate if we miss you at breakfast. It'll be in the back."

"Mr. Atis, I never apologized for making fun of your decorating that first day. I want you to know I'm sorry about that."

"Good night, Janzen."

"All right, Mr. Atis."

Janzen exited and fingered the pill. It was marked with no number or designation, and its shape was made from a mold not concerned with uniformity. He swallowed it and found the stairs down to his room and was asleep within an hour.

10

"I need you to fuck me."

A table away, someone choked on his green bean. Janzen waited across from her hoping for clues. She offered only the grind of her teeth.

"Before I undress, you need to know one thing."

"Not now!" Helena covered her face and shook her head. "That's what you give me?" Janzen smiled at her. He was genuinely shocked at the request, well, demand really. "You'll need to tell me some things?"

"I'm a crier," said Janzen.

"I don't care."

"I'm kidding."

"It won't matter."

"That's sweet of you."

"No, I mean it won't matter if you do or don't. I won't watch."

"You're confusing your lover."

"You're not my lover."

"What am I?"

"You are a fuck."

"Like something to be used?"

"Yes," she replied. Janzen weighed whether or not he should appear to be concerned with such a proposal.

"I'm okay with that." He was not concerned with the details of such a proposal.

"What kind of porn do you like?"

"Something with a story."

"You're an asshole. Do I have to ask you again?"

"All of it."

"I'll figure it out."

"Can you tell me what this is about?"

"No. Movie Night is coming up. We'll talk after that, and then we can move forward with this if you still want to."

"Well, that's certainly cleared things up," he said, wiping the errant salt off the tabletop.

"You said you worked construction before?"

"I'm just gonna go with this. Yes."

"I need you to help me build something."

"Anything."

"Can you put up a wall?" He said that he could. "Can you cut a big hole in that wall?" He nodded. "Okay," she said.

"That's what you give me?"

"I'll find you." She left him.

"I'll probably be lifting weights." Suddenly, Janzen's re-warmed eggs and sausage tasted pretty fantastic. He was out of the commissary with a hop and a skip to attack those five hundred words. He would also do forty push-ups, too – no, forty-five.

As Janzen kept up his side of the arrangement with

Mr. Selby, the miniature log cabin continued to rise piece by piece. After a few days following his blunt discussion with Helena, the supplies to frame a wall arrived. Scoop provided the tools needed, and the lumber and Sheetrock were delivered early one morning along with the normal weeklies. Scoop had not included Janzen in the delivery but was helpful enough to assist in carrying the supplies down a floor to the eighth. Mr. Atis eventually requisitioned the help as Scoop was told that Mr. Selby had something to discuss with him. With Samuel's assistance, Janzen was able to move the remaining wood via the elevator by opening the hatch in the ceiling to accommodate the length. After wrestling off the first load, he turned back to Samuel, and as the elevator doors closed upon him, he said, "Han, I love you."

Samuel played Solo and responded with the appropriate, "I know." It was only the second and third time that Janzen re-enacted the famous scene that made Samuel jiggle with glee. Janzen was not allowed admittance for his final load, much to the delight of the fat man.

The room on the eighth floor more than likely once served as a mid-level executive's office. It offered no window view, but there were a single desk and a few chairs that Janzen moved in with Scoop's growing piles of supplies. During construction, Helena acted as both architect and foreman. Janzen guessed that the room's purpose had something to do with developing film. The opportunity to share such close quarters with her had its perks, though. Their time together afforded him fortuitous insights into her taut figure on display during her squats and stretches.

After a few hours, the ceiling joists were now exposed and the framing for the new dividing wall was ready to be lifted into place when the alarm first sounded. Janzen had never heard the sound before, and he held his hammer motionless until the forthcoming explanation.

"It's just the security gate outside. It's probably just a kid passing by or that drunk lawyer dropping something off," she said.

"You mean out front?" She grunted a 'yes' as she pushed some drywall out of the way.

"So you heard that when I pressed it?" he asked.

"Yeah. You'll get used to it."

"You ready to put this thing up?" They both lifted the framing into place and Janzen began securing it to what acted as a header with a slew of nails. "How big does this hole have to be?"

Helena grabbed the two center studs of the wall and walked straight through without turning to her side. "This should work."

"Do you know what my next question is?" asked Janzen.

"Is it about sex?"

"No."

She looked him over and perceived what was swimming around upstairs. "Mr. Atis will get on the speaker system and make an announcement. Unless something has been arranged beforehand, everyone will go to the second floor where you so kindly threw a chair at us. Mr. Selby will be lowered out the back of the building in his guard suit, and speak to whoever is out there. We should be able to watch a streaming of the interview onscreen while it happens." Janzen nodded and took some measurements to fit the first piece of Sheetrock. "Scoop will be up top packing away the crane arm under the pathway and making sure the banner is set to go."

"So where does Selby go after the interview?"

"Scoop says he just goes out back and hides behind a tree in case it happens right away. It's set up so a single button from a remote triggers the mechanism that pops the banner out and catches whoever. Then Scoop works the side of the building open and in he goes to the dark hallway with the one-legged man."

"How does Selby get back in the building?"

"Scoop connects another line and lifts him to the top."

"It's a goddamn show. It's impressive though. What happens if someone comes back later? Hops the fence or something."

"Selby can still control everything from his office. The place is covered in cameras, so he can do everything from his desk." They were then interrupted by the speakers overhead.

"Ladies and gentleman, will the residents please report to the second floor immediately. Felix, be sure everything is ready to go and the lights are out and the screen is down. Helena, please keep everyone in line down there." A click through the speaker system ended Mr. Atis's instructions.

Helena moved with a purpose and took the stairs two at a time down to the second floor. Janzen fell behind, and he tried to bridge the gap with questions she either ignored or didn't hear.

Downstairs, the group began filing into the space

and congregated before the stage. Helena called for the chairs to be arranged in curved rows of an amphitheater, and her voice gained an administrative edge amid the excitement of the others. Daryl was hoping for someone good on a saxophone, and Kenneth clapped loudly in his charged state. Janzen helped Helena arrange the room until Felix asked him to connect a cable run from the projector to a jack in the wall. Felix pressed a button on the remote that gave power to the suspended device. He realized he had not yet dropped the screen and did so with another remote. The blue menu displayed by the projector could now be seen clearly. He toggled through some prompts before changing to a different input. Now visible was another feed, but this one had a vertical black line running down the middle.

"Let's settle in," said Helena. "Felix, you got the lights?"

"Yes ma'am." He hustled through the velvet curtain, and the room went dark except for the projected bright blue. He returned to an end chair that had a computer tablet resting on it. He swiped his finger across the device, and the glare lit his face flushed with concentration. Everyone but Kenneth had settled into a quiet state of anticipation. He continued his applause until the screen came to life with two shots of the guard shack's interior. The views were of the blinds, and the other was trained at the midsection of a man.

Felix maneuvered his fingers on the tablet and initiated the second floor audio. Over the speakers, Janzen and the others heard the voice of Mr. Selby but couldn't make out what he was saying.

Mr. Selby grabbed the camera filming the blinds and repositioned it while he looked directly into its lens and consequently at the group. He offered a quick wink before turning back to whoever was there with him. "He should be here any minute. I appreciate your patience, young man." Mr. Selby, as the security guard, finally moved out of the way revealing a man in his late forties with perfectly placed hair and a manicured beard.

"Holy shit, you know who that is?" said Felix.

No one recognized the man.

"It's Chase Berger!" If you were from the area and you had a television, chances were that you had seen Chase Berger. For the first few years of his service, he was an on-location reporter for WMAR and was known for that stylized hair that maintained its cemented coiffure even in live stand-ups from the champagne drenched celebrations of the Ravens locker room and in gale-force winds of incoming tropical storms. Whenever he threw the action back to the studio, he did so with such bravado, you'd think he'd received his journalistic training from George Armstrong Custer. Similar to the willful General, Chase also moved up the professional ladder with a flair all his own despite his own academic shortcomings.

He eventually landed an evening co-anchor position at WMAR, and for the next few years, he grew into a serious and trusted newscaster; however, with the promotion came money, a sort of local celebrity and a dependence on prescription opiates and amphetamines. His last appearance on the evening news was his now infamous mug shot taken after he was arrested for attempting to buy pills from an undercover cop on North Avenue. At the time of the arrest, he was supposed to be away on vacation, but his greasy hair and dumb open mouth told a much different story. Initially, he had only been suspended from his job, but the rumor was that he turned down the opportunity to enter a rehabilitation program during his hiatus and his contract was therefore terminated. Following his arrest and firing, he disappeared from the public eye. It was only until the proliferation of the internet that the people of Baltimore heard from their wayward son again. He resurfaced online as an investigative reporter uncovering the seedier stories of Baltimore's back pages. ChasingBmorenews.com was his online address and with his newly bearded face and gonzo disregard for news etiquette, he shined a light on the city with his exposés covering prostitution rings, moonshine runners, unlicensed pain management centers, shifty lawyers and other such stories – all of which lacked credible research but offered bleeding graphics and near-nude re-enactments.

"Can you give me your full name, please?"

"Lucian Chase Bergerfeld." He sat with an on-air poise with his elevated chin and an insistence on addressing the camera lens instead of his company.

"Can you please tell me why you're here today?" asked Mr. Selby.

"I am here to make arrangements in the case of an untimely death."

"Whose untimely death."

"My untimely death," responded Mr. Berger.

"And is it true that you've filled out, signed and properly completed the paperwork needed to accomplish this goal?"

"Yes, I have."

"Mr. Koontz, will you please verify that this is true, and will you please administer the BAC test? Mr. Bergerfeld, do you declare that you are of a sound mind and are under no duress from those present to complete and notarize your last will and testament?"

"I am under no duress, and I am of a crystal clear mind, sir."

"Thank you. Mr. Koontz, please." Mr. Berger blew into the Breathalyzer, which registered a 0.0.

Janzen and the group watched the matinee play out, their film a confessional documentary. "He's about to get his Oprah on," said one of the residents.

"He loves this part," said Felix.

"Well, Mr. Bergerfeld, if there's nothing else, I believe we're set. Please have a good day."

"Something's up," said Felix.

In the shack, Chase finally broke contact with the camera lens and focused his attention on the guard. "How long have you worked here, sir?"

"Years really."

"I can't shake the feeling we've met before."

"Can't see how that's possible, Mr. Bergerfeld. You have a memorable face."

"You know, years ago there was a string of suicides off the top of this building. I remember because I covered the story. I recall the piece. It was a terribly unfortunate situation about a man who had closed this building after the suicide of his own young wife, who threw herself off the top. Afterwards, the once national headquarters for Selby Industries was moved up to the county, and things totally shut down here, which was when the bodies started flying off the top. But there were rumors about the man who owned it."

"I can't give credence to those, sir," said Mr. Selby, who could be heard busying himself with something offscreen.

"And the bodies kept flying off the top, but it wasn't just here."

The man was right. The CDC hadn't used the word 'epidemic,' but it had cited a "significant uptick" in the number of suicides in the past five years. The concern wasn't just about the overall numbers but the ages of those deciding to end their lives. The statistics revealed more and more people under the age of forty were "causing a disproportionate increase in the number of suicide-related deaths."

The fence around Mr. Selby's Formstone building was erected after the first four people had scaled the empty building only to make a final leap to the concrete slab below. The deaths took place over two months, and the fence and guard shack were soon in place. The building on Formstone soon gained a notoriety along the lines of the Golden Gate Bridge and the Aokigahara forest in Japan, places where people went to end their lives. There were nationwide studies and articles published about the phenomena investigating the reasons behind the increase. The left blamed the disproportionate wealth and the disappearing middle class opportunities. The right proclaimed it stemmed from shrinking ideals and morals. Some of the scientists cited the escalating number of hours in front of different screens and the chemical imbalances in the brain that followed. The parents never saw it coming. The police were tied up in litigation, rising murder rates and the threat of another school shooting – and all this was before the IEDs started blowing citizens to pieces, right on their own soil. The foreign interventions and the accidental bombings overseas no longer held a firm place above the fold. The news had become more domestic, and volatility underscored the headlines. Blood and threat ran rampant on front pages, and the spike in suicides was but a side note, and they became the disagreeable Crohn's disease of American society's ills.

A man like Mr. Berger had likely kept up with the news, both locally and nationally. Though sitting there with the guard and lawyer, he offered not a touch of desperation one might expect from a man considering death. He leaned in closer to Mr. Selby and continued. "And surely, a man who loses a wife has suffered. So what's that man to do?"

Mr. Selby could now be seen turning his back to Mr. Berger. "Thank you, Mr. Koontz. I can finish up here." The lawyer collected copies of the paperwork and exited through the front. "So are you a man who has suffered a loss, Mr. Bergerfeld?"

"I have. My livelihood – my profession – my life was taken right from me, and it was then that I learned the difference between friend and acquaintance. Well, that's not altogether true. I learned what a friend wasn't. I learned that everything you worked for could be snatched from you at any minute."

"Yes it can."

"I've also learned that there are people willing to help. There might even be someone out there willing to help me. I've spoken with the lowest of the lows, sir – drug dealers, pimps and prostitutes. One girl I came across even spoke of how she came to get clean because of a most special type of treatment she received in the area. I mean, she's back on the stuff, but if someone had it in him to see to her, well, that's something I'd want to know about. It's something everyone should know about."

"Maybe you're right, Mr. Bergerfeld. I appreciate you sharing your story, and I wish you the best." Mr. Selby opened the front door and showed his guest out. He turned off the power to the one camera before doing the same to the other. The screen inside was once again relegated to standby blue.

"Well, that was different," said Felix, and Janzen lifted a puzzled eyebrow. "He always does the two door thing – both the front and the back door left open. He leaves out the back while Koontz finalizes the paperwork. And then they either take the red pill or the blue pill."

"We used to see him around the neighborhood," said Ms. Patterson.

"I thought he looked familiar," added her son. "He used to buy from Peachie all the time. His brother worked maintenance up on York Rd. at the station."

"We almost had our first celebrity!" added a despondent Daryl.

"Define celebrity," said Helena.

"Hey, the '84 Mustang was still a sports car," quipped Daryl. "What I mean is none of you were ever on TV."

The idea of celebrity took over, the perfect subject that

both differentiated and coalesced without any real fallout. The opportunity gave Janzen the chance to survey his fellow residents more or less surreptitiously to distill from their quirks and opinions who among them might be capable of running around the grounds as a masked tormentor.

He had such few details to go on in which to elicit anything other than a blind guess, and he couldn't even rule out the women given the inconstancy and absence of the eyewitnesses. Mr. McCullough was an old coot in the early-to-middle stages of dementia. The other victim allegedly made the plunge off the top soon after the first incident, and that was months before Janzen's stay in Mount Selby.

The anonymity of the perpetrator made each resident seep with culpability. Over the past weeks, Janzen had learned the tales of what led some of them to their dramatic final step, and much of their courageous honesty and forthrightness now rusted over into something suspect.

Some of the residents began leaving the cavernous open space of the second floor, and Janzen stood up to head back to the elevator to ask Samuel about which of the residents were in the building for both occurrences. The situation was bizarre enough to investigate further, but questions for the big man would have to wait until Mr. Atis's fumbling words found their proper place through the speaker system. "Everyone back to the hall! The fence is breached. He found the ladder. Everyone back to their positions!"

Everyone who had left came rushing back into the great hall. Felix worked the projector remote feverishly with one hand while manipulating the camera feeds on his tablet with the other.

An image finally appeared, and it was a split screen shot from the point of view of two exterior cameras attached at different elevations on the same side of the building. Janzen remembered passing two such devices and the red light of each, not knowing all these drive-in eyes had watched his vertical ascent.

Projected for everyone to see were the empty views of black iron vines coming to their pinpoint ends. If not for the dead, flickering remnants of plant life from years past, the image could have been an accidental photograph. The lonely length of their journey was finally interrupted by the small, grainy figure of a man hugging the outer façade from a floor up off the ground.

"He's gonna climb!"

A collective cheer caromed throughout the space. With the expectation of another body in the building, the group discussed how they would reveal themselves once Helena led Mr. Berger through the darkness and then left him alone on the stage. Apparently, Felix engineered specific lighting plans for different scenarios. The slow reveal was chosen by the time he reached the midpoint of his climb. This decision won out slightly over the strobe light effect.

Onscreen, Mr. Berger approached the first camera and flicked the lens playfully as he passed. Once he reached the second camera just below the rooftop, he was smiling.

Felix switched the bottom camera's feed to one on the roof and everyone saw Scoop stealing away to Mr. Selby's office below through a moss-covered hatchway. Moments later, a second rooftop feed flashed in place of the one Mr. Berger had just passed before he arrived up top. The angle captured his drop into the dense greenery.

Felix tapped into two other feeds, one of which looked down above the yellow banner and to the loading area far below.

They watched as Mr. Berger shook his head at the sight of the flora around him. He invited something up above him to share in the experience. His head began to bob, and he danced closely with an invisible partner, negotiating the landscape with deft feet. He bowed to his partner with a hand held out to hers.

"This motherfucker is going to make breakfast really interesting."

"Okay, what's his reaction going to be onstage?"

"Did you all watch me?" asked Janzen.

"YEEEESSSSS," the entire room replied.

"No one thought you'd throw chairs."

"I'll throw you."

"Ooooooooo!" Everyone laughed.

Helena leaned in and said quietly, "Can we finish the wall tonight?"

"The hole, too?"

"Yeah."

"Yup. Will you tell me what we're doing?" asked Janzen.

"It's where you'll fuck me," she said while watching the screen. If Janzen hid his surprise, his wide eyes were a betrayal.

Meanwhile, Mr. Berger found his way to the gap in the rooftop. He looked down below him and then jumped in place a few feet back from the edge. He yelled out to the woods below, but none of his exclamations were audible to the group. The silent footage was straight out of a black and white dream. He leaned out over the edge, and one of the cameras showed him once again yelling out to the quarry below him. He appeared to count to three before he pushed off.

His landing was captured with an unexpected immediacy. Janzen's stomach turned at the ruffling of the banner against the building and the body so far down below. The broken figure on the slab of concrete was only a blob of blackness onscreen, but the blackness soon expanded with the escaping blood. Then, walked the figure of the guard below. It hovered over the motionless body until it waved for a line to be lowered.

"What just happened? asked Janzen. "How often does this happen?"

Someone said, "It has never happened."

11

Mr. Selby was missing without much explanation after the Chase Berger incident. In his absence, Mr. Atis ran the sessions and deflected questions about that afternoon. He reassured the others that Mr. Selby had contacted the police about the body and complied with the cursory investigation that followed, but after sharing the paperwork the recently deceased had filled out, there wasn't much to uncover. Also, the security footage Mr. Selby allegedly played for the detectives in the guard shack showed a man scaling the side of the building only to jump off its summit minutes later.

With Mr. Selby absent, copies of *The Sun* that sometimes came in with the deliveries were passed around between the residents. It was understood that Mr. Selby thought the outside world was nothing but a distraction for those in the building, but he was gone now so Scoop read aloud the article covering the news of Mr. Berger's death. It was written in economical fashion, focused mostly on the man's early television career and the city's climbing suicide statistics. The article was on the bottom of the front page because the headlines were grabbed by the kidnappers' demands for the return of yet another abducted governor.

Mr. Atis carried on bravely, but he didn't sit so tall on his machine and his responses and directions were filled with deep spaces and long, silent gaps. He no longer ate his meals with the group in the commissary, and he mostly sat behind his desk outside Mr. Selby's office. Each morning, Janzen slid the pages from his word processor under his locked doors. On the fourth day, Mr. Atis no longer pretended to busy himself at his desk when Janzen delivered his end of the bargain.

"You sure he's in there?" asked Janzen. Mr. Atis shrugged and nodded at the same time. "Listen, if there's anything I can –"

"I do need something, Janzen," he said. He rubbed his forehead before going on. "Leonard needs his meals taken down twice a day. They'll be ready to go in the back of the kitchen. You'll have to warm some things up, but I'll have Christian and Amber put on some instructions. Mr. Selby usually takes it down to him, and I just can't do it anymore. It's too much. I don't think he's well."

"Mr. Selby?"

"Leonard."

"I can help."

Mr. Atis was right about a couple things. Instructions were left by Amber to heat the food at a certain level for a certain amount of time. He was also right about Leonard's health. He did not seem well.

Janzen still had flashes of Leonard's wraithlike figure slowly closing in on him during that first night in the building. He was the pale, near-naked man sitting on his bedside, the dead ringer for a backgrounder on a Romero shoot. Besides their initial interaction, Janzen had never spoken to or seen Leonard again and learned of his cancer only through conversations with the other residents.

Janzen knocked at his door and waited in the hallway, holding the tray of food. He heard something hit the other side of the door and fall to the ground. He knocked again. "Housekeeping," he said in his highest register. He turned the knob and walked into a pit of a room he remembered from the first night. A single bedside light illuminated a cluttered room filled with trash, warped books, scattered puzzle pieces, dirty dishes, blankets crumpled in corners and a man sitting off the side of his bed, just as Janzen had seen Leonard positioned once before. He wore clothes this time – clothes that might've fit him years or months earlier – but his skinny arms now stuck out of sagging sleeves. The two men locked eyes and played chicken. Janzen squinted in that dipshit manner of his. Leonard presented a face that disintegrated into something both loathing and threatening.

Even with the menace and drudgery of the place, Leonard's eyes twitched with a bright quickness. Janzen kicked at the carpeted ground below him to locate the specific piece of trash that had been thrown at the door.

"You know, it's impolite to –"

"Shut up."

Janzen shut up. For a second. "You know it's impolite to leave me standing here with *your* food."

"I recognize you."

"And I you, Leonard. I'm Janzen."

Leonard covered his face with a pillow and yelled a prayer to himself. Janzen was only familiar with the Catholic service and could therefore not place this curse-laden invocation. "You nearly shit your pants that night, didn't you?"

"I'll have you know I haven't shit my pants in over three years," said Janzen.

And there it was: a reprobate rapport established.

"Sit your ass down." Janzen followed the instruction. "You get high?"

"Why not."

With weed, Janzen never suffered any compulsion when using it. It always left him dumb as a stump, a repercussion that kept him from becoming a regular user. What was the harm? He was already on one strange trip, and the man offering his medicine was as certified as a Peruvian shaman in the deep recesses of the jungle.

Leonard located a vaporizer from his bedside table and showed Janzen how it worked. It was the tiniest little device and could've passed for an intricate fountain pen. After the first hit, Leonard put on some acid jazz from an uncovered turntable, and they floated along with each other. He eventually picked at the food, and Janzen helped him finish the rest.

"I don't eat if it wasn't for this stuff."

"How do you get it?"

"It comes down with the food. Selby's into trying different strains and oils, and I write about their effects. He charts everything in that notebook of his."

"Where does he get it?"

"It's from here. There's a grow room somewhere

upstairs. You listen to jazz, man?"

"Not on purpose."

"You know, you seem like a real prick."

"Yeah man. You seem like a real prick, too." In this way, the two men weaved in and out of conversation, its rhythm and trajectory guided only by the tips of tongues and wandering minds. They spoke of their climbs to the tippy-top of the building – not what actually led them there, but the climb itself.

Leonard had agreed to be the focal point of Mr. Selby's medicinal experiments as long as he was physically able. It was agreed that Leonard could take leave of the experiment whenever he decided it was time. In return, he kept a journal about his reactions to the different strains – to what extent each helped his nausea, whether one may dull his faculties more than another, anything that could be useful to someone dealing with such a medical condition.

Janzen told him about the goings-on in the building: the anonymous attacks, Mr. Berger's death, Mr. Selby's disappearance. Leonard followed along for a while, and then he'd lose focus and allow his finger to tap along with the bastard beat. He asked no follow-up questions. When Janzen spoke in this room, he felt like the monotonous creak of a chain on a patio swing, and that was okay with him.

Janzen turned down another hit and cleared Leonard's room of leftover dishes. Some of the meals hadn't been touched. He couldn't help but connect the untouched food to the cancer in the man's bowels, giving the plates full of food a melancholic heft. He shook it off. For now, they were two pricks in a pod, and that would have to be enough. Janzen even extended Leonard an invitation to Film Night, which would be held later that evening. Leonard politely responded that he would prefer to stay in and eat a pile of dog shit.

Later that evening down on the second floor, Janzen realized he had never seen the expansive open space with proper lighting. The heavy curtains were wrangled with pretty knots in each of the four corners; they were dark, but in the light they showed their madder accents. They anchored the room exquisitely in their staid and regal flow. The walls were what must've given the room its fragrance. They were made of a paneled mahogany, stained handsomely to highlight their grain. The ceiling was raised and finished with sumptuous tiles inlaid with golden lines that stretched from tile to tile. Janzen mostly appreciated the light wooden flooring and the geometric patterns embedded throughout.

He was the first one to arrive for Film Night, so he had the room to himself. Across from where he entered, he saw a familiar image of his likeness on the wall opposite him. He headed first for the great big portrait of Mr. Wayland Selby framed as an emperor. On either side of him were smaller portraits, each one executed in its own distinctive fashion. As he walked down the line, he recognized the pen and ink of Helena and the oil painting of Leonard. Monroe's hyperrealistic countenance was taken straight from a central booking mug shot. Ms. Patterson was next to her son and her depiction was of the right side of her face with her hair braided in cornrows. On the far right hung Janzen in his dolly-propelled rapture.

He walked to the other side of Mr. Selby and found both familiar faces and those of strangers. Was this a timeline? If so, the person he recognized as being in the building the longest was none other than Mr. Atis. That had to be him, but what was it that led him to offer that slack and open mouth as his best face? He walked the wall again before Felix appeared and yelled over to him to help set up for the movie and soon the room started to fill with residents.

Janzen learned not to ask too many questions because most were answered in good time; besides, the tiny surprises rarely failed to disappoint, and so Movie Night was left as another gift at the bottom of this eleven story Cracker Jack box. Felix played music while Janzen set up chairs and distributed the beanbag chairs and pillows that Scoop delivered. Christian then wheeled in a sparkling carnival popcorn machine and put it to work. The aroma of the stained wood and the popping kernels delighted Janzen. Monroe taught Amber a waltz, and Daryl entertained Ms. Patterson and Mr. McCullough with a detailed account of his latest dream. Kenneth Polk hung around Felix, who was happy to explain the details of his operation. The rest were comfortably reclining in chairs, wandering about, or dancing alone.

Mr. Atis rolled in as the screen was lowered. Felix attached a wireless to his collar and asked for everyone to grab a seat. Mr. Atis nodded, and Felix powered on the mic.

"Good evening. Let me first thank everyone who pitched in to help with…things. Tonight, we are lucky enough to have a double bill. We will start out with the next in line of our regular series, and upon its completion we had a request, which I was more than happy to accommodate." The crowd cheered Mr. Atis's announcement, and Felix dimmed the lights. "Ladies and Gentlemen, please settle in for tonight's first feature: The Misadventures of President Polk." The room swelled with hoots and applause. Kenneth stood up from his seat and took a deep bow.

The screen showed color bars and then the count-down from four to one and next a fade to black. Layered over the blackness was the audio's room tone. Then the shuffling noise might have been someone's feet on the floor or the mic against fabric.

"State your name for the camera, please." The voice was familiar.

"Kenneth Michael Polk." The room once again erupted in celebration with some chanting "The Prez." Video of Kenneth appeared onscreen of him in the guard shack.

"Can you tell me why you're here today?"

First came the quick collective inhale, and then: "Because I'm ready to die!" The entire group proclaimed the words that Janzen could see but not hear from the mouth of Kenneth Polk. Even Kenneth, the one sitting a few chairs over from him, celebrated the line with everyone else. A few jumped to their feet and hugged him from behind. Janzen caught Felix's attention, whose focus was back on his tablet before Janzen could gauge the proceeding's propriety. Was this the first stop along the freak show's exhibition or a bizarre show of succor?

What Janzen watched wasn't just a replaying of the recorded footage. The video was heavily produced, stocked with reverb, echoes, filters, subtitles for anything not clearly heard and an instrumental number he could not yet place. Most haunting was the grainy image of a man who appeared to be Kenneth standing at the opening in the roof; the image flickered onscreen quicker than a blink.

"What brought you to that particular decision, young man?" Mr. Selby's voice offscreen was steadily paced and kind.

"Do you know what Asperger's is? asked Kenneth.

"Is that the same as Down Syndrome?"

"No." His response echoed hard and the video's capture froze on the face of a man making a point.

"Look it up, motherfucker!" Someone down the row shouted and everyone laughed.

"Well, you should look it up," continued Kenneth onscreen, and the room cheered the man's instruction.

"You're angry."

"Yes, I'm angry. I know I'm not happy."

"About what?"

"My isolation, I think."

Helena walked over and put her arm around Kenneth. He patted her arm but maintained his focus on the film. He was proud of his destruction because of what might follow, or he took pride in reliving his courage to change what was his own torture. He told the guard of his alienation. He told the guard that he would never truly understand the people he spoke to whether he was in a guard shack, at a kitchen table, on a city tram, or maybe even one day on opposite ends of a single pillow. Kenneth spoke of his addiction to confession, not because of his devotion to the church and sacrament but because of the divider in between the priest and him. There was so much comfort in that screen because there were no mysteries to decipher. There was no worry about how his face should be arranged, but the sins he confessed were not his own. They were what he had seen on the television or read in a book. It didn't matter that the sins weren't his. He was happy to have found someone to talk to.

The group settled in and cheered some of his lines and preempted the others with their own renditions. Janzen could do the same with only a few films. How long had he rambled on during his own guard shack interview? He didn't remember much from that part of the day. The honesty in what he said required nothing of him; typically, there was the deceit necessitating his active imagination. Would he be the next video? If so, who requested it?

"On Eagle's Wings" played ironically over Kenneth's interview. Onscreen, his eyes followed the man leaving out the back door. The guard's footsteps played through the speakers along with the turn of the door handle. There was no sound of the door closing. Kenneth homed in on that opening, right past the camera's lens while the lawyer wrapped up explaining the final details of the paperwork. The lawyer shook Kenneth's hand and exited out the front door. He was left alone, and the camera continued to record. He stood and the image froze and faded once again to black until the grainy image from before filled the screen. No more music played, and the only sound was that of the wind. Kenneth shot both his arms down to his side and leaned forward and out the opening until there was only the gap. Janzen did the only thing that felt appropriate: he applauded. Soon after, everyone else joined in. Tears streaked down some of their cheeks. Kenneth beamed once again and was surrounded by people who blanketed him with their love.

After everyone had returned to their seats, the sounds of the blips counting down from four, three, two, and one were once again onscreen. A date already passed faded in and out. Close to a year had gone by since this mystery footage had been captured. Again, the audio of the empty room tone could be heard over the blackness. Finally, a familiar voice was heard: "If I asked you what time it was, how would you respond?"

"You want to know the time?" It was Helena's voice.

"Yes," answered Mr. Selby.

"It's thirteen thirty-four hours."

"You still keep time that way?"

"It's how I've always kept time."

"Even after everything?"

"Yes."

"Why?

"It's what I've always done." Footage of Helena finally appeared for this last line, which echoed among the residents. Janzen looked over at her, but she looked down to her hands in her lap. Others also avoided what was onscreen.

"Can you state your full name please?"

"Helena Wanda March."

"Your rank?"

"Private first class, United States Army." Her responses came with a practiced military cadence, and she addressed Mr. Selby with an appropriate focus without eyeballing her questioner.

"Did you serve overseas?"

"Yes. Afghanistan."

"Are you in line to serve another tour? Is that why you're here today? To be sure you have things in line in case something unfortunate happens?"

"I will not be serving again – not ever."

"Mr. Koontz, can I speak with you outside please?" The two men could be heard exiting the guard shack, but the camera still rolled on Helena. The bangs of her hair trembled across her forehead. She now appeared on the verge of catastrophe. Quite possibly, it was her training that denied such a public spectacle. The two men could be heard re-entering the shack, and Helena straightened her back.

"Are you currently AWOL, ma'am?"

"No. I am in no trouble with the law or with any armed forces."

"Then why are you here today?"

"I'm here to get organized and set things straight."

"Are you going somewhere?"

"Possibly."

"Why?"

The image of Helena froze onscreen and faded to black. The audio of her voice played over it. "My mom told me that my dad enlisted when he was 18. I've seen pictures of him holding me, but I have no real memories of him. I was too young."

Helena reappeared on the video.

"How long did your father serve?"

"Until '91, before I was born."

"What happened to him?"

"He took his life when I was three."

"Is he why you enlisted?"

"Maybe."

"Did your mother remarry?"

"Yes."

"To a soldier?"

"No. He was a banker, whatever that means. He came later. He was older. He is older. There were lots of others before him."

"Are you close with your mother?"

Helena sat in the familiar chair and lifted her body off the seat an inch or two with her strong, straightened arms. "I don't know. I really don't know. I'm not sure anyone really escapes childhood undamaged. It's only to what extent you get fucked up. I think she did her best with me, but I never really saw her as this strong person even though it had to be hard raising a girl like me by herself. It wasn't really fair that a dead father I never really knew would always be this standard of a perfect parent. You know, he was this image that could never be tarnished simply because of his absence, which wasn't really fair to her, but I would just see her fucking bow to these men who just preyed on her. She had it coming because she just invited it with her weakness and submission."

"Do you know how to clean and maintain an M-16?"

"Yes."

"Were you a good shot?"

"Best in my unit."

"Did you take any live fire?"

"Yes. I was one of the first women in my unit to take fire and record a kill – should've happened a long time ago if you ask me."

"Was it difficult being a female?"

"Not really. I mean, I went through what everyone else went through and better than most. There wasn't anything I couldn't do. I kicked ass in basic training – earned a lot of respect. When I was in Kabul, I always thought about how the local women were treated over there – as Afghanis – and I guess I wanted to help move things forward in a positive direction. I was there while the Afghan soldiers were training, and I felt proud to be there – as a woman – as a soldier, too."

"So it was a positive experience for you?"

"It gave me purpose. It fulfilled something in me that I was somehow conditioned to complete."

"Because of your father?"

"Yes," she said. Janzen scanned the room, and those who previously avoided what was onscreen were now locked in to the footage. Only Helena resisted with her head now in her hands.

"You still must've seen some terrible things."

"I did. I've seen what a direct mortar hit can do to a body. I know what an IED can do to an armored vehicle. Part of me understands the other side and the allure of giving every part of you for something – without questioning anything. If I was raised the same way with someone I trusted telling me that the greatest thing I can do is to give my life for something bigger than me, well, there's a nobility in that. Most people here don't think in those terms when considering the enemy. I mean, we were the foreigners there."

"Was it hard to see some of your fellow soldiers injured or killed in combat?"

"It was difficult, yes."

"Is that why you won't go back?"

"No. There was a time when it was the only thing I wanted to do. Part of me still feels that way. I didn't care what happened to me."

"So, what's stopping you?"

Onscreen, Helena shook her head. "I don't know why I'm telling you this."

"What happened?"

Helena looked directly at the camera lens. "I was raped."

"Jesus. I'm sorry, young lady. When you came back to the U.S.?"

"No. Over there."

"Were you held captive?"

"He was in my unit. There should be some record of this out there."

"You mean you didn't report it?"

"I did – to my commanding officer."

"And what came of that."

"There was an inquiry," said Helena with a look of disgust.

"An investigation?"

"I wouldn't call it that. The entire system is broken for dealing with something like this. There's zero accountability."

"So what did you do?"

"What could I do? I followed the chain of command."

"And what became of him?"

"Transferred to another base. And then everything changed, and no one wanted anything from me. Everyone knew why he wasn't there anymore, and they were angry."

"At you?"

"Yes."

"Did you try to speak to someone else?"

"Yes. My appointment at the VA is in a month."

"But you're here."

"Yes."

"Can I speak to you outside?" The voice came offscreen from Mr. Koontz. Once again, the two men exited the guard shack, and the camera remained on Helena. In her company's absence, she hugged her legs tightly into her chest and dropped her forehead to her knees. She muffled her anger through a clenched mouth. She dropped her feet to the ground and threw her head back to fight what swelled in her eyes. The two men returned to find Helena fidgeting with her watch.

"Ms. March, my colleague here has a connection with the VA in Annapolis and can see if there's anything he can do to expedite your case."

"No. Why should I get that opportunity? It's not fair."

"It really wouldn't be a problem, Ms. March," interjected Mr. Koontz.

"Can we finish up here?" she responded without emotion.

Mr. Koontz reappeared and indicated where Helena needed to sign. She finished her first signature and then addressed the camera directly. "He fucking did it. And I don't forgive him. I don't forgive any of them." Mr. Koontz took a step away from her and the footage once again froze and the mains hum of a taut power line filled the stillness until everything went black and silent.

Amber moved quickly over to Helena and hugged her. Janzen remained sitting in his chair at a distance from her. They found each other through a gap in the group until it closed. Next to her, Kenneth rubbed her back a little too hard, and he smiled a confused smile.

Janzen marveled at the collection of folks around her. Ms. Patterson smoothed Kenneth's rough caresses with her own kind touch while she held tightly to her son's arm next to her. Scoop held out his bag of popcorn for Helena until she politely declined. Mr. McCullough asked Felix how long until the next movie.

As the one to fuck her, what was his place in this? Was he supposed to move closer and stare just as stupidly?

Felix powered down his tablet and began shutting down his production. Christian announced that he'd be up in the commissary for anyone who wanted mini grilled cheese and tomato soup shooters. Scoop encouraged everyone to take one more helping of popcorn.

In the mix of the chairs being returned to their rolling rack and the effort to clean up the remaining clutter, Helena approached Janzen and stood in front of him before she planted her foot through his chest, leaving him in a crumbled mess on the floor.

By the time Felix and Kenneth lifted Janzen back to his feet, she was no longer with them.

Staring stupidly from a distance was not the correct

decision. To be clear, staring stupidly from a distance was not even a decision.

12

"So every person came into the building the same way?"

"Yes."

"And after the first handful of people that went splat from off the top, he's been bringing them in?"

"Yes."

"Why?"

"That's the tricky part, Janzen. I think he just wants them to find some peace before taking that next step." Samuel spoke earnestly, but it was something else that had brought Janzen into the elevator. "You know his wife was the first one to jump?"

"I had heard something about that. What happened?"

"Apparently, she was never well. Mr. Selby thought it would do her some good to get out of the house, so he brought her in to design the garden up top. The building was still open at that point. She was the one who made Mr. Selby put those iron vines up when the building first opened. She thought that the façade needed life, something beautiful. She was much younger than him. I used to hear everyone talk about it, but he was totally in love with her. She was so private, so Mr. Selby arranged for the crane to be installed and delivered everything she wanted lifted up to the roof. She spent weeks up there. When she was done planting the last flower, she jumped off. It was horrible."

"You were here?"

"Yeah. The building closed later that week with most everything and everyone moving away to the property up in Cockeysville. He just stayed locked up in here after the service, and not long after, the other jumpers started."

"Samuel." Janzen inhaled and turned to face the elevator operator.

"Janzen." Samuel laughed and turned to face Janzen.

"You told me everyone was here for the same reason."

"Yes sir."

"Everyone?"

"What are you getting at?" asked Samuel, not fully understanding the line of questioning.

"Why isn't there a picture of you with the others on that wall?" Samuel's hesitation was enough to compel Janzen on. "Why aren't you in any of the sessions?"

Samuel sat back down on his stool and no longer looked at Janzen. "Mr. Selby was the only one who offered me work coming out of the recession. No one else was hiring and he gave me a shot."

"What was your job?"

"Same as it is now."

"And you've been here since?"

"Yes."

"What about when he closed the building?"

"Who do you think helped him? Who do you think

cemented up the bottom floor and secured every single exit? He needed help."

"And he pays you?"

"Direct deposit. I've been saving everything since."

"For what?"

"What?"

"What are you saving for?"

"What do you mean?"

The elevator doors opened, and Daryl stepped in and asked if Samuel could take him up to Mr. Atis on the top floor. Janzen slipped out as the doors closed behind him. He walked down the corridor now filled with the mud and guck of Samuel's suspect place among them, but he needed to be light on his feet. He needed buoyancy and a lift in his system because of the small chance that a tiny circular object would drop down from above and rattle about in that birdcage like a pebble in a pop can.

He waited days for that sound, and it finally came.

The time written on the first marble read 4:15. By 4:19, Janzen was fucking Helena through the gap in the wall. Janzen really had to give it to Scoop. He had designed a rudimentary but clever communication system by which Helena and Janzen arranged their meetings. It was true that he had not actually spoken to Helena since absorbing her size seven with his sternum, but when Scoop installed the other end of the tubing through the ceiling in his room, he soon became privy to most of the necessary details. As Scoop told it, Helena had bartered a few of her studio electronics in exchange for his help. Scoop was growing increasingly worried about the safety of his various piles of supplies – so much so that he planned to position a few motion-detecting cameras in and around his bedroom office. He was, therefore, more than willing to help Helena with whatever she asked in exchange for some cameras.

The clear plastic tubing was just wide enough to allow the marble's passage. Scoop told Janzen that the other end was run up to "some gawdammed room wit a hole in da gawdammed wall." Scoop had rigged it so Helena only needed to insert the marble at her end and gravity took over. The marble's journey wound down through the previously installed piping that housed the wiring for many of the building's newer amenities. Because Janzen's room was positioned almost directly below the room with the new wall, Scoop only needed to drill a few new holes to facilitate the project.

In Janzen's room, Scoop cut the ass end of the plastic tubing to a reach that extended from the ceiling to about chest high. At the end, he displayed an unexpected dash of panache when he attached a decorative and most diminutive birdcage. He took the time to snip open the domed vault, creating an open-air top that fit snugly around the end of the tubing. When he attached this final touch, its meaning was made muddily clear from Scoop's explanation. "She said she needed to drop somethin' round and small through it so you'd know what to do. Thass what she said. I don' ask no questions, Jay-man. I juss do da job."

When that first marble made its journey through the plastic chute from above, Janzen was writing on the machine at the desk, and the little thing rattled into the brass birdcage and startled him with its tinny report. He opened the alloyed entrance and retrieved the marble swirled almost completely in a milky white. On it were the handwritten numbers 4:15.

Since their last official interaction involved such violence, Janzen was somewhat surprised to hear the marble. He had since adopted a primatologist's approach toward an under-socialized silverback when around Helena, avoiding direct eye contact and deferring to her wont of space and travel.

But now, he was fucking her; well, now he was most assuredly fucking someone. When he first walked into the room, he was taken aback by the amount of work done to the interior. The walls were painted a dark royal blue, and the only light came from a computer monitor on a small tabletop. He walked atop the same rubber tiling he recognized from the gym floor. As the room was now divided in two, there were doorways on either side of the installed wall that led to other offices. It was a room entombed in its own peculiarity between two other useless rooms.

The monitor was on a stand in the corner adjacent to the divider. On it was a porn flick featuring two girls and a guy. Both females had breasts stretched to a tanned translucence with silicon relegating them to the role of tits rather than breasts. A few feet from the monitor sat a metal folding chair, and a condom waited on its seat. Poking out from the hole in the wall were two naked legs spread wide. The light emitting from the monitor bathed the room in its dissipated haze and shadowed and highlighted enough of the splayed legs in front of him to verify her complete state of undress. The upper arch of the hole in the wall was curtained with a silky fabric that hid any view of the adjoining room while providing enough space to allow her hand to fit through comfortably. When he first entered the room, the moon and Venus of her palm rested atop her pubic arch as her fingers circled below. The smell was new, familiar and raw.

Janzen's mind went to Raisin Bran: better get a move on before he's mush. The bench she lay on displayed the ragged hallmarks of something bought from a medical surplus store. The design was clunky, and the bracings that connected the footrests squeaked its antique squeak with every move of her body. Her legs twitched from the startle of his first touch, but the way he reached under the bend of each leg and held her outer thighs reassured her. She relaxed once again, and he was then inside her. She gripped the bench underneath her, and her body offered him no clues as to what she wanted. He either couldn't hear her on the other side of the wall or she was quiet throughout.

Once Janzen finished, he fought his cramping right calf. He stepped back to stretch the clenching muscle, and she slid her legs swiftly back through the hole. After her feet disappeared, a rubber flap replaced the opening and hushed the sound of movement on the other side of the wall.

He really was just a fuck.

He backed toward the folding chair and collapsed in it like a journeyman across from the young prizefighter. The man on the computer held up one of the women against a wall while the other pawed at his swinging testicles. Janzen pulled a handful of his toes toward his body to relieve the cramping in his leg.

He threw the used condom toward the wastebasket in the corner but the end of the scene on the monitor brought with it a black screen, which made him unsure of his aim in the unlit room. He was also uncertain how to process this event. For years, he had chased the nameless nights with numbed and drunk girls, all the while protective of passing along too much information for fear of conveying something that resembled intimacy. After the earnest heartache of his early twenties, he wanted nothing more than the raw act of sex. He had it now, and the retreating blood of his cock coursed back up north and transubstantiated into something wicked thanks to that Catholic upbringing that clung to his being. He no longer possessed the libido to chase away any shame after the initial blast of his climax, so he was left limp-dicked, staring through the monitor now full of raging dicks and gaping pussies.

That was the first time but not the last.

The marbles continued to drop, and the wonder of routine alleviated the initial anger, confusion and guilt. He now kept a glass of water at his desk to fight the cramps, and he settled into his role as the stepping stone fighter, proud of his collapses of exhaustion into the folding chair.

He even privately laughed at the erection he hid while in the commissary. Someone dropped a fork, and the sound was similar enough to the bounding marble in the brass birdcage, rendering him a part of some Pavlovian experiment gone wrong – not totally wrong, gone somewhere.

Helena still had not spoken directly to Janzen, but he could tell that the anger she harbored was receding. While her looks at him during the group's morning and afternoon sessions weren't coquettish, they were wonderfully calm. She permitted her face to fall in such a way that she might've been reading a good book, blinking languidly as she turned a page. Janzen once again looked forward to these sessions because he knew he'd see her. This morning, she even gave him a playful snarl with the lift of half her upper lip and a flare of her nostrils when she found his attention a tad too protracted.

The afternoon session was a follow up to one Janzen had not attended because he had not yet been admitted into the building. It was a Q&A exercise between Monroe and his young mother, Ms. Patterson. They sat face to face in Conference Room A, and in Mr. Selby's absence and Mr. Atis's subsequent decline, Amber refereed the session. It was explained that the activity would consist of two parts. First, Monroe and his mother could only communicate through the posing of questions. During the second half, the Pattersons could only respond to one another through declarative statements in an effort to anticipate the other's inquiries or concerns.

Mother and son sat across from each other in the center of the room. Attendance for these sections had dwindled since Mr. Selby's disappearance, but the only incentive Janzen needed sat right where she usually sat.

"I don't know how to start, Amber." Monroe hesitated to adjust his chair towards his mother.

"Think *Jeopardy*, Monroe. Everything in this round must be in the form of a question, and your mother will respond the same way," said Amber, whose leadership in the group seemed to provide her with a much needed lift after her latest video call with her parents.

Monroe steadied himself and crossed his feet at the ankle. "How did we get here?"

Ms. Patterson paused before responding. "Why didn't you talk to me?"

"Why are we every cliché?"

"What do you mean?" she said, imploring her son for understanding with pleading eyes.

"Why the handouts? Why the food stamps? said Monroe, wanting to say more. "Why the single mother? Why the constant moving? Why the clothes that never fit?"

"Do you have any idea how hard I work? Do you know how much I make? Do you know that even with my two jobs, we still can barely cover the bills?"

"No." Monroe broke eye contact with his mother and shook his head in frustration.

"Monroe, questions only," interjected Amber.

"Can you understand how hard it was to have a child at my age? Do you think I'm proud of needing help?"

"Why were you so young?"

She struggled to explain her childhood cut short to her son while still following the rules of the exercise. "Why do you judge me?"

"Why do *you* judge me? Can't you see this isn't me? Can't you see that this is why we're here?" Monroe searched his mother perhaps for something resembling compassion.

"What would your grandfather say?"

"What do *you* say?" he asked.

"What would the church say?"

"Fuck the church."

"Monroe!" Amber and his mother chastised the young man in unison but for different reasons, one for the flouting of rules, the other for his sacrilege.

"Okay," Amber continued, "let's breathe a second. That was productive. This next round will only consist of statements of fact. There will be no questions or statements beginning with 'I feel.' Do you both agree to these terms?" Mother and son nodded. "Ms. Patterson will start."

"I had you too soon."

"I am a cliché."

"You are my son."

"I am your child."

"I don't know you."

"I will let you know me," he said. They had fired responses back and forth to each other until this last statement. Ms. Patterson grew uncomfortable in her chair as the object of attention. She probably wasn't accustomed to such scrutiny.

"I was raised a certain way."

"We are both clichés."

"I am a single mother. I am a young single mother with little schooling, but I love my son."

"I do not know how much you make. I do not know how hard it is to keep the power on. I do not know how much my cereal costs. I don't even know how much a gallon of milk is."

"I don't want you to know that. I only want to provide

for you."

"I need more than that."

"I love my son."

"But do you love your child?"

"Monroe – statements only," reminded Amber. Mother and son paused while Janzen scanned the room to witness a group of men and women completely enthralled with the proceedings.

"I want us. I want us to be together," said Monroe, reaching out for his mother. "I want to know your struggle. But you'll have to understand mine. We need to break through."

"We need to break through."

"We need to break through," he reiterated and wiped the tears from his face.

"I will try for you."

"You will?"

"I will try for you."

"I will still be your child."

"I love you, Monroe."

Mother and child embraced. The group celebrated their effort. Janzen applauded but with an incomplete understanding of their backstory. The mysterious emotion was still something, though; it was bioluminescent. For Janzen, the embrace he witnessed was the misunderstood brilliance of the neon blue signals he had seen as a child. There was magic in mother and son tonight, and there was magic in the surf he remembered on a night during which he and his mother ran along a deserted beach while the electrified water full of light-bright phytoplankton entranced them. Both events were special in the way a child might recall the first occurrence of déjà vu and the hint of something unknown at work. Amber joined the embrace between Monroe and his mother. Tears ran down their cheeks, and the rest of the room looked on at the beautiful alien sea. Immune to the emotion surging in the room, Helena sat in her corner with her eyes glazed over and her lips repeating something over and over.

The room gave way to breezy conversations and folks lying about. There would be no more work that day, and Janzen took to the hallways led by the memory of his long-dead dog he had named Troubles. He soon found Kenneth and Daryl in the middle of a game of chess.

Janzen had never known a pedophile before his time here; well, that wasn't true. He had never met a person who admitted to being one. He understood the idea of compulsion and empathized with the man because of his condition. How was he to weigh the differences of one's addiction compared to another? Would Daryl have thought of following the brave and brazen lead of the Spartan named Timycha, whose self-mutilation assured her silence under the duress of her torture? Would Daryl have pierced his prick like Timycha had bit off her tongue to preserve her Pythagorean beliefs? What integrity would be left for Daryl when the affliction infected both brain and body?

Janzen headed toward the fourth floor office, preserved in the deep blue of its blocked windows. He walked past adjoining cubicles and noticed that the desktops were no longer wiped clean of their dust, and many of the chairs were no longer placed under their desks. On every previous visit to this office, the room had been kept in immaculate order.

He knew he would end up here. There was the matter of the toy penguin to resolve. The last time he walked through this office he had stashed the cute little bird in the ceiling above a desk. He remembered the specific cubicle because of the water-stained panel above and the framed photograph of a woman with windswept hair. She was on a beach and she looked directly at the unknown photographer. The image was stunning. What compelled a man or a woman to leave such a vision behind? Why was the upkeep of this room so important? What could be understood by a photograph of this beauty left unseen? Janzen jumped up on the desk and pushed through the ceiling panel and felt around for the toy. It wasn't there. He jumped down and walked toward the one corner of the office where he'd originally found it.

When he rounded the corner, there it was – right where he had first found it – resting atop the rim of an employee's UMBC coffee cup. What kind of game was this? The toy's location struck in Janzen nervous, dissonant energies. Someone was indeed watching him; someone was watching everyone.

He grabbed it from the cup and tossed it in the air, but it was before it came back to his palm that he knew a clue was forthcoming. The black of the writing on the underside of the penguin was hidden when it rested on the mug. Janzen read the message:

I knew myself
no longer.

The message was a speck of fly shit in his

understanding's rémoulade. He'd never taste it, but he knew it was there. There was no sense ditching the dish for such an innocuous offense, so his spirits were somewhat encouraged by the ink's obscurity. He held onto the toy because the little thing needed to travel outside this office to test the watcher's range. He held it high above his head and twirled around for anyone to see before he stowed it in his flannel's deep front pocket and strode out.

13

"I want you to come find my cancer."

Janzen was unsure how to respond when Leonard had made that request about an hour earlier. He was still uncertain what was to come after he took the capsule given to him by Leonard, which he said contained properties of psilocybin and lysergic acid. He assured Janzen that Doc concocted such a controlled and precise amount that they would be back to where they started – Leonard's room, of course – in a matter of hours.

About 45 minutes following ingestion, Janzen's jaw loosened and he spoke warmly about his previous trips in dorm rooms and on rooftop decks. Even the first few hours of the DTs expanded his consciousness before everything came crashing down.

Leonard's room began to drip, and the Animal Collective Janzen recommended for their music was a hit. Even with a clear head, the band's psychedelic sound and reverberating lyrics were a pleasant escape. Leonard shook out his neck and no longer held his one arm across his midsection. He leaned back and laid his head between two pillows.

Janzen stood and moved with the music and was able to emit fluttering arcs of color from his smooth and active arms, which splashed against Leonard's walls and did so in time with the music once Janzen figured out how to control their speed.

With his new power, he chose what became enclosed in quivering concentric circles. Leonard smiled and Janzen sent a string of what had now become bubbles in his direction, each one moving at an easy pace and changing its translucent colors along the journey. Leonard lured them in and washed his body with them until they popped along with a drum snare or a hi-hat into something soothing and mild.

Leonard thanked Janzen and then held his hands to his chest so he might take in their power. Janzen, too, held one hand to his chest and everything that flowed from his fingertips hit the bloodstream and the fibers of his muscles and filled him with such pleasure and gratitude. Leonard tried to send his own waves, but his hands offered none of the potency of Janzen's. The sick man jerked both his hands with so much energy, but only limp streams of gray lurched from his palms. He wiped the dull color off his pants before it permeated the material and then shook both hands out in front of him until the gray finally exited his system. The pool of discharge disappeared, and before either could dwell on the spectacle, Janzen sent a burst of color across the room with the flick of his middle finger that hit Leonard right on the forehead. Both lost themselves in laughter at Janzen's aim and Leonard's surprise.

Janzen rolled on the floor, which moved beneath him and he swished the constellations hovering out in front of him. He asked Leonard what shape his cancer would take and Leonard responded that they would both know it when it came. "It's not far from us now."

Janzen remained on his back and continued to manipulate the heavens above him. If he closed his eyes, he was able to rush through some of the closer galaxies but he wanted to stay close enough to Leonard in case the cancer made an appearance. He opened his eyes back up, and everything that he flicked out in front of him began to swirl. He tried to reverse its course but found he no longer had control over any of it. The stars and planets and galaxies merged into something brighter and brighter until everything swirled faster and faster in the space between them.

He leaned to the side to see if Leonard saw the same heavenly light before him, and it was clear that he did. He nodded at Janzen and now it was he who did the conducting. Leonard's finger moved in circles until the brilliant ball of light was something solid. He held out his hand, and it stopped spinning but still pulsated with its radiance.

Janzen instinctively reached out his hand but stopped himself. Leonard wordlessly urged him to touch it. He sensed its warmth in front of him and reached out again and felt a toy from his childhood – the one with hundreds of silver pins that allowed him to press his face or his hand into their prickly mold to capture a 3D image. Janzen wiggled his fingers and what was around them bounced off his fingertips until they settled back against his skin if he held them steadily enough. He turned away and placed his hand to his chest, and everything flowed directly into him. He shook his head in awe and disbelief. He pounded his heart for Leonard to acknowledge the man's generosity. Leonard understood and nodded back at Janzen.

Leonard then drew in the orb until he was able to wrap both his arms around it. He positioned his body over it like a child would a beach ball in a pool. It lifted him slightly off his bed before disappearing in his embrace. The light within him twinkled at first, but it quickly gained power and Leonard's body began to glow. He shined so brightly that Janzen was forced to hold his hand in front of his face before he moved farther away in the skies where he found a cloud that diminished the power of Leonard's light. He found peace on the cloud and knew he was close enough to Leonard if the light became too much for him to bear, but everything was fine.

Janzen floated up there and when he sat up, Leonard was off his bed looking for a pair of shorts in case they came across a sparkling body of water in which they could swim. They heard only the rushing of the river but couldn't find its source before the sounds and colors and bubbles disappeared. The room eventually occupied its normal place and held its normal shapes, but their trip provided for Janzen some tranquility in knowing that his friend wanted to share such an experience with him.

The weeks before he met this cancer, Janzen was having a harder and harder time maintaining his con-vivial spirit around Leonard, whose own humor and weight was sinking and shrinking at a steady rate. There were still good days; in fact, this one had to go down as the best, but through it all, Leonard never complained. He only struggled. He was one tough man, and Janzen appreciated that about him.

If they had been boyhood friends, they would share recollections of ding-dong ditching, ghosts in the graveyard and backyard sleepovers, but as it was, the increasing cough that Leonard attributed to the high-grade marijuana rang of something much more alarming.

When Janzen wrote later that evening, the words were colored in preoccupied ink. Between blocks of paragraphs, he wrote in italics, slanted in the subconscious of his narration. The story that he had started during that first week in the building had changed so much over the months. It was now both everything and nothing he set out to compose. He was pulled to letters and words across the keyboard by Samuel and his elevator, by Leonard and his sickness and by Mr. Selby and his disappearance. The words came to him because of Amber's degradation and through Monroe's kindness and Daryl's heart and affliction. He wrote because of the tube that extended down from a floor above through his ceiling panel. And that night – much later that night – when he exceeded word six hundred, another marble dropped down into the cage and indicated a time twenty minutes from then.

Six hundred words were plenty. A bit of sex did a body and mind some good. The elevator never ran at this hour, but lately Janzen had been taking to the stairs almost exclusively. He was still troubled by Samuel and his presence in the building. The close space he shared with the fat man that was once authenticated with a feeling of brotherhood was now relegated to a deferential distance. He wasn't sure what he had to say. He wasn't sure if it was his place to say anything. Janzen understood the panic of losing one's job. The recessions had hit so many people hard and guaranteed them years of dependence. It led to years of deferring debts and bedrooms in basements, and so Samuel held close to what was his on a life raft in the middle of Death Valley.

Now was not the time to worry about him; around corners, his pecker pointed straightaway to impending pleasure. He popped out from the stairwell and ran his finger along the wall, blazing chipper zigs and zags on his hop and a skip upstairs. He had learned to love the sound of that metallic rattle in the birdcage.

When he walked into the main unused office that led to the split room, he already heard the grunting and moaning from the monitor and its movie. He smelled something odd – something chemical – and it derailed his mind until he absorbed every pound of that heavy weight plowing straight through him from behind. Even before he was smashed to the ground, the laced towel wrapped around his head dispatched him into unconsciousness.

When he came back around, he first noticed the ligature tied tightly around his wrists. He felt nothing below his waist. Where was his sight? His eyelids were dull, and he could barely lift them. His vision returned in blinks, and he was in the right room. He still heard the grunting. With his sight came a sickness. He wanted to vomit. There was the video. It was sideways; no, he was sideways, lying on a shoulder and hip. He saw the light of the monitor and focused on it to steady his sight. But that grunting – the audio of it was off. Why weren't things matching up? He saw the fucking and the mouth of the man on the monitor, but it didn't sync up to what he heard. The smell of whatever enveloped him lingered, and he tasted it in his mouth. He hit his head against the padded floor and waited for an audible delay of sound that would explain his confusion, but when his head hit the flooring and was once again lifted from it, the action came with the properly timed sounds.

He pushed himself against the wall and willed his head up, but that movement sent waves of nausea deep in his gut. He had to gnash his teeth tightly to keep his stomach. He steadied the dizziness in his head and saw the silhouette of the man. Janzen was unsure of what he was seeing. What was that man wearing?

The scene on the monitor changed and in the new light, Janzen saw that the man at the hole in the wall was completely naked except for something over his head. He was thin but his body arched with the flex of his muscles. He saw their flex as the man penetrated in and out. He could hear the effort of the man's fucking.

Janzen's mind worked in spurts, and he wanted the man away from the hole – away from Helena. He inhaled the dank air of the room in an effort to yell out, but the act left his throat scalded in pain. His dragging mouth worked to form the W of his *What the fuck*, but upon the first quiver of his vocal cords, a sensation of such agony combusted in his throat with a searing heat. His body shook with pain, but his silence soon quelled the suffering. An agitation in his throat forced him to stifle a cough but even that brought back the horrible sensation.

The man thrust in and out, but the covered head turned slowly towards Janzen. It moved as if triggered by remote control. The mask he wore was transparent enough to see through, but the fitting of it was so tight that it pulled his skin in strange directions and distorted everything under its pressure. There were drilled circles for eyes and Janzen saw through the holes to the glinting inside. The mouth had a similar hole, but only the far edges of his mouth were visible behind what looked like a filter. The man saw that he was being watched and the edges of his lips rose on each side, the mask compressing his grin into an expression of lunacy.

The head's focus moved methodically away from Janzen and fell back toward the spine. It faced the ceiling as his body spasmed with its climax. The man clutched at Helena's legs. He finished and his head hung down toward his chest. He positioned his two hands against the wall in front of him. The half-body that he was fucking disappeared through the hole and the rubber flap replaced the gap, concealing the view through to the other side.

Janzen kicked at the man, but his feet were also bound, and the throbbing grew stronger by the second. The mask looked back at him, and Janzen fought through the sickness to take it all in. If he survived this, he wanted to remember this image.

The man pushed away from the wall and stood over Janzen with trails of his effort running down his chest, midriff, thighs and shins. He closed his wide stance so that his heels were pressed together and raised his arms to the sides, holding his ten fingers out so they shook with the strain. He stood above Janzen, fed by something powerful. He removed the condom and gauged the weight of its contents. He shook it for Janzen. He shook it again closer to his face before he tied the open end in a knot. He walked toward the door where he had stashed his clothes and a duffel bag. He turned away from Janzen and dug through the contents of the bag. He returned to Janzen and held something behind his back. Janzen made to yell again when he caught a glimpse of a doused towel but was hit instantaneously with the heat of his tormented throat. The man held the towel over Janzen's face until there was no more mask, no more anything.

Once aware again, Janzen trudged through the snow in the bowels of a Kurosawa dream. With each step, he pushed a foot through the new blanket, and his weight would break through a bottom layer of crust that had frozen over days earlier. The whiteness around and beneath him was somehow familiar, but the driving snow in his face made it difficult to see. The wind through the Western hemlocks and Sitka spruces whistled desolate strains throughout the white wilderness. He heard only the crunch of his progress when the wind died down.

There was no sign of anyone. The only evidence of man was the tracks he left and the clothes and supplies on his back. His beard had grown long having tended this trapline for as long as he could remember. His warm exhales froze the whiskers around his mouth and muzzled his ability to speak. It was no matter – the jagged and powdered land absorbed every sound for its sustenance during this bleak season.

He stopped and unclasped the top of his pack stuffed half-full of marten and ermine. He wondered how much they'd go for and if he knew how to process their hides. He wrestled his arms through the straps and tried wiping away the ice from his mouth, but as soon as he cleared his beard free, crystals froze again with his next exhale.

The sting of the cold on his face was superseded by the fullness of his bladder. How had he not noticed that before? There must be better cover from the wind at his next set, but he needed to alleviate the pressure now. He unbuttoned his parka and pulled down his layers. The relief was instantaneous. His relaxed head found the racing clouds above him, but the falling urine began to clink against the frozen yellow of the snow. The fluid crystallized more and more quickly from its source. He couldn't stop the flow, which was now freezing as soon as it hit air. He yelled an absent yell and fell back into the snow to stop the freezing pain now inside him. He yanked at his pants and hiked them back to his waist. He lay in the snow until his shivering forced him to move.

Currents of hidden water made walking the river too dangerous, so he veered from its path and fought the overgrown game trails littered with fallen boughs. He trekked through the bush until a coniferous wall surrounded him and his footsteps crunched louder now they were enclosed. He didn't see any arc of the sun when he was out by the river, so night must be coming soon. He would follow the remainder of his line and hopefully be back at his camp before nighttime took over.

The next few sets were for bigger game. A lynx or

wolverine pelt in good condition fetched a pretty price. He fingered the knife at his side. If there was something over forty or fifty pounds, he would build a fire and process the animal right there. He must have miles to go until his camp, and the full weight of it would slow him down. He'd leave the gut pile and any organs he couldn't stomach for the scavengers.

How long had he been out here in the backwoods? He remembered the note in his pocket, checked it, but was unable to read it. He would try again later. The handwriting kept shifting places but the script was familiar – from a woman – from her.

He stowed the letter back in his pocket and then heard something in the distance. He lifted his hat above his ears to better hear what it was. The wind through the needled trees allowed only broken sounds of something up ahead, but Janzen knew it was where he had placed his next set. He'd heard that sound before.

It was a cry, one of distress. He had caught something. He moved at a steady pace and gauged the wind's direction by the snow falling from the trees. With his urine on his pants and fur in the pack, he gave off quite a scent so his approach required some deftness. It wasn't uncommon for an animal to pull loose from the bite of the metal only to charge the approaching trapper. He even heard of some that had gnawed off their paws to free themselves. He threw some of the newer powder into the air but it twisted and flew off in every direction. He had never seen that before. It wasn't a terrible problem if the animal caught his scent so long as the set held. He listened again for the cries but was unsure of what he trapped. The bait was set in such a way to ensure the animal's neck would be snapped instantly, but whatever was caught in its grip must've come upon it accidently, its paw likely snapped up between the metal teeth.

In between his next steps, he no longer heard the cries. It was possible that the animal had bled out or gone into shock depending on how long it struggled. Out in the isolation of the wild, Janzen experienced no remorse for taking a life. Back in civilization, he wouldn't wear the hide of his catch or revel in the details of his hunt to anyone. Back among people, he agonized over the cruelty of his prey's death. He read somewhere that it might take hours for animals to die in the traps he used, but out here, there was no judge.

He recognized the copse of yellow cedars and knew the fur was close. He was a fool not to wear any snowshoes through this terrain. His thighs burned with the effort, and the animal in this trap ensured calories, warmth and strength.

He veered off the trail and slowed his progress. He planned to come in at an angle behind a cluster of alders he knew to be about a hundred feet ahead. He loved this part. The anticipation was a ritual. It had the strength of an addict's flame, spoon and needle. The beating in his chest replaced the sound of his footfalls. He navigated through the dwarf birch and over the hidden reedgrass. The alders were within sight.

He found cover behind some willows and looked for his set. Through the stubborn growth poking up from the snow blanket, he saw it: a wolf. Its hindquarters faced him, so it was impossible to see how the trap caught it, but it was big – a healthy wolf. Its coat was thick over the muscles of its hind legs. Janzen waited a few minutes before approaching. He ran a thumb along his knife's bolster and looked around for a fallen limb that he might use to throttle the animal if there was still life left in it. He found nothing long and thick enough to do the job. He decided that this wolf deserved the dignity of his knife.

He worked his way through the thicket. He waited for a reaction but saw none. Once he cleared the brush and stood within thirty feet of the animal, he stopped, the snow thigh high; however, it wasn't the depth of what he stood in that halted his advance. Were the hackles on the wolf's neck now bristling? Or was that the work of the wind standing those hairs erect? What was that foreign bump off its head? The blow of the wind parted the fur on the wolf's haunches, but about its scruff, the hairs still stood skyward.

The wolf pushed up onto its hind legs and growled low and angrily. When it lifted its body to its full height, Janzen realized it was a male because of its huge frame and that the foreign bump was a young pup, caught in the trap's grasp. The elder wolf was comforting it during its fading gasps for breath. Janzen unsheathed his knife, and the animal turned to face him. Its four legs shook with ferocity, and it lowered its head and flattened its ears.

Janzen took a slow step back to brace for a fight. He brandished his knife and swung it wildly. The wolf bared its canines and advanced steadily towards its prey. Janzen wiped away the ice from his mouth, but it kept freezing over. Given his normal power of speech, he would've raised a ruckus to scare off the animal; instead, this confrontation would deal only in grunts and blood. Inside, he was wailing in noises familiar to both man and beast.

The newest layer of snow coiled unnaturally between the two. The same wind that lifted the crystals into perfect cyclones bullied the tops of trees, which thwacked about like sails amid a tempest. The force threatened the trees themselves, and the pops of straining trunks blasted around them.

Janzen took a knee and the gales stopped. Everything hushed. He found the grip he wanted on the knife. The tremor in the wolf's legs stopped. It lowered its haunches and charged straight ahead, cutting a path through the snow. Janzen waited until the full impact of the animal crashed into him.

The collision knocked Janzen into a tree with the back of his head absorbing the shock. His senses were confused until he finally found his voice. Were his eyes the first target for the animal? He swiped at the wolf in his blindness with his hand smashing into something. His knife was lost. He brandished only his fists. Both the cold and the wind were gone. He trembled and pushed himself up against the tree. Had the wolf bitten his arms first? Both of his wrists were on fire. The ground beneath him was neither covered in snow nor ice. Gone were his gloves, too. In his confusion, an intense heat burned him from the inside out. Had he finally found his voice or was that someone else yelling at him?

When Samuel finally opened the door to a cleaning supply room, Janzen was pressed hard against the corner of the space with the carnage of his battle spread out before him. The big man helped his friend from the corner. Janzen didn't understand why Samuel was with him and why he was in this small, dark room. The ligature around his wrists no longer held his arms behind his back, but the tightness of them was unbearable. Samuel lifted him into the elevator and held him to his hip. They took the ride down to Janzen's floor without speaking.

As they struggled out of the elevator and down the hallway, Janzen held close to Samuel because his feet were still tied together. Samuel lugged him through his doorway and onto his bed before cutting the bindings from his wrists and ankles with a pocketknife. He took off Janzen's soaked shirt and covered him with the cool sheet. When Samuel left the room, the memories of the masked man spread thickly back into Janzen's consciousness. Sleep came to him only because his body gave out.

The next day, Samuel brought Janzen his lunch and dinner. Janzen was able to speak once again, but he had nothing to say. Janzen thanked Samuel for the food and asked if he would also bring Leonard his meals. Samuel arranged Janzen's cutlery and cleaned up the room, but not much could be done for the desecrated man.

He sank even lower while sitting at his desk when Helena called him by name on the other side of his door a day or so later. The knock she offered was delicate, a sign of tenderness he had wanted from her all along, but he didn't respond to her call. He didn't respond to her because of what it meant to see her face. It meant making a decision and probably his evasion. He needed to eliminate the chance of another marble dropping into the brass enclosure. What could she possibly gain with the knowledge of that night?

Days passed and Janzen began pacing the length of his room. He pissed in water bottles, and his penance of self-loathing for failing Helena bubbled into something much different – something familiar. An old friend had come back to him. It coursed through his body, and he had to tire himself with squats and pushups to keep it at bay. One thing was certain: he was going to get that man. He was going to find him and kill him – brutally.

14

Janzen was a maniac the second he left his room. "COME ON!" he screamed. "FUCKING COME ON!" It was a challenge. He wore no shirt, and though he hadn't planned on stepping out of his room, there he was. The instinct that had led him down so many dark paths took over. He had no real plan, but who needed direction when you were filled with such bile? He put himself behind the mask and marched a psychopathic trail throughout the building. He dangled himself out there and waited for the man to show himself.

It was a course that confused some of his fellow residents. Janzen provided no explanation for his pacing or for that deranged look on his face. He scoured the eyes of every white male resident for hints of the hidden threat. Each responded with different degrees of fear, a witness to a new wildness from their newest resident.

After an hour, he came up empty, and Janzen punched whatever concrete wall was in front of him until it was stained red and his knuckles were on fire. He needed a plan, and Scoop might present a solution. Janzen recollected the snippets of conversation between them when he had installed the tube in his room weeks earlier. He remembered the cameras that Scoop was given to protect his stash, which was the reason he now approached his room. He pounded at his door and then did his best to wipe it clean of the blood before it opened.

Janzen pushed his way in the room and bombarded Scoop with a string of questions about cameras: How many could he get? Was Selby still okaying purchases? Could the cameras be hidden? Could they be viewed live on monitors? Did he have any monitors? What was that smell?

The beauty of Scoop and his particular Baltimore rearing ensured that he was accustomed to different types of chaos, so the sight of an angry white boy busting into his room wearing only a pair of cut off shorts and shouting a string of suspicious questions led to only one question from him: "You wanna try dis stuff?"

The smell that had struck Janzen as pungent was the fermenting mash Scoop was preparing for his moonshine. Without a thought, he drank deeply from the Mason jar, and his body shook from the liquor's proof. Scoop was already dragging him by the forearm to where he had his security base station installed with multiple monitors transmitting the different shots his cameras were currently recording.

Scoop's time in Jessup inhibited him from asking any incriminating questions, though he was most alive when a part of any hustle. Janzen asked Scoop to redistribute some of his cameras to the main corridors of each level, including an extra one on the eighth floor hallway covering the doorway that led to the room of Helena's and his assault. Scoop required no explanations, but in exchange for his help with the cameras, he requested that Janzen speak to Mr. Atis about ordering a few sheets of rolled copper. Janzen assured Scoop he'd make it work, Janzen left him shouting from his room about the specifics of the materials he needed for a new still. "Yup, yup. Got it." His voice was cut off from the closing of the stairwell door. Time to check if she was around.

When he saw that her studio door was open and heard the music playing inside, he knew then that further action was necessary before he revealed what happened. He wanted to see her, though. In the moment, he wanted to tell her, but bringing her the truth was not yet an option. Tales of immediate ruination had been written with much fainter ink. He needed a proper ending to such a story, one punctuated by the final period following the retribution for the masked man's evil.

He walked back up a floor to the office full of cubicles. His plan was to wait. He was done playing games. He lowered himself to the floor, exhilarated and exhausted at once. The liquor swam in his head and dulled his edge. An hour or two passed. The familiar ping of the elevator rang and Samuel exited with a bucket full of cleaning supplies. Janzen had no idea what time it was.

"Why are you sitting on the floor?"

"Why did you tell me I should visit this floor if I wanted to understand this place?" asked Janzen. Samuel sat down next to him in his elephantine way. "What are you cleaning?"

Samuel exhaled and pushed the bucket out of his way

so that he could extend his feet out in front of him. "Mr. Selby usually cleans it, but he hasn't since Mr. Berger's death, so I'll do it for him.

"Why does he do it?"

"I have my theories. Why are some stations cleaned out while others could've been used just yesterday? It's a place he used to love. I think he always thought he would reopen this place. He still might, I hope. But he can't now."

Unlike the other residents, Samuel wasn't halfway buried with an impending date to step off the building's ledge. He came in through the front door and had simply never left. He was a kind man. He was there to help Janzen with his closeted nightmare, having saved him from the attacking wolf.

"Samuel, are we friends?"

"Well, yes."

"Okay. Good," said Janzen, who tried smoothing out the wrinkles of his cutoffs. "Samuel, I'm worried about you."

"Janzen, please."

"I'm worried about your health. I think you and I should do something – to help us both. I want to know if you'll ride with me."

"To where?"

"Just here. You and me. Every day. On the bike."

"I have a job to do here."

"Let me worry about that," said Janzen while Samuel pulled in his legs to get to his feet. "Are you with me, man? There's no trouble for you. Let's move!" A gloss of moisture began to wet the big man's brow. "You with me?"

"Okay."

"Damn right it's okay!"

"You been drinking?"

"I think I might, Samuel. Call it the final tour. Like Elton John." Janzen patted Samuel's hand. "Thank you for helping me the other day. You're no Svengali. We start soon." Janzen jumped up and helped his friend to his feet. "You'll need some shorts. I'll get Monroe on that."

That poor Samuel would require a pair of sturdy bicycling shorts made with flame retardant fabric considering the impending friction. Early Neanderthals had created embers with less. Janzen was slightly sentimental because of the liquor and thought that Samuel was true-blue – the best out there. If Samuel was genuine, it was Scoop who was resourceful, and Janzen figured he should head back to see him and take another quaff before his next move. Back to Scoop. No, Monroe. Scoop first, then Monroe.

The next three days passed in an expected fashion. Before Janzen would drink himself into a heap, he fired around the building in constant motion. He secured the order of copper for Scoop after a furtive agreement with Mr. Atis, who agreed to place the order if Janzen attempted to contact Mr. Selby. The proprietor of the building was allegedly stowed away in his office and had been accepting whatever food Mr. Atis could slip underneath the door.

As opposed to a judicious approach, Janzen pounded on the heavy oaken doors that separated Mr. Atis from the one he missed so desperately. He cursed the old man for his absence and left blots of blood where he had opened wounds on his fists. Mr. Atis rolled close to the double doors and waited for a response that never came.

"Come out here you fucker!" hollered Janzen in his drunkenness. "Is there a way to see below, Mr. Atis? Can we take a look outside?" The idea that the mission had transitioned from one of rescue to one of recovery must not have crossed Mr. Atis's mind, and a plague of silent desperation descended upon him.

"He's in there. He'll be out," said Mr. Atis, now in a panic. "I'll have Mr. Scoop check the pavement below right away."

Janzen assured him that Mr. Selby was just stubborn and he'd be out soon enough. "But I need something else from you, Mr. Atis. I need your set of keys to the elevator for tonight. I told Samuel I would help him." The need for any further explanation had passed weeks ago, with Mr. Atis's sole responsibility having shifted to Mr. Selby's well being. He removed a chain with the keys from around his neck and remained at the door as Janzen exited the room.

Janzen stopped back in to see Scoop for some liquor and came by a lightweight remote controlled generator, which ran on a rechargeable battery. He gulped and resurrected an old conspirator that served more as a shot caller than an accomplice. He was flying high, and the rate at which he moved bounced the keys on the chain against his chest. There were two keys: one to operate the elevator and another that opened – or locked – everything else.

Minutes later, he opened the door to the makeshift

pharmacy and the scent of marijuana rushed him with the same robust power of the McCormick spice factory in Hunt Valley. He entered through a series of doors and located an inner grow room with thriving plants bathed under the blueness of the halide bulbs. Beds of plants were raised off the ground, and the floor below them was sealed and coated with a watertight substance. There were sprinklers hung from the ceiling, and a drainage system had been installed below. In the corner of the room was the computerized nerve center of the operation, which monitored everything from temperature to humidity.

He wanted to see Leonard again, that old crank, and tell him about the wonders of his weed's origin. The blue from the bulbs along with their oddly peaceful hum held Janzen in the room, but the little bottle in the first room marked *MDMA* bewitched him back into its orbit. Were those the same little pills he was given, how long ago, by Mr. Atis in the room with the mics and visions and streams and skies when Helena had come over and sat down right next to him? She had given him her drink, and they had kicked at each other's feet. Janzen popped two of the pills and chewed them into pulp before he pocketed a wider variety from the pharmaceutical buffet in front of him.

Things went a tad hazy soon thereafter.

Janzen guessed it was the middle of the night, so Samuel was stowed away somewhere in the building. Hours passed like minutes, and Janzen climbed through the elevator's ceiling panel and installed the generator – really more of an oversized battery – to a bracket crossing above the carriage. He taped the remote starter to one of the paneled interior walls so that he could start it while underneath the power source. Scoop had loaned him some stingers and they reached the tail end of each of the exercise bicycles he had moved into the elevator. With a push of a button, the world's prettiest roads were now accessible for Samuel to enjoy. Overhanging branches with falling leaves, desolate stretches through the Badlands, or maybe a familiar neighborhood all awaited the big man. Janzen swapped out the seat to give Samuel's backside additional support, but the setup worked.

He crashed when he brought down more weed to Leonard. Time moved forward in flashes until his body collapsed. When he awoke in Leonard's room, he was unsure how long he had been out. One of Leonard's blankets twisted around his body with sections of it damp from the sleep he wrestled through. His scorched head and his empty stomach doubled him over. Did he eat yesterday? Or was it the day before? He sucked deeply from Leonard's vaporizer to lure out his appetite.

Leonard forced him to eat before he left. The hit from the vaporizer quelled the nausea, but inside his head was a kiln-hot katzenjammer that was cured with the same potion that caused it. He found the stashed Mason jar in his room. He found more capsules in his pocket and choked back two more for good measure. He'd see where some chem to the head led him.

When the elevator doors opened, Samuel stood dead center – right in between the two exercise bikes. The way he held his arms tightly alongside his wide frame maximized the equidistance between both machines. Janzen stifled a laugh and punched a series of uppercuts to keep his hands from shaking. The amphets he took had found receptive receptors, and he was functionally high enough.

Monroe had left three pairs of cushion-lined spandex shorts outside Janzen's room. They were triple-stitched and made of enough material for a quilt. Samuel regarded Janzen in his current state like little Timmy confronted by a frothed and feral Lassie. But that Samuel, he was true to his word. After ascending away in the elevator to change, he reappeared in workout gear stretched so tight he could've been played as a snare drum. Janzen hopped on his bike and tested the limits of his body's endurance.

Samuel found pleasure in the comfort of the seat and the different settings he could fiddle with on the screen. He found that he could adjust just about anything on the bike and burned more calories elevating and then lowering the seat than he did pedaling. Janzen rode with his arms in tight and his forehead down on his forearms. He licked what bubbled up from his arms in the off chance any chemicals were carried from the body in his perspiration. With the strength still in his legs and the drugs in his system, Janzen settled into a steady trance. He broke from his spell when Samuel asked if he had ever seen *Breaking Away*. "You maniac! Of course, you fucking Cutter!"

Samuel laughed, and Janzen talked about that quarry in the movie and then the Tour de France and the different stages and how the spectators would crowd around the breakaway riders as they climbed through the mountain stages. He spoke through quick breaths about the sport's dirty history of doping and cheating but how at its core, it's really something beautiful. "It's just a man powering a machine." It was hard not to learn something about yourself when the bike's capacity for remaining upright depended directly on that power. Eventually, for those with a certain mind, the clicking in of the shoes to the pedal cleats implied an agreement to go until you could go no more. On a bike, Janzen learned as much about courage and grit bombing a hill at 45 miles an hour than he did climbing up that same hill at a fraction of that speed. He loved the torture of it and wanted Samuel to find something in it, too. For now, though, the hefty fellow would need a period of acclimation.

Janzen tugged the drenched shirt from off him and wiped up what he could from the puddle on the elevator floor. He left Samuel happy to be sitting and fidgeting with new buttons. He'd take another glug of diesel fuel and see what came of some work on the word processor. The writing was slow going and god awful, but he maintained his agreement and word count with Mr. Selby. He continually slid the pages under the unseen man's doorway.

Back in his room, he smashed the birdcage at the end of the tubing and then tore all the plastic down from the ceiling. He needed to be sure there would be no more marbles coming his way. He later tracked the plastic's journey and ripped it down, too. He took all of it down.

When he finished what was left in the Mason jar, he headed back to Scoop's room to find his doorway open a crack. Janzen still knocked, having gone through amorous periods of solitude so intense that he assumed all doors led to chronic masturbators and madmen. His knock went unanswered, but he heard movement on the other side so he stepped through the doorway to find the place a wreck.

He passed through scattered piles of Scoop's stashes and found him motionless and unresponsive on his tiled floor, streaked in a crimson struggle. He still had the pallor of someone with life in him, and a trail of blood fell from a split on his forehead, swollen and purple in the light.

The smell of burning plastic caught Janzen's attention, and he rushed to the smoke rising from behind a line of shelves. Even in his state, his investigative instincts collected dots. He left Scoop on the floor and ran off to find the security base station in a smoldering pile of rubble. There were gashes in the monitors likely made by an axe or hatchet. Most of the smoke came from a flaming computer cord still plugged into its socket. Janzen tugged it free and rifled around for something close to smother the heat. He found a full glass of clear liquid and stopped himself before he poured it over the mess. He took a gulp from the glass and nearly lost his balance from the liquor's power. It burned his throat and pierced his gut. The container was probably used to collect the moonshine's foreshot, which would've contained a high enough concentration of methanol to sucker punch a donkey. Instead, he found a canvas tarp and beat out the flame and unplugged all other hazards. He stemmed any other threats of a conflagration and wondered what the monitors that lay in waste before him had captured.

Scoop would know what to do.

Scoop was leaning against one of the shelves but his head fell forward in a drunkard's pose of respite. His shirt stuck curiously to his chest, and there were spots of darkened fabric from the wetness. Janzen lifted his shirt and discovered the source of the seeping. His trunk was awash in red. Some of the gashes gaped, and Janzen was forced to look away. Blood covered Scoop's entire torso.

Janzen dragged the short but heavy man to his bed in the corner of the room. Scoop stirred and initially fought Janzen's help. The singular rumble of his first groan caused Scoop to hold his neck as if it was about to explode. In his confusion, he tried speaking again, and the pain sent him barreling off the side of the bed. Janzen yelled at Scoop, "Shut up! Shut the fuck up man!" and Scoop revealed a different man in his fright. Both Scoop's hands were on his throat, and Janzen held his own palm over the man's mouth to ensure no sound crept out. He kept telling him to shut up and that he was safe and not to talk. Janzen remembered the same shocking pain when he tried to call out to Helena while the mask fucked her. He told Scoop that he should breathe through his nose because that was what dulled the pain for him.

"Look at me, man. Just keep looking at me." He didn't want Scoop to see the swelling blots of blood on his shirt. "You're going to be okay. Just don't say anything. You'll talk to me later, but right now just calm down." Scoop nodded and removed his hands from his throat and fingered the welt on his forehead. He felt another lump on the back of his head before he noticed the stinging from his midsection. Janzen held Scoop by both wrists, preventing him from exposing his chest. He told him not to panic but it was too late. When Scoop bared his body, both saw that some of the wounds required stitching.

At first, the smearing of the blood scrambled the message. Janzen grabbed a towel from nearby and wet it with a bottle of water. Scoop retched in his growing panic and shook his head from side to side to avoid what was becoming legible. Janzen cleaned his chest enough so that he could decipher what was written. Etched into Scoop's body were the words: *You next*.

15

"A few years after the Arab Spring started really heating up, there were experiments with different types of chemical warfare." Doc sat at the end of Scoop's bed. He was a man of about fifty with a full head of silver hair and a freshly shaved face. He wore the plain clothes of someone on a walk on a New England fall day. As far as Janzen knew, Doc and Leonard were the only two residents who never made appearances at the morning and afternoon sessions, so this was the first time Janzen had spoken to him. He'd seen him in the commissary before but only on occasion. The former dentist had allegedly become so engrossed in his grow room and pharmaceutical experiments, that he was better served concocting medications and cures the FDA would never approve.

Janzen paced back and forth while keeping a vigil over the sedated and resting Scoop, stowed away deep underneath his covers. "I've read about compounds that paralyze the vocal chords, and it was rumored that the Muslim Brotherhood had used it in Cairo. Assad was also said to use it when the protests got really wild after it was found he was poisoning his own people with the chlorine."

"What would it be used for?" asked Janzen.

"That's a good question. I imagine that when it was first developed – it was probably an accidental discovery – that someone in power thought it could be used to silence protesters. It had to be frightening to feel that type of sensation when you wanted to speak. It's supposed to be really painful, but imagine the effects wear off and everyone is still there in Tahrir Square or wherever and they release it a second time. This time, the people don't speak, but they don't go anywhere either. Imagine that goddamned scene – the power and unity of that silence. It had to be a real trip – might've ended up working against those who released it, but I can see how someone would want to use something like that on a whole different level," continued Doc. "Think about robberies, home invasions, rape, you name it. It's horrifying."

"Where do you get it?"

"The internet – some offshoot of the Silk Road. If one shuts down, another pops up. It's the way the world works. It can be difficult to trace those sites. Others probably made it in basements with commercial cleaners. The world is a mess, young man, but I guess it's always been that way." Doc had a forlorn way of speaking. He almost ran out of steam at the end of his sentences. Had his paragraphs run a mile, they'd cross the finish line on hands and knees.

"Is Scoop okay?"

"Yes. He should be speaking again when he comes to. I'll see after him about changing those bandages. Some of his hooch will probably take the edge off. He just needs to take it easy. Will you make sure he gets these meds?" Doc shook a bottle full of pills.

"What are they?"

"They'll manage the pain."

"Opiates?" asked Janzen. Doc nodded and Janzen grew visibly uncomfortable with this responsibility. "Don't give them to me. Scoop needs them."

Doc understood the power of those pills. "I can respect that."

"I plan on getting clean again, Doc. And what do you say we keep this whole thing between us. You read the message. He's coming after me next. I plan on taking care of this on my own. You got some type of protection for yourself up there?"

"I have the only locked door in the place."

"You and Selby. I'll speak to everyone at breakfast about sticking together from now on. Everyone's been alone too long. I'll tell them it's a preventative measure," said Janzen. Doc wished him luck and left him to tend to Scoop.

The thought of the upcoming confrontation sent tiny charges to his fingertips. He held out his shaking hands. He was excited at their movement because he knew it stemmed from neither detoxification nor fear. No, the tremble was more akin to a hunter's shake before the squeeze of the trigger.

He held a half-filled jar in his hands and took his last gulp of the liquor – that final kiss goodbye with a disinterested lover. He let it sit in his mouth and trickle down his throat so that it burned real nice. He had thought a life without the liquor meant a life without romance or music, but that wasn't true. There was still romance, and the music sounded just as good. And soon enough he was going to find out if that old fiery friend of his was still present in his sobriety – that transformative anger.

From his spot at the end of Scoop's bed, he saw a spilled set of billiard balls on the floor, which had probably been knocked about in Scoop's earlier struggle. Janzen picked up the cue ball and wiped it clean. He scouted around the room until he found a marker and continued to pace the room until he summoned the appropriate correspondence. He took his place back on Scoop's bed and decided to chum up the waters. On the ball, he wrote:

Find me
Find you
In Drool

He waited until Doc returned hours later with clean bandages for Scoop, who was still under the spell of the tranquilizers. Doc insisted that Janzen take a break from his watch. He lifted his shirt and showed Janzen the stun gun he intended to use for his protection. Months earlier, Mr. Selby had ordered Doc different models when they were first experimenting with the current TMS system. Janzen headed back to his room and placed the cue ball in the center of the hallway directly outside his door. He would have left his door ajar but decided against it for fear of a visit from Helena.

He sat at the word processor that night and wrote pages he'd never recall. When before he had written to race the sound of the marble down the plastic chute, he now clacked the keyboard to hush the piercing anticipation. He heard the shuffle of feet down the hallway and muffled sounds of conversation through his door. He heard the quick yet heavy footfalls of Kenneth, more than likely heading back to his room after a visit with Daryl.

An hour passed and he was back at the word processor; only now, he was without a shirt and his heart rate was up from his shadowboxing in the center of his room. Janzen had always been grateful for the boxing lessons his father had given him as a child. The tutorials seemed excessive at such a young age, but could it be that his father had anticipated the inevitable fistfights his son would eventually find himself in given his own foul temper? Even as an adult, special bumps against something hard reminded Janzen of the slaps on the back of his baby soft hands whenever he had left his thumbs tucked into his tiny fists.

The footsteps he expected came during the dead of the night. Janzen had already moved to his bed and was minutes away from giving up the wait when he heard the slow and deliberate steps. There was no attempt made to mute their passage. Janzen pushed himself up from his bed and knew the bedsprings would sound loudly enough to be heard from the outside.

Whoever was in the hallway was now standing directly on the other side of the door. He heard no more movement and wasn't sure who was there. Janzen stood facing the entry with each hand flexing in unison from five wide to a clench. Because his door was not outfitted with a lock, he rolled his neck in anticipation. He shook out his arms through a quick succession of punches, muffling none of the effort coming from his grunts. He saw no shadows through the sill of the door's framing, but whoever was on the other side was shifting his weight from one leather boot to the other. It was another thirty seconds – could've been longer – when the footsteps once again resumed and trailed off down the hallway from the same direction they had come. Janzen decided then that he would hunt from the cover of his room no more. He barely slept that night from a simmering that percolated from his inaction. In the morning, he would not find the cue ball outside his door.

Janzen brought Scoop a plate of food the next morning and found the man up and arranging the mess from the attack. He moved slowly on account of his injuries. He had retained his ability to speak, and his mood had stabilized to its normal level – that is he dwelled on none of the horror around him because he said, "What da fack good iss dat gonna do me anyways?" He had yet to wipe clean the blood-stained floor he worked to clear. A knife attached to the tool belt he wore hung from his side.

Janzen asked him if he had captured any of what happened to him on his cameras, and he responded that he might be able to access the video footage from one of the hard drives left undamaged. Scoop had yet to look at the video on the new monitor he had just installed in place of the previously destroyed station. The obvious cause of hesitation to see what was recorded was still carved into the man's chest. Spots of blood leaked through his shirt the more he organized his things.

"What do you remember?"

Scoop sat down in front of the screen and attached a

line from the hard drive to the monitor. "He came outta nowhere. I smelled somethin' first and it was stuck in my throat. It starned ta burn like fahr and then he was owun me." Scoop navigated his way to the footage as if playing a game of solitaire. He was that child who marveled at his own crooked and broken arm on the playground, where the same sight would've spun Janzen into a nauseous panic. Maybe it was Scoop's time in prison or his time running the streets from White Marsh to Glen Burnie that had tempered a wild reaction to the violence around him. He had told Janzen that he'd never seen "Tha Wire" because he "watched da damn news erry night." He didn't have to see that show "cuz I dun seen it ware I came up. An' I don' need ta see dat damn show if Stan Stowv'l tells me wassup."

Four rectangles of static spread across the computer monitor. With a few keystrokes, Scoop brought visuals to two of them. On each were frozen black and white images of his room, captured at different angles. Scoop was unable to access the other two feeds because of the destruction and fire that followed the attack. He played the two catty-cornered videos as the time stamps on each began to roll.

The internet had offered Janzen enough real-life videos of shocking train crossings, street fights, beheadings, and jihadists strapped with explosives and camcorders in the past two years, so when Scoop appeared onscreen, the shock of knowing what was to come didn't have the sting that it might've years ago.

On the video, Scoop crouched down over a wooden stool to hammer out a stripped screw from an old piece of equipment. Almost as a shadow, the man in the mask walked in slowly and stood at a distance behind Scoop, watching him work. The man then aimed a small canister of something and compressed the top, which sprayed something at Scoop who wheeled around, and they stood facing each other. Scoop grabbed at his throat and backed away from the man who placed on the ground whatever he had sprayed. The two stood a few feet from one another until the man produced a baton, which was tucked in his pants.

Scoop held out his arms to keep the other man at bay, but the attacker was relentless with his strikes, beating him until he no longer protected himself. The man stood over his prey and poked at him to ensure his submission. He looked around the room from where he stood and the red light of the security camera caught his attention. The one angle captured the mask scrutinizing the lens. He turned his body towards the camera to give a shot of his entire being. He then walked out of view and returned with an axe and swung at everything within its reach. He moved with the jerking motions of one compelled by something strong and uncontrollable. When before his movements were so precise, he was now wild with rage.

Onscreen, Scoop was motionless and the masked man was out of each camera's view, likely continuing his parade of destruction. A minute passed and Janzen made his appearance on the monitor. He pawed at his downed friend and tried to shake some life back into him until he hustled out of view because of the smoke. The masked man then double backed and walked the same path from the entrance of the room. He stood over Scoop and looked toward the direction of the monitors. He no longer gripped the axe in his hand; he now held a box cutter. He leaned down on top of Scoop and worked quickly with his back to the camera before walking out of the room. Scoop struggled to his feet, and Janzen reappeared and guided him towards his bed.

Scoop thanked Janzen for coming when he did and offered Janzen some whiskey. Janzen declined, and Scoop asked for some time alone. He obliged and left to work out with Samuel for an hour in the elevator.

The big man had taken to the riding after the initial bouts of soreness from basically every muscle from the waist on down. He had lost seven pounds in the first week and was thrilled with the extra length of belt reaching around his waist. Janzen mentioned nothing to Samuel about what happened to Scoop and was content to ride and talk with Samuel when his labored respiration let him do so. He spoke in vague terms about things he *had* wanted to do and see, and that past form – so perfect in its uncertainty – at least gave the indication of hope. Janzen, on the other hand, thought only of his immediate future, which dealt only in vengeance.

In the following days, he continued to walk the halls brazenly, alone and defiant, waiting for each turn of the corner to bring forth his adversary. The preoccupation proved a valuable tool in toppling the chemical dependence he had reintroduced into his life. He was surprised at how quickly the recidivism of his habits took hold. What he ingested hadn't simply called the shots; it changed him completely. It changed the idea of hunger into something that nothing but another hit would satiate. Janzen now wanted his wits about him. He wanted to feel the rawness of what was to be absorbed and inflicted. There was honesty in such an act, and it was time for him to be upfront – with everyone.

He worked with Mr. Atis on the day-to-day operations that went unchecked with the absence of Mr. Selby. He returned Mr. Atis's keys, and the man had found strength in running the happenings of the building just as his mentor would have. He oversaw the morning and afternoon sessions with an authority more befitting a man with such a voice. The group recognized his efforts, and the attendance at these meetings once again grew to numbers of prior months. Janzen exchanged polite words with Helena as he left one of the afternoon meetings, and the enormity of those platitudes were immeasurable from the way they shook every part of him.

Janzen continued to bring down the food and medicine to Leonard. His six-foot frame had dwindled down to about 120 pounds. While staying to visit, Janzen opened up about his problems with addiction. Leonard accepted this information with a sympathetic ear, though Janzen's erratic behavior during the past few weeks told enough of the story, making the admission unnecessary.

Leonard even surprised the group when, during a breakfast, he showed up dressed in his draping clothes. Everyone turned towards the skinny man in disbelief, but Janzen was quick to wave him over. This was the start of Leonard's integration into the family. "It's good to see you, Leonard."

"Fuck you, Janzen. Everyone is staring."

"You're a giant squid, man. What do you expect?"

Janzen stood and introduced him, and the group responded with a sing-song, "Hello Leonard" that proved welcoming enough to bring the man back to the commissary for another breakfast and then another.

While Scoop recovered from his wounds, Mr. Atis enlisted Janzen to lift the pallets of supplies from the loading dock to the ninth floor. Mr. Selby had presumably set up the crane on the rooftop, so all the controls could be handled from the panel where Janzen stood.

Some of the items were wrapped in *The Sun*'s recent editions, and the headlines were dominated by the admission of the State of Washington, Douglass Commonwealth as the 51st state. It was reported that there were already antagonistic responses from many representatives in Congress unhappy with the statehood. Consequently, some were backing the idea of annexing Cuba as the 52nd state to maintain a more balanced Union.

Janzen read the articles aloud to Leonard, and the newspaper's reporting transitioned into Janzen's mock cable news coverage of the events. He held Leonard's vaporizer as his microphone and communicated with another talking head in the studio. "Yes, we're here live now, Thad...I can, yes...well, having already been bestowed the honor of paying federal income taxes, serving on juries, and contributing to the national economy, it seems the residents of D.C. still wanted more – representation. This is a travesty, Thad. Trending online and gaining traction in Congress is the idea of splitting Wyoming into two autonomous states to maintain the balance of power. What's that? Well, the leading names are West Wyoming, trailed only slightly by Whiter Wyoming, no doubt a glorious reference to the snow-capped Grand Tetons. And just today, that national treasure of a congresswoman from Georgia has reached out to the Emir of Qatar to invite him and his country into the U.S. as the first true satellite state." Janzen pressed his pointer finger to his ear. "I'm sorry, what, Thad? Qatar is where? And filled with who? Oh dear. Someone should've told her that. Well, back to you in the studio. God bless you, too."

Leonard fell to his side in laughter, and Janzen ended his transmission only because a coughing fit overtook the sick man's delight. Despite his failing constitution, Janzen noticed a lightness taking hold of him. He saw a man not so much resigned to his fate but rather someone sampling bits of life that still remained: the occasional taste of his eggs over medium, the lampooning of the nation's politicians, the camaraderie of their intersecting journey and the choice to put to rest what would soon become a waking nightmare. During these good moments, Janzen witnessed a man still holding on to his dignity – fighting for it, in fact.

Similar weeks followed. Janzen continued stalking and provoking the masked man, and he continued to turn in the pages underneath Mr. Selby's door. During breakfast one morning, Mr. Atis announced that the holiday season had arrived and there was to be a Christmas gala in the ballroom of the velvet-draped second floor. No doubt, he sensed the tension building within the grounds that coincided with Mr. Selby's disappearance. The group not only lost its head of state, but it lost the one crucial option that had brought each of them to the building in the first place. The only known exit was up through the steep stairway leading to the roof by way of Mr. Selby's office. The choice to step off the edge of that rooftop bonded all the residents, and when that option vanished, the building turned into a repository, which was that much closer to imprisonment. None of these words were spoken, but Mr. Atis – ever concerned with Mr. Selby's ambitions and welfare – perhaps thought a shindig would be a topical remedy or at least a distraction for the frayed nerves of his inherited subjects.

Monroe was busy following the announcement of the event because Mr. Atis requested that the collective attire reach a certain level of sophistication as a gesture of respect for those putting it together. As expected, not everyone scaled the building concerned with leaving behind a finely dressed corpse. The work, though, invigorated Monroe, and Janzen offered his untrained hands for whatever would lighten his workload. Fortunately enough, the wardrobe racks were already filled with meticulously constructed dresses of varying lengths and fashions, so the focus of Monroe's labor was the duds of the sartorially challenged dudes.

Monroe's workspace became the social epicenter of the building. Couches were brought in, and Mr. Atis allowed an allotment of the methylamphetamine to work its way through the room. Janzen fingered a pill from the bottle without guilt. If he stayed away from Scoop and his drink, he'd be okay. He took the pill with a glass of water and found himself steeped in the music playing, conversation and busyness around him. He thought that everyone should experience such a tingle. The meds worked, and Janzen made the cuts Monroe asked of him.

Notably absent was Amber, who earlier in the day had made another video call to her mother. Janzen sat in on the meeting and flinched at the painful exchanges between mother and daughter, which reiterated what everyone else understood. The scripture verses that her mother recited distanced whatever existed between them years earlier and extinguished any hope of absolution or understanding. The daughter was a whore, and the mother was too far down her ecclesiastical path to remit a penance that would permit them to move forward. Both Amber and her mother finished the call with no plans to follow up with one another. Her mother said that she had family staying with her, "so things were going to be hectic for the holidays and we're going to be pulled in a million different directions." Amber said that she understood. "Maybe things will be different down the road, Amber."

The only solace she received that morning was the confirmation from her mother that the majority of her school loans were federally subsidized. When Amber had broached the subject with her mother, she appeared confused at the non sequitur – a reaction shared by those in attendance. After the call, she explained that those specific loans would be forgiven in the event of her death. Amber also asked Mr. Atis if he would get in touch with Mr. Selby's lawyer, Mr. Koontz, to find out the termination clauses of her remaining private loans along with the community property laws of Maryland. Amber had already read countless articles about spouses, co-signers, estates, or parents mixed up with collection agencies of private lenders following the suicide of the primary borrower. Amber did not believe her parents deserved the task of having to repay $20,000 because she had strayed from the righteous path. She dispensed these details with such a detached practicality, leaving some of the residents distraught.

In Monroe's studio, Christian sorted through fabric in his own corner of the room to prepare just the right dress for Amber in the hopes of lifting her spirits. Helena popped in and out whenever she heard a song she liked. She was playing chess with The Prez, Kenneth Polk, in his room a few doors down.

During one of her appearances, Monroe dragged her gently by the wrist so he could get all the measurements he needed. Helena tolerated the attention, and her playful exasperation signaled an improved temperament. Every few songs, a holiday number played, and the cauldron full of their mutual sentimentality was stirred into a warm and bubbling brew. Even Mr. Atis appeared in a lighter mood, if only for a night. He still wore his pressed suit while he worked out the details of the second floor décor with Daryl, Felix and Ms. Patterson, who all wanted to decorate the event. The three of them smiled not at his loosened tie, which had now dropped uncharacteristically below the first button; rather, they smiled at the Santa hat perched crookedly on Mr. Atis's shaved head.

Scoop reappeared back into the community after his chest healed enough. He explained his head and face trauma as a result of a blackout from the contents of the jar he made available to the group. Mr. Atis believed the story and maintained the coldness he typically reserved for his interactions with Scoop. Maybe because of the holidays or on account of Scoop's injuries, Mr. Atis allowed the liquor's appearance a temporary stay. It would've been a shame to tarnish the contentment of the evening, so Scoop stowed the homemade whiskey in short time after one or two of those Mr. Atis glowers rested a little longer in his direction than the ones before them. Janzen tasted not one drop of the drink.

Leonard showed up and politely declined the chance to be measured for anything he needed tailored. Monroe saved the histrionics he used when Helena dared walk out without succumbing to his measuring tape. The numbers for Leonard would've been too small, and Monroe – in his effortless presence – pressed him no further. Leonard invited "all my new friends down below if you're looking to get a little lifted." A few of the residents followed Leonard out the door and returned to the studio with eyelids a tad lower than when they had left.

The drugs wore off, and Janzen made sure that people left in groups to assure their safety. He herded Monroe from his studio and back to his room. Janzen walked the halls and made his way back to the fourth floor office where he would wait through most of the night under the vigilant surveillance of someone. He had waited there for each of the last three nights, and every night he expected his opportunity for recompense would come walking in, masked and ready.

16

Rumors of Amber's death came as a surprise to no one. There even seemed to be a collective sense of relief that she would no longer have to suffer through her mother's coldness and the dissolution of her past decisions. The residents talked of missing her and wanting to say one final goodbye, but most of the conversations that morning concerned the details of her leaving. Her friend and fellow chef, Christian, had not spoken to her since the previous night and did not find her in her room after she had not shown up for the morning meal's preparations.

When Mr. Atis rolled into the commissary, he confirmed her death. He had been contacted by Mr. Koontz, who said that he would be the one contacting the police to recover her body down below and that any peculiarities with the building that might be seen from the outside should be completely avoided. What Mr. Atis didn't say was that Amber's leap off the rooftop confirmed Mr. Selby's presence – alive and well – inside the building. The only way up top was through his office, and Mr. Atis, who had now taken to sleeping outside said office, swore that during his sleepy state he had heard conversations behind those closed doors in the middle of the night. Mr. Atis spoke in the most proper of solemn tones, but he sat lifted slightly higher on his perch with the knowledge of Mr. Selby's well being. "He's still alive!" his eyes shouted while the rest of his face mourned accordingly.

Some had met his position as the de facto leader in the building with apprehension, and Mr. Atis was smart enough to recognize this. In Mr. Selby's stead, he struggled with the inherited power. When he was typically authoritative and full of bombast with Mr. Selby at his side, he at times wilted in his absence, but today saw a strong Mr. Atis. His big hands were more animated, and his voice hit increasing decibels while he authored the few particulars of Amber's demise. Janzen processed the words he spoke and considered them a performance Mr. Selby would've enjoyed.

After hearing of Amber's past and seeing her mother's disgust, Janzen was surprised only that she endured her shame for as long as she did. Maybe now she'd have some unspoiled time in which to exist, or maybe she was lucky enough to have her lights eternally extinguished.

Janzen mirrored Mr. Atis and wore a face full of grief, but if someone cracked open that skull of his and walked around amid those whooshing thoughts, that someone would be shot full and through with only one preoccupation: the man in the mask. He was ready for the violence to come. He thought back to those first few fights in high school and how frightening they were and how he had no real control over what he was doing in his movements; however, the more he did it, the slower the fists and angles flashed themselves. He developed a drunk-ard's poise and flailed less. He began to anticipate and made sure to take the shortest route from launch point to target.

Each night among the fourth floor cubicles, he'd wait long enough until the soporific drone of the lights above him threatened his vigilance. To combat the list-less hours in wait, he took to calisthenics and yoga. He also approached the resident technology guru, Felix, about borrowing one of the tablets he used to control the in-house audio-visual setups. Janzen explained that his job was to write about the inner workings of Mount Selby as dictated by the agreement made when he first entered the building.

Janzen asked if he could watch all the video footage of the guard shack interviews from his fellow residents. Felix organized the raw footage of them in one folder and the edited pieces played on Movie Night in another. The former's contents were filed by date and provided a basic timeline of who had entered the building and when.

Janzen sat with his back to one of the cubicle divid-ers and, file by file, learned the motivations behind each of the subject's presence in the guard shack and, sub-sequently, the building. First on the list was Mr. Atis. He clicked on his file and barely recognized him. The black figure on his screen had the exhausted face of an addict, and his mouth chewed on nothing while his head twitched from his sickness. When he spoke, his words were sober and slow as though the mind had detoxified well before the body. He spoke carefully, and some of the more formidable utterances revealed missing teeth. The video panned out, and his one good leg bounced. The other leg was freshly bandaged under the soiled pants he had rolled above the knee.

He spoke of the heroin that had taken over his life and things he had to do to maintain his habit. He spoke of the inability to find fresh veins and the infection that had spread from the injections into the now missing leg. He was never arrested for the theft of his friends' and family's belongings but was shunned and no longer permitted to visit the grandchildren who once played on his lap. The last he heard, they had all moved down South, and he was given no number to reach them.

He spoke of an honorable death, one free of the opiates that had ruled his life for longer than he could remember. When his two grandchildren were born, he had started a $200.00 savings account for each to put towards their college education. He had taken out all the money from the accounts because he had nothing left to support his habit, and he would need something to stave off the withdrawal. On the video, he reflected on how difficult it was to keep from spending that money – the same money that remained in his pocket while his dope body begged for deliverance. At one of the shelters where he sometimes stayed, he was told about the Selby building and how he'd be able to arrange everything for his granddaughters before he spent what he had saved for them. A year earlier, he had also seen the article in *The Sun* about the string of suicides from the top of the adjoining building and how the operations of the Selby company had moved into a nameless square structure in Cockeysville following the first suicide off the roof – the woman understood to be Wayland Selby's own wife. That particular newspaper had been left as trash on the ground, and Mr. Atis read the article while he waited for his dealer in an alley off Route 40.

The video showed Mr. Atis handing over the money as if it carried the infection that claimed his leg. A voice off camera promised to find the proper destination for the $400.00 with an accompanying note informing his family of his untimely death, if that was what he wanted.

Janzen watched all of Mr. Atis's raw footage and then the produced and edited piece that would've played on Movie Night in the building. The effects added to the latter only enhanced the rawness of the former and remade a closed circuit capture into a scored art house short.

The security footage from the top of the building that looked down the twisted metal showed the one-legged man struggling up his ascent. The words he spoke were mixed over the slow and dedicated climb to the top. At times, he clung so close to the iron that Janzen could see the shake of his body. The music playing in the background was familiar, something by Henry Cowell whose atonal clusters played a perfect complement to a man who had lost his battle to addiction.

The cameras on the top of the building captured Mr. Atis pulling himself over the capped parapet edge. The rooftop garden looked different from when Janzen had made the climb. The rolling greenery of the moss had yet to be installed, and in its place were trellised archways laced with flowers. Mr. Atis dragged himself around the rooftop with a doper's army crawl during which time his voiceover narrated his descent into heroin. He reached out to the softness around him. He moved clumsily as he had only recently lost his leg. The gap in the rooftop seduced him towards the edge overlooking the loading dock. He pushed himself up on his one good leg and leaned out into the nothingness with the quickness of someone moving through a subway turnstile. He disappeared from the camera's view, and his final words echoed over the image of the abandoned rooftop. "It's time for me to do something good – time for me to do the right thing."

The men and women in all of the videos were rubbed raw with circumstance. Next was Daryl, his hair combed and his shirt tucked into his pressed pants. He sat in front of the camera with his hands clasped calmly in his lap. Besides the polite 'yeses' and 'noes' and 'thank yous' in response to Mr. Koontz's questions, he was mostly withdrawn until he was asked about allocating his belongings in the event of his death. This process was much lengthier compared to Mr. Atis's interview and his poverty. Daryl had recently sold his house in Locust Point, and the money from its sale would go to his mother, who was living in a nursing home in Pensacola. He asked that a donation of $10,000 be sent to New Song Academy in the Sandtown area of West Baltimore. Amid the dilapidated housing and drug corners, the school had provided a safe and positive haven for local residents whose alternatives were seriously lacking. Daryl mentioned no affiliation with the school and asked that the donation be made anonymously, with the hope that he might "be of help to some kids who could use it."

Per the guidelines of the Maryland state law, Mr.

Selby asked if there were any outstanding warrants issued for his arrest or if he had done anything to justify the attention of law enforcement. Daryl responded, "I haven't done anything. I've broken no laws." Janzen had always assumed the worst after hearing of Daryl's pedophilia, but he now understood the sympathy of his fellow residents after seeing the conviction in his proclamation. Janzen compared all his past proclivities to Daryl's inclination and discovered a new appreciation for his plight. What was Daryl to do when the lapping waves of his affections endlessly wet his toes like King Canute and his powerlessness to stem the incoming tide? Janzen remembered what Daryl had said in one of the previous sessions: "I wasn't sitting on playground benches or outside elementary schools. I was inside and alone. I even canceled my internet connection, but in the morning, there it was, again and again."

Years ago, Janzen had also woken up from his shallow sleep only to hear the siren call of whatever he drank the night before. To indulge it would have appeased the monster. To ignore its beckoning would've only delayed what came later, lengthening the sickness's grip. An addiction or an affliction wasn't so much a preoccupation; it was the reason for everything. Janzen found salvation in a bottle. Daryl thought only of youth. Felix, it turned out, couldn't escape the lure of a screen and lived in an online world of warcraft and make believe that drew him only further and further from a life unplugged – a life he was not interested in joining. Amber's mother, Mrs. Vanetti, found her addiction bound in leather, which provided her the strength to hold fast to a line in Matthew's gospel that demanded "whoever loves son or daughter more than me is not worthy of me."

The files filled in many of the gaps in his fellow residents' former lives. Christian's video was, by far, the most perplexing. It offered no clues or reasons for his presence in the guard shack. He mentioned his job as a lawyer for a well-known family-run local firm. He had no children and no wife, and all of his belongings were left to his only brother, who could "use the money more than me." Mr. Selby had asked him if he was sick or stricken with something that might end his life prematurely. Christian responded, "There's only what's been inside me from about the time I was twelve years old." On the video, Christian chose to exit the shack the same way he came in – back out to Formstone Ave. Later that night, he returned to Mount Selby having then scaled the security fence and the sculpted metal. The fluorescent green of his body shone eerily in the night vision footage scored by Daniel Johnston's "Some Things Last a Long Time," a somber and otherworldly anthem for the mentally ill and pop lovers alike.

Janzen listened to the video and song on repeat until the tablet dropped to the floor, and his head fell softly between his crossed arms. The lyrics melted into the droning of the lights above that no longer provided any useful illumination. The electric purring morphed unnoticeably into the field recordings of the snowy white backwoods of the forest. Janzen lifted his head and found himself amid black spruces. The only sound was the ringing in his ears and the distinct and continuous splatting of something close. He looked in between his legs and saw a pool of blood. A trail traced down his face and fell off his chin. His one hand was gloved while the other was naked, torn open in parts to the soft tissue. He inspected the hand, and the once familiar terrain was now torn up as though a coulter had ripped open swerving tracks.

Sometimes, the rifle he carried was strapped across his chest, but it was not there. His exposed hand burned with pain, and he buried it in the deep snow. The spruce he sat against was bare at the bottom from the moose and deer feeding from its lower branches. He pressed his back hard against the tree's trunk on account of the thing that hunted him. He slowed his breathing and exhales of his breath crystallized and sprinkled to the snow in pieces. The clustered clacks with which his breath hit the ground reminded Janzen of the Newton's cradle he kept at his bedside as a child. With his one good hand, he was able to collect half of his falling crystals before they ruined the silence once again.

From somewhere behind him, he heard the soft compression of snow and was forced to use his mangled hand to collect the blood that still fell from his chin. The drops echoed across the stark landscape with increasing volume. He would need silence if he hoped to escape with his life.

The wolf had already lost its pup to the trap so Janzen was unsure of what sustained the lurking animal's hunt. He sensed a savage intelligence in the beast, which assured its motivation as one of vengeance alone. He twisted his body and saw the wolf positioning itself in the center of a clearing in the brambles. Its fur stood erect along its spine, and it snarled deep in its throat.

Janzen stood to face it. He saw where the knife had penetrated the wolf's side, but a rib diverted what would've been a lethal shot of the now missing blade.

The animal inspected Janzen, looking for injuries it could exploit. Janzen no longer caught his breath in his hand, and the blood dropped freely from his face. He smeared his forearm across the one corner of his left eye, which had become a receptacle for the wound opened right above it. The noise of dropping blood rang out past the tundra. The Arctic wind picked up, nearly knocking Janzen over. The wetness of the drifting snow hit his face and whipped harder and harder until it found its way down the back of his parka. The cold spread around his body and constricted him with such power that he grimaced audibly from its strength. The pain shifted up his spine and into his throat. In all of the smothering white of the snow, a heat began strangling him. He collapsed in the snow and heard the advance of the wolf but was blinded by the tears and blood.

Janzen held out frantic hands in defense before the snow disappeared. The cold was gone, and he recognized the cubicle across from him. The tablet on the ground played the same song on repeat. He ran his tongue around the inside of his mouth and swallowed. It was there. He permitted the slightest noise to crawl from his mouth, and the agent burned his throat. His vision tripled, and he once again held his hands out in defense while he fought the nausea. He recovered and looked down the aisle towards the center of the room and resting at the main intersection of the aisle was a solitary cue ball, a spherical herald of menace.

Janzen turned off the power to the tablet. His body shook. He would give the man the silence he sought. If someone else was still there, he couldn't hear him. He stood up and scanned the perimeter of the office but saw no one. He walked toward the center of the room and picked up the cue ball. The same message he left for the masked man was still scrawled on it in marker. He thought to continue down the aisle to reach the opposite wall, but he would have to pass a battery of cubicles, each providing a space of safe harbor for a stealthy assailant. He expected the pain, knew he would absorb the inevitable blows. He made his way to the far wall while crouching low, better to take on what was to come. He reached the wall and turned back quickly toward the office. He would now see any attack that came for him.

He held the cue ball in his hand and rolled it back down the aisle toward where he had just fallen asleep. He hoped that the ball would either divert or draw the attention of the man. The ball hit the opposing wall with a smack and ricocheted out of sight.

The man then showed himself.

He stepped out from the cubicle where Janzen had fallen asleep. He wore the clear mask, which covered all of his head. His midriff was bare, and his black pants were tight down to the leather calf-high boots. From behind his back, he pulled a metal rod. The contortion of the skin underneath the mask revealed a man in rapture. He hit the solid metal against his head and the sound was dull.

Janzen bounced up and down, shifting his weight from each foot to the other like a prizefighter. He took off his shirt knowing it would be easy to grab. He was not alone in his fight. The friend he wondered about so many weeks ago had, in fact, joined. It shook him with its potency. Janzen dropped to the ground and pounded the floor with his fist. This fury needed a release. He pushed himself up to his feet and stood with his hands clenched at his side. He then lifted his pointer finger against his lips.

Janzen picked up a mug from the nearest cubicle as he strode towards the man. He threw it at about ten paces from his opponent, which was enough of a distraction to take the fight in close where the rod could do less damage. Their clash was hard and violent. Janzen found space in the struggle to land some sharp elbows. He pinned the man to the wall behind him, reducing him to only glancing blows with his weapon. Janzen caught one of the man's swings and pinned his arm in close to his rib and twisted his tendons. He grimaced and was forced to drop the metal to free his arm.

Janzen then landed a straight leg to his midsection, dropping him to the ground. He found the rod and picked it up, waiting for him to find his feet and smiled when he saw that he was hurt. Janzen threw the rod across the room and hit him hard with a straight right. The man was unfazed by the punch and followed with his own right to Janzen's mouth. Janzen's hand throbbed, but he smiled with a bloody mouth at taking the punch. He allowed another strike to land and held his pulsing arms out in a manic show of provocation. Janzen's eyes bulged, but he maintained his silence and rushed him again with the only sounds coming from flesh pounding flesh and the collateral damage inflicted on the office cubicles.

Janzen took his back and secured a chokehold, but he slipped out but could not get to his feet. Janzen kicked him hard in the face and heard the crack of the mask, causing an explosion of blood that now laced the inside left section. Janzen kicked his face again. The man struggled to keep himself upright on all fours. Janzen kicked his face again, and the man dropped to the floor in a ragdoll collapse.

Janzen crouched low before him and lifted his chin to his own and looked straight into the dazed eyes, only inches away. The man's wobbly head would've dropped to the ground if it weren't for Janzen. He had never snapped a man's neck and had no idea how much pressure was needed. It must be easier than ripping off a steering wheel. He smashed the man's head to the ground before going to work on his back with a shelling of punches. The body softened and went limp with each ensuing strike. Janzen's shoulders burned, but he couldn't stop.

In the midst of his rage, he never noticed the other person approaching from behind. He only heard the dull thud of the rod against the back of his head ushering in a blaring tinnitus.

So close. So slow. Bye now.

Janzen did not remember being dragged to the elevator and up to Doc's office. He had been knocked unconscious multiple times in the past, a product of living the life of a dope. For each subsequent concussion, the unconscious gaps grew longer and longer. When Janzen was lifted onto Doc's examining table, the dead weight of his legs spilled to the side and carried the rest of him off the table.

It was the voice cursing his negligence as a caretaker that brought Janzen back to himself. This was a voice of a man he used to know. He found himself wedged between the examining table and a heart rate monitor. He hit his head once again on the way down, and the jarring knocked something back into place. He still maintained little control of his body and moved as though in slow motion, and a man once again lifted him up on the table, which was when Janzen finally saw the face of Mr. Wayland Selby. He smiled at Janzen and told him that he should rest easy and that he was going to call on Doc to check on his wounds.

Janzen moved his lips to speak but only uttered a syllable on account of the chemicals he had breathed in. The pain in his throat brought with it a sudden nausea that required a wastebasket. Before Mr. Selby left, he held fast to Janzen's shoulders so he would stay in place. Janzen nodded, threw up and soon blacked out from the exertion.

When he came to later, Doc had already dressed his wounds and was waiting on his patient at his small corner desk.

Janzen tested his voice with a quiet hum and experienced no pain. "Where is the fucker?"

"He just came in to check on you, Janzen."

"Not that one. The masked one."

"You saw him?" asked Doc. Janzen edged himself off the table, unsure of his stability until a few shimmies of his body assured him of his full faculties. "Mr. Selby said he found you on the ground and brought you up here, but he didn't say what happened. I figured you and Scoop got after it with the whiskey."

"I'm going to find him."

"Which one?"

"Thanks, Doc" He exited the office and traced the circumference of the bump on the back of his head. The skin of his scalp held tight and required no treatment other than an ice compress. The blow left Janzen with a humdinger of a head-ringer, but he had sustained worse beatings.

He was closer to the staircase but called on the elevator. The doors opened and there was Samuel, perched atop his rider, flinging sweat in all directions. He had lost another fifteen pounds in the last week, and his normal cheerfulness took on an air of confidence that was missing in the previous months. Samuel noticed the scrapes and swelling of Janzen's face and dismounted his bicycle. "What happened?"

Samuel held on to Janzen's wrists. Their form could've passed muster at any remedial dance class for the blind or hearing impaired. "Samuel, it's not safe here anymore."

"But Mr. Selby's back!"

"I know."

"You look beat up."

"Samuel," said Janzen, placing his busted up hands on either of Samuel's shoulders. "It's time."

"Time for what?"

"It's time. As your friend, I'm telling you it's time." Samuel looked through Janzen. His face fell and his jaw hung open. Janzen pulled in Samuel and the two embraced. "Promise me one thing."

"What is it?"

"Come to the party. We're all going to be there. And you should, too. Okay? Then it's time." Samuel pushed away from Janzen and stood there unsure of how to arrange his body, so everything just hung there. "Just think about it. Now can you take me to Selby?"

The ride down to the second floor was silent save the plops dripping from Samuel's hands. The two stood side by side, distanced by what had just passed. If they were once painted in a portrait, *The Portly and The Pugilist* would've sufficed for a title. Now, Janzen recognized Samuel's hurt and wasn't sure his companion would share the canvas with him. Their conversation had spawned a second portrait and required another frame with another hanger on which to hang the two solitary figures.

Janzen left the elevator without a word and walked into the spacious second floor where the residents flew around with their bustling activity. Some of the velvet hung freely while other sections were drawn at the corners. Most everyone was there making all the preparations for the big formal to be held the following night. In the center of the activity was Mr. Selby, and he worked the reins of his command with the effusiveness he had shown on his best days. The men and women whirled around him, caught up by his long-awaited return.

Mr. Atis wheeled about the room from project to project to check on the progress. Mr. Selby was the first to acknowledge Janzen with a smile and a nod. He held both of his arms out to his side – palms up – to showcase the excitement around him. Janzen understood the gesture to mean there would be a better time for questions.

He nodded at him and approached Mr. Atis who mentioned nothing of Janzen's injuries. He had either already been apprised of the situation or was unconcerned with the aftermath of a drunkard's bumbles. After watching Mr. Atis's entrance video, Janzen better understood the man's devotion to Mr. Selby and his meticulous approach to everything, knowing the stationary minutes of his hours might lure him towards all things hazardous.

Mr. Atis asked what took him so long to show up and sent Janzen to help Scoop and Felix rig the stage's lighting system. Felix was preoccupied with the wiring of the lights, but Scoop froze upon seeing Janzen's face. "What da fuck?" Janzen hushed him and nodded, and Scoop realized that there had been another incident. Not wanting to spread word of the fight, Janzen whispered that he was okay and proudly lifted his swollen fists. Scoop mouthed a "fuck yeah" and included Janzen in their project, which served as an effective diversion from what bounced around in his swollen head.

All around them, the room swam in a nice, warm tenderness. The seasonal standards played over the speaker system, and the pleasant singsong murmurs of the conversations were interrupted only by joyous bouts of laughter. Janzen fell in and out of Scoop's digressions and kept lifting his head to find her. She worked with Kenneth on the hanging of the garlands. Janzen excused himself from Scoop and Felix and sat with his legs extended out in front of him with his swelling hands propping him up. He watched her as if she was the one onstage. She finally looked over at him – a momentary glance. An ambiguous gesture. An accident.

Janzen wanted to get some ideas down on paper.

Scoop assured him they'd handle the rest of the job and practically pushed Janzen offstage and towards the door. He returned to his room and set to work. The story was there, but he needed to slog through the muddy sections to provide enough of a polish. He wrote about truth and honesty. His work had become completely unguarded.

Mr. Selby's insistence that Janzen document his time here was an agreement between the two men and had been sealed with a handshake. His dedicated work shook off the rusted remnants of past promises Janzen was unable to keep for so many different excuses.

He wrote late into the night knowing the door behind him was without a lock. While the prickle of hairs shook him to chills at the sound of passing footsteps, he neither paused nor turned to face any would-be intruder. He worked until he awoke with his head cradled in his arms atop the desktop. Later that night after sleeping off his exhaustion, he found himself wide awake when the slow footsteps stopped before his door. Janzen stretched his legs and turned on his side with his back to the door. He fell back to sleep long after the footsteps trailed off.

The next morning, he woke to more sounds of the season playing over the speaker system. He opened his door to make his way to the commissary but kicked something on the floor where he found a tiny wrapped box with his name written on a slip of paper inserted under the small bow. He did not recognize the writing. He unwrapped the gift in the hallway and found two keys on one modest ring. Nothing about them distinguished themselves from any other house or apartment key except the word written on the one: *Home*. Janzen's fuzzy head made no sense of the word, and he dropped the keys in his pocket before he threw the box on his desk and headed up for breakfast. He avoided the elevator and took the stairs instead.

Leonard held court while his audience ate casually and listened to him. Janzen could tell that he'd inhaled some of his product before leaving his room. Whenever he was high, he grew all the more voluble, and his body did as much of the talking. The points of his elbows and shoulders broke the flow of his shirt. His plate of food went untouched, but his spirits rivaled any of his good days during the past month.

Janzen sat next to Monroe, who ate politely but quickly. The designer in residence said that he had too much left to do before things kicked off tonight. Janzen offered his help but was politely turned away. "Just stop by in another hour and pick up your things." He nodded and put his arm around the young man. Monroe dropped his head on Janzen's shoulder – only for a beat – before he was up and out the door.

He was left sitting across from Mr. McCullough, the older gentleman who was previously attacked by the masked man. Up until this morning, the conversations between the two had been pleasant enough in that they typically revolved around the same three topics: his job as a postal clerk, his trip to Aruba to visit a cousin and his forty-year marriage to his wife, who had died a courageous death years ago.

Janzen learned that Mr. McCullough's best days were

now filled with a restless reticence. When the elderly man began talking at length, the symptoms of his Alzheimer's were apparent. This morning, though, the active eyes were there, and he scanned Janzen's injured face.

"Did that son of a bitch get you too?"

"Excuse me?" asked Janzen.

"That psycho get you?"

Janzen smiled. "I got *him.*"

Mr. McCullough sat up straight in his chair and leaned in toward Janzen. "Did you get him good?" Janzen nodded nice and slow, enjoying McCullough's delight. "Did he get you with that stuff? Could you feel it in your throat?"

"Yes."

Mr. McCullough sat back in his chair and looked off past Janzen. "It happened to me, too."

"I know. I got him. I bashed that mask in good."

Mr. McCullough reached across the table for Janzen and grabbed at his shirt. "Today's a good day."

"I think so, sir."

17

During the afternoon before the party when Janzen walked through the workout room to track down Monroe, he noticed that both the exercise bikes had been returned to the gym. Cycling inside the elevator with Samuel became such a normality that the pieces of equipment now looked oddly out of place. He would speak to Samuel tonight – tell him *why* he needed to leave and why he *deserved* to leave.

He would make him understand.

The hour had finally come, and Janzen stood in his room fully dressed for the formal. He had never before worn a tailored jacket and shirt, and they fit around him like a rind on pith. Outside his doorway, excited taps of dress shoes and heels clicked and clacked on their way to the ballroom. He adjusted his tie and thought back to many months before. He had last worn a tie on his last day of work at Tappert Publishing where he had said his final goodbyes and shifted the necktie's responsibilities from one of dress code to sweat band. He had survived his old job in daily increments. The energy that barely sustained him through to lunch flagged and evaporated by three o'clock until his five o'clock body and mind died its recurring death.

The ride he took down the Jones Falls Expressway was not one he honestly expected to finish. It was a ride that he suspected might finish him. He would've been all right either way. The silly part about that day was that Janzen had originally thought of testing the flow of oncoming traffic as opposed to riding along with it. He had liked those two black fellas in the SUV and how the driver didn't mind that Janzen's damp arm had used his open window for support. The thirty-second conversation was enough to dissuade him from any extended game of dodge the Dodge. Those guys were all right, and they seemed to think that he was all right, too.

He took the stairs down to the ballroom and pushed open the doorway. The view was blocked by the drapes, so he walked around the perimeter of the room, the same route he had taken with Helena on his first night in the building. Over the speakers, "A Tender History in Rust" played, a song Janzen had added to the evening's playlist. He figured that the post rock of Do Make Say Think was appropriate for the residents in their post-leap life. It unexpectedly put a lump in his throat as he turned the corner to the open end of the ballroom.

A video of a fireplace shone brightly with its flickering flames on the descended screen with its pops and crackles complementing the music. The edges of the fireplace blended with the wood-stained walls behind it. The stage was dressed in rustic accoutrements similar to what might be found outside a well-to-do Westminster home up in the more affluent parts of Carroll County. On the stage were trees and toy reindeers wrapped in multi-colored strings of soft light. A weathered fence had been installed around the perimeter of the stage from which wreathes of all sizes hung. The platform was smothered in fluffy white cotton, and in the corner was a nativity scene with a jack-o'-lantern swaddled in the cradle. Long strings of metallic snowflakes dangled at different heights from the ceiling. The blow of the heating ducts and the suspended fans spun them, and the lighting reflected off their surface and gave the room its heavenly glimmer. Tables were scattered and covered with the deepest red linens. The smell of the hors d'oeuvres waiting on their serving platters stoked Janzen's appetite. A few of the residents sat quietly next to each other enjoying the atmosphere. Mr. Atis zipped around, fine-tuning every last detail.

Janzen spotted the back of Helena's head and walked straight over. She sat by herself and stared at the fire-lit screen with a drink held loosely on her lap. She wore her typical jeans and hoodie, and her black boots were tied low on the ankle so they flared out around her calves. He sat next to her and said, "You know you're going to upset him." She maintained her gaze towards the fire and told him that he looked nice. "You know you're going to upset him, right?"

She finally turned her head toward him. "I couldn't get the zipper up."

"Bullshit."

"The fabric kept getting stuck."

"Do it for Monroe. Let me help you."

"No."

Janzen stood in front of her and held out his hand. He waited until she could no longer ignore him before relenting. Her studio was only a floor up, so the silence of their walk was manageable. Janzen expected to follow her into the room across from her studio, where she typically slept and hid away, but he followed Helena to her darkroom in which her dress was hidden from sight. She held it nervously in front of her, and Janzen lifted it from her grasp to admire the handiwork. "C'mon. Turn around." She turned away from Janzen, and he lifted her sweatshirt off. She wore only a bra underneath. "Will you wear this under your dress?" She said no. Janzen unclasped the bra and draped it over the back of a nearby chair. He put his hands on her hips and held them there. She kept her back to him and crossed an arm across her chest. "You can't wear those jeans, Helena Wanda."

"Don't call me that. Only my dad called me that."

"What should I call you?"

"Just call on me."

"Okay. I will." He felt the goosebumps on her skin. "If I take your jeans off, are you going to kick me?"

"I don't think so. Get those leggings over there – on the table." With her clothes stripped away, her edge disappeared. Janzen returned and handed the leggings to her before he reached around her waist and unbuttoned her jeans. He pulled them down with his version of delicacy, the kind of movement better described as precise. She placed a soft hand on his shoulder to keep her balance while he slid each foot from her pants. "The dress." Janzen slipped it over her head and down her body. She adjusted the fabric into place, and he zipped up the back.

"I'll see you up there, Janzen."

Janzen stayed in place a beat too long.

"Helena." She still had her back to him, and he wanted to erase the distance.

"Not in here, okay?"

"Okay."

He left the studio and returned to the party.

In the ballroom, Janzen approached Mr. Atis, who sat behind a rollable bar top. The drinks he poured were divided into blue and red cups, each containing a promise of either serotonin bliss or sobriety. "Good evening, Mr. Hakkinen. Care to wet your whistle?"

"What's on tap tonight, Lloyd?"

Mr. Atis was confused by the reference but had long ago learned to press forward in his conversations with Janzen. "In the blue, the good doctor has concocted a potion guaranteed to liven those toe tappers and loosen that quick tongue or yours. In the red, is Christian's brew consisting only of the freshest fruit and some simple syrup.

"Will you share a drink with me, Mr. Atis?"

"Not the kind you want."

"Is it possible there's no wrong choice for me tonight?"

"Seems unlikely."

"It's good to have you back, Mr. Atis. We've missed you."

"It's good to be back."

Janzen selected one of the blue cups and enjoyed the pharmaceutical wash of its aftertaste. He mulled over the bottom of the cup but not because of some anticipatory chemical bump. He knew the power of its contents to expedite truth. He was unashamed at the notion that sometimes, you need a quick kick in the ass to get you going. Janzen was simply sticking an oar in the river to help navigate his journey downstream. That current would grab a hold of you either way.

Everyone in the building made an appearance that night – even the newest member, Madeline. When she first walked around the velvet corner, most of the residents already filled the ballroom. Janzen was talking with Leonard when she appeared. At the corner of the stage, Felix lowered the volume of the music and focused a single light on her. She hid her long, clasped fingers behind her and looked down to avoid the light's intensity.

Janzen saw through the cosmetic transparency of her thick makeup and extended hair and padded curves and discovered someone finally unencumbered. The glow of her brilliance swooshed around the ballroom, and Janzen whipped around looking for her mother. Madeline walked toward the center of the room and shielded the spotlight with her manicured hand as she, too, searched for her mother. She walked so easily in those heels, no doubt a product of years of practice.

Ms. Patterson placed her cup down and walked out to meet her. She reached for Madeline's hands and held them out so that she could take in the elegance before her. Everyone in the room watched them under the spotlight. Ms. Patterson pulled her child in close and held her like only a mother could. Felix lifted the volume of the music and everything surged and swelled.

The residents converged around them until there was one mass in the middle of the dance floor swaying back and forth together. Janzen hopped in place and beamed while he waited for his turn to congratulate mother and daughter. By the time he reached them, both of their faces were streaked in joyous trails of eyeliner.

That night marked a watershed in the trajectories of Janzen and his closest companions. Caught up in the confluence were Janzen and Helena, who found each other in the playful scrum to reach Ms. Patterson and Madeline, formerly Monroe. Helena had let her hair fall freely around her face instead of her usual ponytail. The decision showcased a new nervous gesture of tucking the stray hairs behind her pretty ears.

Everyone spread back out, and Janzen dragged her to a lively table where they were both swept up in conversations that he both ignored and indulged. The lines of her body were much too distracting to ignore, and twice she kicked him in the shin because of his loitering eyes.

When the right song played, some in the group would pop up and drag the others to the open floor where they danced as one and with one another. Even Mr. Atis rolled around while Mr. Selby watched on alone from one side of the stage.

As soon as the floor cleared, Mr. Selby nodded to Felix and the music tailed off, allowing the graybeard to approach the decorated lectern at center stage. The rowdier ones shouted curses of tribute while others applauded. Janzen waited quietly for the old man to speak. The questions he had surrounding Mr. Selby's disappearance and reappearance and subsequent rescue of Janzen kept him from offering a more enthusiastic welcome.

"Thank you all for your effort in coming together for this celebration. It was only a week ago when I was still hidden away, mired in thoughts of why I closed this building in the first place. Ultimately, what you all do for one another is what helped me through and the reason I stand before you tonight, so thank you for that." Mr. Selby spoke with sincerity and was forced to collect himself before continuing. "Anyways, enough about that. I understand that we have both lost and gained a new member of our community tonight, and it is my pleasure to officially welcome Madeline to our group." She stood up and curtsied modestly, much to the crowd's delight. "You look stunning, my dear."

"She's a hottie!" Scoop was drunk.

"Yes she is," agreed Mr. Selby playfully, "but life has a way of balancing itself sometimes, and it is with my most absolute gratitude that I hand the floor over to one of our own – to one who has meant so much to me. He asked to say a few words tonight. Samuel?"

Everyone in the room waited for their faithful elevator operator to cross the stage. Mr. Selby looked over at Felix, who swiped quickly at the tablet in his lap. The fireplace on the screen disappeared and was replaced by flames of a lesser intensity dancing inside another fireplace. "Samuel, are you with us?"

The footage onscreen moved with an amateur's grace, and whatever device recorded the new video feed dropped to the floor. A muffled "Did it look cool?" was heard through the speakers. Video of Samuel came into focus. He sat looking into the lens, and now behind him were the gentle flames. "Hi guys. Can you hear me?"

"We can hear you just fine, Samuel. You're doing wonderfully."

"Thank you." Samuel did not appear to know what he was about to say. He shook his head from side to side in either trepidation or as a response to a query only he heard. "I'm on this camera because I thought it would be easier this way, but it's not." Samuel spread out the comforter he sat on. Janzen had never before seen inside his room. "I've called the same place home for years now. I was there the day Mr. Selby shut the front doors. We bricked up all the accesses to the ground floor those first few days, and I knew something different was happening. I wasn't sure what it was, but I wanted in. So I stayed. I stayed initially because Mr. Selby needed the help. And then we both settled into our roles, and routine took over." Janzen looked around the room for someone's tacit understanding of what was happening, but everyone watched the screen. All you came into the building with the same idea in mind. I mean everyone, and that's what separated me from the rest of you. It wasn't anything you did. Please don't think that. I've been closed off myself. I used to be scared of everything. I was scared of never finding work again. I was scared of all the violence. I mean, I read the paper today and the murders and deaths are everywhere. Our own senators aren't even safe anymore. It's crazy. It doesn't make any sense!" Samuel seemed to regret his emotion and looked off past the device before he held the camera's lens against his stomach. He lifted it back to show his face and struggled to find the right words. "But it's time I try to make sense of it all – or none of it. It really doesn't matter yet. I'm here tonight because I want to say thank you. I want to say thank you to Mr. Selby for hiring me when no one else would. And I want to thank all of you for your courage. You've inspired me every day with it, and courage is the reason why I'm not sitting there with you tonight. I'm somewhere else. Let me show you something." Samuel walked over to a set of sliding doors, pulled one aside and stepped outside to a balcony. "Look at this!"

The camera's focus was lost in the darkness of the night, but what finally came into view was a shot of the Druid Hill Reservoir, lit up in the colors of Christmas. "It's really something isn't it?" Samuel steadied the camera and spoke over the video of the tranquil body of water. "It's where I'll be from now on. Thank you, Mr. Selby." Samuel's voice trembled as he spoke. "It's really scary, you know? But I'm not sure it's supposed to be any different. Here's a picture for you. And thank you, all. Thank you." Samuel captured a still image of the reservoir. The image remained on the screen as the audio connection cut out.

"Samuel, you there?" asked Mr. Selby. "I believe he's off." He looked over towards Felix, who could only shrug. "We will miss him dearly, that Samuel. *I* will miss him dearly. He didn't tell me what he was planning to say. We wish him luck." Mr. Selby held tightly to the sides of the lectern. "Things are changing." He walked off the backside of the stage and disappeared from sight. Mr. Atis followed after him.

"She's a hottie!" Scoop was still drunk.

Felix resumed the night's soundtrack, and the group rebounded well after the news of Samuel's departure, but Janzen grew more and more irritated that the night should proceed without further acknowledgement of his friend's leaving. He wanted to talk about Samuel and wanted everyone else to do the same.

"I'm going to miss him, too," said Helena. She stroked his thigh and dropped her head to his shoulder, and the bile bubbling up in his throat leveled off with her touch. "You get pretty fired up, don't you?"

"Yes."

"You worried you might hurt someone?"

"Yes."

"That's good." She held his hand in hers and tried to steady what trembled. "Let's dance."

No one else was on the dance floor, and the music playing was a forgettable pop tune. Helena pressed herself against Janzen and rocked from side to side. The music was the screaming of a child. She rocked back and forth and gradually quelled the cyclone inside him. He would miss her – Samuel, too. Things were going to change.

Janzen then quietly whispered into Helena's ear everything she needed to know. She deserved the truth. If she was strong enough – and he believed that she was – if she was just strong enough, she would fight on.

Her interlocked fingers fell from around Janzen's back and down to her side. He held her tightly and her body began to shake. The music was loud and obnoxious enough to muffle anything coming from her. He carried more and more of her weight in his arms, until his hands were locked around the small of her back. She pushed him back and held every bit of fabric she could twist in her clenched fists. She pushed him away and drove him back until he hit the wall. She held him there and almost said something before she left him and everyone else.

He followed her, the echoes from the ballroom fading between floors. She barricaded the door to her studio before he could walk in. He told her that he wouldn't kick the door down but he would wait for her in the hallway if she wanted him.

He waited another hour – or was it only ten minutes – before the chemicals in his body required some type of release, and the more he labored under the idea that it was he who failed to protect her only led him once more down a familiar path: incapacitation.

He ran back to the ballroom and picked up every blue plastic cup that wasn't held by a hand and downed them in gulps. Some had the kick of Scoop's new holiday moose milk. The ingestion was over in a flash, and he sat with his head on a tabletop until the doses took hold.

By the time Janzen sat back up, the numbers in the ballroom had dwindled. Scoop was still drunk, and Felix still fawned over his tablet and kept the music playing. Mr. McCullough was nodding off, and Daryl was in an involved conversation with Madeline. Daryl also might've been Leonard. Was Kenneth there, too? Janzen's vision throbbed and contorted. He'd have to try a walk about to test his constitution. The rush of the drugs jerked him all over the space. He spoke, and the words poured from his mouth with pinpoint exactness. He joined the others, no longer harboring the anger against them for their indifference towards Samuel's departure. They were fine. Intoxication filled them all, and they reveled in it – a revelers' communion – the chemical transubstantiation from wine and drug to dopamine reward.

Music continued to play and Janzen took to the dance floor and moved freely and alone. He thrashed his head until his balance failed him. He drenched his clothes. He danced with Madeline. They were both wild and wet when all the power to the room was cut.

In the blackness, Janzen caught his breath. Felix called out that he wasn't sure why they lost everything but said he knew where the breaker was. The only light in the room was what emitted from his tablet. Janzen paced until he ran into a table. He heard Madeline calling out for Kenneth so she could sit.

"Everything was either tripped or turned off!" yelled Felix to no one and everyone. "Hold on." The lights popped back on, and the projector's screen was filled with a restart blue.

"The fuck is that?"

In the middle of the dance floor, only a few feet from where Janzen now stood, was the mask. It rested upright and translucent as if its phantom shoulders and remaining body continued down to the lobby below. Janzen looked around the hall for signs of the man.

"He was just here."

"Or he's still here."

"Don't say that!"

"It's none of us." A few wondered aloud at how Janzen could be so sure of that fact. "Any of you recently sustain a major head wound – a broken rib or two?" No one followed his questions, and he gave no explanation. Janzen picked up the mask and looked it over. The split where his foot had connected was either flawlessly patched or this was a new mask. A latching mechanism on one side of the neck allowed it to open at a transparent hinge on the opposite side. Janzen closed it and latched it shut before he dropkicked it against the wall. The force of his strike lifted him off his feet and sent him flat on his back. The impressive show of inelegance played well with his audience, and what could've been a portent of terror was turned quickly into a show of slapstick buffoonery. Who would've guessed that under-coordination could combat such an evil token? Kenneth helped Janzen off the ground and struggled to wipe the pleasure from his face at such a spill.

The music came back on, and their insouciance, their narcotic bodies, their collective spirit deflected – at least temporarily – the presence of the mask.

With his teeth grinding nonstop, Janzen's feet no longer touched the floor. The music wrapped around him and controlled him in new ways. Scoop wore a wreath around his neck. Janzen located the mask and put it on and circled around the remaining residents in a lunatic skip. Was that Helena he saw standing in the corner? He couldn't see so well through the holes of the mask. Had she seen him circling out there – going nowhere? The mask fit perfectly over his features. It pulled somewhat at his skin, and there were requests for him to take it off.

Janzen was gone, and he was soon the only one there. He punched his masked face and slammed it into the wall. He crawled under a table and found it to be a sacred place. He pressed his face close to the ground and found a tiny cluster of earth. The unnatural way it curved meant it must've come off the tread of someone's shoe. He took off the mask and blocked one nostril and snorted the dirt with the other. There must be magic in it. How did it get in the building? The mask was back on. The music had stopped, and the space under the table was no longer sacred. He stood and challenged the man one more time with a yell before he staggered off to his room. He plunged head first into bed and lost consciousness before the mask bore too uncomfortably into his face.

The next morning, Janzen suffered the penance of his poor behavior. The mask he still donned wore the crust of his drool but became lubricated once more with his sick morning sweat. In the past, Janzen had typically forced himself to face such days in reconciliation for his past sins, and so he was up and out of bed. There was, after all, still a code of honor among a certain brand of addicts. He would take on the day the way he used to at the beginning of his degenerate journey: straight on and without the benefit of any more chemicals. He would still need to get his five hundred words in, and food in his stomach would do him wonders – and then some push-ups as a fuck off to himself.

He looked for Helena and asked about her, but no one had seen her since the party. After eating, Janzen knocked on her doors again but received no response. He returned back to his room and tried his luck at the key-board, fighting for the words to appear on the antiquated screen.

"Ladies and gentlemen, the session scheduled for this afternoon has also been canceled," Mr. Atis announced through the speaker system. Janzen had not heard the previous announcement on account of his convalescence. "Of course, all the facilities will be open for your use, so please enjoy your evening."

Janzen had come to look forward to their sessions. He performed well within the structure and the routine they provided, but a day alone to sit and dwell with his intemperance was a just sentence. He held the mask in his hands and looked into the eyeholes. Some real craftsmanship went into this piece. He put it on again and marveled at how snugly it fit him.

18

Mr. Selby made the announcement of "Helena's passing on" two days after the Christmas party. As he described it, Helena had requested a private ceremony, meaning she was alone on the roof when she pushed off the building's edge. Mr. Selby thanked her for her year of service as the resident photographer and artist. What passed for a eulogy took place in the commissary while the group sipped coffee, and it was finished before a pat of butter could melt completely on a piece of toast. "We can never predict when it's going to happen, but that time will come for each of us. It already has in a way," he said. "There's no forecast – no prognostication, ladies and gentlemen – and we'll all know that time when it comes calling. It called for Helena Wanda, she came to me, and she was ready. Thank you. And we'll need someone to continue her artistic responsibilities in the studio. Please see Mr. Atis if you're experienced and/or interested. If we do *not* get an applicant, the role will be assigned. Thank you." The coldness with which he spoke to those in the commissary erased any of the shared goodwill that had bloomed over the previous few days.

Mr. Selby walked out the room before anyone could ask any follow-up questions, and Christian announced the meal ready through his tears. Those present lined up quietly and filled their plates. Janzen sat stunned in his seat – stunned not so much at the news of her death but at the distant manner in which it was announced. He'd need some words with Mr. Selby. It was time they talked.

The flights of stairs he covered in a flash only sent his simmering to a full boil. Mr. Atis sat at his desk and regarded Janzen with the look of someone who had just encountered a copperhead.

"Is he in there?"

"Janzen."

"Fuck that. Is it locked?" Mr. Atis looked over towards Selby's double doors and revealed the answer with his outstretched pleading palms. "Selby!" Janzen burst through the door and found him standing in front of his monstrous desk. He held the metal rod that the masked man had used. Mr. Atis attempted to wheel his way into the office, but Janzen quickly locked the door behind him. He positioned himself only feet from Mr. Selby and stood with arms and legs spread wide, a comic book stance for a rawboned aggressor. "Did you hit me with that goddamned thing?"

"Only for your protection, young man." Mr. Selby could've loosely held the middle of the rod, mitigating any second-guessing about his intentions, but he held tightly to its one end and seemed willing enough to swing it if Janzen moved any closer.

"Why would I need protection?"

"He would've hurt you."

"He was done!"

"He would've come back. It would've been worse." Mr. Atis called through the door for Mr. Selby. "It'll be all right, Mr. Atis."

"Will it?"

"Easy, Janzen."

"You know who he is?"

"I used to."

"What does that mean?"

"It means exactly what I've said."

Janzen moved a step closer. "I'm going to take that thing from you, and you're going to tell me what the fuck's going on, and I want to know about Helena."

Mr. Selby looked down to the weapon in his hand and flipped it in the air with the hope of catching it. It fell to the ground, though he picked it up quickly. "Helena requested that the details surrounding her passing remain private, and I intend to keep my word. Other than that, I've been nothing but up front. And no, you will not take this from me lest it does any more harm."

With surprising quickness that superseded the gray-beard's reaction, Janzen seized the metal. Both men regarded the proceeding as an act of unexpected presti-digitation, and Mr. Selby responded in his own deliberate way and grabbed the rod at either end while Janzen held fast to the middle. What followed was a grunting exer-cise that mixed part judo with old world butter churning. The two men flung themselves about the room, knees-a-knocking and elbows grazing chins. There was only one sensible destination for the melee, and Janzen powered all his might towards the table supporting what was now a massive Lincoln Log fortress. It was clear that Mr. Selby had kept up with its construction even while he was stowed away after the death of Mr. Berger.

"No, no, no, no," came forth the crescendoing string of exclamations from Mr. Selby, but he would not let go and they flew across the room together. They both barreled into the table, and their combined force sent the entire castle to the floor. They fell hip-over-head in a bastardized cartwheel, and the metal rod flew from their grasps as cranial considerations prevailed over disputed property. The crash left both men woozy and bereft of any further offense.

Face-first on the floor, Janzen pushed himself up to a sitting position. The table they flipped over lay broken in pieces on the floor. Mr. Selby adjusted his pant leg back down to his ankle and twisted his pants so the zipper no longer held firm at his hip.

Between them was the wooden castle, upturned but still completely intact. Not a single Lincoln Log had been shifted out of place! On one side of the fortress was an unfinished wing, but that would've been because Janzen had not yet turned in the requisite number of pages for its completion.

Janzen reached a leg towards the structure and kicked it hard enough to test its structural integrity once again. "You glued it together? Why the fuck did you glue it?"

"It would've fallen to pieces if I didn't."

"That's not how these work, man."

"I bought them for my son years ago. I thought we'd build them together." The structure held Selby hypnotized under its upside-down power. "I never got around to it. I thought you were supposed to glue it all together. How else could I keep it all together?"

"Jesus, Selby."

"He's my son," he said, all the more exhausted by this simple declaration.

"Who is?"

"The man you fought – the one in the mask. It's my son." Mr. Selby rubbed his eyes either in vexation or possibly to hide what welled up in them.

Janzen fell to his back and stared up at the ceiling. "He's a monster, Selby."

"It's what he's become. It's what I raised – or didn't raise. And now he's coming for me. It's been coming for a while now – before you were ever here. I lost him after his mother died, and then the religion just took over. It already had him. I even tried it – thought I could reach him with it – show him I cared. But it turned into something ugly along the way, and I've just been watching it unravel." Mr. Selby spoke flatly of his failures as a father and his inability to reach his wife. Son and mother had been so close, and he couldn't come close to either of them. "She was so sick but wouldn't see anyone and wouldn't take anything. Her sickness could've been managed, but she was unwilling and drew even further inward with my son who never left her side. But then something happened."

Janzen sat up and looked at Mr. Selby. "What was it?"

"I can't be sure," said Mr. Selby, and Janzen believed him.

On the inside, the Lincoln Log fortress was divided

into rooms and levels. It was grand and elegant; it was upside-down and empty. "Come on, Selby. Let's pick this thing up." He helped the man to his feet, and they grabbed either side of the structure, placing it on his desk. "How did you know your son and I were getting into it?"

"I see everything, young man." Mr. Selby moved the structure to one side and lifted off the central section of his desktop. Hidden underneath the stained panel was an enormous computer screen, the bulk of which displayed security footage both inside and outside of the building. On one of the feeds was the fourth floor office where Janzen had fought and been knocked out. "All these cameras are fed to a similar station on the ground floor."

"The bottom floor? The one blocked out?"

"Yes."

"It's how your son watches – how he knows?" asked Janzen. Mr. Selby nodded his head slowly as if it was twice its normal weight. "How does he get up?"

"I don't know. I haven't figured that out. I'm not ready for that."

Janzen believed him. "He needs to be stopped." Both men looked at each other. Janzen waited for an affirmation from him, but none came from the conflicted man. "I'm going to stop him. I'm going to hurt him, Selby."

"I need to speak to him first. Please."

"What are you going to do?"

"Try."

Janzen walked away and unlocked the door into Mr. Selby's office and found Mr. Atis waiting outside. He turned back into the office. "What about Helena?"

"What about her, Janzen?"

"Did you try and stop her?"

"Of course not."

Given the transcendent power of demolition, calmness overcame Janzen after the first few swings of his sledgehammer against the cinder block barricaded wall in the hallway leading to the bottom floor lobby. Scoop had provided the tool without question, and Janzen walked out of his newly organized stockroom with it stretched across his back. He tested his arm's strength and raised the sledgehammer out before him by holding the lowest possible portion of the handle. The iron of it was straight up to the ceiling, and with his arm held stiffly out in front of him, he slowly brought the iron end down to his nose and back up again. He still had it.

The first swing sent a shockwave through his arms and torso. The ensuing strikes thundered through the hallway, and his ears rang at a pleasant pitch. He could've bypassed the wall by either going through the ceiling or stripping the adjoining wall of its drywall, but surreptitiousness was not a priority; in fact, each of Janzen's successive swings was harder than the last to build on the echoing racket.

A man conserving his strength would've taken out the top corners first, but Janzen pounded at the heart of the wall before him. He pulverized the concrete into a widening dent. Cracks spread to the edges, and chunks of the material fell to the ground. The cloud of material stung his eyes and mixed with his sweat. He sucked the newly made plaster back into his body. A cinder block wall and a sledgehammer were as good as any therapy session that morning.

Once he opened a big enough hole, a draft from the other side swirled the hallway with the once-loitering dust. Janzen crouched and looked through the gap. The hallway led into the building's lobby. No lights were on, but sunlight streaked through the open area. Outside of what he had seen in Mr. Selby's office or when he helped with the ninth floor deliveries, he hadn't seen true natural daylight since he was first swallowed into the building. The dust fluttered around like schooling silversides before he smashed open the wall wide enough for him to fit. The urge to step through the gap was strong, but he would give Mr. Selby the time he requested. For now, he'd be content watching the light and wondering not so much at its source but what effect it would have on a pool of spreading blood.

When Mr. Selby called Janzen to his office a day later, he assumed it dealt with his marauding son, but it was Mr. Atis who met him off the elevator – now run simply by a key turned to the right and the push of a button. Mr. Atis informed Janzen of the evening's ceremony. He told him that he had been invited to the roof at sunset to celebrate Leonard's departure. Janzen was both certain and uncertain what would happen later that night. He asked about the time and what he should wear.

Hours later, he again met Mr. Atis outside Mr. Selby's office, and he picked the lint from Janzen's shirt before straightening the collar. "Mr. Selby is already off the premises, and our select security cameras will be rolling. Of course, Mr. Selby will handle the body's discovery and call the proper authorities, but you will have to follow certain protocols or else you would be involved in what should only be a hasty investigation. Mr. Selby will attend to the body in about an hour's time, and he will pass over the security footage along with Leonard's initial interview and last will and testament. Are you following me?"

"What protocol?" asked Janzen.

"Do you remember the roof's layout and the fountain and the small patio table and chair?"

"Yes."

"When the time comes, you are required to stay next to the fountain. If you venture any farther away along the path, you will show up on the security footage and would consequently become involved in Leonard's passing, thereby complicating your standing here and the safety of the others within the building. Is that clear?"

"Yes."

"You will be free to walk around the rooftop until Leonard tells you it's time. Then, he will climb over the edge of the railing to appear as if he has scaled the iron vines of the building. It is then that you must remain out of sight. Our cameras will only record video so you are free to speak, but it must look as if he is alone on the rooftop. It is Mr. Selby's preference that these ceremonies are handled without others involved, but Leonard insisted on your company." Mr. Atis wheeled through Mr. Selby's office doors as he continued to give instructions. "Be sure to close the roof hatch when you're through and be mindful of the grounds up there. Mr. Selby goes to great lengths to maintain the florae."

"Maintain the florae?"

"He waters the pretty flowers, Janzen," Mr. Atis deadpanned.

"Was that so hard, Mr. Atis?"

He led him through an office door and once through, Janzen was surprised to find a space large enough to fit the furnishings of a one-bedroom apartment. The décor was feminine and floaty, replete with the embellishments of pearl, lace and brushed nickel. Over the single bed hung a diaphanous canopy, and seashell colors offset the whites. The duvet was pulled crisply into place. In one corner of the room was an enclosed shower next to a modest but modern pedestaled sink. In the other corner was an enclosure that likely hid the commode.

Janzen now understood how Mr. Selby was able to spend all that time stolen away in his office. "Did you decorate this, too?" Mr. Atis said he did not and moved through the room as though a single touch to one adornment would spoil its preservation.

"Did she stay in here?"

"His wife, yes. She stayed in here while she designed the rooftop garden. Samuel told me once that he would bring Mr. Selby her food, but no one saw her. I can only imagine what that man went through with her."

"Why would you say that?"

"Because all he wanted to do was help her."

"What difference does that make?"

"It's different."

"It's not. You didn't know her. None of us did."

Mr. Atis was a thoughtful man and gave the impression of someone stuck in cogitation. "It's different when you have no one – no one left."

"You can't be fucking serious. I've – " But what was the point? The two probably understood only one thing: that they would never fully understand each other. They were two men waiting in line for a confessional with nothing worth saying. Mr. Atis rearranged his face from a look of exasperation to that of a stoic. Both softened their rigid frames and the brewing argument dissipated into something resembling respect. "Mr. Atis, I believe we've had ourselves a moment."

Mr. Atis nodded. "Come on. Let's get you up there." Janzen followed his wheeled path through the room and saw that the bed's canopy concealed an ornate spiral staircase on its other side. "You'll need some warmer clothes." He retrieved a thick overcoat from off the back of a chair and held it open for Janzen, who slipped into it and scratched at the embroidered Selby Inc. insignia to the right of the lapel. The coat was thick but flexed easily with its wear. "One more thing." Mr. Atis pulled down a wool toque over Janzen's ears. "It's cold out there." He flattened Janzen's lapels and brushed pieces of Mr. Selby's dandruff off the fall of the worn collar. "Do you remember the instructions?" Janzen nodded and headed up the staircase.

When he pushed his way through the roof's hatch, January's breezy current hit him hard. The winter tears hadn't cleared by the time he lifted his legs through the opening. After a pinch of his fingers against his eyelids, he could see clearly again. What he saw laying there on the rooftop nearly leveled him.

Leonard lay on the ground, motionless in the cold air. His body lay crooked off the pathway with his head facing away from Janzen. His chest was to the sky, and Janzen was unsure if he had collapsed or if he had found an embracing curve in the soft moss. He walked over to him, and a smile crept across the man's skinny face. Leonard's hands were clasped loosely on his chest, and he wiggled his feet languidly. He wore a heavy down jacket and buried his chin deep into its cushion.

Janzen took the path straight towards the gap and looked down to the paved delivery entrance below. He turned back toward the roof across to the fountain, still bubbling despite the frigid weather. With most of the flowers hidden away until spring, the blooms of the mixed hellebores and Christmas roses defined enduring beauty. Compared to what he saw on the day of his climb, the setting was no less winsome – the way a wild meadow might look from a dense forest's edge. Heated lamps clinging to garden trestles warmed his stroll around the perimeter.

Janzen dipped his fingers in the cool water of the fountain's basin and enjoyed the smudge of Leonard's clothes against the rooftop's plant life. Janzen couldn't help but soften amid the stretching shadows of the waning daylight. The winds no longer stung as much because they had changed back to zephyrs, and it wasn't Arvo Pärt that played in his head. He heard only the fountain and its numbing flow.

Janzen lowered himself down next to Leonard. There was just enough room for the both of them to lay snugly next to each other in the indent between two of the mossing hillocks. Janzen buried himself in his coat and found himself nestled comfortably next to Leonard, who had barely stirred with his presence.

If he was forced to guess at the sensation of floating on a cloud, the softness of the thick moss underneath him now served as an appropriate example. It sucked none of the warmth from his body, and despite his condition, Leonard still emitted the body warmth of someone with more bulk. Janzen sank deep into his surroundings so that he was no longer conscious of his twitching arms and legs.

The bubbling of the fountain transformed into effervescence, which morphed into the murmur of a rolling stream. The water had only touches of cold, and Janzen needed only to flicker his fingers beneath the surface to keep afloat. He mastered this effortless buoyancy with the twists and turns of his wrists. He picked up speed with a wiggle of all ten fingers and slowed almost to a stop with the clenching of fists. The gray of the sky was filled with clouds, but they soon took on the many colors of the refracted light off the water so that everything around him glimmered.

Janzen steered his way down the stream, not the least bit concerned about rapids or rocks. Leonard playfully maneuvered past him, splashing Janzen with his quick cuts and turns. He, too, had his chest in the water, and he steered himself with his arms out in front of him. Leonard ducked beneath the waterline, and Janzen flipped over and did the same. They both found each other underwater. Their joy and speed magnified their shared exhilaration. Leonard's pinniped agility tested the limits of his body with his fingers blurred in their quickness.

Janzen propelled himself into the air for a breath

but found he didn't need it. From the height he reached, he could see the rapids up ahead crashing against the shimmering rocks. He dove back under and nodded for Leonard to head back up to take on the river's new challenges. Janzen needed a better view of what was to come so he held his palms out against the now surging water, his angled hands lifting his body out of the water. For the first few times, he managed to rise about thigh high, but he eventually gathered enough speed while perfecting the angles needed for a proper breach with the increasing intensity of the river rush. Leonard did the same. Both were now standing atop the steep waves, and Janzen found that he could drop into the wave and harness its power, building more and more pace. He tapped into his days on a skateboard and controlled his direction with a staggered stance. He slalomed through the rocky sections with ease and crouched low to join Leonard up ahead on his wave.

The strength of the rapids transformed Leonard. He was no longer burdened with a deteriorating frame. His body was now thick and strong in the thighs and shoulders. The wave they rode grew taller and stronger behind them and sent both barreling down their winding course. Leonard fell back and ascended the steep wall of water and lifted Janzen up by the arm. Even if they wanted to speak, nothing could be heard over the river's tumult.

The higher Janzen rose, the farther he could see ahead of them, and both realized that they approached the river's descent over the precipice. The swell they rode began to break, and Janzen and Leonard were propelled off their feet and sent crashing under the weight of the colossal wave. Janzen flipped and twisted in the depths of the river and lost sight of Leonard during the throttling. Something dull and heavy smacked his head, and he could no longer harness the water around him. His slow-motion focus moved from a ruptured bed of pebbles below him to the wash of the breaker that had caused his discombobulation. His head pounded with the absence of oxygen, but his building panic only slowed his movements. His vision blurred, and he sank deeper until the light of the surface faded to a dark gray.

The burning in his lungs wasn't unbearable. The water was colder at this depth, and it numbed his aching organs. He was ready to accept whatever came on the other side of a drowning. His insides crinkled their slow, frozen goodbye. Everything started to freeze with even his eyelashes trapped shut. He no longer sensed the rush of the water or its gelid stranglehold. He lost all feeling in his arms and hands, so he rubbed his chin against his chest for some type of sensation, but there was none. Janzen was a fighter, but there was nothing he could do while paralyzed by the river's grip.

He detected the rush of water pass by him again, but it wasn't the direction he expected. He had been flipped around so many times in the crash, and with no sight and no feeling in his extremities, he gave himself over to the will of the water. With his depleting oxygen he fought the urge to gulp for air. He was confused as to why he had been able to breathe earlier while submerged but not now.

Suddenly, the water warmed, and he was able to open his eyes. Leonard was above him, and he pulled Janzen by the wrist towards the surface only feet away. Leonard swam at such a rate that when they broke through the choppy surface waters, Janzen flew through the air to the farthest bank and crashed into the river-washed sand and debris.

With his head half-buried in the embankment, he sucked in sand and air in violent gasps. The water at his feet pulsed with the frothy whiteness of its rapids. He dug his fingers and toes into the earth, and their tunneling brought back their senses, one pinprick after another. The sun broke through the gray sky and warmed his back. He lifted his head and cleared his face of the bank's sediment. With his sight came his hearing, and what had begun as a muffle grew into something roaring.

He sat up and looked for any sign of Leonard at the waterfall's edge. He was mid-stream, held perfectly in place between the river's two banks. He was only twenty or so feet from the fall's precipice but moved not an inch forward despite the water's swift current and depth. Leonard lifted his arms out to his sides. The back of his head pivoted into the water, and his feet broke through the water downstream. The river's force crashed all around him, but he didn't move from his place. Janzen called out for him, but nothing he yelled bested the sound of the river.

Leonard bent both his arms at the elbow, sending each of his hands up to the sky. He then crashed both palms back down atop the river, and the concussive impact lifted his head, torso and legs clear of the river. With his palms held out flat, he harnessed the torrent beneath him, lifting his feet clear of the current. He looked back at

Janzen, who threw a celebratory fist into the air. Leonard nodded, turned and then ran atop the water towards the fall's edge, and he hovered momentarily with his body held open wild and wide before he disappeared.

The cold that had gripped Janzen a minute earlier thawed. He sat back into the bank's natural incline and traced his fingers through the washed up silt. He nuzzled his head into the earth so he could watch the passing sky while he warmed himself in the sun's fading rays. But the forest on the opposing side cast a shadow across his naked toes. He positioned his feet in closer but a new cold and its shadow now covered his entire body.

He sat up, and across the river was the wolf – only now, it was taller than the pines it sat between.

On its hindquarters, it took in Janzen's scent with a flex of its nostrils. Janzen stood up and approached the water's edge. The malice that had once filled the animal was gone, and in its place was something benevolent. The wolf leaned towards Janzen, and its nose reached nearly halfway across the river.

Janzen started to wade out into the water, but the current was stronger than before. Its rush threatened his place along the shore, and his feet began to slide. Ignoring the peril of the falls, he held his hand out to the wolf. It, too, leaned out even farther, but there was still too large of a gap to bridge. The bank on which the wolf stood gave way under its massive weight, and it pushed back deeper into the trees. The animal peered down to the river's end and after, leaned its head low over the water and said, "It's time." It then turned and leaped back into the woods and disappeared with two of its great strides.

"Janzen!" The old graybeard stood over Janzen and shook him by the lapels. "What are you doing out here, man? Didn't Mr. Atis give you the instructions?" Mr. Selby's inquiries knocked free some of the languor from Janzen's sleep. He was unsure exactly how long he had been out, but the sun had set. There was no sign of Leonard.

"Where is he?" asked Janzen.

"Where's Leonard? You fool, you fell asleep right next to him! Don't you see he's wrapped your legs with his jacket? You were supposed to be at the table, Janzen! We're going to have to get creative with the security footage before I call on the police. Damn it, Janzen." Mr. Selby removed the jacket from around Janzen's legs and helped him up. "We need to get you out of sight, young man." Janzen walked to the gap in the rooftop and looked down upon his friend and his smashed skull. "Janzen! Now, man. Let's go! Copy that, he's coming down now." Mr. Selby spoke the last line into a walkie-talkie.

At the bottom of the spiral staircase waited Mr. Atis. He welcomed Janzen back with a soft nod of his head before guiding him through the bedroom, Selby's office and into the elevator.

Janzen went to Leonard's floor and cleared the man's room of dirty dishes and unwashed clothes. He stripped the bed and scrubbed the walls and floor with cleaning supplies from Scoop's cache. He played the role of healer, ridding the place of its sickness. He didn't want someone else to come upon Leonard's room and misinterpret the mess for the work of a man prone to squalor, when in fact, Leonard had been remarkable in his courage the entire way through.

19

A week passed without provocation from Mr. Selby's son. Each morning, Janzen stood before the hole he made and waited. Some mornings he sang whatever song was in his head, and his melodies bounced down the hallway for him to hear; other days, he'd kneel silently with his head and torso framed in the opening. He saw no sign of the man and had memorized the smashed wall's crumbling material like a tracker would a game trail. He studied and obsessed the scene just as he had done to a print of Edward Hopper's *Hotel Room*, which had adorned any bedroom wall he had slept near since finishing college. He threw himself wholly into the morning and afternoon sessions and wrote in between and after. He ate well and exercised before every dinner. He exhausted himself to ensure a block of sleep before he would wake once again with the live current flowing through his body at the prospect of an encounter.

Days after Leonard's death, Mr. Atis had assured Janzen that they – whoever that might involve – had been able to manipulate the different cameras angles of the event to appease whatever officer had been assigned the lead on the paperwork of yet another Baltimorean's suicide. Janzen would not be involved or implicated in any way, but his cavalier disregard for the rooftop rules had frosted the warmed relations between Mr. Atis and him.

Janzen's main two focuses were to finish his commitment to Mr. Selby in the form of his written work and to redress the wrongs that the masked man had done to Helena. His manuscript was nearly finished, and another week was all he intended to give Mr. Selby to reach his son before he stepped through the gap and hunted the monster. During his manic moments, the end of his time in the building played out in artistic shots with clever depths of focus – all of it so cinematic – and culminated in an exciting build up to someone's fantastic demise. The script was nearly done until that evening when yet another soul scaled the wrought iron vines to the top of Mount Selby.

The buzz of the front gate blared throughout the building, and as Janzen was told months earlier, this interruption would be a sound to which he would become accustomed. Since Janzen's arrival, he'd heard twenty-plus drones through the speaker system, and only one had precipitated an interview in the guard shack: the rather odd occurrence featuring Chase Berger, former television personality. Of course, Mr. Berger had then climbed to the rooftop and thrown himself down to the landing dock below, a shock to the residents, as there had never been a jumper who had not been admitted to the building going back to Mr. Atis and the many who followed.

That night with Chase Berger commenced Mr. Selby's month-long disappearance and left the residents to speculate as to why he did not press the button to catch the man in the banner. Commissary conversations had offered a series of believable reasons, but there was one that satisfied the majority of the folks' suspicions. When Mr. Berger walked into the guard shack, it was argued that his presence there was not to allocate property and valuables to loved ones. No, it was generally accepted that he was after yet another storyline, one that would detail the inner workings of a closed building that had once served as the hub for Selby Industries. Some in the commissary thought Mr. Selby was unwilling to jeopardize the secrecy and isolation he desired. There were also those who held firm in the belief that he had decided not to catch the falling man in an act – or inaction – of wickedness.

Janzen had not come to his own conclusion on the matter when in-house speakers blasted a second buzz of the intercom. Mr. Atis's voice followed and instructed everyone to his or her place. Janzen understood this to mean he should head to the second floor ballroom to watch the spectacle on the big screen.

The prospect of a new person in the building lifted the energies of those collected in the big room. The losses of Amber, Samuel, Helena and Leonard had sullied the palliative waters that had flowed around and through the earlier therapeutic sessions, turning them into somber flotillas around islands of grief. Present also was a morbid curiosity at what might happen if and when this next visitor were to step off the perch atop Mount

Selby. Besides his own entrance into the building, Janzen had witnessed only one result from that particular leap. When the projector illuminated the lowered screen in the ballroom, he studied the woman onscreen. The way she moved the one corner of her mouth and that crease between her eyebrows reminded him of someone he knew years before. It couldn't have been her, though; she was much heavier then.

Was that the woman who had provided Janzen a safer passage through the DTs while he was strapped to a gurney and sure only of the existence of the next terror to come? This woman looked much thinner in the face, but it was one still coated in the thick concealer and makeup. How could she know about this place? Janzen struggled to locate any memory when he had mentioned this final destination during his benzodiazepine stupor.

Vanessa Williams had spent hours next to Janzen during his stay in the ICU, but he recalled only flashes of her amid his battles with the nefarious and penetrating infestations of his mind. This woman's skin now had the appearance of someone who had lost significant weight. Her head tilted to one side, not purposely coy but more so a gesture that resembled a collapsed dorsal fin of an orca in captivity. Janzen filled in the blanks of a woman who had searched for answers and even went about solving a couple of life's 'what ifs' before she finally recognized that what was inside of her wasn't a monster but a companion. Stronger men and women had been broken by much less.

"Can you please say your name for the camera?" asked Mr. Selby.

"Vanessa Jane Williams."

"Fuck! I need to get to Selby." Janzen panicked and knocked his chair over with how quickly he popped up. "I know her. How can I reach Selby?"

"If you find Atis, you can reach Selby," said Felix.

Janzen ran out of the room and climbed the nine flights of stairs to the top floor. He yelled for Mr. Atis, but he wasn't at his desk. He pushed through Mr. Selby's doors and found him sitting at the big desk watching the interview on the monitors installed in the desktop. "Can you get in touch with Selby?"

Mr. Atis took his time with his reply. "It isn't the best time."

Janzen slammed his fist on the desk and leaned in close to him. "Listen to me, Atis. I know the woman down there." Both men could hear Vanessa's interview through one of the monitor's speaker.

"Did you tell her about this place?"

"I don't know. That's not important."

"It's terribly important, Janzen. She could be here because of you."

"Can you get in touch with Selby?"

"Yes."

Both of them then heard Janzen's name come from Vanessa.

"Mr. Atis, can you please show me how to reach Selby?"

Mr. Atis scanned Janzen's face, maybe for signs of edification. "We can try. It doesn't usually work this way. I'm only supposed to contact him if I uncover any red flags, but she's totally clean. No arrest record. Perfect credit score. Steady employment."

"Please, Mr. Atis." Janzen paced the room and tried shaking out the apprehension from his hands.

"What should I tell him?" asked Mr. Atis. The tone of his voice let Janzen know he was willing to help.

"To see her off. To keep the back door closed."

"So she can go somewhere else?"

Janzen crunched his eyes shut and worked through what to say next. "Just please tell him to catch her if she climbs. He has to catch her."

After a deep breath, Mr. Atis nodded and lifted the phone's receiver to his ear. Janzen could hear the ringing of the phone through the computer monitor. One camera feed showed Mr. Selby's arm quickly cross the screen, but instead of picking up the phone, he either turned off the ringer or disconnected the phone's cord. Mr. Atis called again, but this time there was no ringing through the monitor. "What's he doing?"

"The line's not working, Janzen. I'm not sure what to do."

"Is he on walkie?"

Mr. Atis tried the device. "Atis to front gate. Atis to front gate. Do you copy?" Only the first part of Atis's transmission went through before the volume on the receiving walkie was extinguished with an audible click.

"Can you get me to the roof?"

"Janzen, what would you do?"

"I don't know. I'm not going to sit here and watch her die. Can you get me on the roof?"

He turned away from Janzen. "I can't."

"Or you won't?"

"Both," Mr. Atis responded. He appeared crushed by having to go through this with Janzen. "You have to trust him, He will do the right thing."

"He will do what he wants to do."

"Yes."

Janzen walked away from Mr. Atis and over to the door leading into Mrs. Selby's old bedroom and the staircase to the roof. The door was locked. "If she climbs to the top, do you know where I'm going to be?"

"I don't understand the question," responded Janzen.

"Where was I when you were first pulled into the building?"

"You were in there with me – in the hallway."

"Yes. Now ask me where I'm going to be if she climbs to the top."

"Where, Atis? Where?" Janzen smashed the heels of his palms into his temples before trying the office bedroom door once again.

"I'm going to be in the hallway because I believe that's where she'll be. She may simply sign the papers and leave, but that's where I'll be if she makes it up."

Janzen rushed out of the office, not quite sure where he was going. He found himself in the stairwell and knew he at least wanted to watch her in the hope that she would leave out the front door and back out to Formstone Avenue. He headed down to the second floor.

Vanessa Williams did sign all the paperwork that afternoon, and when everything was signed, initialed and notarized, both Mr. Selby and Mr. Koontz left her sitting alone in the guard shack with both doors open. Janzen watched with the rest of the group on the ballroom screen. It was almost ten minutes before she stood up from the chair and walked out the back door. Felix was already on a second tablet editing together a more polished version of her interview in the event of her climb.

Within another two minutes, the side-mounted cameras caught the first time she lost her footing. Janzen could barely stand to watch while she held on with her fragile ferocity. She would catch herself from falling two more times, but by the third time, Janzen was not part of the audience. He was done spectating.

When Vanessa finally stepped off the gapped edge of the rooftop, Mr. Atis was not waiting for her in the ninth floor hallway. No, he was still in Mr. Selby's office trying in vain to reach the man on the walkie – the man who was out back in the meager tree line that speckled the rocky landscape. He had not bothered to turn back on the power to his walkie, a possible act of obfuscation, or maybe it was to focus better on what he watched.

He would've heard her sobs when she leapt, and he would have heard her body tumble around in the hold of the yellow banner. But what Mr. Selby would not have heard were the words of compassion and fear and fright and love shared between Vanessa and Janzen in that ninth floor hallway. He would not have seen their embrace, one trembling and the other shaking.

During the following week, Janzen served as a tour guide, ambassador and protector for the broken woman. Vanessa walked around dopily in a suspended state of shock at her extended existence. She kept repeating to him that she always thought she would run into him again. "I mean, I just knew I was going to find you." Janzen stayed at her side and purposely omitted the threat Mr. Selby's son played with her admittance. The work he had devoted to cleaning Leonard's room proved well spent when she genuinely thanked him for her new lodgings. He had applied a lighter paint scheme weeks before, and both he and Vanessa worked together to arrange and update the décor to fit her tastes.

Janzen would swing by her room and walk her to breakfast, and they attended both morning and afternoon sessions together. She was hesitant to join in but soon began to surprise the other residents with her soft and polite contributions.

One quiet night after dinner, she revealed that it was Janzen's ramblings during his stay at St. Joseph's that had led her to Mount Selby. He had no recollection of mentioning the building or of his plans to scale the Formstone Ave. fortress, but she assured him that he had gone into such specific details pertaining to his sobriety, the completion of his novel and the eventual climbing of the building had the novel not materialized into anything other than a file saved on his computer. Of course, she said that she had to weigh the truth of his words against the other sentences that flowed from his mouth – maledictions against the plague of his mind.

She confided to Janzen that she had only been on the job for a week and half when she first met him, and his confused and deteriorated state was such that she took a piece of him home with her, and she did the same with her other suffering patients. All those pieces eventually coalesced into something ponderous, which lay deep in her gut. She said it was there even after she lost the weight and began to dance again. All the pieces she brought home from her shifts led her down a familiar path. In what should have been the altruistic and self-edifying profession, her new career only magnified the derailed endeavors of her past. She told him that she couldn't hack it, but she kept it up. She had gone back to school to study nursing when everything else hadn't worked, and it turned into another checkmark next to her expanding list of failures.

The group responded well to Vanessa's presence. They were warm and inviting. Christian was particularly pleased with her nutritional knowledge and asked if she would be interested in helping prepare some of the group's meals. She was happy to help. At the close of her first week, her portrait was presented – an original piece of work drawn by Felix, who had completed the task on his tablet – the first piece not to be cast in one of the classical mediums. Her portrait was printed and framed and hung next to Janzen's in the great ballroom.

Many of her early days were spent in the haze of Doc's sedatives under which she rose and fell from its undulating waves. Vanessa would ramble on, lost down her mind's well of abstraction, elucidating only upon phrases she fished out when she exhaled as if her respiration was tied to her digressions.

Mr. Selby had recommended this medicinal course of action after his discussion with her on the top floor. In her more salient asides, she revealed a focus still wrapped in the stranglehold of suicide, but as those first days passed, she responded positively to her new surroundings and eventually cast her own stories' needle and thread into the collective fabric of the residents' warp and woof.

Vanessa was told nothing about a masked man because there was nothing to report. Since Janzen had opened up the barricade to the lobby, the only sign of the man showed on the anxious faces of those he had already encountered. During his free time, Janzen continued to sit there, looking through the gaping hole on a folding chair he borrowed from Scoop. Each time he sat down, he expected to find the man on the other side. It was his monomaniacal obsession for vengeance that possibly deflected the idea that the man on the other side might have priorities that existed beyond, or more appropriately, above Janzen.

20

It wasn't that Janzen hadn't done exactly what Mr. Selby had asked of him. On the contrary, he *had* set out to do just what he had asked of him as a stipulation of his stay in the building. He *had* intended to document his time in Mount Selby and to create a portrait of life of one swallowed as a yellow glob through the ninth-floor window. His original intention was to handle his written responsibility from a first-person account, one in which there was no external pressure to lionize or demonize the building's paterfamilias. He had been assured that his work would remain unread and unquestioned so long as he met his daily deadlines of five hundred words, and he had done just that. Even when wrecked by his intoxication, he had done the work.

Sitting at his desk, he printed his story's final five pages. He had always printed two copies of his work – one going to Mr. Selby and the other added to the growing stack in the bottom desk drawer. There were only two more words to write: the title. He started a new page and wrote those two words that were mentioned so many years ago in a class he could barely remember, but the one word – the main word – was a role that had stuck with him throughout the years – a dark, mythological word. He printed this page for himself and laid it atop all the others.

Maybe Mr. Selby would find significance in that title as a role he played or tried to play. Maybe it wasn't his to play. In all, what Janzen wrote over those months mentioned neither Mr. Selby nor his building on Formstone Avenue. Instead, what he wrote was a piece of fiction. Janzen wondered if Mr. Selby would find his legacy's documentation in the diverted waters of these pages knowing the eddies all swirled from the same unseen spring.

Janzen climbed the stairs to the top floor with his pages. He believed in Mr. Selby's word. He believed his work went unread until its completion. Janzen believed in him when the other residents were still unsure of the man's standing. He might even tell the old codger if things went well.

At around the ninth floor, a deep murmur grumbled below. He felt it in the railing he held onto and against the soles of his shoes, a shudder from the percussive depths. The building had spewed out so many different noises since Janzen's arrival that he was no longer shocked by anything new, but this one was different. This sound shook the building with its steady chuffing of an enormous, approaching locomotive.

He doubted that it was anything coming through the speaker system. Nothing that had been previously played had such an effect. Janzen sensed that it must be time. This had to be the masked man's siren song. Janzen's hands began to shake, and the pages scattered in the stairwell. He collected them and flew up the remaining flights and burst his way to the top floor.

Mr. Atis was not at his desk and Mr. Selby's door was open only a crack, an aberration because it was typically either locked shut or opened widely. He walked straight in and saw the deep scarlet blood trail against the lighter colors of the rug. The faint smell of that sickly familiar chemical hung in the air. He checked around the desk and found the chair knocked over. He ran over to the door that led to the rooftop exit, but it was locked. A clumsy noise back towards the elevator caused Janzen to run out where he found Mr. Atis pulling himself up from behind his desk. Across the side of his head stretched a wound that was bleeding all over his face.

Janzen found a chair and dragged Mr. Atis's limp body onto it, for the one he had been using was smashed from whatever violence had been unleashed. Mr. Atis fought his assistance in his groggy state, but he relented after Janzen spoke a few words of reassurance. Mr. Atis composed himself enough to utter Mr. Selby's name.

"Where is he, Atis?

Mr. Atis shook his head and felt the different wounds on his body and face. "He took him."

"Down?"

"Yes."

"All the way?" asked Janzen. Mr. Atis shook his head with more animation, which caused him a jolt of pain. "Are you going to be all right?"

"Find him. Save him." Mr. Atis pushed him away. "Go!"

Janzen streaked down the stairwell yelling in an indecipherable language. What he yelled was from an earlier time. It might've been the Hakkaa Päälle howled for the service of King Adolphus. It could've been a Cro-Magnon wail. The exhilaration overtook him. He had missed this so much in his sobriety, but he could not release everything yet. It was pouring out of him, though some of it must be saved for the man in the mask. He stopped on one of the switchback's landings and waited for calmness. He focused on his hands, which shook less and less with each controlled exhale.

He recalled the press clippings that were delivered to his room in boxes so many months ago when he flipped through them from page to page with lukewarm interest. His only knowledge of the bottom floor came from what he had learned from those articles. He knew Mr. Selby had dedicated the base of the building to the fabrication of the company's first products whose designs had come from the mind and hands of his father. Could it be that the grandson had started the dormant machines? Janzen recalled *The Sun*'s article on the building's opening and the photograph taken of a younger Mr. Selby with his even younger wife and the small boy, perhaps just five at the time, who hid his face in his mother's dress.

The article had detailed Mr. Selby's insistence on featuring the heavy machinery and the workers who ran them "as the foundation from which everything else is possible." While the first floor had only produced a fraction of Selby Incorporated's overall product, the gesture and the symbolism had undoubtedly endeared many of the employees to their homegrown leader and boss in their new Baltimore headquarters. Janzen started to understand his son's plan: to destroy his father in the only place he held sacred.

He walked the remaining flights of stairs with precise deliberation. The sounds of whatever had been powered on grew louder and louder as he descended, and it was clear that it was coming from the first floor.

Once there, he noticed that the gap he had sledge-hammered open was not as it was a day before. In the hallway, everything was now out of order. The hole had been widened, and through the dust and debris, a set of footprints, swathes of blood, and tracks of what might have been dragged heels dirtied the photograph in his mind. He stepped through the opening and ran down the hallway.

In the lobby, Janzen passed the welcome desk, which was fitted with flickering security monitors like the ones in Mr. Selby's office. The man had enjoyed a view of every camera feed in the building. Janzen looked for more tracks, but the floor shined with such an unblem-ished brilliance, nothing could be detected. He looked down the rows of equipment used for processing, bend-ing and manipulating the Selby product line, but the reach of what he could see was limited in the darkness. The turning of gears, the hiss of hydraulics and the roll of a central conveyor belt gave Janzen the only idea of the space's depth as the sounds caromed around him. He walked toward the industrial center and was startled over and over at the machines' popping and clanging.

The reach of whatever light was in the lobby reflected weakly off the sharp angles of the moving machines, surrounding Janzen with dull and mechanized threats at every step. Above him, a single auxiliary light suddenly shone, and the ceiling's exposed exhaust system came to life. He could see down to the other end of the floor to a glass-enclosed storage room and the roll gate that would have opened to the pavement delivery dock below the yellow banner. He saw no sign of either Mr. Selby or his son.

Janzen walked toward the opposite wall and began to hear the arrhythmic sounds of shuffling feet. He passed an aisle of grinding machines and metal presses. He moved slowly and peered around an older bulky brake press and saw the masked man working hurriedly near the railed bucket of a compressed scissor lift.

The man then moved towards Mr. Selby, his father, who stood by watching him. Mr. Selby would approach the other and lay a hand on his son's bare back only to be moved farther back with a straight arm to the chest. Based on the way he moved, Mr. Selby was hurt, but this did not stop him from approaching his son, who in turn would once again push him back. Even with the noise of the machinery, Janzen could tell there were no words spoken between the two.

The son attached something to the scissor lift's platform. The one auxiliary light above them did not fully illuminate them because of the stacks of cellophaned Selby products that had sat undelivered for so many years.

Janzen was confused by what played out before him. The son held a rectangular controller in his hands, which raised and lowered the platform of the scissor lift. Janzen thought that he might try and string his father up, so he looked around for anything to use as a weapon. He found nothing nearby. Not a problem. He didn't need one.

Once more, Mr. Selby grabbed at his son, but was thrown to the ground this time. His son shoved something into his father's chest. As Mr. Selby gathered himself, his son walked away from him spreading his hands out wide. Mr. Selby shook his head wildly from side to side and motioned for his son to stop whatever it was he intended.

"Now!" shouted his son. "Now!" Mr. Selby shook his head and shrank before the extended arms of his son.

Janzen moved out from behind the machine and yelled at him to stop. The son looked from his father to Janzen and instantly advanced toward the intruder. Mr. Selby turned and spotted Janzen. It was then that the scissor lift rose, and the masked man could move forward no more. He was forced back toward the lift until he was finally lifted off his feet from the rope around his neck, which his mask partially hid. He tugged frantically at the rope to free its hold while he strained to confront Janzen, but with the other end of the rope rising and rising, the man moved farther and farther from Janzen. He was slowly lifted ten and then fifteen feet in the air. He held his arms out wide with his hands outstretched, and the mask muffled his choking. His hands then clawed at the rope around his neck as he gasped for air. He began kicking and his body jerked horribly.

Mr. Selby threw the scissor lift's controller aside and dropped to the floor before his son, who continued his prolonged ending. The mask he wore unclasped and was pulled off to the side by the rope revealing a mouth stretched in anguish.

Mr. Selby jumped up from the floor and pulled on his son's legs. With the added pressure, the neck snapped, and it was finally over. Mr. Selby hung onto his legs until Janzen picked up the controller and lowered the body to the ground.

Each of Mr. Selby's whimpers was met with a convulsion of pain from the chemicals he had been forced to ingest. His silence magnified the machines' clunking repetition around them. Janzen loosened the knot and laid the body into Mr. Selby's lap, who held him tightly to his chest.

Janzen backed away and saw Mr. Atis approaching. He was without his transport, hopping along the best he could. The wound on his head was still untreated, and twice he fell to the ground in his rush to reach Mr. Selby. Janzen recognized the addict's desperation on his face and walked toward him to help his progress.

Mr. Atis stopped where he was when he saw Mr. Selby against the lift's chassis. His one good leg buckled beneath him, and Janzen swooped under the man's arm and supported all of his weight.

Mr. Selby motioned for the two of them to approach. Mr. Atis found strength in the gesture and threw his arms around the old man, who fought for some distance but still held his aide close enough to mouth something to him. Mr. Atis, still overwhelmed and certainly relieved at seeing his friend alive, tried translating what was being mouthed to him but failed in his first few attempts. Finally, Janzen said the words Mr. Selby tried to speak. "We need to get rid of the body." At that, Janzen walked away and left Mr. Atis to fret over these muted instructions.

No one saw Mr. Selby in the weeks following his son's death, though it was made known by Mr. Atis that he was "off site" to see to "final arrangements." On one of those quiet afternoons on the top floor of the building, a convalescing Mr. Atis assured Janzen that Mr. Selby had dutifully called the police about the hanging. He alluded to concocted details that included Mr. Selby's happening upon the swinging body of his son on the property of his defunct horse farm up in Monkton, where his wife used to spend months of her life hidden away from everyone but her son. Apparently Mr. Selby's lawyer, Mr. Koontz, played a key role in the body's transport from Mount Selby to Monkton. Mr. Atis peppered in words like "harrowing," "courageous" and "perseverance" in the retelling, but Janzen knew how to translate an editorial and imagined himself raising and re-raising a single eyebrow to deflect those words coloring the basics of the story.

Mr. Atis leaked the news about the Monkton suicide and explained that the threat was no longer present in the building. Janzen added nothing to the conjecture of the residents and mentioned no part of the role he played that night.

He no longer accompanied Vanessa everywhere she went, but her looks of gratitude conveyed her understanding that his vigilance was tied to something real and dangerous. He always smiled back at her and she would shake her head sometimes, possibly in wonder at both of their journeys.

While Mr. Selby attended to his son, he made time to send word back to Mr. Atis that he needed Janzen to handle one extra duty during his absence. Mr. Atis explained that since winter's hold on March had broken early, the rooftop garden would need specific attention to ready it for a promising spring. Mr. Atis bypassed any further explanation and handed Janzen a dossier with pictures, names, descriptions and instructions of care required for each plant. "He fully expects you to follow these guidelines, Janzen. I'm not sure you realize how much that garden means to him." He didn't doubt what Mr. Atis said, but he couldn't help but wonder at Mr. Selby's true intentions. Mr. Atis handed over the spiral-bound notebook and the key that opened both the office door and the other one leading into Mrs. Selby's old bedroom, which gave him access to the staircase up to the roof.

Janzen hadn't been up there since the winter evening with Leonard. He climbed through the hatch and was welcomed by a mild afternoon. The fountain bubbled behind him, and he scanned the garden for signs of life. In sections, some of the moss had lost its color and lay flat where the winter snow had tamped it down, but there were other patches of deep green that stretched for the sun after a frosty slumber.

Years ago, Janzen had built retaining walls that encircled gardens and ground cover, but the extent of his experience of tending to plants dealt only with a dead ficus and illicit buds bought by the ounce. The binder given to him by Mr. Atis was filled with pictures of the plants he saw before him with handwritten notes written in two distinct scripts: one possibly female and the other in Mr.

Selby's hand. The latter's notes were written in bulleted lists and organized by detailed watering cycles, trimming recommendations, soil and fertilizer amendments and suggestions on sun exposure. The other notes were made in elegantly written penmanship, organized in passages over and through the pictures including references to the "vainglorious vines of the wilting bougainvillea."

Janzen found a dry spot in the moss, sat and read through the pages of the binder not for any horticultural instruction but for a lyrical walkabout through the mind of the former Mrs. Selby. He came upon one of the more organized passages, still fraught with crossed out words and bending lines:

He said her blood might sour the compost pile,
But an anemone thrives in the wild,
Where the dirt is stained and the dead turn vile.
"We're part of the earth!" she told her child.

The blood she'd spill was stored still deep within,
And the boy grew amongst the heathers high,
Held tight to her side 'til after his chin
Did sprout wild 'long with his unyielding eye.

Next, he quotes a Lot and The Word obscures.
"What you tell me cannot be so," she cries.
He bares her in time and still she endures.
His venom now hers will fill her doll's eyes.

She buried it all from her man most lost,
For she said, "I do" to Richard Cory.
Then her blood inside turned to permafrost.

"What good's a young bulb down in a quarry?"

Janzen read it over and over and counted the sylla-
bles and recognized the allusion to another poem from
his school days. How many times had Mr. Selby read
these same words?

They were all doomed. The desperation of the poem
portrayed Mr. Selby possessed by his sadness. Janzen
pushed himself up and approached the gap in the roof.
He looked out at the surrounding land and saw the elms,
ashes and oaks tired from the long winter. Jagged out-
crops of limestone cut paths between the trunks, and
some of the lower lying shrubs were beginning to flower.
The thwacking of the yellow banner below lent an
uneven and unpredictable soundtrack – something that
struck Janzen as hopeful, like a spinnaker blasted full of
warm Pacific currents.

He turned around and focused his attention on tending to the garden. When the sun set, he returned down
into the building where he found Mr. Atis sitting at his
desk, smiling a beekeeper's March smile.

When Mr. Selby returned from his absence, he
deflected any solicitous attention and focused the group
back into the routine to which they were most accustomed. He employed Scoop as the contractor to help
rebuild the concrete wall Janzen had smashed open.
Mr. Selby assisted, trowel in hand, laying the mortar evenly between bricks. While they worked, Janzen
used the opportunity to maintain the garden. Each time
he descended the rooftop stairway and made his way
through Mrs. Selby's old apartment, Mr. Selby would

be conspicuously absent in the adjacent office. He and Janzen had only shared space and pleasantries around the other residents during their sessions, where he was back to his mystic ways – running things for the group with his chin pinched between his fingers as if he were surveying a chess board. He'd whisper to Mr. Atis who'd execute his laconic murmurs with a string of his own expansive instruction.

The rooftop provided the only haven for Janzen's restive state, which now made him squirm if he thought about it too long. It might've been a coincidence or specifically because he recognized Janzen's growing agitation, but Mr. Atis approached Janzen and requested that he please meet with Mr. Selby on the rooftop on the evening following the next. Mr. Atis had been waiting for Janzen in the big office. Janzen had spent the previous six hours tending to the flowers. "And I'll need those back, please." Mr. Atis was referring to the keys to the rooftop access hanging around Janzen's neck. "Do you still have the others?"

"What others?"

"Did you not receive a tiny wrapped gift box with another two keys on a ring?" asked Mr. Atis. Janzen remembered those keys. They had been placed outside his room around the time Samuel left. He nodded and handed the rooftop keys back over to Mr. Atis. "Bring those with you when you meet with Mr. Selby. He'd also appreciate the return of the garden journal, too." Janzen handed it back over to Mr. Atis. "He was quite pleased with your efforts, Janzen." Janzen nodded again and headed down to his room. "Shall we say five o'clock p.m.?"

"We shall."

Mr. Atis no longer wore the smile of a spring bee-keeper; Janzen only saw Spurinna's ancient countenance bear down upon him. What was it that this soothsayer foresaw?

Janzen spent much of the next day and half walking the different floors with a pace and manner best suited for a museum. Most regarded his unexpected company with such warmth, but it was Monroe – now Madeline or Maddy – who surely understood the reason behind his visit to her studio. But rather than lingering on what was to come, she showed Janzen her latest collection for Vanessa.

She moved so much more freely as Madeline, and her passion and happiness lifted Janzen. His stomach fluttered and tears threatened his eyes. She turned her back to him and pretended to make a few measurements before she skipped over to Janzen, and the two embraced. She kissed him plum on the lips and ran away even before Janzen could drop his arms. They both laughed from opposite corners of the room, and she wished him a "positively wonderful night."

Minutes later, Scoop asked him, "Why da fuck you need da sledgehammer again?" He spoke with the subtlety of a road grader.

"Scoop, it'll be the last time. I promise, good buddy." Janzen gripped Scoop by the arm. "You've been a real son of a gun, Scoop. I appreciate it."

"Juss bring it back, Jay man. I'm juss gettin' things back in order."

Scoop had responded well to the near evisceration he received at the hands of Mr. Selby's son. Since the news of his hanging, Scoop no longer carried any weapon with him – at least that one could see. He had, however, developed the unconscious habit of tracing the lines of his scars through his t-shirts whenever he was anxious about something. Since none of the other residents knew of the pectoral inscription, the thumb that now ran all over and about his torso might've appeared mildly lecherous, the product of a man obsessed with his own touch.

"Janzen."

"Yeah, Scoop?"

"Barn door's open." Janzen looked down. So it was. He lifted it shut.

"Scoop, sometimes it looks like you're pinching your nipples when you're feeling that scar."

Scoop placed his hand flat against his chest. He, too, looked down. "I sometimes think it'll split wide open."

"It'll get better."

"You ever get that fucker?"

"I got him pretty good, Scoop."

"Good."

"See ya, man." Janzen turned to go.

"I'mma need dat back," he called after him.

Janzen carried the sledgehammer back to his room and set its head down in the corner. He looked through the drawers of his desk and found the small box that held the two keys on the ring. He pocketed them and returned the word processor to its original box. He cleared the desktop of its contents and organized everything else so that it could be hauled out easily in under an hour.

He made the bed and lay atop the covers with his hands behind his head. It was still another hour before he was scheduled to meet Mr. Selby. He spent the remaining time reading through his manuscript. It wasn't bad. He would bring it up with him to the rooftop.

The roof hatch was already propped open before Janzen lifted himself up through it, though the move was made more complicated with the sledgehammer in tow. Mr. Selby chuckled at the heavy tool's presence. Janzen found him in the final stages of setting up the rooftop crane. The design was truly inventive. From either side of the gap unfolded the framing for what became a jib arm. Each side was hidden from sight within the building's cornice, and both sides could be manipulated and locked at ninety degree angles – one right next to the other – thus coming together to bridge the gap to extend out over the pavement below. A line of cable came up from under one of the pavers along the walkway in an embedded winch system. The cable then ran out over a spooling attachment, which also held both sides of the framing tightly to one another. It was a quick and effective set-up.

"You going to bash me over the head with that thing?" asked Mr. Selby, holding up his hands in mock submission.

"You heading somewhere, Selby?"

"Not me, young man." Janzen paced back and forth in front of the old man. "But I think it's time for you to go."

Janzen looked at the head of the sledgehammer and laughed out loud. "This wasn't for you."

"I know. But I'm glad to see you have it with you. You won't need it though," said Mr. Selby.

"No?"

"No."

Janzen leaned out and looked over the edge of the framing down to the concrete below. "One way in, one way out?"

"You got it," said Mr. Selby. He then lifted another section of the cornice and withdrew a three-foot length of cable with a carabiner on one end and what looked to be a nylon harness attached to the other. He attached the carabiner to the end of the winch's cable, and both watched it dangle over the edge of the building.

"Is this how it goes every time?"

"Everyone had a choice. Except in Leonard's case. He was very open about how he wanted things to end, including your participation," said Mr. Selby. Janzen smiled and shook his head and let the sledgehammer fall to the ground. "Do you have those keys?"

"Yes."

"Do you remember the building where you last saw Samuel – on the video at Christmas?"

Janzen fingered the keys in his pocket with the one marked 'Home.' "I remember." He laughed and shook his head again.

"Samuel's there now. He's waiting for you. I'll need to clear out your room here, but all your things will be there by tomorrow – your clothes, your word processor, your marbles."

"You don't miss much, do you?"

"I miss quite a lot actually. Now come on. It's getting

cold out here." The winch cable separated the two men. "You were going to go through that wall again, weren't you? Then out the back?" asked Mr. Selby. Janzen smiled. "This'll be more fun. C'mon, slide yourself right down in the harness."

Mr. Selby held his hand out over the wire and helped Janzen ease himself over the edge of the building so that he could slide his legs through the nylon. Janzen was then suspended eleven floors over the concrete landing. Mr. Selby disappeared from his view and came back with a remote that let out the cable from the winch. Janzen slowly descended the backside of the building.

"Janzen, I've arranged a meeting with an old friend of yours – right around the corner, okay?"

"Okay." Janzen had just passed the yellow banner when he yelled back up to Mr. Selby, who watched him from above. "Did you read the book?"

"Yes! It was wonderful! I don't recall seeing my name anywhere in it, but it was brilliant!"

"You were in there, old man."

Mr. Selby leaned out over the building's edge and continued lowering Janzen. As he took in the sight of the old quarry, Janzen believed he was descending at the right speed. He would have time to build up some more momentum. Once he was on the ground, he saw Mr. Selby waving from the top before disappearing from view. The cable then slowly made its way back up top. The ground beneath him was nice and solid, and he jumped in place a few times. He looked down to his hands shaking in anticipation of whatever was to come.

He walked around the corner and resting against the

building was his old bike. The note he had weaved in between the brake line was still there: *For whoever needs it.* Janzen reacquainted himself with the grip of his drop bars and then banged the seat with a quick drop of his fist. He looked up at the roof, but no one was looking down at him. He removed the note, folded it and put it in his pocket. "Hi, old friend." With the squeeze of his fingers, he checked the pressure in both tires, which were recently filled. That man had thought of everything.

He walked with the bike by his side, and as he passed the guard shack, he triggered the front gate to open. He realized the freedom before him. He could go either left or right. He could really go either way.

"Hey."

Janzen heard her before he saw her. She stood with one hand laced in the fence. She wore the same black boots, but her hair was now a wild violet, and the wind pushed it across her face until she tucked it delicately behind her ear.

About the Author

Sean Byrne is the author of *The Psychopomps,* his debut work of literary fiction. A former award-winning English teacher in Baltimore, Sean used his summers off to complete the book. He has a B.A. from Boston College and a master's from the University of Southern California.

Apprentice House Press

Loyola University Maryland

Apprentice House is the country's only campus-based, student-staffed book publishing company. Directed by professors and industry professionals, it is a nonprofit activity of the Communication Department at Loyola University Maryland.

Using state-of-the-art technology and an experiential learning model of education, Apprentice House publishes books in untraditional ways. This dual responsibility as publishers and educators creates an unprecedented collaborative environment among faculty and students, while teaching tomorrow's editors, designers, and marketers.

Outside of class, progress on book projects is carried forth by the AH Book Publishing Club, a co-curricular campus organization supported by Loyola University Maryland's Office of Student Activities.

Eclectic and provocative, Apprentice House titles intend to entertain as well as spark dialogue on a variety of topics. Financial contributions to sustain the press's work are welcomed. Contributions are tax deductible to the fullest extent allowed by the IRS.

To learn more about Apprentice House books or to obtain submission guidelines, please visit www.apprenticehouse.com.

Apprentice House
Communication Department
Loyola University Maryland
4501 N. Charles Street
Baltimore, MD 21210
410-617-5265
info@apprenticehouse.com • www.apprenticehouse.com

CPSIA information can be obtained
at www.ICGtesting.com
Printed in the USA
LVHW081829150322
713510LV00004B/126